A bit of a Nomad herself, **K.A. Finn** has wandered around Ireland and the UK for decades before settling back in Ireland with her husband and kids (two and four legged).

Visit K.A. Finn online:

www.kafinn.com
(trailers, excerpts, artwork, playlists etc)

Facebook: kafinnauthor

Instagram: kafinnauthor

Twitter @K_A_Finn

Also by K.A. Finn

Nomad Series (Space Opera)
Ares
Nemesis
Perses
Chaos
Mania
Cronus
Talos (TBA)

Blackjacks Series (Paranormal Romance)
Breaking Phoenix
Reviving Davyn
Defying Shep (2023)
Unraveling Fallon (TBA)

Broken Chords (Rockstar Romance)
Broken Rock (Tate)
Fractured Rock (Gregg)
Split Rock (Tate – 2023)
Crushed Rock (Luke – TBA)
Shattered Rock (Dillon – TBA)

CRONUS

NOMAD SERIES – BOOK 6

K.A.FINN

Cover design by Deranged Doctor Design
www.derangeddoctordesign.com

Published by Cooper Publishing
www.cooperbookservices.com

Edited by Desert Mystic Literary Editing
www.desertmysticliteraryediting.com

ISBN: 978-1-914177-35-4

To Gryffin and his Nomad.
Six books on and I'm still enjoying the ride.

1

EARTH SECTOR

Sayber looks out the window at the large station in front of them. 'Readings?'

'Nothing, sir,' Gaige reports. 'As far as I can tell it's a hunk of scrap metal.'

Sayber turns to face Avoca. 'You sure about this?'

Avoca nods. 'Readings can be deceptive. Trust me, this is the right place.'

Sayber examines the floating wreck again. 'How can you be so sure your mates won't run straight to the Foundation as soon as we make contact?'

'Not everyone in this Sector follows the rule of the Foundation. These people have opposed the Council for as long as I've known them. We'll be safe here.'

Sayber leans over Gaige's shoulder and checks the readings again. He's stalling but it's not a decision he wants to rush. Putting his faith, his crew, and his ship in the hands of a Foundation admiral goes against everything he is, but he's not too proud or stupid to dismiss Avoca's help. He's out of his depth in this Sector. 'Don't have much choice I guess.'

Avoca squeezes his shoulder briefly then nods at Gaige. 'Uncloak and bring us a little closer. Ask *Lir* to do the same.'

Gaige glances at Sayber for confirmation. Sayber pauses for a few seconds then nods once. Gaige relays the message to Rua as he guides *Perses* towards the station. 'We're being contacted, sir.' Gaige frowns as he reads the message on the screen.

'What is it?'

'Either the system is screwed up or there's someone just as screwed up over there. It just says, "JAM." That's it.'

Sayber glares over his shoulder at Avoca as the man laughs. 'He's screwed up all right. Reply with - PLUM.'

Gaige looks to Sayber for help but the Hunter just shrugs. 'Do what he says.'

Gaige takes a deep breath then relays the message to the station. 'Sir, the cargo doors are opening. Still no power readings coming from the station. I don't understand.'

'You and me both. Avoca?'

The Admiral nods towards the station. 'I suggest we get in there before someone sees us.'

Sayber shrugs and nods at Gaige. 'What the hell. We're sitting targets out here. Take us in.' Sayber leaves Gaige to guide *Perses* in and lowers onto his chair again. 'Who are these people?'

Avoca leans against the console behind him. 'Evie and Felix Dixon. They lived next door to me and my family for years. They'd both dutifully followed the Foundation ideals for...' he blows out a breath, 'it must be about fifty years or so. Then one day, they decided they'd had enough. They sold everything they owned and vanished from the

Foundation system. I heard nothing more from them for about two years.

'Knowing I was as disillusioned about the Foundation as they were, they reached out to me. I still remember the first time I came here. I was amazed at how they had managed to build a life out here completely off the grid. They used their saved credits to transform this place and built up a network of black-market traders to supply the border worlds with whatever they need.'

Sayber whistles. 'Impressive.' Anything else he is going to say is cut off as *Perses* enters the station. Lights guide the ships towards a large landing platform. About a dozen transports of various sizes, condition, and age line the far side of the platform, but it's the mammoth vessel to the back of the station that gets his attention. He's never seen something so big. The enormous Foundation symbol plastered on her hull gives him reason to pause.

'I don't like the look of this. Why is there a Foundation ship here?'

'Whatever the reason the Dixon's would not betray us.' Avoca slaps Sayber on the back. 'Just follow my lead.'

'Yeah, sure,' Sayber scoffs. 'Gaige, stay here. If anything looks off, get *Perses* out of here. Got it?'

'Yes, sir.'

Sayber walks with Avoca to the cargo hold and tries to steady his nerves as the back opens. He steps onto the ramp and looks around him. He nods at Rua as the captain waits at the base of *Lir*'s ramp to his left. Both captains examine the inside of the facility. The derelict station deception is effective. From the outside you would never guess at what is really going on inside. State of the art atmospheric units circulate fresh, cool air around the cargo hold. A team busily works on a platform to his right, unloading crates stamped with the Foundation logo from a transport. Sayber smirks. There's no sign of any Foundation personnel, meaning the ship and the cargo must have been stolen. He likes these people already.

Two double height doors ahead of them burst open and a couple walks out. Evie and Felix Dixon couldn't be further from what Sayber had envisioned. After only spending a few minutes on the station and seeing a small part of the operation, Sayber had pictured an imposing couple. The truth is a far different picture.

Dressed in a red blazer, white shirt, green cargo shorts, and black boots, Felix doesn't fit his surroundings. Evie follows after him in a knee length skirt, heavy navy jumper, and brown sandals. Her greying, wiry hair is stuffed under a wide brimmed hat with a large flower sticking out of it.

'Different,' Sayber mutters as they approach.

Avoca smiles and laughs. 'They prefer eclectic.'

Felix waves his arm at the security. 'Get out of my way. Move!'

The men step aside, giving the couple room to pass. 'Well, well, well. Think I may finally be losing it. Hank Avoca?'

'You're looking well, Felix. Evie, you haven't aged at all.'

'And you're still a lousy liar, Hank.' She smiles and embraces him.

'No hugging yet,' Felix interrupts. 'Payment first.'

Sayber tenses at the comment, but Avoca merely nods and walks back up the ramp. He opens one of the crates he brought from Ultar and takes something out. He passes it to Felix who takes it from Avoca as if it was pure gold. 'Plum jam.'

'What?' Sayber asks.

Felix glances at Sayber. 'Plum jam.' He repeats each word slowly. 'Did you get it that time?' Felix looks at Avoca. 'What's his problem?'

Sayber grinds his teeth as the two men laugh at him. 'You brought a crate of jam from Ultar? I told you to pack essentials.'

'And I did. I thought we might need some help. The Dixon's are partial to plum jam.'

'Can't get it out here. Plums are reserved for the elite Foundation fat-cats.' Felix gestures behind him. 'Unload it. If even one jar goes missing, heads will roll. Now, dinner is just about ready. Can I presume there are more than just the three of you on these ships?'

Avoca nods. 'There's a full crew on each.'

Evie steps closer to Rua. 'Apologies, we've been ignoring you. Rogue?'

Rua nods. 'That a problem?'

Evie laughs. 'Heavens no. You the only woman?'

Rua shakes her head. 'My crew is all female.'

Evie squeals and claps her hand. 'You've made my day, Captain. It's a little testosterone heavy around here,' she says, waving her hand at the group of men standing beside Felix. 'Hey, you with the gun.'

'They've all got guns,' Felix responds.

'That one there. What's his name?'

Felix shrugs. 'How am I expected to remember?'

'You hired them all.'

'Yeah, but they look the same. Big men with guns.'

She nudges Rua in the side. 'The small ones didn't work.' She leans closer. 'Can you imagine having a protection detail full of men that looked like Felix. He couldn't scare a fly off a corpse.'

She waves at the man beside Felix again. Something about his stance tells Sayber he's the leader of the protection detail. Dressed in black combats and a green t-shirt, the tall, broad, menacing looking man with short, dark brown hair takes a step forward. 'Yes, you. Big guy, would you be a dear and make sure we've got enough room in the mess for the crew?'

The man sighs as he walks over to Evie. 'It's Heath.'

'What is?'

'My name, Evie.'

She pats him on his arm. 'Whatever you say.' She turns to Rua. 'He's been keeping us safe for years now. He's a big softy really, well, unless you get on his wrong side.' She leans closer and lowers her voice. 'Saw him kill someone with his bare hands once. Best security in the Sector. Isn't that right, fellow?'

He groans as he gestures to the rest of his men standing beside Felix. 'And you still don't know my name.'

'What was that, dear?' Evie asks.

'Nothing.' He addresses Rua and Sayber, 'Unload your people. After you eat, we can have a look at your ships, see if anything needs to be done.'

Rua looks over at Sayber who shrugs. 'I'm game if you are.' Rua turns her attention back to Heath and quietly examines him.

Heath holsters his gun and holds his hands out. 'I get why you're wary, but Hank is a friend of the Dixon's. We got your backs while you're here.'

The door behind them opens again and Sayber spots someone he honestly didn't think he'd see again. Bray smiles at Sayber as he approaches his captain. He stands in front of Sayber and salutes. 'I can't believe you're here.'

Sayber smiles. 'Couldn't have you going AWOL on me. If I needed to come here personally and drag you back, so be it.' He gestures over his shoulder at the hulking Foundation ship behind him. 'Should I ask?'

Bray grins as he proudly looks at the ship. 'I didn't think the Foundation deserved her.' He shrugs. 'You never know, she might come in handy.'

'You don't say.' Sayber looks around the group of mismatched people. 'Where's your mate?'

Bray's face drops. 'Still on Earth. It's a long story. Fill you in over dinner?'

'Sounds good.'

Bray looks over Sayber's shoulder at Rua, standing on the loading ramp of *Lir*. 'Captain.'

A whisper of a smile crosses her lips before it disappears. She nods at him then turns to the Rogue beside her. 'Regan, assemble the crew. I want a team on board at all times. Take it in shifts.'

Seeing that everyone is in agreement, Evie claps her hands together. 'Fantastic. Time for dinner.'

'Couldn't agree more,' Felix says. 'My stomach feels like my throat's been cut.'

'Oh you're always hungry. Don't think I won't be keeping an eye on those jam jars too. I know what you're like. I haven't forgotten about the cake.'

'Seriously, woman. Can you not let that go? We have company.'

She thumps him full force in the arm. 'Do not call me 'woman', and no, I will not let it go. It was my birthday cake.'

'And it was delicious.'

Evie glowers at her husband for a moment, then turns away from him with a snort. 'Big fellow, I'll leave you to organise the people.'

Heath closes his eyes and mutters under his breath. 'I swear she does it on purpose.' He moves away to speak to his team while Avoca, Sayber, Bray, and Rua follow the Dixon's through the large doors.

Sayber and Rua fall into step beside Avoca. 'They always like this?' Rua asks.

Avoca nods. 'Don't let them fool you. Heath and his men are the muscle, but the Dixon's are, without a doubt, the brains behind this station. Anything they don't know about smuggling, hacking systems, or evading detection isn't worth knowing.'

'You're putting a lot of faith in them,' Rua says.

'They haven't let me down in the past.'

Sayber stops Avoca. 'You've used them before?'

'Of course.'

'Why would an upstanding Foundation admiral need smugglers?'

'How do you think I got Bray out of Tyrat?' Avoca puts his hand on Bray's shoulder. 'They organised everything for me.'

Bray leads them down the corridor to a large open-plan mess. 'I spent a few weeks here recovering after Tyrat. They're good people.'

'Will they be able to help with Garvan and Gryffin?'

Bray takes a deep breath before answering Sayber, 'I hope so — for all our sakes.'

∞

FOUNDATION HQ - EARTH

Garvan wakes from his nightmare and sits up suddenly. He gasps in pain and presses a hand to his stomach as his wound protests. A few sessions in the rejuvenation pod has helped, but it's still bloody sore. Harvey said that he'd need just one more session in the pod before he's strong enough to undergo some mods.

Garvan rubs a hand across his face and swings his legs over the side of the cot. That's something he'd prefer to put off as long as possible. After checking he's not about to have any company, he throws himself against the cot, ramming his wound against the corner.

He bites back a scream and somehow manages to stay conscious and convince the little food in his stomach to stay put. He squeezes his eyes shut and focuses on breathing instead of throwing up or passing out. When the room stops spinning, he crawls on to his bed and slowly lies back on the hard surface. Blood seeps through his scrub top, the material sticking to his wound with every laboured breath.

With each passing day in this place, Tyrat looks more like a holiday resort. He misses the nice, cosy, foul smelling, dank cell he spent three years in. At least there he knew he had a fair chance at survival. If any of the prisoners got in his face, he'd be able to deal with it - fair and square. Man against man. Fist against fist.

Harvey isn't playing by the rules, and he doesn't have a clue how to prepare for his games. All he can do is keep his head and not let the bastard think he's getting the upper hand. Which he is.

He thought Harvey had done his worst when it came to tearing his life apart. It seems he was wrong.

And that's more than a little irritating. When he had survived his first few days in Tyrat, he swore he'd never let anyone control his life again. The guards tried, but after a few broken bones - theirs not his - he made his case. They left him alone for the most part, only pushing him around when their bosses visited. Then Bray burst into his cell and took him from that monotonous hell.

He has no regrets throwing himself off the back side of *Alpha*. It helped to get Bray and his family to safety. He'd re-paid his debt to the Hunter and that's the most important thing. With all the lies and deceit plaguing the Sector thanks to the Foundation, it was damn important to stick to your word.

He stares up at the featureless ceiling and resists the urge to scream and beat his fists against anything and everything. It would be too easy to let the situation take over and drag him down to a dark place. He forces himself to think about Erin instead. Leaving aside the fact she's Bray's cousin and a fair few years his junior, he can't deny the attraction.

He looks down at the ring on the chain around his neck. He loves his wife, but if he's being really honest, he was never in love with her. Like everything else on Foundation Earth, their marriage was arranged by a computer somewhere deep in the bowels of HQ.

Whatever attraction he feels for Erin is real. It hasn't been engineered by the Foundation or decided by a computer. A little bit of him regrets turning her down when she tried to kiss him. Given his current predicament, having that pleasant memory to focus on would be nicer than some of the thoughts running through his head.

Roman walks down the steps leading from the side of *Infinity* and looks around the base. He was only gone two days, but it felt like a lifetime.

If someone had told him he'd be happy as a rebel commander in the Outer Sector, he would have thought them crazy. Yet here he is. Up against the Foundation but also truly happy for the first time in his life. Well, the first time since Maggie, his first love, left him and had his son in secret. A son who is occupying many of his thoughts recently.

His second in command, Tanner, a fresh-faced officer who was finding life in the Outer Sector as easy to adjust to as Roman had, stops at his left shoulder and hands him the report from their latest mission. 'Debrief now, sir?'

Roman takes the report and tucks it under his arm. 'Ten minutes. I want to see how he is first.'

He turns away and makes his way through the hustle and bustle of the hangar. *Ares*, with her unusual metal sails, sits to the left, her cargo ramp open as personnel move supplies around her hold. The menacing purple griffin glares over at him as he passes the back of the ship. *Nemesis* and *Epsilon*, along with one of the Rogue ships, *Dannan*, take up the rest of the bays. The rest of the Nomad, Hunter, and Rogue ships are on patrol or ferrying colonists to safety.

Roman nods at any personnel he passes on his way to the belly of the facility. He finally reaches the heavy metal door and places his palm on the security pad. The door slides back and he steps into the holding cells. Four out of the five cells are empty, the occupant of the first cell is someone he's become somewhat close to over the last few weeks.

From the first moment over a year ago when he discovered he had a son, life had spiralled out of control for him. Too many things had come to light, and to remain as level headed as possible, he pushed some of those revelations to the back of his mind. Dealing with the fact he had a grown son, who had been kidnapped by his best friend, Callum, was too much to handle at the time.

His friend's jealousy of Roman's relationship with Maggie had put their son in danger. Callum had targeted Gryffin and spent years modifying him, altering the boy, making him a highly volatile cyborg. Unsurprisingly, Gryffin didn't want anything to do with his Foundation father and, at the time, Roman had whole-heartedly agreed with his decision.

Finding out about their relationship was a surprise to both Roman and Gryffin. Neither of them had been overly enthusiastic about the situation. Thirty-five years is a long time to make up for, but something changed over the last few weeks. Perhaps it was the events on the New Colony with the Scientist, but Gryffin seems to be warming to him. It is far from a typical father/son relationship, but the Nomad leader is at least acknowledging him. It's a small and welcome start. Unfortunately, unless a miracle happens, they may not get the time they need to develop anything more.

His son is dying. Piece by piece, the modifications his twisted friend made are failing, taking more of Gryffin with them each time.

Roman settles on the chair in front of the cell and dismisses the Nomad standing guard. He leans forward, resting his arms on his legs. From what he can see, Gryffin's condition has worsened over the last two days.

He seems to be asleep, but his rest is far from soothing. There's no comparison between the intimidating man he met a year ago and what's facing him in the cell. Apart from the damage the implants are causing to his body, they've also had to remove his prosthetic arm. After nearly electrocuting Milla it was decided, for his safety and theirs, to take it off. Even without his lower arm, small sparks of electricity still race across the surface of his exposed stump.

His pale face is damp with sweat, the few days growth of facial hair helping to mask his sunken cheeks. He had cut his hair, losing the long locks that hid his facial implant and scars from view. The short, dark spikes helped keep him cool through his frequent raging fevers, but even they are soaked in sweat.

The anger still burns in Roman's gut when he sees the damage to Gryffin's face. The more serious of the two scars, the one that stretches from over his right eye and across the bridge of his nose to his left cheek was done with a broken bottle while he was in Tyrat prison. At least that's what Desyl told him. Gryffin never spoke about the myriad of scars on his body. Something that Roman can't help but be somewhat grateful for. He's struggling with the little he knows about the torture his son has endured over the course of his life.

Gryffin mumbles in his sleep and thrashes in the bed. The black t-shirt rides up, exposing much too visible ribs. The 'W' shaped implant embedded in his chest seems to have sunken creating a hollow that gives him a skeletal appearance. Not training or eating much has withered the once strong body. The rare times he's been interested in eating usually ends with the food making a reappearance. Milla was reduced to giving him high doses of nutrients to keep him going. Not being able to restock *Infinity* or *Epsilon* with Foundation grade supplies leaves her trying to utilise what they have left on board with the meagre and primitive offerings of the Outer Sector.

The metal brace supporting his right leg rattles against the bars as he moves on the small cot. It's his damn leg that's giving them the most sleepless nights. For reasons he will never comprehend, Roman's dear psychotic friend decided to add cybernetics to Gryffin's leg. He had left the lower leg as it was, choosing only to replace the outer layers of his upper limb with metal.

Apart from leaving him with a near useless, excruciatingly painful leg, the living tissue imprisoned under the metal is so riddled with infection it is putting a huge strain on his system - both organic and artificial. Nothing they try makes it any better. The last update he had from them ended with the mention of amputation. It is something Gryffin is dead against, but it is getting to the stage where he loses his leg or his life.

His other implants aren't faring any better. His robotic eye shut down before Roman left on this trip a few days ago and the other is less than reliable. He's also battling a brutal headache and nothing Milla does offers any relief.

Unable to watch Gryffin struggle with sleep, Roman pushes to his feet and paces the small room. He's actually surprised Terra isn't here, keeping Gryffin company. While he hopes she's taking time out for herself, he knows she's probably under a console somewhere on *Ares*. She's another person occupying his thoughts. Her feelings for Gryffin are plain as day - which in itself is troublesome.

She's in love with him in spite of everything he's said and done to try to convince her otherwise. Roman knows she's going to get hurt. Whether thanks to his brutal childhood or something the implants did to him, Gryffin struggles with emotions. There is no question

Gryffin cares about her, but Roman doubts it goes beyond that, or if it does, whether Gryffin comprehends what the feelings mean. It's not his fault, it's just how things are with him.

'How'd it go?'

Roman stops pacing and looks over at Gryffin. The Nomad is propped up on his remaining arm, squinting at him through unfocused eyes. 'I didn't realise you were awake.'

Gryffin uses the bars to pull himself up and manoeuvres himself against the corner. He collapses back between the wall and bars looking exhausted by the effort. 'How'd it go?' he repeats.

Roman sits down. 'Surprisingly well. The leaders of the colonies are going to continue working with us. Admittedly, at the initial meeting having the Nomad involved didn't fill them with confidence, but they came around.' Gryffin looks away and Roman knows he blames himself for destroying the relationships he spent so long forging. 'Hey, this isn't your fault.'

'I was the one holding the gun. I attacked Ultar. I betrayed the colonies.'

'That gun was put in your hand by the Foundation. When they sent you to destroy Ultar, it was as much a tactical decision as it was a plain old attack. Everyone heard about it. They know it wasn't your fault. They know the Foundation programmed you—'

'Doesn't make a damn bit of difference and you know that. Might be best if I back out. Leave it to you and Desyl.'

Roman shakes his head. 'Give it time. So far, the leaders seem to be happy with me taking charge. They know the Nomad are still involved, but they'd prefer if it was behind the scenes for now.'

'You good to do that?'

Roman gives a half-hearted shrug. 'With you stuck in there and Aleena dealing with the colonists here, I don't have much of a choice. I'm not built for the political life, but we all have to adapt to the circumstances. You just need to give them time, Gryffin. So, how are you feeling?'

Gryffin smirks. 'Peachy.'

Roman laughs and leans back in the chair. 'Sounds like you've been spending too much time with Milla.'

'She suggested I try a response other than fine.'

'Can't say it suits you.'

Gryffin closes his eye and rests his head against the wall. Staying awake is a constant struggle for him lately. 'Think I'll stick with fine.'

'Have you been able to eat anything?'

He shakes his head. 'Terra's taking it personally. Like I have a problem with her cooking.'

'Please don't say she's cooking for you?'

'Don't tell her, but I tasted better in Tyrat.'

'Burnt beyond all recognition?' Gryffin nods. 'Always happens when she cooks. Can't for the life of me figure out how she does it.'

'Yeah, well I wish she'd stop trying. Food is in short enough supply without her ruining what little we have left.' He winces and looks over at him again. 'Anything from Earth?'

The question is innocent enough, but Roman can't help but feel there is a little brotherly concern at its core. His brother, Bray and the ex-inmate Garvan disappeared through the port two weeks ago after hitching an unplanned ride to Earth on a Foundation vessel.

Gryffin hooked to the nav system on *Ares* and brought himself to the brink of death trying to catch up with them before the Foundation ship entered the Port. He wasn't successful and he's still paying for it. To get his man back, Sayber had taken his ship *Perses* along with a Rogue ship to find them and bring them back.

'I've only just got back, but I'm sure someone would have told me if there was.'

Gryffin nods and readjusts his leg on the bed. 'If Sayber and Bray don't make it back, they'll need to appoint a new leader and flagship. Quinn still here?'

'And not too happy about it. I'm getting the impression he'd much prefer to be on *Perses* then a grounded Hunter representative.'

'Can't blame him. The Nomad and Hunters on the surface haven't spent this long on solid ground before. We prefer to be on our ships.' He takes a deep breath and closes his eye again. Roman knows he would give anything to be at the helm of *Ares* again. 'You should talk to Quinn. Make sure he has a back-up plan in case *Perses* doesn't make it back. Wouldn't want some other group taking them down while they're getting their shit together.'

'Should I be keeping an eye on your Nomad, Captain?'

Gryffin opens his eye and smirks slightly but doesn't reply. He readjusts his brace again and lets out a deep breath. 'I need you to do something.'

'Sure.'

Gryffin pushes himself further upright and looks at Roman. 'Talk to Terra. She's brushing off my condition like I've got a damn bullet wound. I've tried, but she won't listen to anything I say.'

Roman had noticed her clear case of denial before he left but he was hoping, with time, she'd allow the truth to sink in. 'I know Milla's tried a few times. You can't blame her for having a bit of hope. She's in love with you. Not giving up hope of a miracle goes hand-in-hand with that.'

'Hope is fine as long as she accepts it will probably go the other way. I'm not going to beat this, Roman.'

'Gryffin—'

'I'm not. You know that. She needs to understand. Milla thinks I have two weeks left at most. Terra needs to accept that.'

Roman leans forward and laces his fingers together. 'I'll talk to her but I'm not promising anything.'

Gryffin shuffles down the bed, bringing him closer to Roman. He takes a few deep breaths, the exertion of moving from the top to the bottom of the bunk wiping him out. He leans his head against the bars and meets Roman's eyes. 'There's something else. I've said this to Terra, but she wasn't taking it in. I don't want to die in a cell on Ultar.'

Roman swallows as a sour taste appears in his mouth. He was expecting this conversation. That doesn't mean he's one bit ready for it. 'I've spoken to some of your crew about Nomad traditions. An honourable death is to go down fighting. As captain... being on your ship in your command chair is also acceptable. I'm taking it you want the latter. The first could be... well, an unfair fight.'

Gryffin laughs. 'Yeah. Takes the honour out of it when it's a slaughter. I'm not saying you let me out yet. Not much of a threat like this, but not going to risk it. But when the time is... right, I want to be moved to *Ares*. Even if she stays in orbit. Just as long as it's not here... like this.'

'Of course.'

Gryffin nods and begins the task of moving back up the bed again. He lies down and closes his eye, quickly giving in to exhaustion. Roman slumps back in the chair and watches his son sleep. Never in his life has he felt so completely helpless.

Roman takes out his comms, but stops himself. Pressuring Milla and her team won't do a thing. They're spending every spare minute trying to find why Gryffin's programming stopped him from going through the Port. Until they find out why, they can't risk bringing him through. Even if that wasn't an issue, there's nothing to bring him across for. They're headlining the most wanted list. Earth is closed to them. If anything, they'd be in a worse situation than they are here. At least here Gryffin's got a support system.

There's no point even considering any of that. He knows without a doubt Gryffin would rather die here than go to Earth. All he can do is make sure his death is an honourable one. If he wants to die in his command chair on *Ares*, then Roman will make sure that's exactly what happens.

FOUNDATION HQ - EARTH

One opens the door to the cargo bay and walks purposefully towards the loading ramp on *Beta*. He can't help but sneer at the small vessel. *Beta* is used to ferry Council members around the surface. She is small and certainly nowhere near as impressive or intimidating as her sister.

Losing *Alpha* as they had was a severe blow to the group as well as an embarrassment to his leadership. The rebels took *Alpha* from under their noses. He doubts he will be able to recover from that. His only salvation would be securing the prototype and bringing him back to Earth. With Thirty-Five on display and operating as it should, perhaps the *Alpha* issue will be forgotten.

He watches from the bottom of the ramp as drones load crate after crate of weapons into her hold. Even before she reaches him, One is aware of Nova's approach. The cyborg leader comes to a stop beside him. He glances over his shoulder at her, examining her from top to bottom.

The fall from *Alpha* had broken most of her bones and the resulting blood loss from being impaled had nearly killed her. He's glad they were able to salvage her. It would have been irritating to have to train a different cyborg to take over.

He smiles as the small army stops behind her. A total of thirty-seven of the new model are fully operational and ready to fight for the Foundation. The colony should fall without any human Foundation losses. A few cyborg losses won't bother him in the slightest - as long as Nova and the prototype survive, the rest can be replaced.

He may have told the rest of the Council members that Thirty-Five is not vital to their project, but that was a lie. Without the prototype, they can never hope to rectify the issues with the male subjects. Having an army of female cyborgs is an achievement, but having a male one as well would be quite a bonus - especially if Wade Garvan could be first on the list to be modified.

Besides, a part of him would like to have the prototype back on Earth. Something about the cyborg intrigues him. His defiance and continued stubbornness, in spite of all they've put him through, is fascinating. That in itself is worth closer inspection.

'Is your team ready, Nova?'

'Yes, sir.'

'I know you are aware, but I am going to stress this again. I will be less than happy if anything happens to Thirty-Five. Once you have completed your task, he is to be returned to me in one piece and unharmed. Do you understand?'

'Yes, sir.'

He raises an eyebrow as he glances sideways at her. He's probably imagining it, but he swears he caught a slight irritation in her tone. 'Keep in regular contact. Dismissed.'

She nods and without another word, steps onto the loading ramp, and disappears into the ship. The rest of the women follow close behind, their footsteps in perfect synchronisation with each other. The loading ramp closes and he moves out of the way as *Beta*'s engines power up.

The craft lifts off the ground then moves towards the exit followed by every other available ship they can spare. He stays in position as the fleet clears the base and gradually disappears from view as they rise higher. A few minutes later, they are gone.

One spins on his heel, clasps his hands behind his back, and strolls through the base. He is mere days away from officially being known as the greatest leader in Foundation history. His cyborgs will take over Ultar which, in turn, will weaken the opposition in the Outer Sector. With no defences left, they will submit to his rule. The colonists will provide everything the elite on Earth needs, thus ensuring the survival of the most important people on Earth. With the majority of the populace content, he could then turn to his personal issues. The prototype would undergo a complete rework. Millions of credits would not be wasted again.

He checks the time on his unit. It would take an hour for the fleet to reach the Port and another five on the other side to get to Ultar. As soon as they get close to the rebel planet he'll put the final part of his plan in motion.

If all went as predicted, Nova would return in a day or so with the prototype in custody. This time, One would make sure the control implant could not be overridden by anyone. There's no point having invested that much in a weapon if you then give it free will to do whatever it wants. No, he would fix that problem once and for all.

He smiles and hums to himself as his private elevator carries him up to his office. He makes a mental note to check on the progress with the new lab. It needs to be completed before Nova arrives. Having both the prototype and the troublesome Wade modified to the new specification would give him two powerful bodyguards. With them at his side, fighting for him, he'd be unstoppable.

∞

DIXON SPACE STATION

Bray sits down at the desk in his room and waits as Sayber finds the relevant data. Sayber and Rua had spent dinner filling him in on what's happened since they hitched a ride back to Earth on *Alpha*, or *Cronus* as she is now being called.

He hates the fact that everything Sayber said after hearing about Gryffin's deteriorating health had gone in one ear and out the other. He doesn't want to care about his brother, but it seems he does - and that's really irritating him.

Sayber points to the file on the screen and moves back to lean against the window. 'That's everything Milla downloaded on Gryffin before we left.'

Bray ignores his captain as he reads the information. Every sentence fills him with more dread. 'Chayse and Milla have any ideas how to fix him?'

Sayber shakes his head. 'Nope. They're stumped. Gryffin was pretty much undergoing constant testing while he was unconscious. Bottom line is the implant in his brain is failing which is having a knock on effect on the rest of his components.'

Bray grunts as he examines the readings. 'Milla thinks there's something hidden in his programming that stopped him from going through the Port, but nothing showed up.'

'And they looked, believe me they looked. Whatever it is, it's well and truly hidden.'

Bray scratches his jaw as he reads through the data. 'It's all down to the control implant. If we can remove it, or repair it, all the other problems should be easily fixed.'

'Why do I get the impression it's not that simple?'

'If it was, the Scientist would have done it by now. Maybe the Foundation have had more luck. There could be something on their system that could help.'

Sayber pulls up another chair and sits beside Bray. He strokes his goatee and looks down at the floor. 'You're serious about going to Earth to get Garvan, aren't you?'

Bray glances up at him. 'Just say what you're thinking.'

'I know he's your mate, but...'

'You're not here to help him, right?'

Sayber smiles and nods. 'Got it. I don't know much about the man, but I doubt he'd want you risking your ass to get him out.'

'It's not his call. I don't answer to him.'

'True, but you answer to me.'

'So you're going to order me to come back with you?'

'I shouldn't have to. It's a damn shame about Garvan, it really is. But it's done. What we need to do is get the hell out of here in one piece. If we manage to take out a Foundation ship or two before we go, fair enough. I'm not going to put two ships at risk to save one man.'

Bray smirks and meets Sayber's eyes. 'That's exactly what you did when you came here to get me, Captain. Well, two men but same difference.'

Sayber clenches his jaw, clearly irritated at the truth of Bray's statement.

'Listen, I'm not asking for your help to get Garvan out, but I have to go. I'm not leaving him there to be used as a test subject for the Foundation. I'm also not going without *Cronus*. The information on that ship could put a stop to all the cyborgs. We need to get her going and bring her across the border with us.'

'This is about Gryffin, isn't it?'

Bray makes a face. 'Not entirely. Believe me, there's no love lost between us. It's the information I want.' He silently apologises to his mother for the lie. Just another thing she'd be less than happy with him about. Since his parents' death, he hadn't exactly done many things to make them proud of him. Illegal fighting rings, being arrested, drugs, more fighting. Not model son kind of stuff. Dismissing his brother so easily is just another thing to add to the list.

Sayber frowns at him. 'What good will that do?'

'A hell of a lot if the Foundation uses the data.' He swivels his chair around to face Sayber. 'Think about it, sir. They've somehow figured out how to fix the problem with the control implant. Now there's nothing stopping them from starting a production line. They didn't think twice about fitting a faulty implant to hundreds of prisoners. What's to stop them from fitting a fully operational one? Within a few months, they could have an army of Gryffin's ready to forcefully take over the Outer Sector.'

'Yeah, but the prisons are cleared.'

'Not the ones in Foundation space.'

'They're small fry compared to the ones we took out. There's only a few hundred prisoners in total.'

'That's all they need. If every one of them, or even ninety-percent of them survive, that means a lot of trouble for us.'

'Damn it.' Sayber scratches his head as he looks at the data on the screen. 'You may have a point about helping Gryffin.'

Bray smirks. 'You want to save your old mate now?'

'Not top of my list. I'm not going to deny he's a definite asset to our common cause. If they launch this army, we could very well need him.'

Bray points to Milla's last line of text in the report. 'If we're going to do this, we can't hang around. He's got a few weeks left, tops. The longer he's left to deteriorate, the more damage is done to his body.'

Sayber curses and looks up at the ceiling. 'Can't believe I'm going to save his Nomad ass, yet again. Just for once I'd like to kill him. I created the Hunters to wipe out the Nomad. We're meant to be hunting them, not helping them. If we let his programming fail now, it'll save us a hell of a lot of trouble when we face the Nomad again in battle.' Sayber smiles apologetically at Bray. 'You know what I mean.'

Bray nods and looks back at the screen. 'I understand.' Sayber is right. Once the Foundation issue is taken care of, there'll be another big problem to face. With the Sector free from the Foundation, the Nomad and Hunters will be back to their rightful positions — on opposite sides.

The feud between Sayber and Gryffin is carved in stone. Just because they're working together for the moment, doesn't erase the past. Sayber betrayed Gryffin's trust when they served together. Just as Klay and Rayde did. Gryffin will never forget that and Sayber will never step aside and let the Nomad take the Sector. Bray has to accept the fact that, sooner or later, he'll have to face Gryffin from the opposite side. It's not something he's looking forward to. 'The Hunters will give as good as we get, sir.'

'Yeah, well we'll cross that bridge when we get to it. For now... ' Sayber scratches his cheek as he focuses on a spot on the wall. 'Damn it. Let's find out what the Foundation knows. I'd be fairly ticked off with myself if I didn't try to irritate the Foundation while I'm here.'

DIXON SPACE STATION

Bray pushes the screen away and rubs his eyes, wincing when the pressure sends a wave of pain through his head. He honestly doesn't know how Gryffin puts up with the damn mod around his eye. The fact his brother has had an eyepiece for nearly twenty years doesn't give him much comfort. Getting used to the pain isn't the same as not having it in the first place. He can handle the piece on his chest. He wants rid of the eyepiece though. If he has to tear the Foundation ship apart he'll do it. The information they need is somewhere in there and he's going to find it.

They've been trolling through the data from the Foundation ship continuously since they arrived. The plus side is that they are learning quite a bit about the systems on *Cronus*. The negative is that they have only managed to scrape the surface of the data.

With the majority of the files they need still fighting any serious attempt to access them, they've focused on the smaller unit they found in the med bay. The Scientist's dated unit didn't put up any barriers when they accessed it. Unfortunately, most of the files on the system are also dated. There were a few schematics from some of the newer models and it's these files they're concentrating on.

As a lot of the data is beyond Bray's knowledge of cybernetics, the Dixon's were able to fill in the gaps, helping him get through the information. He was hoping to find something - ideally about a kill switch. It's probably asking for too much, but he's still going to look. If they're to put a stop to the Foundation cyborgs they'd need a miracle.

Taking *Cronus* and the lab full of technicians will have slowed them down quite a bit, but no one was under the illusion they had done anything more than just delay the inevitable. The Foundation would carry out their plans. Bray and the others just had to find some way of stopping them before too many people lost their lives.

People like Garvan.

Knowing that his friend is more than likely going to be first on the mod list when the Foundation gets themselves sorted, gives Bray an extra kick to keep searching the files. Not that he needs the kick. He's all too aware what's at stake.

'I think I may have found something,' Felix shouts from the head of the table, startling everyone.

'Put it on the big screen.' For once, Felix does what he's asked without complaining. Bray studies the information, but all he can see is a garbled mess of nonsense. 'What am I missing?'

Felix's fingers dance over his screen for a few minutes. 'I've highlighted the section.'

Bray reads through the data and curses.

'What?' Sayber asks.

Bray points to a line of text at the bottom of a page filled with numbers. 'Felix is right. The Foundation figured out how to fix the problem with the control implant.'

Sayber leans forward to get a better look. 'You mean the thing that's going to go pop in Gryffin's head?'

Bray rolls his eyes at Sayber, regretting it when the pain shoots through his head. 'Dumbing it down, yes.'

'Not sure how that's going to help us. Gryffin and the Nomad, yes, but definitely not us.'

Felix walks around the table, tutting loudly. 'Do you all have blinkers on or something? With a little preparation, and the right tools of course, this information can be used to stabilise the control implant.'

Bray flops back against the chair. 'Are you sure?'

Felix nods. 'A full overhaul is a bit more than I could carry out here with my team, but with help from a team who are more familiar with the implants we can do it.'

Sayber leans forward on the table. 'I didn't think it was possible to stabilise it?'

'Neither did I,' Bray agrees. 'This is really big, Felix.'

He puffs out his chest and holds on to his lapels as he smiles widely. 'Why thank you. You're still missing the biggest bit. This information can also be used to remove the implant. In time, the cyborgs can be fully human again.'

Bray stares at the screen in silence. Not for one minute did he even consider being able to undo the work the Scientist had carried out. He's only been like this for a few months, but he'd give anything to be one-hundred-percent human again. And Gryffin... it would be a new start for him. A chance to live the life he missed out on. He looks back at the data. 'Are you sure about all of this? It says all the implants can be removed?'

Felix shakes his head. 'Not quite. It says nothing about removing everything. What it does say is how the parts were fitted in the first place and exactly what they do, down to the last detail. Well, it cross-references other files that we don't yet have access to. If we could get that data we could potentially work backwards and remove the other implants. As for the control one...'

He glances back at the screen and his frown deepens. 'It really depends on how long it's been fitted. With the new colony cyborgs, it's a possibility. You too... well, if you have a control implant, but Gryffin...' He shakes his head and meets Bray's eyes. 'Twenty-odd years is a long time to live with something. I'm confident it can be stabilised and possibly even decreased in size. I can't say whether he'd survive without it in some form or another. I'd have to examine him alongside the data. As for his other implants, he'd need a lot of reconstructive surgery, both internally and externally, but it looks like it can be done.'

'If we can access the files,' Bray adds.

Sayber runs a hand over his goatee. 'So, we can just take this data back, whizz him through surgery and make him human again?'

Felix rolls his eyes. 'You and your inane questions. No, it would take a few months to regenerate tissue needed to replace the implants. He'd be out of it for the best part of a year, maybe longer.'

Sayber shrugs. 'Not an issue for me. It'll give the Hunters time to take over.'

Even though Sayber's talking about destroying his brother's livelihood, Bray still smiles. Gryffin would be mostly human again... and so would he. He runs his finger across the throbbing implant on his face. This information offers him the chance to get rid of his own mods.

'So, what's the plan?' Bray asks.

Felix sits next to his wife and, in a rare show of tenderness, takes her hand in his. 'Well, I doubt you have the necessary equipment in the Outer Sector to carry this out, and I certainly don't have the expertise.

'So there are two options — one, we move the station and everyone on it through the Port and we have a vacation in the Outer Sector or, two, you bring the cyborgs to us along with the relevant personnel.' He sits back in his high-backed chair. 'For the record, this station hasn't moved farther than a sedate stroll for decades, just like Evie and me. Probably best to rule that one out.'

Bray laughs, the sound echoing around his skull. 'You want me to go back to the Outer Sector and bring Gryffin here? Are you crazy? If the Foundation even gets a whiff of him, he'll be back working for them before we can stop it.'

'If you've fixed the implant, that won't matter.'

Bray looks at Felix as if he's grown another head. 'Gryffin isn't going to consider coming here. And even if he did, his programming is altered. There's no telling what will happen if we try to take him through the Port. He could easily turn on us, killing us all before we even complete the journey. Bringing him across will give One exactly what he wants.'

'Not quite,' Sayber says. 'One wants Gryffin in the Outer Sector - you said it yourself. Having him over here might just scupper his plans.' He smiles and clasps his hands behind his head. 'Sounds like music to my ears.'

Bray looks around the table of people and can see they agree with Felix and Sayber. 'I... I could be altered too. What if bringing him here... I don't know, triggers something in the two of us. I don't want to go up against my brother - not like that.'

Sayber turns in his seat to face him. 'We will all be here to make sure that doesn't happen. Felix is right. As much as I hate to admit it, Gryffin has to come to Earth.'

'Okay, so say I agree - we've got no way of contacting Ultar.'

Felix slowly nods his head. 'Bray's right. The Foundation still control all transmissions entering and leaving the Sector.'

Bray rubs his forehead but it just makes the pain worse. 'Actually, we hold the other side of the main Port.'

Felix's eyes widen. 'Why the hell didn't you say earlier? We could use that to our advantage.'

'How does that help if the Foundation hold this side?' Sayber asks.

Felix touches the side of his nose. 'Can't give away trade secrets,

Captain. Give me a few hours. I may be able to figure something out.' He shuffles towards the door, pausing before he leaves. 'Heath, why aren't you following me?'

The young man mutters something under his breath before obediently following Felix from the room.

∞

ULTAR

Gryffin sits up, clutching his head and roaring in pain. He falls off the bunk, landing on his injured leg. The pain from that is no match for whatever's going on in his head. He buries his fist in his hair as another vice of pain tightens around his head. Someone tries to pry his hand away but he's sure if he lets go his head will split open.

'Gryffin! Can you hear me?' He recognises Desyl's voice but there's only enough air in his lungs to scream.

As quickly as the pain started it fades, leaving him on the floor with his bad leg twisted awkwardly underneath him.

Gryffin slowly lifts his head to look at Desyl. The Nomad is on all fours on the ground in front of him. 'Sir. What happened?'

He reaches up and wipes blood from his nose. 'He died.'

'Who, sir?' Desyl asks.

'One of the cyborgs. Stefan.'

He closes his eye as Desyl makes the call to check on the cyborg. A minute later he crouches down to Gryffin's level again. 'They just checked his room. He's dead.' Desyl helps lift Gryffin back on to the cot. He kneels in front of him to check his leg brace. 'I've put in a call to Milla. You landed pretty hard on that. Might have done some damage.' Desyl sits on the end of the cot and looks sideways at Gryffin. 'You felt him die, didn't you, sir?'

Gryffin nods once. 'The link between us is getting stronger. Or I'm getting weaker.' He leans back against the bars and looks over at

Desyl. 'I'm not fit to be High Commander. Damn it, I shouldn't still be in command of *Ares*. You need to take over.'

'The last thing the Nomad need now is a new leader. You need to stay put, sir.'

Milla arrives, ending the conversation. Desyl's right. The Nomad need stability. The problem is that's the one thing he can't offer.

'I've just heard from the team about Stefan. I'm afraid he suffered from a terminal aneurysm. Desyl said you felt it?'

'Stabbing pain in my head for a few seconds then it stopped.'

Milla frowns as she places her bag on the floor of the cell. 'You landed on your leg?'

'Landed hard,' Desyl answers before he can say anything.

'Well, let's see what damage you did to yourself.' She unlocks the metal brace and unfastens the side of his trouser leg to expose the dressing over the metal section. He doesn't need to be a medic to know he's messed it up again. Blood is seeping through the dressing. 'Damn it. Right, well, this will need a bit more than my basic trusty bag can offer. Good thing I brought the 'Extreme Gryffin patch-up kit'.

'You're kidding, right?' Desyl says as he looks down at the case.

She points to the writing on the lid. 'Nope. I also have a 'Gryffin nearly killed himself again' kit. Since working with you louts I've had to upgrade my field kit.'

'Yeah. I probably don't blame you,' Desyl says as he drags a chair into the cell for Milla to sit on.

'Trousers off and lie back on the bed. I mean Gryffin, not you Desyl,' she adds with a smile.

'Glad you said that before I stripped.' Desyl helps him to his feet and holds him up as Gryffin pushes his trousers down, carefully avoiding the growing patch of blood, then flops back on the bed, exhausted by the simple task. Milla snaps on a pair of gloves and cuts the bandage off. 'So, exactly what did you feel when Stefan died?'

'Everything. Why the hell is this happening? Why is it only one way?'

Milla grimaces as she cleans his leg. 'I haven't got the first clue I'm afraid. Maybe your control implant is somehow blocking or muting signals from you. I'm only hazarding a guess though. I'll have to—'

'Run more tests.'

She looks up from his leg and winks. 'Said that a few times before, haven't I?'

'Once or twice.'

'Desyl, can you pop on a pair of gloves?' Once he's slipped the gloves on she holds out a handful of bloody swabs.'

'Oh thanks.'

She smirks at him. 'My pleasure. Just stick them in the waste bag in the case then pass me more swabs. This is a mess.'

Desyl grimaces and passes her more swabs. 'Yeah, I don't need to know, thanks.'

'Neither do I,' Gryffin mutters as she leans over his leg again. 'How is it?'

Milla frowns but doesn't reply immediately. 'It's not good, Captain.'

'If I lose my leg, how much time will I buy myself?'

Milla blows out a long breath and scrunches up her face as she concentrates on something fucking painful in his leg.

'Brutal truth is it's not going to make much of a difference. The surgery alone could kill you. For the amount of time you have left...'

'Not worth doing anything.'

'Sorry, sir. How's the pain?'

'It's there. Meds are helping.'

'That's good. I guess it's the silver lining in all this. With your implants failing, they're not neutralising the pain meds as fast.' She grimaces at the look on his face. 'Yeah, not much of a silver lining I know. Sorry, sir.'

Gryffin closes his eye as she rummages in her kit for something to hold his leg together another few days. He's half tempted to tell her not to bother wasting the supplies. If anything, he wants to order her to put a bullet in his head. He's done waiting to see what part of him fails next. He's done being stuck in this cell while everyone wastes time babysitting him. It's beyond humiliating and not the way he wanted things to end.

The only thing keeping him here is Terra. He wants to get on *Ares* and die on the command deck. He wants her as far from him as possible when that happens. Knowing that she's witnessing this is the hardest part for him to deal with. Seeing that look on her face every damn time, the hope in her eyes, it's tearing him apart.

'Sir? Hey, you still with me?'

Gryffin opens his eye and looks over at Desyl. 'Yeah. Did you—Fuck!'

Milla grimaces. 'Sorry, sir. Must have hit a sensitive spot.'

'You're inside my fucking leg. It's all sensitive.'

He swallows deeply trying to keep his stomach in check. 'Desyl, did you get the repairs done on the sails?'

Desyl tears his gaze away from the inside of Gryffin's leg and nods. 'Yeah. Got it wrapped up today. *Ares* is fighting fit again.'

'You need to get her in the air.'

'Sir—'

'Next run Aleena needs, *Ares* should go. Fuck, Milla.' She's dealt with his leg on a daily basis since he was locked in the cell, but the pain today is unbelievable.

'Nearly done, sir.'

Desyl crouches down beside the head of the bed and clasps his hands together as he looks down at him. 'Sir. Roman told me what you want... you know... later.'

'Not going to talk me out of it?'

'Why would I talk you out of it? You deserve to die on *Ares*. No one is going to argue with that, sir. Milla will temporarily transfer to *Ares* so she can be there in case... just to make sure it goes like you want.'

Milla throws another handful of swabs in the waste and looks over at him. 'I'm presuming Terra won't be coming too?'

'No.'

Milla nods and takes more swabs from her bag. 'Fair enough. Can I also presume you want your implants shut off? Let nature take its course.'

'Can't keep going like this, Milla.'

She smiles sadly and nods. 'When do you want to leave?'

'A few days. But don't tell Terra. There's no way she's going to agree to this. She'll just try to talk me out of it.'

'You're the boss. How about you get some sleep? I'll have your leg patched up by the time you wake up.'

He wants to stay awake, but his body has other ideas. A few weeks ago, he wouldn't have considered sleeping in front of his crew but he's gone beyond worrying about that. All he cares about right now is surviving a little longer so he can see his beloved ship one last time.

DIXON SPACE STATION

Bray sits down next to Morgan, takes the offered glass, and empties the contents down his throat. He shakes his head and winces as it burns on its way down.

'Was Felix able to send a message?'

Bray nods and stretches out in the low chair. 'Felix managed to piggyback it off a cargo vessel going through the Port. It'll take a few days to get to Ultar.'

'Do you really think he'll come here?'

Bray sighs as he looks out the window. It's something he's been wondering about since he decided to contact Ultar. Having a rough idea how to help Gryffin's implant issue is one thing. Actually convincing the stubborn Nomad to come to Foundation territory is another matter entirely. And even if he did make the journey, there's nothing to say they can actually do anything to help Gryffin. There's every chance they'll make the journey and it will be a waste of time. No point voicing his worries right now. Everyone has their own set of problems and issues to deal with.

He looks over at his uncle. Morgan and Erin have lost everything. They're facing as much uncertainty as himself and Gryffin. They have no home, no credits, and a future filled with doubt. The obvious plan would be for them to settle on Ultar, but until the Foundation threat has been removed, that's not possible.

He forces a weak smile on his face. 'If the choice is left up to Gryffin, the answer would probably be no. Luckily, he has Roman and Terra. They'll give him the kick he needs.'

'Terra?' Morgan asks. He leans forward in his chair. 'As in Terra Rush? Callum's daughter?'

'You know her?'

'Of course. Callum and Jensen were Maggie's closest friends.' His expression darkens as he clenches his fists. 'Still sickens me to know he was involved.'

'She feels the same about the whole thing - believe me. She had no idea what her father was up to.'

'So, what's her relationship to Gryffin?'

Great, just what Bray wants to talk about right now. 'They're together. You know - like a couple.'

'Is that right?'

'Yeah, she's one of the few people that can get through to him. If anyone can talk him around, it's her.'

Morgan shakes his head as he blows out a long breath. 'Small world. I still can't believe we could be meeting Daegan— sorry, Gryffin. I can't get my head around it.'

Bray smiles at him then turns back to the window. He doesn't have the heart to tell him Gryffin probably won't be interested in a family reunion. His first brotherly chat with Gryffin ended with them beating the living daylights out of each other.

'So, what happens now?' Morgan asks. 'Do we just sit here and wait on the off chance he decides to come here?'

'The new cyborgs are the biggest threat at the moment. There's no way the Council is going to sit back and do nothing. They'll launch a counterattack. We have to be prepared for whatever they throw at us.'

'The Foundation has an armada of ships. That could be a pretty big counterattack. Are you confident we can stop them?'

'If *Ares* and some other ships are here, possibly.'

'They're not going to drip feed ships to the Outer Sector. It's too much of a risk. A handful of Nomad or Hunter ships would put an end to that pretty quick from what I've heard. They'll send quite a few ships to be on the safe side.'

'I don't have all the answers, Morgan. All I know is that we need eyes on the Foundation and their new toys. If Gryffin comes across he'll bring *Ares* and probably *Nemesis*, maybe more. There's no point in us swapping places with them. Better to have a few of us here just in case.'

Morgan nods slowly, but looks less than convinced. Bray can't blame him. It's not a plan. In truth, they've got nothing - just the off chance a faulty cyborg will come to them. Those details will hardly strike fear in the heart of the Council. At most it will give them a good laugh.

He discretely covers his eye with his hand as his vision swims for a moment, then rapidly sharpens, showing him a completely different view than a few seconds ago. He focuses on the far side of the station visible from his seat and gasps as the image gradually moves towards him. He puts out his hand as the station wall seems to rush towards him.

'What's the matter?'

Bray blinks a few times and everything returns to normal. 'Nothing. Just my eye playing up. I'm fine, really.'

His uncle looks less than convinced. 'Are you sure? That's not the first time it's done that.'

'I'm fine, Morgan. Really.' Bray desperately needs to figure out what's on *Cronus'* system. Whether Gryffin can be fixed or not is one thing. Right now, he's worried about his own future. He's no good to the Hunters like this.

He refills his glass and sips the contents as he mulls over what lies ahead. So much depends on their ability to hack the system. Getting Gryffin to directly access with the system is the perfect solution, but he may not be strong enough to do that anymore.

Without that information, they've got nothing. How can they possibly go up against an army of cyborgs without knowing the first thing about their strength and numbers? If Gryffin and Bray have the work reversed along with the other cyborgs on Ultar, they could find themselves at a definite disadvantage.

He looks out at the blackness surrounding the station. For the first time since he was changed, he's beginning to wonder if having the work reversed at this stage is such a good idea.

∞

ULTAR

Roman shuts down the comms channel and leans back in his chair. He blows out a long breath as he swivels around to face Chayse. 'Before we address the content, first things first. Is the message legit?'

Chayse nods enthusiastically. 'Absolutely. I checked it four times. Not sure how Bray did it, but he bounced the signal through the Port when a Foundation ship came through. It was sent a few days ago.'

Roman rises to his feet and paces the comms room, ignoring the strange looks from the other occupants. 'It is worth the risk? I mean, I know you and Milla have done everything you can for Gryffin and the others, but can we really decipher the information contained in *Alpha*'s system? And even if we can, is there a possibility the work to Gryffin can be undone?'

Chayse opens his mouth to speak, but closes it again and frowns.

'I'm not sure to be honest. If it was a few weeks ago, Gryffin probably could have hooked to the system on the Foundation ship and accessed it that way. If he tried in his current condition, it'll kill him.' He looks over at the blank screen and thinks for a moment. 'About Gryffin however, yes, I think it can. Obviously, we'd have to check the data in more detail, but if Bray thinks it's a good idea, then it must be. He knows more about the Foundation work than any of us here — Avoca made sure of that.'

'I never thought there'd be a way of undoing what Callum did.'

Chayse holds up a hand. 'Don't get carried away, sir. Bray isn't saying that. There's a possibility some of it can be undone — definitely not all, but you're right. It's a hell of a lot better than surviving the way he is now. Bray also has access to a rejuvenation pod. Milla's told me about them. A few sessions in one will strengthen his body. In theory, if he's stronger it'll prolong his life. Maybe even long enough for us to fix the damaged implants.'

'Okay, so let's just say we agree this is his best option, how do you think he'll react if I broach the subject with him? I can't see him being too keen about a trip to Earth.'

Chayse scrubs his hand over his blond spikes. 'That's putting it mildly. He'll take it badly. Going to Earth isn't even on the bottom of his to-do list.' He pushes back from the table. 'I fully believe, as his father, you should do the honours.' Chayse quickly gets to his feet and hurries away before Roman can object.

Roman sighs, runs a hand over his cropped hair, and looks at the door. With no other reason to delay and, with no last minute crisis to deal with, Roman decides to get it over with.

This isn't a conversation he's looking forward to having. Even though Gryffin is seriously unwell, the thought of letting his son go anywhere near Earth doesn't sit well with Roman. His son has been through enough procedures without sending him to Foundation space for more.

Roman smiles to himself as he descends to the belly of the

complex. He's still having a hard time accepting the fact he's a father. He'll never get back the thirty-four years he missed with Gryffin. There's no point regretting or wishing otherwise. What happened is in the past and, unfortunately, there's nothing either of them can do about it. However badly Roman wants to go back in time and make sure his best friend doesn't get anywhere near his son, all he can do now is make sure no one gets close to him again. And it's a job he's taking seriously.

He gets to the basement level and salutes the guard standing by the door. The woman salutes back and opens the door for him without a word. Roman suppresses a shiver as he walks along the dimly lit corridor. Even after all this time, he still prefers the clean lines of *Infinity* compared to the cramped tunnels that make up most of the underground base.

Who's he kidding. The feeling of dread has nothing to do with the tunnels. It's because of the upcoming conversation. He runs through his lines in his head, rehearsing for what he has no doubts will be a short and blunt discussion.

He's no fool and neither is his son. He knows Gryffin will say no and he can't blame him. Why would he willingly go anywhere near the people who hurt him? That doesn't mean Roman's not going to give it a damn good try though.

Having the entire cyborg project in their hands is an enormous bonus to the group. He's looking forward to hearing the story of their conquest.

When Bray and Garvan disappeared along with *Alpha*, a bit of Roman thought that would be the last anyone heard from them. It says a great deal about the men that they survived a stay on Foundation Earth and even managed to take the Council's pride and joy.

Roman smiles to himself. He really wishes he could've seen the Council's faces when they realised their ship had been taken by Outer Sector rebels.

'Sir, everything all right?'

Roman jumps slightly and looks at the security guard. He must have walked to the cells on autopilot. 'Of course. Is he alone?'

The security guard raise his eyebrows. 'Are you seriously asking me that?'

Roman smiles. 'Terra, right.'

'As always.'

'Dare I ask how long she's been here for?'

'Only two hours... so far. I heard Gryffin tell her, forcefully, to leave, but she was equally as forceful when she refused.'

'Thank you. We'll be fine for a few minutes, if you want a break.' Taking the hint, the guard salutes and walks down the corridor. Roman holds out his hand to the door, takes a deep breath and places his palm on the lock.

As usual, Terra is working on the small desk against the far wall. Ship and base reports are neatly piled on the floor around the desk. Instead of having her head buried in a report, he's relieved to see her drawing.

Completely engrossed in her creation, she doesn't notice him come in. Every few seconds she glances up at a sleeping Gryffin, then back at her paper. Dark pencil blackens the tips of her fingers as she rubs and blurs the lines, softening the pencil marks. Terra never liked drawing on a unit. When it came to her art, she was very old fashioned. Pencils and paper were her only tools. Luckily, Ultar has plenty of both, more than enough to keep her supplied for many years.

He looks over at his son, wondering what she could be focusing her drawing on. The image facing him is not something he'd want to immortalise in a drawing. This lifeline from Bray couldn't have come at a better time. Now all he has to do is convince Gryffin to take hold of it.

'How long have you been there?'

He smiles at Terra and shrugs. 'A few minutes. How is he?'

'No worse. He's been asleep for about an hour.' Her tone is cheery, but Roman can see the worry etched around her eyes. He's seen her age in front of him the last few weeks. The stress of Gryffin's situation is deeply affecting the twenty-seven-year-old. The sparkle had gone from her green eyes and the shine from her dark hair. He knows a part of her is being destroyed as Gryffin's condition deteriorates — and that worries him. 'Speaking of sleep...'

'I had five hours last night. I'm fine, really.'

'What about food?'

'I grabbed something before I came down.'

'I can go and get you something if you want.'

She shakes her head. 'I don't really like eating in front of him. Food isn't agreeing with him at the moment. He refuses to eat everything I cook him.'

Roman hides his smile as he sits down beside her. Gryffin groans in his sleep and Terra instantly gets to her feet. Gryffin's brow furrows and he buries his head under his flesh arm, grabbing onto his hair as he thrashes in the bed. Terra calls his name over and over until he eventually stills and opens his eye. He looks around the room, then from Roman to Terra.

'Hey,' Terra says. 'You okay?'

He nods once and runs his hand through his damp hair as he takes a deep breath. 'Yeah. I thought I told you to leave?'

'I'm not going anywhere so stop wasting your breath. Do you need anything?'

He shakes his head and slowly pulls himself up the bed, leaning against the back wall for support.

Roman looks away from his son. He looks even worse than he did earlier. 'I have some news. We just got a message from Bray.'

That instantly gets Gryffin and Terra's attention. 'Is he okay?' Terra asks.

'Seems to be. He's hiding out with some friends of Avoca's. *Perses* and *Lir* have just entered the system. It was only a short message, piggybacked on a Foundation cruiser as it came through the Port. He was able to steal *Alpha*.'

Gryffin stares at him as he shuffles down the bed. 'Say that again?'

'He's got *Alpha*. He's also got the Foundation's cyborg lab and all of the data. The Council moved it to *Alpha* thinking it would be safe there.' Roman laughs and shakes his head. 'Guess they didn't count on Bray doing something completely stupid.'

Terra smiles as she looks up at Roman. 'Does that mean Milla could fix Gryffin?'

Roman shrugs. 'We need to get to the data and unlock it first. We're a long way from knowing what exactly we have access to.'

Her smiles only grows. 'But it's a good start, right?'

Roman nods as he looks away from the hope in her eyes. Having access to the information is one thing. Using it to fix Gryffin before he... Well, that's completely different.

Gryffin grunts as he moves his damaged leg. 'There's a catch, right?'

Roman nods at Gryffin. 'There's no way to get *Alpha* here at the moment. She needs a full crew to operate anything faster than her drive engines. It would take months to get her here in drive. So, we either send a crew there to spend the next few weeks learning how she works or... '

Gryffin's eye narrows as he hears the unspoken words. 'Hell no.'

Roman sits on the stool by the bars and clasps his hands on his knees. 'I know it's not ideal.'

Gryffin's lifeless robotic eye stares unblinking at him. 'That's an understatement. I'm not going to Earth or anywhere near the damn planet. Or the Sector. Understood?'

Terra tries to take his hand through the bars but he pulls it out of the way. 'Gryffin—'

'Don't, Terra. I'd prefer to rot in here than go anywhere near the Foundation.'

The smile that was on Terra's face a few minutes ago disappears.

'Now you're just being ridiculous. The equipment on *Alpha* could save your life. Are you really that stubborn you'd sacrifice yourself because of your damn pride?'

His face hardens as he meets her eyes. 'Yes.'

Roman leans forward, resting his arms on his legs. 'There's more you should know before you make any rash decisions. The Foundation have continued the project on Earth. From what Bray says, they have an impressive army of cyborgs ready to attack.'

Gryffin shakes his head. 'Fuck. How many?'

'Hard to say. He's hoping to get a better insight once they hack *Alpha*'s system. Avoca's friends are trying to help him. I don't need to tell you that this army poses a serious threat to the Sector. We have a slim chance if we can access *Alpha*'s files. If we can find a flaw in the new cyborg design—'

'We can possibly bring down the whole program,' Gryffin finishes.

'Exactly.'

Terra reaches through the bars to place her hand on Gryffin's arm. 'As much as I want you to go to Earth, there's a problem. You can't go to Earth — physically. The last time you tried, your programming stopped you.'

'Bray had an idea about that too,' Roman says. 'We still have the stasis pod from Maggie.'

'Oh no, Captain,' Terra protests. 'You can't be serious? That's just... wrong.'

'Trust me, I feel the same, but so far we haven't been able to isolate the specific programming responsible for that. Unless we find a way to counter that issue, you won't be going anywhere.'

'So you want to shut down my cybernetics and let the pod keep my body alive?'

Roman grimaces, not entirely thrilled about the prospect either. 'To put it bluntly. Then, when we get you to Earth, Bray can fix the problem, get you up and running again, and you can have a serious chance of surviving an encounter with the Foundation.'

'That simple,' Gryffin mumbles sarcastically from his bunk.

'Peeled back to its basics, yes.'

Terra gently squeezes Gryffin's arm. 'Milla can't do a lot more to help you here.'

'This army any good?'

Roman nods. 'Bray's report was sparse, but he's seen them in action and barely made it out in one piece. The Foundation are using the Scientist's data to create as many cyborgs as they want based on your design.'

Gryffin leans his head back against the wall and rubs a hand over his flesh eye. Roman and Terra glance at each other, but neither says a word. It's Gryffin's decision.

After a long wait, Gryffin finally opens his mouth to speak, but instead squeezes his eye shut in pain. He sucks in a breath as he struggles to control the pain. Gryffin shakes his head and mutters a curse under his breath. 'Who are the people Bray's with?'

'The Dixon's? He assures me they're trustworthy.'

'I'll think about it.'

Terra gets to her feet and paces in front of his cell. 'Excuse me? What is there to think about?'

'I said I'll think about it. Time you got back to work, Commander.'

Terra opens her mouth to reply but Gryffin's lone eye targets her, cutting off any words that might have been tempted to leave her mouth. She gestures to Roman, who, after shrugging apologetically at Gryffin, follows her from the room. She waits until the door slides shut then kicks it for good measure.

'I could just...' she mimes strangling someone then shouts and kicks the door again.

Roman places a hand on her shoulder. 'Hey, you know what he's like.'

'Yeah. Stubborn, irritating, and did I mention stubborn?'

Roman smiles. 'Give him time. It's a lot to process.'

Terra gestures angrily at the door. 'We're trying to save his life. I don't get him. I thought he wants to live. None of his actions even hint at him wanting to give up. How can he get what he wants but still refuse to cooperate? I swear I'm going to go insane trying to figure him out.'

'We have to see it from his side. He doesn't have any good memories of the Foundation. It's understandable he would be less than keen about going to Foundation space to a commandeered Foundation ship to be worked on with Foundation equipment. Again.' He turns her away from the cell and leads her back down the corridor. 'Perhaps a bit of thinking time would be a good thing for all of us.'

Terra glances over her shoulder at the door. 'Probably a good idea. In my current mood, I could very easily...' She lets the sentence go unfinished, but Roman has no doubts she'd like to beat some sense into his son.

ULTAR

Terra lowers the tray of food onto the small table opposite the cell and turns to face Gryffin. It's been four hours since their heated discussion. She's not disillusioned enough to think he's changed his mind but she's going to give it another shot.

He's awake and sitting against the back wall talking to Chayse and Baila. *Nemesis* and *Dannan* are heading out on a supply run tomorrow. With the Foundation nipping at their heals, most of the colonies have relocated to Ultar, or other secure settlements Gryffin lined up. Unfortunately, with trade being their main source of provisions and income, people are struggling to keep food on the table.

In true Gryffin form, he's putting on a convincing show in front of them. He can do little to hide the tremors, the chills, or the raging fevers that plague him, but he continues the briefing without showing how unwell he feels. He's fighting chills at the moment and is wearing his uniform jacket, his hand tucked under his armpit for warmth.

Terra leans back against the wall and opens her drawing pad as she patiently waits for the meeting to finish. In a change to her usual portraits, she had woken up with the urge to draw a landscape. As she draws, her gaze wanders from the page to his pasty skin, back to the page, then over to the collection of scars crisscrossing the side of his head.

With his hair cut short there's nothing to hide the wounds left by her father. If she looks closely she can actually see the holes his drill left in Gryffin's scalp. She shakes her head and tries to focus on something else, but everywhere she looks, she can see remnants of her father's work on the man she loves. She curses to herself and focuses on the drawing instead.

They finish their meeting and Chayse squeezes Terra's shoulder as he leaves the room. Things are still damaged between the High Commander and his former aide. Chayse has never forgiven Gryffin for leaving him out of the deception which involved Gryffin pretending to kill Milla. Even though Gryffin did what he did for the right reasons, Chayse can't move past Gryffin's decision to leave him in the dark. Hopefully time can heal the rift between them.

She just manages to keep the tears at bay. Time is the one thing they don't have enough of. As if reading her mind, Gryffin meets her eyes and smiles wryly. 'Commander.'

'You hungry, Captain?' Terra asks, returning his formal greeting.

'You cook it?'

Terra smirks. She knows her culinary skills may leave a little to be desired. 'It's fruit.'

'Okay.'

He doesn't say anything else which doesn't surprise her. Having a conversation with Gryffin is frustratingly difficult at the best of times. 'How are you feeling?'

'Fine.'

'Of course you are.' She carries the chair over to the cell and sits down.

'What are you drawing?'

She reaches across and holds up the page.

'Ultar?'

She shakes her head as she swallows a mouthful of fruit. 'It's Earth. Well, a small wooded area about ten minutes from where I grew up. I used to spend weekends exploring with my friends.'

'Right.'

'We'd stop at the shop on the way home. They sold the most amazing chocolate covered donuts. We'd easily eat three or four each and all seriously regret it afterwards.' She smiles as she looks down at the page. It had been months since she'd thought about Earth. The Foundation was always on her mind, but not her actual home.

Friends and family had been left behind when she was forced to stay in the Outer Sector. It's not like she could contact them either. When they made the decision to stand up to the Foundation, she had been declared dead by the Council. Everyone she knows or cares about on Earth thinks she's dead.

She puts the pad down and smiles at Gryffin, but the look on his face tells her he can see right through her. 'Sorry. Just having a donut moment. What I wouldn't give for one of them right now. So, Bray mentioned in his message that he found your uncle and cousin.' Nothing from the irritatingly stoic Nomad. 'You must be curious about them.'

'No.'

'No? Really? They're your family. They thought you were dead, Gryffin. Can you imagine what they must be feeling? I'm sure they're eager to meet you.'

'I've told you I'm not interested. And I'm not going to apologise for what I said. Sending me to Earth is a bad idea—'

'I did hear you the first time.'

'I wasn't finished.'

'Sorry.' She grimaces when he glares at her for interrupting again. Gryffin shuffles to the end of the bed, rests his head against the bars, and takes a deep breath. 'The Foundation didn't create an army to leave them on Earth. They're coming for us. Might already be on the way.'

'Ultar is protected. There's nothing to worry about. The colonists are safe.'

'Roman took their flagship, Bray took the replacement, and they probably still want me back. You really think they'll politely knock at the door and ask for us to give them back their stuff? Our defences won't hold them off for long. I want to be here when they make their move. I'm falling apart but there's no way in hell I want to leave.'

Terra's heart sinks. 'So that's it. You're just going to keep going like this until you fall apart.'

'For a communications officer you don't listen too well.'

'What do you mean?'

'I said I want to be here. Doesn't mean I will though.'

She slumps back in her chair and frowns at him. 'Hang on. Are you saying you'll let us take you to Earth?'

'I don't want to go, but it makes sense. I'm useless like this. If Bray found a way to help get me operational again, I have to give it a shot.'

'I think I may just faint.'

'Don't push it, Terra. There is one condition.'

Her eyes narrow. 'Of course there is. Do tell.'

'I want these people to see if they can upgrade my implants, remove the program block, and use me the way I was designed to be used - as a controllable weapon.'

∞

DIXON SPACE STATION

Heath leans over the desk and glares down at Evie. 'Are you kidding me? You're letting them bring him here?'

'Heath, please. We may live in Foundation space, but that doesn't mean we forgo manners.'

'Screw manners. The last thing we need right now is a damn cyborg on the station. It's bad enough having Bray here without adding to our problems.'

'Oh now you're just being ridiculous. Bray is not a cyborg.'

'Yeah, but his brother is. You know the Foundation based their design off Gryffin. He's the original one and you want to invite him on board? He killed hundreds of people when he destroyed *Omega*. I had friends on that ship.'

Evie waves her hand dismissively at him. 'Well, you could hardly call them friends after their lack of support at your trial.'

'Thanks for reminding me,' he replies sharply.

'And Gryffin destroyed *Omega* to protect the Outer Sector.'

'Who gives a damn about the specifics? He tethered that freighter to *Omega*. He killed them and now you want to work with him. This is a bad idea if you ask me.'

'No one did, dear.'

Heath frowns and slams his gun on the desk in front of him. 'You pay me to protect you. Having that... thing here won't make my job any easier.'

'From what I've been told, he is the way he is due to no fault of his own.'

'What if he turns on you? What's stopping him from bringing the Foundation to our door and letting them in?'

'You have to look at the big picture, Heath.' Felix says as he enters the room. 'He's the key to undoing the hold the Foundation has on this Sector. You know that.'

'You can't expect me to work with him.'

Evie shrugs. 'We're not going to force you to do anything. What I will say is that, to keep your job here, you will work with him. Whether you want to stay here or not is your decision.'

Heath rubs his hand over his head as he curses to himself. 'Not much of a choice, Evie.'

'You really think you're alone in this?' Felix asks. 'I can't say I'm singing and dancing at the thought of having him here either. He's a weapon and unless I can pick him apart I won't be able to trust him in my home, but I will work with him because that's the right thing to do. It will help our cause. Help what we've been working incredibly hard to do for the last few years, which is to destroy the Foundation.

'Think about it, Heath. He's the embodiment of everything the Foundation has been doing behind the back of the public for years. If they knew the Foundation took children and subjected them to modifications and horrific experiments, do you really think they will happily follow their rule?'

Heath snorts. 'You really think the population will believe anything we say? The Foundation has them by the throat. You know that. We do what we do because so many people follow the Foundation like mindless drones. It's going to take a hell of a lot more than a defective cyborg, with a well-publicised criminal record, to convince them otherwise. Even if we parade Gryffin in front of them it'll be a push to get anyone to step away from the rest of the damn herd.'

Evie slaps her palm against the table. 'That's enough cursing, Heath. You know it brings me out in hives,' she adds, scratching her neck. 'We are so close to ending their rule. Closer than we've ever been before. Together with whatever's on the system on that monstrosity of a ship the Hunter brought us, we can do it.'

She gestures out the window towards the Foundation ship in their hangar. 'We could really do with your help, Heath. There is so much more at stake than personal feelings. So many people have been hurt by the actions of the Foundation. Don't you want to be a part of ending them once and for all?'

Heath looks at the ground and shakes his head. 'Fine. If he does come, I'll be keeping as far from him as I can though.'

Evie nods. 'I completely understand. I, for one, will be standing behind you as you keep away from him. So, shall we get back to work?'

DIXON SPACE STATION

'We're missing something.' Bray shoves his chair back from the table and drags his hand through his hair.

Rua massages the back of her neck. 'We've barely scratched the surface. There's a strong chance we've missed something. It'll take time.'

'Yeah, and that's something we don't have a lot of. The Foundation could be on their way there right now.' Bray slams a hand against the table and shouts, 'Damn it. There has to be something!' He marches over to the screen. All eyes in the room focus on him. 'Why would the Foundation leave Gryffin on Ultar? It just doesn't make sense.'

'You've lost me.' Sayber says.

'They put a lot of effort in to getting him back on the table. Why would they suddenly drop all interest in him?'

Rua gestures to the data on the new cyborgs. 'Better models to play with?'

Bray shakes his head. 'It's more than that. The report states that the prototype is in place.'

'Yeah, but that could mean the first of the new feisty women they've changed,' Sayber offers.

'Gryffin has always been referred to as the prototype. No, they mean he's in place. But for what? His programming is as it should be. Unless Gryffin suddenly developed a serious case of Stockholm syndrome, which I doubt, there's no way he's going to just let the Foundation in. Knowing him, he'd personally try to take them all down before that happens... or himself worse case.' Bray winces and steadies himself against the wall as his vision swims.

Rua jumps to her feet before anyone else can move. 'What's the matter?'

Bray slowly shakes his head. 'I'm fine.' He faces the screen, resting his arm against the wall as he leans forward. 'Why leave him there?'

'As a demonstration.'

Bray spins to face Rua. 'What did you say?'

'I heard a lot of stories about what he did the last time the Foundation had him. He was a weapon, a lethal one. The Foundation have created a new army based on his design, right?'

Bray nods.

'What if they want to use him as a demonstration model?'

Evie slaps her hands against the table. 'I think I found something!' She loads the data on the screen at the head of the table. Line after line of code appears. 'This is a section of that fellow's programming.'

'Gryffin,' Felix says.

'Yes, thank you dear.' She scrolls down and highlights a lone line in the middle. 'This is the bit that stands out.'

Bray blinks a few times as his eyesight blurs slightly. 'I recognise that. Lucan and Chayse checked that when Gryffin came back a few months ago. It's odd but doesn't mean anything.'

Evie nods. 'Odd always means something. You young ones are too quick to dismiss things that can't be explained. It's there so it does mean something.'

'I've checked it. It's gibberish.'

'On its own perhaps.'

'What do you mean on its own?'

'I've got something too!' Felix takes over, much to Evie's annoyance. 'My encryption program brought up something interesting.' He pulls a message up and displays it on the main screen. 'It's a message from One to someone with the charming name of Forty-Three.'

'That's the cyborg we killed on *Cronus*.'

Felix nods approvingly at Bray. 'With a name like that you were doing him a favour. Anyway, this Forty-Three reported to One that the alternative programming had been placed in all the new cyborgs. Now, given the time code on the message he was referring to the cyborgs you encountered on the new colony, not the female ones you recently met.'

'What alternative programming?' Sayber asks.

Felix releases a long, dramatic breath. 'If you hadn't interrupted, you would know by now.'

Sayber clenches his jaw and gestures for him to continue. Felix nods and goes back to the screen. 'It seems there was a line of code added to each of their programming. It was dormant but could be activated remotely when needed. They were each reprogrammed. Including your brother.'

Bray's stomach rolls. 'To do what?'

'I haven't been able to figure that part out yet.'

Bray stares at the screen. 'I don't understand. That line makes no sense.'

Felix nods in agreement. 'Not individually, no. If I was a gambling man, I'd put a fair few credits on the fact this is part of a larger piece of programming.'

'What do you mean?' Bray asks.'

'Well. What if they divided a program between Gryffin and the others you took with you?'

Bray wipes a hand over his face, wincing when his hand brushes off his new eyepiece. 'Why the hell didn't I see that?'

Felix leans back and crosses his arms. 'Because it's damn sneaky, that's why.'

'But about half of them have died since we got back,' Sayber says.

'No telling how many need to be operational for it to be completed. Without examining all the remaining cyborgs we'll never know.'

The room falls silent as each occupant thinks about the consequences of having a group of Foundation controlled cyborgs on Ultar — especially if Gryffin is going to lead them. Bray stares at the code on the screen hoping that Felix got it wrong. But he knows he hasn't. It's going to happen again. Gryffin is going to help destroy Ultar. 'We need to contact them again. Now!'

Felix shakes his head. 'You're in Foundation space now, son. It's not quite as easy as just sending them a message. We need to hijack the comms on a ship going through the Port.'

'You don't understand. I don't know what he's going to do, but it's not going to be good.'

'We'll prepare a message but there's not a lot we can do right now. Just keep your fingers crossed they send something through the Port fairly sharpish.'

Bray looks back at the information on the screen. He's got a really bad feeling about this.

∞

ULTAR

Terra stares over at Gryffin, waiting for him to tell her what he just said was a joke. It's absolutely ridiculous to even contemplate he was anything other than serious. She's known him for two years and joking was not something Gryffin did. When he says something, he means it.

Terra gets to her feet, needing to put a little distance between them. 'You have got to be kidding me.' She turns around to face him again. 'This isn't the time for hair-brained ideas, Gryffin. The control implant is killing you.'

He struggles to his feet. 'I'm not an idiot, Terra. I get it.' Gryffin rests his head against the bars and closes his eyes. 'If these new cyborgs didn't exist, I'd consider having the work reversed. That's not an option anymore. You really think we can survive an army of cyborgs more advanced than me? The new cyborgs are strong and damn tough. As a cyborg, I'm going to have a hard enough time fighting them. As a human...' He lets the sentence hang. 'The only way we stand a chance is if I'm at the same level as them technology-wise. My implants are two decades behind theirs. I need to be upgraded.'

Terra stands in front of him, unable to find the right words to say. The main thought overpowering all others is that she'd prefer losing him to death than have him live one day as a weapon just as her father intended. And that terrifies her.

She takes his hand in hers and squeezes it. She looks up at him and his bloodshot blue eye meets hers. 'The most important thing is making sure you're all right.' She reaches up and taps a finger against the side of his head. 'Fixing that will save you.'

'The only way to fix it is to take it out and try to repair it. I'll be in a stasis pod for months. If it can't be fixed I'm done for. I won't be waking up again. I can't survive without it and that's fact. Even if they do manage to fix it, best case, I'll be out of commission for months. I'm your best fighter. Taking me out now is a dumb move.'

She smirks. 'Best fighter, huh?'

'Well, I could be again, with some work. You'll need me and the other cyborgs to fight, not be burdens while we recover. Not while you're facing the Foundation. They've got an army, Terra. What the hell have we got?'

Terra holds on to his hand. 'We'll be fine. You don't need to even consider this.'

He pulls out of her grip. 'Fine? We'll all be dead, Terra. The only way for the colonies to survive is if you have your own operational cyborgs to fight with you.'

'And what if you die, huh? What if overhauling your implants kills you? Where would that leave us?'

'We're going around in circles. I don't have the work done I'm dead anyway. I have the work done and I might die. Which one sounds like the better option? I've spoken to the other cyborgs. We want both options explored or we stay put. Have you seen the footage from the base?'

Terra nods. Roman had shown everyone during the afternoon briefing. The thought of an army of cyborgs like that terrifies her. 'I agree they're strong, but we can deal with them. We'll figure something out. There has to be a dozen other ways that don't involve you considering kissing your humanity goodbye.' She slumps back in the chair and looks at him. 'Did you seriously think I'd be okay with this?'

'It's got nothing to do with you.'

Terra stares at Gryffin as the enormity of what he just said settles on her. In those few words he had summed up how he thinks they work. She knew it was far from a normal relationship. Being with someone like Gryffin made anything normal difficult, but she had hoped he considered her an equal, someone important in his life. It appears she was wrong, and that hurts. 'I can't believe you just said that. Of course it has something to do with me.'

'This isn't the time for this.'

'That's where you're wrong. You're in there and you're damn well going to listen to me.'

'Listen to what? If I decide to get my implants upgraded we'll deal with it.'

'You really think it's that simple? You can't tell me to just deal with it and leave it at that. This is a life changing decision, Gryffin. One that, whether you like it or not, will affect me too.'

'The Nomad come first.'

Terra slumps back on the chair and takes a deep breath to calm herself. If she gets worked up, this conversation is as good as over. He'll dig his heels in and order her to drop the subject. 'The Nomad come first for you, but not for me. You come first.'

That shuts him up for a few seconds which is better than an instant dismissal. 'I'm High Commander of the Nomad.'

Terra nods. That's his way of telling her she has no part in whatever decision he makes. 'I understand that. All I'm asking is for you to think about this from my angle.'

'There can't be another angle, Terra. I need you to get that.'

'We're in a relationship, Gryffin. I'm asking you to get that - even for a moment. You live from day to day, from battle to battle, disaster to disaster. You jump into dangerous situations without considering for one moment how it will affect the people that care about you.' She taps the side of her head. 'There's just you, your ship and your Nomad in there, right? There's no room for anything or anyone else. I thought that after my time on *Ares* we had grown closer. I guess I was wrong because I sure as hell didn't see this coming.'

'I didn't force you to stay on *Ares* with me.'

'I'm not saying that. You're not even listening to what I'm trying to say.'

'So you're saying I don't give a damn about you.'

'That's not what I'm saying either.'

'Then what?'

'I get why you make the decisions you do, but just for once I'd like you to consider me. Consider us. Even for a few seconds before you plan something as life changing as this.'

'Of course I do,' he shouts, startling Terra. 'If I wasn't considering you I'd have shut off my damn implants weeks ago. You are the only reason I've delayed ending this hell as long as I have. All I've done is try to do the right thing by you.' He gives up standing and goes back to his bed to sit on the edge.

His words take a few seconds to sink in. 'Delayed? You were planning on killing yourself?'

'That's still the plan, Terra. I told you I don't want to go out in this fucking cell. I want to be on my ship, Terra. On my terms.'

'You're giving up?'

'Giving up on what? I'm dying, Terra. It's time you accept that and stop pressuring Milla to find a miracle cure.' He sighs and shakes his head. 'Right now, the only options I have are to go to Earth and buy a little more time so I can end Project Conscript once and for all, or I stay here and die on my ship. There are no other options. If I can be a part of taking down the Foundation I'll give option one a go, otherwise I'm back to my original plan.'

'So that's it? An upgrade or turn off your implants. Hell of a choice. But like you said, it's got nothing to do with me. That's how we do things, right? You make all the important decisions and I just have to go along with it.'

'That's not even close to how we work. Stop blurring the lines. This decision is for the Nomad. It's not about us.'

'I'm not even sure there is an us. I'm trying so hard, Gryffin, but I'm running out of energy. Do you have any idea how difficult the last year has been for me? Do you have the first clue what I've lost? My home, my friends, my family. I've even lost my career. Then I have to try to deal with thinking you're dead for ten months.

'When you came back... I thought I found a home again on *Ares*. A group of space pirates became my new family. But ever since I joined

Ares— sorry, was allowed to stay on board, you've been treating me like I'm a... I don't know what. Certainly not a member of the crew. All I'm asking for is a little consideration every now and again. Surely that's not too much to ask.'

'We've all lost something, Terra. We've all made sacrifices. You don't get special treatment for having a shit few months. If we all did, I reckon my six years of being tortured every day beats your few months of having your Foundation life thrown on its ass.'

Terra bites back her terse reply. She's not going to win the 'who's had a worse life' game. He's top of that leader board. That doesn't mean what she's been through hasn't affected her. She may not have been repeatedly tortured, but that doesn't diminish her pain.

Thinking he was dead for nearly a year on top of dealing with forced exile in the Outer Sector was bad enough without finding out her father had faked his death and had been the one who tortured Gryffin for all those years.

They'd spoken of it briefly, but not for a long time. When Gryffin had come up with the plan to use himself as bait to find her father a few weeks ago, it had brought the truth of her father's involvement to light.

He wasn't in the slightest bit excited to see his daughter again after so long. All he cared about was getting his beloved prototype back. He had strapped Gryffin to the operating table and hurt him without any trace of remorse, or hesitation, or disgust. If anything, he had enjoyed Gryffin's reaction to the pain he was inflicting. In no part of her darkest, deepest thoughts had she truly accepted what her father had become. Not until then.

When he embedded a knife in each of Gryffin's thighs just for fun, a part of her withered away. Whatever love, respect, or pleasant memories she had of her father ceased to exist. It was all a lie. The man who stole Roman's son and Bray's brother from his happy life - that was the truth. And was the cause of her sleepless nights.

She wants to talk about it, needs to, but to whom? Roman is harbouring enough guilt about his part in young Daegan being used in the project. He mentioned once that Gryffin only exists because of him. Daegan would have grown up with his mother and Bray on Earth if not for him. It's ridiculous really. Daegan was taken because of her father. Roman couldn't have stopped that. Even if he had known Daegan was his son, he still couldn't have stopped it.

Talking to Gryffin is out. He wouldn't understand. Couldn't understand. She can't even say for sure that he's fully accepted the Scientist is her father. If he did, how could he realistically want anything to do with her?

She knows she wouldn't if the tables were turned. Milla is always there for her but she's got her plate full with Chayse and *Nemesis*. All she can do is try to deal with it herself or do a Gryffin and completely ignore it, pushing her feelings to the back of her mind. It seems to work for him.

'I don't want to fight about this. I really don't. I know what you're saying, Gryffin. I'm just...' Tired. Worn out. Desperately in need of some good news. She looks across at the man she loves and realises things are going to get so much worse. She knows he's dying but is it so wrong to hang on to whatever hope she can? He may have given up and accepted he only has two options. Neither one will give him a long and happy life. Neither one will give him a life with her.

'What I'm trying to say is that there should be two of us in this relationship, but right now it feels like I'm not one of them - it's you and the Nomad. You make all the important decisions and tell me as an afterthought. Tell - not discuss.'

'That's not true.'

'Really? So you're telling me this plan to hand over your brain to the control implant just came to you. Like a flash of inspiration.' He clamps his mouth shut and Terra laughs harshly. 'Thought not.'

'What the hell do you want from me, Terra? You're the most

important person in my life. I'd die for you in a heartbeat. You know that. But what's happening, is bigger than us. Bigger than your feelings. Bigger than my feelings. I'm the Nomad High Commander. That will always come first - not us.'

Gryffin silently stares at her, nothing showing on his face. Terra sighs and shakes her head. 'Message received, loud and clear, sir.' She turns on her heel and storms towards the door, slamming her hand against the control panel.

Milla shouts and drops the screen on the floor in front of her as Terra bursts through the door. 'You scared me half to death.'

Terra sits on the couch opposite her desk, completely ignoring Chayse sitting beside her on the couch. 'He's finally lost his mind.'

Milla bends down and picks up the screen, placing it on her desk. 'Who?'

'I mean who in their right mind would even consider something like this? The whole idea is downright certifiable.'

Chayse pushes himself off the seat. 'Think that's my cue to leave you two alone.'

'No,' Terra says, finally acknowledging him. 'You know him as well as anyone. Do you think he's lost grip on reality?'

Chayse slumps back on the couch and stretches his legs out. Milla stares over at the stunning Nomad who has become her world.

Since Gryffin made him Captain of *Nemesis*, he's taken the role in his stride. In spite of Chayse's initial reservations, it seems Gryffin knew exactly what he was doing when he made that out-of-the-blue decision. The crew love him and so does Milla.

Gryffin's former aide grabbed her attention from the first minute she saw him on Ultar all those years ago. In that instant, she knew she would get to know him one way or another. She's only human after all. Terra had her sights locked on Gryffin and Milla on Chayse.

And now look at the two of them. Both had gotten their man. It's just a shame only one of them would get their happily ever after. If she's being honest with herself, she never expected to fall in love with Chayse or for Gryffin to break all the rules so they could be together. When Gryffin had officially made her the doctor on *Nemesis*, he had also made her the first female Nomad in the history of the group.

She had expected some resistance from the longer serving Nomad, but no one had batted an eyelid. Their High Commander had made a decision and the group accepted that. End of story.

Being on the same ship as Chayse had changed her life for the better. Being a Nomad had done that too. For the first time in her life, she's proud of what she's doing. And she gets to be with a man who makes her happier than she remembers being before.

As a whole, the Nomad were a group that demanded you take notice. With a leader like Gryffin they were difficult to ignore. Chayse may not have Gryffin's 'I can kill you with one look' stare, but each day, she can see him growing into his role as captain. The terrified aide who felt so far out of his depth is gone and a Nomad captain is appearing.

He certainly looks the part too. Rigorous training had turned the once wiry body to an impressive solid mass of muscle. His black leather uniform matches her own, but on his body it is more than a little distracting.

Black Nomad tattoos cover both arms and the left side of his chest. That one he was particularly proud of. The symbol over his heart marked him as a captain. Something he never thought he would see on his flesh.

Milla has a small griffin on her wrist which told everyone she is under Gryffin's protection. From what she's heard, it's a damn effective deterrent. She'd need to work up to getting an official Nomad mark.

Terra waves her hand at Milla. 'Hey? Hello! Are you listening?'

Milla pulls herself out of her wandering thoughts and back to the current conversation. 'What? Yeah. Sorry. Why don't you start at the beginning? I'm not quite following the conversation.'

'Your leader is considering having his implants upgraded so he can fight these new cyborgs.'

Milla blows out a long breath as she focuses on her desk. Terra looks across at Chayse. His attention is on the floor at his feet.

'Say something. Did you not hear what I just said?'

'We heard you, Terra,' Chayse replies.

'So, that's it? Nothing to say?'

Milla leans forward and clasps her hands together. 'I'm as thrilled as you are about this, but it's an option.'

'Option? It's not an option, Milla. I can't believe you're saying that. Chayse, you agree with me.'

'Hey, Milla isn't saying she agrees or disagrees with anything. It's his choice though. What we want isn't going to influence his decision. We all have first-hand experience with his stubbornness. No matter what we think, if this is what he wants to do, there's damn all any of us can do to stop him.' He gets up and crosses the room to kiss Milla. 'I've got other things to do. See you later.'

Milla takes his place on the couch and holds Terra's hand in hers. 'I'm giving you my professional opinion, Terra. Gryffin is dying. There is absolutely nothing more I can do for him. I'd give anything for that not to be the case, but it's the harsh reality. Realistically, having his implants upgraded and adding some additional ones could stabilise his system.'

'If he has the modifications, what then?'

'What do you mean?'

'Do we lose him anyway? Will he be nothing more than a programmable machine?'

'Stabilising the implant will save him from any further deterioration. He'll be alive.'

'You didn't answer my question.'

Milla rolls her eyes. 'Fine. Okay, yes, there's a fair chance he'll be different. Terra, he's not saying this is definitely going to happen. It's just an option. Nothing more. You and I both know he'd consider almost anything if it means he doesn't have to go down that route again. He's being a leader, Terra. Keeping all his options open.'

'I'm not an idiot, Milla. I know he's... I just can't... I can't lose him to more implants. Not that.'

Milla wraps her arms around Terra and pulls her close. 'Hey, there are a lot of super talented people working to stop that from happening, okay. For now, the best thing you can do is be there for him. Whatever decision he makes, he'll need you by his side.'

'Yeah, that may not be entirely true. I don't think we're talking to each other.'

'What? Again? I thought you just made up?'

Terra sighs and drops her head back against the cushion behind her. 'I told him I want to be considered when he makes these life changing decisions. Apparently that's not the way things work. He's the Nomad High Commander first. That leaves our relationship taking a distant second. I may have stormed out of the room.

'Why does this keep happening, Milla? We can barely get through two days without one or both of us saying the wrong thing. I feel like we're going around in circles. I don't want whatever time we have left to...' Terra closes her eyes and looks away.

Milla has never felt more helpless in her life. If they were in

Foundation space, she'd be able to help Gryffin. Watching her commanding officer getting weaker by the day is horrible.

She's only been a Nomad for a few weeks, but she'd quickly adapted to his style of command. He didn't her give much of a choice, but she found it refreshing. Milla's always been a black and white kind of girl. The blurred lines of the Foundation had been driving her out of her mind for years. It only hit her after seeing how the Nomad run their ships.

On a Nomad vessel there was no wondering how well you were doing your job. No weight of uncertainty on her shoulders. The Foundation had a habit of reassigning people instead of giving them any feedback. The first you knew you weren't pulling your weight was when you found yourself in a new role without a heads up. On Gryffin's ships, you knew pretty damn quick if you'd stepped out of line.

Chayse ran *Nemesis* the same way - although with a little less attitude. She loved her new life and loved being a Nomad. With Gryffin's fast approaching demise hanging over the group, things had taken a sombre tone.

Desyl didn't want to take command of *Ares*. He'd flat out refused. With the future of the flagship clouded in doubt, the group was weakening. She could see it. Chayse could see it. No doubt Gryffin could too, but with him stuck in a cell there's not a damn thing any of them could do. They were in limbo.

Like Terra. They were all living from day to day, waiting to see how much longer the High Commander would be with them.

'Listen, it's a shite situation for everyone. You've got an argumentative, awkward, bull-headed, grumpy git locked in a cell. He's angry and frustrated about what's happening to him. In near constant agony thanks to his implants. Worried about the future of the Nomad. I'd imagine scared shitless about his future. Quite possibly going stir crazy being locked in a cell instead of rampaging across the Sector. I'd also bet a fair amount of credits he's worried sick about you.

'Mix all that fun with what's going on with you and it doesn't paint a happy-go-lucky picture. I'm not surprised you're both stressed and irritable. I know we've all said this to you, but maybe some time apart will do you both a world of good. I'm damn sure I'd be fit to kill Chayse if we were stuck with each other all the time. You need a break. You both do. When was the last time you got a decent night's sleep in a bed?'

Terra grimaces. 'Not sure.'

'Well there's a shock. You're exhausted.' Milla stands up and holds out her hand. 'C'mon.'

'Where are we going?'

'You are going back to *Ares* to get an overnight bag. Then you are coming to my quarters. You will have a ridiculously long shower while I prepare - well, collect from the mess, a banquet of the finest Ultaran fare. We will eat and we will drink,' she adds with a wink. 'And then, my friend, you will sleep all the damn night in a proper bed.'

'That sounds great, but—'

Milla shakes her head as she grabs Terra's hand. 'Nope. Do not go there. I'll make sure Desyl sits with Gryffin. He'll be fine. Nothing's going to happen to him. I promise.' Milla stops at the door and squeezes Terra's hand. 'Hey, I promise. All you'll miss is him sleeping and possibly some scintillating conversation.' Milla snorts. 'Not bloody likely. Seriously, Terra. He'll be absolutely fine. You need to take care of yourself. Now skedaddle. I expect you to be in the shower by the time I get back with food.'

Terra nods and walks towards the hangar. Milla stares after her and rubs her hands together. 'Right, Gryffin. Time you and me had a little chat.'

∞

70

ULTAR

Milla lowers onto the seat opposite Gryffin and makes a point of picking fluff from her trousers. He doesn't think he'll ever get used to seeing a woman wearing the Nomad uniform. Milla is the first and only official female Nomad. Desyl was sorting through some of the ex-inmates from the Foundation prisons - male and female, to see if any would fit the Nomad group. Judging by the last report he got, Milla may not be alone for long. He has to admit, she was a solid fit. She even looks the part in her black leather trousers and black t-shirt.

He leaves her to her delaying tactics. He knows exactly why Milla is here and he's not in the mood to go over it all again with someone else. 'Do I need to order you to stop stalling?'

'Stalling? Whatever do you mean, sir?'

'Just get it over with so I can get back to staring at the corner in peace.'

'Busted.' She sighs and crosses her legs as she waves her arms theatrically in the air in front of her. 'Picture this scene. There I was, minding my own business, busy doing my reports for you, when your other half bursts into my room - literally I might add - all in a tizzy.'

He cocks an eyebrow. 'My other what?'

She raises her eyes to the ceiling. 'I really must give you guys a crash course on everyday slang.'

'What's a tizzy?'

'Never mind. I meant Terra and she was more than a little upset.'

He looks towards the edge of the bunk. 'Right.'

'Is that all you've got to say? She thinks your implants may have fried a little too much of your brain.' She pauses and tilts her head to the side as she examines him. 'Somehow, I get the impression that's not the case, sir. I know you're really considering this as a serious option. Are you sure you want to go down this path?'

'I just want another option.'

Milla snorts and slides the chair closer to the cell. 'You know I can see through that tough guy thing you do. Stop being the Nomad High Commander for one minute and attempt to have a normal conversation.'

He glances up at her. 'You like irritating me, don't you?'

She beams widely and winks. 'Girl's gotta get her fun where she can. Especially when there's steel bars between us. Are you going to answer my question with more than a brush off? Having another option isn't a valid response for something this big.'

He slumps back against the bars, giving up on fighting Milla. He doesn't have the energy to go around in circles with her. 'No.'

'No, you're not going to answer or no, you're not sure about going down this path?'

'Second one.' He drops his head against the bars with a dull thud. He only woke up about an hour ago, but he's seriously struggling to stay awake. 'I've been like this for so long. I never thought I'd be anything else.'

'There is a chance we can take more of the implants off. Given a few months, and if Bray can somehow get more data from *Alpha*, we can probably undo quite a bit of what the Scientist did and rebuild your body.'

He opens his eye and tries to focus on her face, but it's a lost cause. 'Chance, somehow, and probably?'

She grimaces. 'You know more than anyone that when it comes to your implants, there's no certainties.'

'Except that the countdown isn't slowing.'

Milla looks at the ground. 'We all have a countdown, sir.'

'Mine is down to single digits.'

'Believe me, I'd give anything to have positive news for you.'

'But you can't.'

She smiles sadly at him and shakes her head.

He jumps slightly as electricity unexpectedly buzzes out of his metal covered stump. 'I never wanted to be a cyborg, but right now, it may just be what I need to be.'

'You don't have to be a cyborg to defeat the Foundation. Between the Nomad, Hunters, New Foundation, and anyone else we can gather together with a Foundation grudge, we can handle this. No one has to go through that horror again.'

'They based the cyborgs on me, on my mods, Milla. I studied Bray's video over and over.' He taps a finger against the side of his head. 'All the information is in here going around and around. As I am right now I'm useless. There's no way I can beat the new models.'

'You don't know that for sure. I've heard some scary things about you, Gryffin. Ever think you're being a bit hard on yourself?'

'It's fact. I can't win while I'm falling apart.'

'And what makes you think having more procedures, more implants will give you the edge you need?'

'I don't.'

'That's reassuring.'

'It will put me on the same level as them and that can't hurt.'

Milla makes a face. 'It's going to hurt you and the other cyborgs here. I'm not convinced about this, Captain.'

'You don't have to be.'

Milla tucks a leg under herself as she opens and closes her mouth a few times before finally speaking. 'Fair enough, I'll give you that, but you have to realise other people will have an issue with this.'

Gryffin sighs. 'Terra, right?'

Milla laughs. 'Yes, Terra. And Roman. Chayse too. Desyl. Ooh and Aleena.'

'I get it.'

'Lucan would be less than impressed I'm guessing. We can't forget Bray.'

'I said I get it.'

'You're considering having more metal attached to you. Please tell me you're not surprised she's a weensy bit upset.'

'What the Foundation are doing—'

'Isn't on Terra's mind right now. She loves you, Gryffin. Can you really blame her for being terrified she's going to lose you again?'

He gives up on the fight to stay upright and shuffles down the bed. He lies on his side and tries to get comfortable, but everything is aching. 'You think I don't feel the same? I don't want to do this, but it might be our only option. If I decide to do this I sure as hell won't be asking for anyone's support.'

'I'm damn glad to hear that because you'd be hard pressed to find someone who does.' She gets to her feet and stuffs her hands into the back pockets of her leathers. 'Well, I've done my bit for the cause. Now I'm going to do my friend duties and treat your girlfriend to a proper meal and a good night's sleep. Desyl is on his way down. You won't be seeing Terra until the morning.'

'Thanks. She needs a break.'

Milla smiles. 'I'll look after her, sir. Make sure she gets it.'

'I don't need a babysitter. Cancel Desyl.'

'Not a chance in hell, sir. I had a hard enough time convincing her to leave you for the night, even after your best efforts to completely piss her off. Desyl will sit with you.'

He doesn't reply. Instead he gives in to the pull of sleep.

Foundation HQ

Garvan takes a deep breath and turns to face the opposite direction. He takes five steps to the far side of his cell and repeats the walk. Thanks to his handiwork on his wound, each step is agony and helps convince more blood to ooze out of it. He probably should be lying down but staring at the sterile white room is hurting his eyes. The bright lights coming from the ceiling seem to reflect off every surface. Even the polished bench serving as his bed, reflects the light. Give him the dingy darkness of Tyrat any day over this.

Adrenaline builds in his body as footsteps echo off the bare walls of the corridor, heading in his direction. The hairs on the back of his neck stand to attention. He knows it's One coming to gloat. He expected a visit before now. Perhaps Harvey was preening himself in the mirror to make sure everything was in place before he paid his prisoner a visit.

The man himself steps around the corner and stops in front of the bars. Garvan faces him, his shoulders back and his face blank. He doesn't say a word. Let Harvey do all the talking. Even though the years in prison have changed how Garvan looks, he still reckons he's fairing a lot better than Harvey.

His unmasked face is heavily lined. If Garvan didn't know any better, he'd put him in his late-seventies. His thinning, brown hair is scraped back from his face with a little too much gel to keep it in place. Either his heavy, velvet robe is adding pounds to his weight or Harvey has been enjoying the finer things in life a little too much. If this is what being the head of the Foundation does to you, Harvey can keep his position.

A few minutes of silence stretch on before Harvey's shoulders drop slightly and he sighs dramatically. 'Nothing to say for yourself?'

Garvan smiles but doesn't respond.

One paces in front of the cell, his robe trailing after him like a faithful companion. 'I feel for you old friend. You escape being modified only to be recaptured and placed in the exact same position you were in before. I have to admit, I am glad you were foolish enough to allow this to happen again. I am grateful for the chance to have a chat with you. A catch up if you will.' He stops in the centre of the doorway and clasps his hands together. 'The years have changed you, Wade.'

Garvan steps closer to the bars and gets a little kick of satisfaction when Harvey takes a step away. 'You too.' Garvan rests his hands on the top of the cell door and leans closer to Harvey. The smaller man's eyes focus on the large bulging muscles in Garvan's strained arms. Garvan smiles again. 'Council life suits you. You've become an impressive... specimen.'

One sneers up at Garvan. 'It seems sending you to Tyrat has not had the effect on you I thought it would.'

'Sorry about that. I did consider lying down and dying, but I reassessed my situation. I thought it would be much more fun to survive and one day repay your hospitality.' Garvan holds his arms out to the side and smiles. 'How about a thank you hug?' One steps back again and Garvan laughs. 'What's wrong? Don't fancy stepping in here with me?'

'I should have killed you instead of making the mistake of sending you away.'

'You can't kill me.' Garvan lowers onto the rock-hard bunk and clasps his hands on his knees. 'You see, if you kill me, you'll never know if I've kept your little secret.'

'Who have you told?'

Garvan laughs at the panic in One's voice. 'Couldn't possible say.'

One's face takes on a strange purple hue. 'You know, I can do a lot worse than kill you. You think Tyrat was bad? I can bury you in the worst places in the galaxy. I can leave you to rot alone in the dark.'

'Been there, done that. You just described Tyrat. What else you got for me?'

One is silent as a sly smile spreads across his face.

'Looks like you've found a winner. Don't keep it to yourself.'

'I might just have a use for a strong animal such as yourself.'

'Hey, you don't have to be mean.'

'With a few tweaks to the design I could use someone like you.'

Garvan grimaces and shakes his head. 'Not sure metal would look good on me.'

'We've been avoiding fitting the control implant to males we've acquired. Perhaps it's time to change that.'

'The old mind control didn't hold too well with Gryffin. What makes you think you can do any different with me?'

One nods his head. 'We have perfected the control implant so I have no doubt we will succeed in that regard when we capture him again. He was strong enough to survive, perhaps you will also come through the procedure. Once under my control, I will have no difficulty getting the truth from you.'

'Is it really that important no one knows you weren't legally assigned this role?'

'Perception is everything in this position. It took me a lot of hard work—'

'And lies. Don't forget lies,' Garvan adds.

One ignores the interruption. 'I earned this role and nothing will destroy that for me. Especially you.' Harvey smiles as he spins on his heel and casually strolls down the corridor. 'I suggest you get some rest old friend. You'll need your strength if you're going to survive what's heading your way.'

∞

ULTAR

'You wanted to see me, sir.'

Gryffin looks up at Chayse and bites back a groan. Chayse is furious and doing a bad job of hiding it. As if his clipped tone wasn't enough of a hint, his clenched fists and strong stance helped him figure it out. 'You know.'

'Know what? That you're thinking of having your implants upgraded?'

'What the hell is it with everyone? I just said I wanted to look into it - not sign up to get modified again.'

'You shouldn't even be considering it.'

Gryffin gets to his feet. 'I may be in here but you still answer to me. What I decide to do or not do to my body is my decision. I get it's not what everyone wants, but, if I do go that route, I want you all to keep your mouths shut and get in line.'

'That easy, huh?

'While I command the Nomad it is.'

'It's always the same with you, isn't it?'

'I didn't catch the sir anywhere in that.'

Chayse slowly approaches him, the frown on his face deepening as he walks. He stops in front of Gryffin and crosses his arms. 'You and your selfish decisions are really pissing me off, sir. First you decide to kill off my girlfriend and now you're offering yourself up as a martyr to the cause.'

Gryffin runs a hand over his hair, still not used to the feel of the short spikes. 'Milla's alive.'

'Don't, Gryffin. You know exactly what I mean. You made me think you killed her right in front of me.'

'She's alive. I don't get the problem.'

'That there is the problem. You pretended to kill the one person I love and you don't get why I'm pissed off at you.'

'We needed to do something convincing to flush out the mole. It was her idea. Go shout at her.'

Chayse jabs a finger in Gryffin's chest. 'It was your idea not to include me. Just like you've made this decision about your future without including Terra, or me, or anyone else for that matter.'

Gryffin glances down at Chayse's finger, still resting on his chest. 'Hit me if you want but if you poke me with your finger one more time I'll break the damn thing off and shove it down your throat.'

Chayse accepts Gryffin's suggestion, reaching through the bars to strike him in the jaw with a blow that knocks him back a step. Gryffin wipes his mouth, smiling at the smear of blood on his hand. 'Feel better now?'

Chayse lunges at him again, but Gryffin steps back, leaving Chayse's fist swiping through empty space. Before he can recover, Gryffin grabs him by the arm, twisting it behind his back. Chayse hisses in pain as the bars dig into his arm. 'It's done. Move on.' He shoves Chayse away, sending the Nomad stumbling forward. Chayse massages his limb as he glares up at Gryffin.

'I can't just move on. You still don't trust me enough to let me in.

I've had your back since I stepped foot on *Ares*. You know what the rest of the crew put me through. You know they avoided me cause they thought I was going to report back to you if they said or did anything they shouldn't.

'But I didn't mind. I was reporting directly to the leader of the Nomad. The privilege of being trusted to be that close to you more than made up for not being part of the crew. You told me you trusted me. Damn funny way of showing it,' Chayse scoffs.

Gryffin drops onto the end of the bunk. He can't figure out exactly when it happened, but lines are being blurred. He's Captain of *Ares* and High Commander of the Nomad. Whatever else people think he is to them comes second to that. Always. He's getting sick and tired of people questioning his orders. He's already losing control of his body, he doesn't need to add losing control of the Nomad under his command to that.

'I'm still High Commander. Until I appoint someone else or die, that stands, so less of the fucking attitude. You want to hold a grudge — fine. But if you speak to me like that again or disobey me I'll personally remove you from *Nemesis* and the Nomad, and this time it'll be permanent. Understood?'

Chayse stares at him for a few minutes while Gryffin holds his gaze. He meant every word of what he just said and Chayse needs to know it. His former aide is one of the best Nomad Gryffin has known, but if he lets personal issues get in the way, he risks losing *Nemesis* - and not because Gryffin takes her from him.

'Understood, sir.'

'And you'll follow my orders without question?'

Chayse clenches his jaw but nods.

'Will you follow my orders?'

'Yes, sir.'

Gryffin slumps back against the bars and closes his eye for a minute before he focuses on Chayse again. 'I need you to help me save the Nomad.'

'How?'

'I've got something in place that'll help secure the future of the group. I need you to go and get it. Go to Desyl. I gave him two data files a few days ago. He should have locked them in the safe in my office on *Ares*. The smaller one is for you and has coordinates in it. Follow them and give the other file to the blacksmith you find at the location.'

'The blacksmith? You're not making any sense.'

Gryffin pulls himself to his feet and hobbles over to the bars. 'I don't have to. I'm giving you an order, Chayse. No questions, remember? Just go and give the file to him. I can't tell you anything else right now. You're going to have to trust me.'

'*Nemesis* will head out in an hour, sir.'

Gryffin smiles and drops his head against the cell wall. 'I'll clear everything with Roman. Make sure she's battle ready and fully stocked. You'll get further orders once you get to the coordinates. Don't say a word about any of this to anyone. Understood?'

'Understood.'

'You better go. You've not got much time to get ready.'

Chayse leaves the cells, locking the door behind him. Gryffin slumps back on the mattress and stares at the ceiling. It'll take *Nemesis* two days to get to the location. After that he'll be free to make a decision about his future without worrying about how it will impact the Nomad.

∞

FOUNDATION HQ

Garvan licks his lips and tries to steady his racing heart. The footsteps are loud and the pace is brisk. No way his mate, Harvey, could move himself that fast. It must be one of the cyborgs. That means he's not going to be having a fun time.

The woman stops in front of his cell and quietly stares at him. Garvan lifts his hand and waves cheerily. 'Hey. What's a nice cyborg like you doing in a place like this?'

Her only response is to open the cell and step aside to let him out.

'Care to tell me where our stroll will take us?'

She doesn't reply. Garvan shrugs. 'Mystery tour. Fair enough.' He steps out of his cell, feeling a hell of a lot more anxious than he hopes he's showing. He's not an idiot. He knows this isn't going to end well for him but he'll be damned if he's going to give Harvey the pleasure of knowing he's getting to him.

He glances over his shoulder at the petite woman, and for a moment, considers trying to overpower her and make a run for it, but it seems they're prepared for that. The main cell block door is opened by three women who take up position around him. 'You're making me feel mighty special, ladies.'

One of the new cyborgs shoves him in the side and he stumbles forward as he loses his footing. 'Easy there. I'm going.'

The rest of the walk through the facility is made in silence. Garvan tries to get his bearings, but it's nearly impossible to keep track. Each corridor looks the same as the last and the cyborg's path to wherever they're going leaves him completely lost.

With no distractions, Garvan's mind wanders to the inevitable. Harvey had made it clear that he's going to be modified. The bastard had taken pleasure taunting him with that fact. Maybe today is the day he's going to begin the procedures? Garvan swallows deeply as he follows the lead cyborg down a long corridor to a room at the end.

His feet come to a stop just inside the entrance. A gurney is bolted to the floor in the centre of the room. Three figures in surgical scrubs are sorting through a table of instruments and discussing readings on the screen in front of them. Harvey is sitting on a chair at the far side of the room. His ornate robe and mask of his station are in place, hiding his less than memorable face from view.

Harvey gestures to someone behind Garvan. Firm hands pin his arms to the side as the lead cyborg roughly pushes a gag into his mouth, securing it with force behind his head. He breathes heavily through his nose, trying to get enough oxygen to his lungs.

He's beyond terrified but is determined not to give Harvey the satisfaction. He stares at the man and wills his body to stay as calm as possible - which is a fucking big ask. He doesn't bother struggling as he is guided past the gurney to a smaller side room.

Slightly relieved he's not staying in Room A, he doesn't immediately notice the heavy chains hanging from the ceiling of Room B. The women quickly and efficiently secure his arms over his head, painfully stretching the wound in his side. After they fasten his ankles in chains on the floor, they step back to the main room, disappearing from view.

Harvey strolls up to him and pulls his mask off. 'I have to say, it's nice to be able to speak to you without having to endure one of your irritating rebuttals. It makes a pleasant change.'

Garvan braces his feet, taking some of the weight from his wrists and releasing pressure from his side. It's doesn't do much good. Between the pain from his wound and the gag blocking his airway, he's going to be unconscious in a few minutes. Not that it would be a bad thing. At least he wouldn't have to listen to Harvey prattling on.

Harvey smiles and clasps his hands in front of him. 'Now, I don't know how much detail you know about the cyborg program and the prototype.' He reaches into his robe and takes a box from a pocket. He opens it and holds up a piece of metal about the size of the tip of his thumb. 'This is the control implant the prototype has in his head. Well, not the exact one of course. This is the latest version, but the principles are the same.

'So far, the prototype is the only male to survive having this fitted.

I'm hoping you will be the second. You are certainly as stubborn as he is. So, in order to give you the best possible chance of surviving this, I have decided you should undergo the same pre-surgery care he did.'

He slips the implant back in its box, then strolls in circles around him. 'As with the prototype, we need to deal with the stubbornness first. The implant requires the subject to be compliant in order for it to take hold. I read countless reports from the admirals who began this project and one in particular was of interest.

'The prototype was beaten into submission before the control implant was repaired and activated. He was weak, unable to put up a fight - both mentally and physically. It did take quite a bit of punishment for him to get to that level, but it worked. How long do you think it will take for me to break you, Wade? One day? Three? A week?' He stops in front of him and slips the mask back on. 'There's no rush. Ladies.'

Three of the cyborgs step back to the room as Harvey backs away from him. 'Try not to do too much permanent damage.'

He spins theatrically and leaves the room. Garvan stares at the woman and knows he's in serious trouble. There's nothing in their dead eyes. Nothing except a dull purple glow that brightens as they collectively move towards him. He closes his eyes and focuses on the faces of his children as the cyborgs attack.

∞

ULTAR

Gryffin jerks awake and stares at the ceiling. He lies perfectly still, just breathing in and out for a few minutes. He rolls onto his side, wincing as the ever present headache takes a few seconds to readjust to his new position. He rubs his eye and eventually his vision clears, but instead of seeing the bars of his cell he finds himself in a room surrounded by banks of computers.

'What the hell?' Ignoring the pain, he tries to use one of the units to pull himself to his feet but instead of a console his hand hits metal bars. He rubs his eye again and finds he's back in his cell. He hears someone moving beside him and turns quickly surprising Desyl.

'Captain, are you all right?'

His vision blurs again and he's back in the computer room looking down at the unit controlling the planet's defences. He squeezes his eyes shut as his vision blurs, throwing him back to his cell.

Desyl frowns as he steps closer to the bars. 'You're freaking me out, sir. What is it?'

Gryffin spins around when he hears a voice whispering behind him. Seeing no one there, he turns around to look at Desyl again.

'Gryffin—'

He shakes his head briskly. 'Shut up.' Gryffin spins quickly as the voice whispers behind him again. He looks over his shoulder at Desyl, but it wasn't him. The voice sounds again, and he grabs the bars to stop himself from falling as he pivots. With his implants failing, there's nothing to stop his heart racing in his chest in time with his breathing.

He places his palm to his chest, sure his heart is about to beat right out of his rib cage. He's not used to these strange new sensations. Until they started failing, he didn't realise how much his implants masked his body's reactions. A throbbing pain builds, working form the base of his neck and around the top of his head.

He's vaguely aware of Desyl calling for help as he tries to figure out what the hell is going on. He hears the voice again and finally realises where it came from - deep inside his head.

'Damn it.' Gryffin slumps against the bars, wincing as the metal brace holding his leg together bangs painfully against the wall. Something is wrong with the control implant. Either that or he's somehow been compromised. He freezes as the pieces slowly fall in to place. 'The control room.'

'What about the control room?' Before he can answer Desyl, the base alarms screech to life.

'The defences are down.'

'How the hell can you know that, sir?'

He throws an exasperated look over his shoulder at Desyl. It's all the confirmation his first officer needs. Desyl activates his comms again. 'This is Desyl. What's going on?'

Gryffin watches Desyl's expression change from confusion, to anger, then the cold calm of a Nomad commander in a crisis. 'Got that.' He looks over at Gryffin. 'Defences are down. Foundation are minutes away.'

ULTAR

Terra hurries after Milla as they head to the control room. They burst through the door of the command room to find one of the cyborgs from the New Colony slumped in a chair surrounded by eight security personnel, each one with their weapon trained on him.

'What's going on?' Milla asks.

Roman takes the offered weapon from an Ultaran and pulls the holster over his shoulders. 'He turned off the defences. The Foundation are on the way. Appears he got the order from Gryffin.'

Terra looks at Roman. 'What? You must be wrong. He wouldn't do that. His programming was checked.'

Roman slots another gun in the holster on his hip and then slips a knife down his boot. 'That's what I'm afraid of. We must have missed something.'

'But none of the cyborgs have been anywhere near him since he got back.'

Roman pushes her towards the weapons locker. 'Take as much as you can carry. Two more of the cyborgs have attacked security teams guarding the perimeter. We have to assume they've all been compromised. Gryffin included. He's admitted the order came from him, but he's got no idea how. He was aware of what the other cyborg was doing.'

'I don't understand. He's been checked twice a day for weeks. His programming is clear.'

'Unless it was dormant,' Milla says.

Terra looks at Milla. 'What do you mean?'

She blows out a deep breath. 'They had him for ten months. They could easily have hidden something until it was time to use it.'

'What can we do?'

'We've got a Foundation carrier minutes away. We've been told to stand down. Needless to say that's not happening. A few of us are going to run interference while *Nemesis* and *Dannan* get as many civilians off the surface as possible. They were about to take off so they're good to go.

'Milla, clear the med bay. Load everyone on *Nemesis*. Chayse is taking as many as he can from the hangar. As soon as you're clear, *Nemesis* will leave. Terra, you're with me.' Roman hurries down the stairs, closely followed by Terra as Milla rushes off to clear her area.

Terra watches in horror as families with young children and couples clutching each other's hands, hurry through the large hangar towards the two ships. They had planned for this, practised evac drills on a daily basis, but seeing it like this is a different thing. Men, women, and children disappear into the large cargo hold on *Nemesis*, while the smaller *Dannan* is being loaded with non-essential base personnel.

Aleena rushes up to Roman and takes one of his weapons before he can say anything. 'Where do you need me?'

'On *Nemesis*. Now! She's ready to take off. Go!'

She shakes her head. 'My place is here.'

'Your place is on that ship. Listen to me,' he says as she begins to argue. 'You need to go.'

'But I can stay and fight with you.'

He shakes his head. 'You get on that ship. I need you on that ship.' He brushes her blonde hair away from her face and cups her cheek. 'Please, Aleena. I need to know you're safe.'

'And what about Terra and Gryffin?'

'They'll be following on *Ares* as soon as you get away. Now get on that ship and stop wasting time. Please.'

She pauses as she weighs up her options, then leans forward to kiss him deeply as tears fall down her face. Terra looks away from the couple, feeling like she is intruding in a private moment. Roman pulls away and gently guides her towards *Nemesis*. 'Now, Aleena.'

She nods and blows him a kiss before she disappears in the crowd moving towards *Nemesis*. Roman keeps watching her until she enters the ship.

Terra looks around the hangar feeling slightly detached. The base is lost. There's no way they can defend it against the might of a Foundation attack. That doesn't mean they'll give up without a fight though. Roman looks over at Terra. 'Let's get you and Gryffin to *Ares*.'

'But—'

'Don't, Terra. If they get their hands on him again, we might as well line up and let them put a bullet in us. I don't know about you, but I don't want to die by my son's hand. He needs to leave and get to Earth before they realise what's going on. Lucan and Desyl are securing Gryffin and bringing him out. *Ares* will be ready to leave as soon as you're on board.'

'What about you?'

'Vance, Lucan, and I are going to irritate the Foundation long enough to get everyone off the surface. Buy you all as much time as possible.'

∞

OUTER SECTOR

Chayse watches as the battle continues on the screen beside his chair. His orders were clear - they had to find the blacksmith. That was all Gryffin wanted him to do. It goes against everything he is to walk away from a fight, but he risks seriously pissing off Gryffin if he disobeys. Whoever this blacksmith is, he better be important.

'Tret. Push her as hard as she'll go. I want to get to Gryffin's coordinates as fast as we can.'

Milla rests her hand on his shoulder as they speed away from Ultar and their friends. 'You okay?'

'No, I'm not fucking okay. We should be back there with everyone else. This feels wrong. *Nemesis* can more than handle herself against the Foundation. We shouldn't be running.'

'You're following orders. You've just got to trust this is more important.'

Chayse lowers his voice so the rest of the crew can't hear him. 'I took those orders from someone who's been locked in a cell for weeks because he's unpredictable and potentially dangerous. Where's the logic in that?'

'You took those orders from someone you've known for years. Someone you trust.'

Chayse snorts and looks down at the screen again. 'Not so sure about the trust part. None of this makes any sense. I mean what the hell can a blacksmith from a remote colony possibly do to help us?'

'I guess we'll just have to wait and see. It'll be worth it though.'

Chayse looks up at her. 'What makes you so sure he's not sending us on a wild goose chase?'

'Because it's his body that's falling apart.' She taps the side of

Chayse's head. 'Up here he's our High Commander. If he wants you to go to this delightful sounding colony it's for a good reason.'

'Delightful? You know it rains there - as in most of the time.'

'From what I read it actually rains there all the time. I forgot to mention when I said delightful, I was being as sarcastic as I can be. I strongly suggest you try to grab this mysterious blacksmith from the ship without actually setting foot on the surface.'

'Sir, I got Baila on comms,' Tret says. 'Apparently Gryffin asked her to back us up.'

'Baila? What's going on?'

The Rogue captain appears on the screen in front of him. She shakes her head, clearly as pleased about leaving the fight as Chayse is. 'Ask your High Commander. He told me he wanted *Dannan* to go with you. So here we are. I'm going to assume he's got you on some important mission or else you wouldn't be running like this.'

'He gave me coordinates - that's it. Apparently there's something there that'll help the Nomad.'

'Yeah, 'cause that's what I live for - helping the Nomad.'

'You don't take orders from Gryffin. Feel free to head back.'

Baila shakes her head again. 'Given a choice between the Hunters and the Nomad, I'll go for the Nomad. I've got you, Captain. Give me a shout if you need anything.'

Chayse cuts the connection and looks at the readings from the area around Ultar. The Foundation have landed. Ultar has fallen. He considers turning around and heading back. There's nothing to say Gryffin is still alive. There's nothing to say any of his friends are still alive. Is he really doing them and the Nomad a service by saving his own ass?

Milla squeezes his arm again. 'Follow his orders, Chayse,' she whispers before kissing him on the cheek and leaving the command deck.

He slumps back in his command chair and rubs a hand over his face. 'We at top speed?'

Tret nods. 'That's all we can get from her.'

'How long until we get there?'

'About thirty hours or so.'

Chayse turns off the screen. No point watching a battle he can do fuck all about.

∞

ULTAR

Gryffin resists the urge to break open the cell door - not that he'd be able to, but it would make him feel better to at least try instead of just standing here. 'What the hell is taking so long?'

'On it, sir,' Lucan replies. 'Do I need to restrain you?'

'Shoot me if I do anything I shouldn't.'

'You mean do anything you shouldn't, again, sir.'

Gryffin grimaces. Lucan is right. He's already opened Ultar to the Foundation. 'Shoot me in the head then.'

Lucan shrugs. 'That'll do. Right, so I guess we're good to go.' Lucan takes the gun from its holster then opens the cell door.

'Where are the other cyborgs?'

'Only three are still with us. The others were... well they had to be taken out, sir. The survivors are being loaded on *Ares*. We need to get her off the ground as fast as we can.'

Gryffin stumbles as he leaves the cell for the first time in weeks. 'Is the evac underway?'

'Sorry, sir. You're on the don't need to know list. I don't want to hear anything from you, Captain. Whether you were aware of it or not, you and the other cyborgs killed our defences. You need to do as you're told.'

Desyl stares at Lucan then at Gryffin, expecting an argument, but

Gryffin is all out of those. Lucan is right. He's the reason the Foundation is coming. He'd give anything to stay and fight on the ground, but in his current condition, he'd be worse than useless. The best place for him is on his ship.

He tries to take a step on his own but his feet have other ideas. Lucan and Desyl slip under his arms to help support some of his weight. Desyl blows out a breath as he adjusts his position. 'Why are you still so heavy? You haven't been eating.'

'His implants aren't going to lose weight. You'll need to help us, sir. You're too heavy for just the two of us.'

Gryffin nods, ignoring the fact the room doesn't want to stop moving. Leaning as little as possible on Desyl and Lucan, they finally make it to the corridor leading to the main hangar. Desyl props Gryffin against the wall so he can check the area ahead. He rejoins Lucan and holds up his weapon as someone comes barrelling around the corner. Terra skids to a stop inches from Lucan's weapon. 'It's just me.' Terra frowns as she looks up at Gryffin. 'Hey, you okay?'

He nods, not trusting himself to speak and breathe at the same time.

She frowns as she continues to examine him. 'We'll get you on board as quick as we can.'

He must look like he feels. He squeezes his eye shut and nods again. Heavy footsteps echo through the corridor so he opens his eye again, blinking to clear his blurring vision. Roman joins the group and wipes his forehead with his sleeve. 'Everyone's loaded. *Ares* is ready to fly as soon as you're on board. The ships have just landed so we're running out of time.'

'Is *Nemesis* gone?'

'She's clear. Baila's ship too.' Roman stops the group as they approach the main hangar. All they can hear is gunfire and shouting. 'Damn it. They're here already.'

'I need a gun.'

Roman looks at Gryffin and shakes his head. 'Don't think that's a great idea.'

'I want them dead, not you.'

'No offence but you can't stand on your own.'

'I can still shoot.'

He looks over at Terra who shrugs. 'An extra gun would come in handy.'

'Fine. If you feel anything off you tell me immediately, preferably before you shoot me in the head.'

Lucan gives his captain a gun. 'Try to point that away from me, sir.'

Gryffin frowns at Lucan but doesn't respond.

11

Gryffin peers through the smoke in the hangar and sees a faint purple glow. The strange whispering starts in his head again as he stares at the approaching cyborgs. Are they trying to communicate with him? Trying to give him orders? Whatever it is, he could do without the added distraction. Staying on his feet is taking all of his concentration. 'They're here.'

'Who,' Terra asks.

He nods to the front of the hangar. 'The Foundation cyborgs.'

Terra and Desyl don't argue. They herd any stragglers towards *Ares* and hurry up the ramp. Gryffin looks over his shoulder, counting three sets of purple eyes in the gloom. He registers the red glow from a gun sight and throws himself at Terra, grabbing Desyl's arm on the way down.

The three of them hit the ground in a heap, sending knives of pain through his leg. The round buries itself in the wall where Terra's head was seconds ago. They get up and pull Gryffin to his increasingly unsteady feet. There's no way they can make it without taking hits. He leans against the wall and watches the approaching cyborgs. He can't make out any details yet, but they're heading in his direction.

'Desyl. get Terra to the ship.'

'What the hell are you talking about? I'm not going anywhere.'

Ignoring Terra, Gryffin directs his order to Desyl. 'It's not a request, Commander. We'll hold them off. Get her to the ship.'

Terra hesitates, but accepting he's not going to back down, nods and kisses him. 'I'll see you on the Command Deck.' Gryffin grabs Desyl's arm as he passes. 'Get *Ares* in the air and protect the colony. Keep *Ares* and Ultar out of Foundation hands.'

Desyl opens his mouth to argue, but Gryffin cuts him off. 'It's an order. Clear the hangar and keep the Ultarans safe from the air. Understood?'

Desyl nods and races towards *Ares*. Gryffin glances over his shoulder at Lucan and Roman. 'I want you both behind something solid. Now.'

Lucan has the sense not to argue. He grabs Roman's arm and shoves him into an office to Gryffin's left. Gryffin concentrates on his implants, knowing if he gets this wrong it will probably tear a hole right through him. Hell, even if he does it right, it could still take him out.

He reroutes all the power from his implants to his arm, hoping the damaged metal stump can handle everything he's going to send its way. The pain builds in his body as his implants rally to obey him - maybe for the last time.

He opens his eye to find the room bathed in a purple haze. He lifts his arm, then sends everything he has left out of his body. The blast is deafening as it rips out of his arm. Crates of supplies, boxes of machinery, consoles, anything in its path is knocked to the ground. A smile crosses his face as he watches half a dozen cyborgs get blown off their feet and away from the waiting ship. Then his world goes black.

∞

FOUNDATION HQ

One sits on the chair the guard places outside Garvan's cell. Garvan hasn't acknowledged him and that causes him a great deal of irritation, which no doubt causes Garvan a great deal of pleasure. One clears his throat but Garvan continues to ignore him.

He clenches his jaw, trying not to lose his temper. He's sure that is what Wade wants. Instead he takes a few discreet breaths to calm himself before he speaks. 'You survived your first session. I'm impressed.'

Still nothing.

'Very well. Who was on board *Alpha* with you?' Garvan's chest rises and falls, but the man remains motionless on the bed.

'We have footage of a security officer called,' he stops speaking and checks his notes. 'Erin Richards. She unlawfully gained entry to *Alpha* with another man. I want you to tell me who he is.'

No response.

'I have sent a team to her house in the city and a farm her father owns on the outskirts. We will find the answers sooner or later.' The continued lack of response finally gets to him. He stands up and beats his fist against the panel at the side of the bars. 'Answer me!'

Garvan slowly turns to face him, a big grin on his face. 'Oh, hey Harvey. How long have you been there?'

One hits the panel again. 'You will respect me!'

Garvan rolls over and sits up on the bed. Harvey is momentarily shocked when he gets a proper look at the prisoner. The women had been ruthless in their attack. His left eye is bruised and swollen shut, his right cheek has a deep gash and his lip is split and bleeding. Deep bruises cover his arms and chest. His hand is pressed firmly to his old wound as the other hand clutches his thigh. The injuries are not life threatening but are intended to be painful.

Wade takes a few attempts to push himself to his feet and unsteadily limps across the cell. He rests one hand against the wall, keeping the other pressed to his wounded side. 'Ah come now, Harvey. You can't really expect me to respect you? Hell, I don't even like you.'

In spite of his cheery tone, Harvey can hear the pain in his voice. Another few sessions like that and he will be more than ready to accept the control implant. 'Who is the other man in the footage with you?'

'You're not jealous I was spending time with someone else, are you?'

One turns his back on the cell as he composes himself. He cannot let Wade know he's getting to him. He turns back, irritated by the large grin on the prisoner's bruised face. 'Is everything a joke to you?'

Garvan shrugs and winces. 'Just trying to make the best of a bad situation.'

Harvey laughs and shakes his head. 'You're right, old friend. You are in a bad situation. Perhaps it can be improved by telling me what I need to know.'

Garvan grins widely at him. 'Where's the fun in that? Besides, you said you can find the details all by your lonesome. I'm not going to take that from you.'

Harvey steps closer to the bars and sneers up at Garvan. 'I will take great pleasure in watching you take the first steps towards a new and more useful existence.'

Wade coughs and curses in pain. 'Do whatever you have to, mate. Make me stronger. Make me more resilient. I'll use it all to destroy you.'

'You really think you'll have free will after you go through the procedure? I will own you.'

Garvan shrugs again. 'Did they say the same to Gryffin when your mates were doing their worst to him? Didn't end too well for them. You just got yourself a pissed off cyborg intent on taking you all down. To be honest, I'm a tad confused why you'd create more of the same?'

'He was malfunctioning. Thanks to years of research, this issue has been taken care of.'

Garvan laughs as he slowly makes his way back to the small cot. 'Issue? That's one word to describe him. Can't say I'd fancy being in his sights. And now you're in my sights too. You're a popular guy, Harvey.'

Garvan groans as he lies back and rests his head on his hands. 'Spending a few years locked in what you affectionately called a prison, for something I didn't do... well, it gave me clarity.' He turns his head slightly to look at One. 'It's kind of ironic if you think about it. If you hadn't thrown me in Tyrat I wouldn't be the man I am today. I worked hard to survive both mentally and physically. Your actions resulted in me being a bigger problem than you could have ever imagined.

'The old me couldn't have cared less about who your parents are or about your position, title, or any of that meaningless fluff. I just wanted to get on with my life. But this new me...' Garvan sits up to look him in the eyes and One takes an involuntary step back. 'You see, this new improved me has one objective. That objective is at the core of my being and there's not a damn thing you can do to me that will ever stop me from carrying it out.'

'And what's that exactly?' One asks before he can stop himself.

'Keep up, Harvey. I plan on killing you, mate. I'm going to look in your piggy eyes as your fat chest rises and falls for the last time. And I'm going to be smiling as I do it.'

∞

ULTAR

Roman groans and pushes onto all fours. Rubble falls off his body, landing on the ground around him. He blinks, but a searing pain shoots through his left eye. He slowly touches his fingers to his eye and they come away covered in blood. 'Shit. That's not good.'

He forces a foot to the ground and tries to push himself upright. Dust fills his lungs, bringing on a coughing fit that does nothing to ease the pain in his eye.

'Roman?'

He looks around the gloom, but can't see farther than a few feet in front of him. He opens his mouth to answer the call then stops. If it's the Foundation, telling them his position probably wouldn't be a great idea. He stumbles forward, catching his foot on the masonry covering the floor. Bracing himself for the upcoming pain of hitting the ground, he is surprised when someone catches his arm, keeping him from falling. He smiles when he sees Lucan instead of a Foundation cyborg. 'Am I glad to see you.'

Lucan frowns as he checks him out. 'Bit surprised you can see anything. Your eye doesn't look too good.'

'My legs work. You okay?'

Lucan smirks. 'I'll be every colour of the rainbow tomorrow, but I'm good.'

'Where's Gryffin?'

Roman crouches down, searching the darkness for his son. 'Gryffin?'

'Over here,' Lucan whispers from somewhere to his left. Roman follows his voice and nearly trips over something on the floor. He focuses on the space in front of him and shapes begin to take form. Lucan is crouched on the ground beside the prone body of Gryffin. 'Is he hurt?'

'Don't think so. I'm guessing using his arm like that knocked him out.'

'How do we wake him up? We can't just sit here and wait to be found.'

Lucan pauses then slaps Gryffin's face.

'Is that the best you can come up with?'

'Do you have any better ideas cause I can tell you there's no way we'll be able to lift him. He weighs a hell of a lot.'

Roman looks around them but Lucan is right. He doesn't have a better idea. The Nomad repeats the process and much to Roman and Lucan's surprise, Gryffin coughs and rolls to his side as he tries to catch his breath.

'Are you okay?' Roman asks as Gryffin groans.

Gryffin curses instead of answering. 'What the hell happened?'

'The compound collapsed.'

'Did I do that?'

'I don't know. I think you may have knocked me out when you did that trick of yours.' Roman coughs again, tasting blood in his mouth. He looks down at Gryffin. 'Can you walk?'

'I'll need help to get up.'

After a few failed attempts, Lucan and Roman manage to get him upright, but he's not going to be fighting anyone anytime soon. Roman can feel the tremors working through his body as he leans heavily on the two men. 'Did the ships get away?'

'I hope so. Until we can get out of here we have no idea.'

Lucan adjusts his grip on Gryffin's arm and nods to the gloomy corridor ahead of them. 'There's a store room along this corridor. Would that have anything useful in it?'

Roman nods, then speaks when he remembers the others can't see him, 'There'll be torches at the least.'

'My night vision is working... sort of,' Gryffin says. 'I should be able to guide you. Head straight.'

Following Gryffin's directions, they work their way through the rubble to the relatively clear corridor beyond. With the path clear from debris, the going is easier, but Gryffin still struggles. His feet drag along the ground, loading his immense weight on the men's shoulders.

They get to the store room and lower Gryffin to the ground outside the door. Roman gropes around in the dark and finds the shelf housing the torches. Taking three, he turns his on and goes back outside to the others. He plays the light over Gryffin and his breath hitches. Blood is seeping from his son's nose and from a gash on his cheek. His good eye is dull and his hand is pressed to his side. Roman moves Gryffin's hand aside, uncovering a wet patch on his t-shirt. 'Lucan, can you see if there's a first aid kit in there?'

Lucan grabs a torch from Roman and hurries inside.

Gryffin pushes himself upright. 'I'm fine.'

Roman laughs in spite of their situation. 'You could have a shuttle embedded in your chest and you'd still say you're fine.'

Lucan reappears with a basic kit which he tears open and passes to Roman. 'I'll get some bits together while you patch him up.'

Roman pulls Gryffin's t-shirt up and examines the wound finding it's not deep. He cleans as much of the dirt from it as he can then presses a thick gauze pad over it. 'That should keep you going. Any other injuries you're hiding?'

Gryffin shakes his head. 'Is it just your eye that's hurt?' he asks as he examines Roman's face.

'I guess we're a matching pair now,' Roman says with a smirk. 'Are you okay to move? I'd prefer to get going while we still have the advantage.'

'Think it'll be better if you go alone. I'll only—'

'Now don't you even consider finishing that sentence,' Roman says. 'We get out together or not at all. Do you understand me?'

'Terra was right.'

Roman frowns, a little surprised by Gryffin's reply. 'About what?'

'I get my stubbornness from you.'

Gryffin holds out his hand for Roman to help support him. Roman smiles to himself as he struggles and eventually aids the Nomad in getting to his feet.

Lucan reappears empty handed. 'Nothing else worth loading ourselves with. We ready to get out of here?'

The men pause at each doorway to check for personnel who may have been left behind, but Roman is relieved to see the evacuation seems to have been a success - at least for the moment. They have no idea if the back door to the facility was breached when the Foundation attacked. Or if personnel attempted to leave and were captured. Perhaps there is an army of cyborgs lying in wait.

'What are the odds of this exit being clear?' Gryffin mutters in between gasping breaths. Roman laughs as he readjusts his grip on Gryffin's arm. 'What the hell is so funny?'

'I was just wondering the exact same thing.'

'Did you come up with an answer?' They stumble as Gryffin loses his footing. 'Sorry. Damn feet won't move in the same way at the same time.'

'Do you want to stop?'

'No.'

Roman nods to himself. 'Well, as for what's waiting for us. It could be a lot of trouble or a lot of nothing. Personally, I'm keeping everything crossed it's the later.'

Gryffin grunts and continues his shuffle down the corridor. Roman doesn't have a clue how the Nomad is still upright let alone walking. This is the most exertion he's had since he was locked in the cell. The walk alone could kill him and that's before they even attempt the assent to the surface.

They continue in silence for another ten minutes, slowly making their way deeper into the base. The further they go, the weaker Gryffin feels in his arms. He's barely able to offer any support leaving Roman and Lucan struggling under the weight of Gryffin and his implants.

They stop in a corridor and lower Gryffin to the ground then Lucan seals the door behind them. If the cyborgs have access to the base they'll be able to open it, but it might slow them down for a few minutes. 'You catch your breath. I'll check the coast is clear.'

Roman sits on the ground beside Gryffin and looks over at him. The High Commander's eye is closed and his complexion is the same shade as the off-white walls. His short hair is plastered to his head and he's pressing his metal tipped elbow against his wounded side, trying to keep pressure on it. 'I want her to leave me. You know that, right?'

Roman glances up at Gryffin's face. 'What?'

'Terra. I never wanted her to be with me. Not like this. I tried to change her mind, but she's stubborn too.'

'I know you only want what's best for her.'

'And I know you're not happy about us being... whatever we are.'

'Initially, no. I'm not over the moon about what she's facing once you...'

'Die.'

Roman clears his throat. 'I guess I'm trying to shield her from being hurt. After her father's death and horrific return, I probably worry about her more than I should. I know one thing for sure. I doubt she could be safer with anyone than she is with the Nomad.'

'Her place is secure even after I go. If she wants it. I'm not going to force her to do anything she doesn't want to do. Losing battle.'

'And what about you? Were you serious about having your mods upgraded?'

'Yes,' he replies without hesitation. 'If it helps take down the Foundation I'll do whatever I have to. Besides, I want to be there. I want to witness the Foundation being torn limb from limb. I think I deserve that much.'

'And more. Listen, I know this is probably the last thing you want to hear, but I have to say it now before I back out.' Gryffin doesn't try to stop him talking. Instead he turns his full attention on Roman. His son's lone purple eye locks on to his. 'I can never apologise enough for what the Foundation did to you because I did nothing to stop them.' Gryffin doesn't say anything as his eye remains focused on him. 'I know I've made countless unforgivable mistakes—'

'Did you sell me to the Scientist and the project?'

'What? No! I've already told you that.'

'The Scientist told me that so many times while he had me. That's the lie that killed the idea of a family for me. And that woman, Maggie, she didn't tell you about me. That lie meant you never knew you had a family. Neither lie was our fault. Your loyalty was with the Foundation. Can't fault you for that.'

'So you can just forgive and forget so easily?'

'It's done. Fuck all either of us can do about any of it now.' He grunts and squeezes his eye shut.

'You okay?'

Gryffin nods but it's blatantly obvious he's far from okay. 'We were both screwed with.'

Roman wants to say so much more to his son, but with thirty-five years to make up for it's a daunting task. A part of him will never forgive Maggie for keeping Gryffin from him. What right did she have to make that decision for him? But like Gryffin said, it's done. Absolutely nothing he can do about that.

Lucan hurries back around the corner. 'Coast is clear. We probably should go before that changes.'

Roman gets up and both men haul Gryffin to his feet. Lucan supports Gryffin while Roman moves towards the wall and opens the panel. The air beyond is damp and carries the slight smell of rust. The tunnel opens into the forest a few miles downriver from the base.

They just need to make it that far. After working with the Nomad for over a year, he knows without a doubt that *Ares* will be hanging around to collect their Captain. It's also a certainty that Terra won't budge until she gets both of them back.

Moving quickly, he slips back under Gryffin's arm. He meets Lucan's eyes as he adjusts his grip. Lucan glances at Gryffin and shakes his head briskly. Roman doesn't need him to explain. Gryffin is deteriorating in front of his eyes. He's not going to survive being moved much longer.

12

Gryffin shouts as his leg gives way, dropping him to his knee with a painful jolt. 'Fuck. I'm done.'

Roman crouches down in front of him. 'No you're not. C'mon. Get up.'

'My leg is fucked and you can't carry me. I'm too heavy. I want you both to go.'

'Not happening, sir,' Lucan replies. 'All this will be for nothing if they get you. Get up, sir.'

Using the wall and the assistance of the two men, Gryffin finally gets up, but he can't help them much. He can barely see straight let alone put one foot in front of the other.

'Don't move!'

The woman's voice brings them to a stop.

'Turn around.'

They do as they're told and face the cyborg. She's alone, for now at least, and is pointing her gun at Gryffin's chest. The woman takes a step closer, her purple eyes targeting Gryffin. 'Put him down.'

Roman slowly releases his hold on Gryffin. He slumps against the wall but manages to stay on his feet. Gryffin summons energy from somewhere and straightens. He takes a step forward, putting himself between the cyborg and Roman. 'I'll go with you. No fight. Let them walk away.'

'Gryffin. What the hell are you doing?'

He ignores his father and firms his stance, willing the brace around his dud leg to support him a little longer.

The cyborg ignores him and tilts her head to the side. She must be telling the others where she is. 'I'm to bring you all back.'

'That's not happening. Let them go and I'll come with you.'

She fires, catching Gryffin in the side. He grunts and has to steady himself against the wall. 'You can survive that. If I shoot them they won't. Stop delaying and walk. All of you.'

The next few seconds go by in a blur for Gryffin. His body was fucked before he was shot, but the blood loss isn't doing him any favours, making him sluggish and drowsy.

Roman and Lucan attack her before he gets a chance to react. Someone fires at the same time he is dropped by another body barrelling into him. Pain explodes from his body as it hits the ground. He hears a gun going off again, but thanks to whacking his head off the wall he can't tell which direction it comes from.

As the ringing in his ears dies away he looks up. Roman is lying across him, pinning him to the ground - not that he'd be able to get up anyway.

'All clear,' Lucan calls from somewhere further along the tunnel.

Roman looks down at him. 'Sorry about that. You okay?'

Gryffin nods. 'Yeah. Head fucking hurts, but it did anyway.'

Roman smiles and pushes off Gryffin. He slumps back against the wall and winces. It takes a few seconds for the blood to pool on his chest from the wound. Gryffin pulls back Roman's jacket and curses. 'Why the fuck didn't you say you were hit?'

'I just realised.'

'Lucan! Get over here. Why did you do that?'

'I wasn't keen on her taking you. Seemed like a good idea at the time.' He laughs and blood dribbles out of his mouth.

'I can survive being shot. You can't.'

'I wasn't going to let them take you. Not again.'

Gryffin pulls off his t-shirt and holds it against the wound on Roman's chest. Lucan drops down beside Roman and sucks in a breath. 'Oh shit.'

Roman looks up at Lucan. 'Get... get him out... of here.'

'But—'

'Now, Lucan.'

Gryffin shakes his head. 'You touch me Lucan and I'll fucking kill you. I'm not leaving him behind.'

Roman smiles and lifts his head off the wall. 'You need to get away from here. There'll be more coming. Lucan can't get us both out. You've got... to go.'

Gryffin shakes his head again. 'No. Lucan, I'm ordering you to get him out of here. Now, Lucan!'

'Sir. Gryffin.' He turns his head towards Lucan. 'He's not going to make it. He's right. We have to go.'

'And I said no. We're not leaving him. Nomad don't leave people behind.'

'I can't help both of you.'

'Then go and get help. I'll stay here with him.'

Roman grabs Gryffin's arm and squeezes it. 'Daegan.'

His original name meant nothing to him until that moment. For some reason, hearing it from his father hits him like a kick to the gut. Gryffin shakes his head. 'I can't leave you.'

'Yes, Daegan. You can. Don't let them take you again. Got... to survive.'

His eyes close and Gryffin shakes him. 'Don't die. Not because of me. Don't you dare die because of me!'

'Proud of you, son.'

Roman's arm goes limp and falls to the ground. Gryffin shakes him gently. 'Roman. Wake up.'

Lucan rests his hand on Gryffin's shoulder, but Gryffin shoves it away. 'Get off me. Roman? Roman! Dad!'

Lucan crouches down beside Gryffin. 'He's gone, sir. We really need to go.'

Gryffin stares at the body of his father. He can't be dead. Life can't be that shitty, can it? He's only just gotten used to having a father. And he was starting to like it. He places his fingers on the side of Roman's neck, knowing he's not going to find a pulse.

They need to go. The commander in him knows they have to go, but he can't convince his body to move. There's no way he wants to leave his father behind like this.

Gryffin looks over at the cyborg lying on the ground a few feet from him. He doesn't bother trying to get to his feet. Ignoring the wound in his side, he drags himself over to her. He peers in her artificial eye and smiles when he sees the inner workings spin as she focuses on him.

'I hope whoever is controlling you is listening. You fucked up today. By killing him you've put yourself on my list and now I'm going to kill every single one of you.' Gryffin lifts her gun and aims it at her eyepiece, then fires.

∞

ULTAR

Terra keeps low as she pushes through the undergrowth. In the distance she can hear *Ares'* engines fading as she moves away. Desyl and three Nomad stop in front of her. The exit from the tunnels is just up ahead. She's hoping Roman, Lucan, and Gryffin will head this way but it's a gamble at best. One Desyl was more than happy to take.

Terra keys in the code and pulls back as the door opens. Desyl raises his gun and steps around the corner. He relaxes and lowers his gun when he sees Lucan on the other side. 'You good?'

'Not really.'

'Where's the Captain?'

He steps aside and Terra pushes past Desyl. She drops to the ground beside Gryffin and places her fingers against his neck. 'He's barely got a pulse. What happened? Where's Roman?'

'He took a bullet meant for Gryffin. I'm sorry, Terra. He's gone.'

She hears the words, but it takes a few seconds for them to sink in. 'He's dead?'

'Gryffin wouldn't leave him. I had to stun him. I didn't have a choice.' Lucan looks over his shoulder and curses. 'We've got company heading our way. Get him out of here.'

Desyl and three Nomad pull Gryffin out of the tunnel and towards the shuttle. Terra looks back down the tunnel. 'Is Roman close?'

Whatever answer Lucan was going to give never materialises as the side of his head disappears. Terra screams as he falls to the ground where Gryffin was lying less than a minute ago. Desyl appears behind her and grabs her around the waist. Terra struggles against him as he hauls her out of the tunnel and towards the waiting transport.

'We can't leave them.'

'They're dead, Terra. Nothing we can do for them.'

She loses sight of Lucan's body as Desyl manhandles her into the back of the transport and slams his hand against the hatch control. He unceremoniously dumps her on one of the benches and sits in the pilot's seat.

Terra stares down at Gryffin's prone body on the floor at her feet and then at the blood on her hands. Lucan's blood. It's on her face too. She can feel it on her skin, taste it on her lips.

Terra gets to her feet and pulls open the compartments above her head.

'What the fuck are you doing?' Ryder asks as she empties supplies onto the floor.

'I need to clean this off me. His blood everywhere. I need to wash it off.'

The ship lifts off the ground and swings around sharply, bringing them over the tops of the trees. Terra braces herself against the wall as she continues her search. Ryder shoves her back on the bench and empties a bottle of water down her face. He quickly wipes her skin then deals with her hands. '

'All gone. You okay?'

She nods, unable to get any words out.

'Good. Now sit the fuck down and let me deal with Gryffin.'

Terra nods again then wipes her tears away. She got Lucan killed. Why had she delayed? She should have gone straight back to the ship with Gryffin.

Terra glances at Gryffin's chest. Something's not right. It's not moving. 'Ryder! He's not breathing.'

'I know. Shut up so I can keep him alive.' Ryder pulls the monitoring device from the first aid pack behind him and carefully inserts the probe in one of the ports on Gryffin's chest implant. Ryder taps in a few commands then curses loudly. 'We gotta move, Desyl. His implants are fucked. Nothing is in sync. Must have messed them up when he blasted the place.'

'How long?' Desyl asks, while hitting the controls, forcing as much power as he can from the engines.

'Minutes.' Ryder hooks a small terminal to the chest implant then throws an oxygen mask at Terra. 'Stick that on him. I can override his programming, get him breathing, but it'll only work for six minutes tops. After that I'll damage what's left of the implant.'

Desyl doesn't respond. There's nothing to say. Terra tries to keep her hand steady on the mask as Ryder closely monitors his improvisation.

Terra is so fixated on the mask, she doesn't realise they've docked until the ramp lowers and a gurney is wheeled in. Pushed out of the way, Terra can only watch as Gryffin is whisked away to a room at the side of the main engine.

Desyl shouts orders at whoever he left in control of *Ares* and the ship accelerates away from Ultar. Terra ignores the guttural growl of *Ares'* mighty engines beside her. Right now, her sole focus is on Gryffin and how he appears to be dead. It takes her a few seconds to realise they've stopped beside the stasis pod that housed Gryffin's mother for years. 'Why did you bring that?'

Desyl shoves the empty gurney to the side. 'We weren't sure if he'd have the same trouble with his implants that he had before. If he was blocked going through the Port we'd be screwed.' Desyl attaches monitors to Gryffin's chest implant and Ryder passes a thin needle to Terra. 'Push that in his ocular implant, just beside his ear. There's an access point.'

She takes the probe and looks with horror at the metal needle. 'What?'

'You want him to live? Do it now!'

Terra places the end of the probe against the connector on his implant, takes a breath and pushes it in to his head. Ryder nods approvingly then takes the end of each monitor and attaches it to a handheld unit. He looks at the screen and grunts. 'Up and running, sir.'

Desyl wipes his hands on his leathers then takes a large syringe from Ryder. 'What the hell is that?' Terra asks.

'His implants are more or less keeping him alive, but we need it the other way around.' Without explaining further he stabs Gryffin in the heart with the syringe and empties the contents. Less than a second later, the reassuring beep from the monitor signals a heartbeat. 'That's good. The pod is regulating his vitals. Shut him off, Ryder.'

He taps the screen and the faint glow from Gryffin's eye dims until it's gone.

Desyl pushes Terra out of the way and secures the lid of the pod in place. They fix each of the large locks down and check the monitors again.

'I need to get to the command deck. You watch his vitals closely, Ryder.'

'Yes, sir.'

Terra leans over the pod and stares down at Gryffin. His heart is beating steadily but that doesn't put her at ease. He'd nearly died trying to save them. If they didn't have this pod, Gryffin would be gone.

'You can't do anything here. The Captain won't be getting out of the pod any time soon.'

'I should stay with him in case he wakes up.'

Ryder humourlessly laughs. 'He's dead, Commander.'

'Desyl just—'

'Desyl just gave him a heartbeat so the pod could take over. As soon as we take the lid off, he's a goner again.'

She looks at Gryffin then back at Ryder. 'What?'

'His only hope is the med bay on the Foundation ship his Hunter brother found. Anyway, like I said, you can't do anything here.'

'I'm not leaving him.'

Ryder crosses his arms and Terra notices that, while he's wiry, he's all muscle. The tattoos on his arms only help to highlight his lean biceps. 'I'm not a fan, Commander. Just want you to know. Never been too keen on having the fairer sex on board. Makes things complicated. But here you are, and for the most part, you've chipped in. But just because you share the Capitan's bed, doesn't mean you get treated different.'

The ship shudders as something hits it.

'If you want to be taken seriously by the crew, you'll get your arse to the command deck and do your fucking job. I'll do mine and keep our dear Captain away from death's door.'

Terra wants to stay. She also wants to thump Ryder in the mouth, but she has to admit he has a point. She wanted to be counted as a member of the crew. She's had numerous fights with Gryffin about that very point.

She gets up, and before she can stop herself, her weapon is out of its holster and pressed to the side of Ryder's head. 'If anything happens to him while I'm gone, so help me, I'll make any punishment Gryffin could dish out seem like a slap on the wrist. Do you get me?'

He nods and she walks away, without looking at Gryffin again.

Ryder leans against the wall and checks the monitors again. 'You got a good one there, Captain.'

∞

EARTH

Harvey pours himself a large measure of scotch and sits in the chair behind his home desk. He spent the day interrogating Garvan, but the irritating man refused to give him any information. His responses were limited to smart comments and snide remarks. His inability to make his old friend see the seriousness of his predicament is beginning to grate on One's nerves.

He takes a sip of the liquid as he stares out the window at his grandchildren playing in the garden. It will take them at least two days - possibly three - to set-up a new facility. While he'd like nothing more than to add Garvan to the top of the modification list, he'll just have to wait.

He spins his chair around when a light knock sounds on the door. His step-daughter pops her head around the door. 'Dinner's ready in five.'

'Thank you, Liza. Has your brother arrived yet?'

'About ten minutes ago.'

'Could you send him in?'

She closes the door and Harvey opens the top drawer of his desk and pulls out his personal unit. While he waits he locates the document he needs, then places the unit on his desk beside his glass.

Zeke enters the room a few minutes later without knocking. Harvey forces a smile on his face, trying not to let his irritation at the lack of manners show on his face. 'Take a seat, Zeke.'

The tall, blond-haired man slumps in the chair opposite him and crosses his arms. Unlike his sister, Zeke has never fit in his family. His decision to take a new wife so soon after Liza and Zeke's mother's death had never been accepted by the young man.

The fact that he still allowed him in the house should have made Zeke grateful, but he did nothing to hide his disdain at the situation. It was a feeling that Harvey fully understood and completely agreed with. He would have no issue if he never saw Zeke again, but that would affect Liza. Her younger brother may be an ungrateful irritant, but his sister, her husband, and their children mean the world to Harvey.

Zeke slumps back in the chair and yawns loudly. 'You called?'

Harvey forces his jaw to unclench and puts what he hopes is something resembling a smile on his face. 'How was work?'

Zeke shrugs. 'Same as usual. It would be nice if someone actually attacked the HQ from time to time. Make my life more exciting.'

'Who would dare to attack us?'

'I'm sure there are one or two groups out there who'd love to give it a shot.'

Harvey shakes his head. It's disturbing how true that statement is.

'I've been thinking about what we discussed a few months ago - about changing your name.'

Zeke's blue eyes turn dark. He brushes the loose hairs back from his face, but they refuse to stay in place, too short to be captured with the rest in the stubby ponytail. Another thing that irritates him greatly. Men should not have long hair. He swears Zeke does it to annoy him. 'Yeah, and the discussion ended less than a minute later. My answer is the same.'

'Your family name is greatly important. Think what it would do for you if you had my family name. I have a good position on in the Foundation HQ. It could mean a promotion for you.'

'I don't want a promotion and I sure as hell don't want your name. I'm only here because, for some reason, Liza cares about you and so do her kids. I don't. We agreed to be civil for their sakes.'

Harvey pushes the unit across the table towards Zeke. 'It's just a name.'

'Exactly. What different does it make to you?'

Harvey rests his elbows on the desk and steeples his fingers. 'Consider it.'

Zeke shakes his head as he rises to his feet. He pushes the unit back to Harvey then rests his hands on the desk. 'I will never turn my back on my family name. Do you get that? I am and will always be Zeke Garvan. End of conversation.' He straightens and grins widely. 'Now, dinner's ready.'

Harvey remains composed until he hears Zeke joining his sister in the kitchen. He gently closes the door to his office then kicks the chair Zeke was just sitting on.

Having Wade's son take his name would be such a kick to the convict. It didn't bother him either way but it would greatly annoy Wade, and that was worth it. The fact that Zeke refused to take his name or even be civil with him isn't ideal but there's not a lot he can do about it.

Zeke and Liza will never know what happened to their father. As far as they and their late mother were concerned, he committed treason and died in prison during a fight. That didn't mean he wouldn't use them to hurt Wade as much as possible.

He activates the security screen on his comms unit, shuts down the two-way video feed then contacts Leeson. After less than thirty seconds, the man's thin, lined face appears on the screen. 'I want the prisoner moved to surgery tomorrow.'

He isn't surprised when Leeson impersonates a fish for a few seconds before he speaks. 'But, sir. He's male.'

'I'm well aware he's male. I don't care about longevity. I just want him to undergo the procedure.'

'But should he not undergo intensive interrogation first? He escaped Tyrat. We need to know how. Perhaps he has information on the rebels from the Outer Sector.'

'Nothing is to be gained by questioning him. He designed the New Colony. He knows too much to take any chances.'

'If you're sure—'

'You recalled the remaining technicians?' he interrupts.

'Of course, sir.'

'And the temporary facility is operational?'

'Well, yes, but—'

'I have never explained myself to anyone before. I'm not about to start now. I don't care what you have to do, I want that convict modified with as much pain as possible. Do I make myself clear?'

'I'll see to it personally.'

Harvey shuts down the comms and leans back in his chair. Finally, something is going to plan.

13

Zeke turns off the unit, slips it back in his pocket and quietly makes his way to the kitchen. He smiles at his sister and takes the tray of food from her hands, placing it on the table.

'Are you all right, Zeke? You look like you've seen a ghost?'

'Yeah, Liza. I'm fine.'

'What did Harvey want?'

He pulls a chunk of bread from one of the plates and rolls it in a ball before popping it in his mouth. 'Same as always.'

Liza pulls the plate away before he can help himself again. 'You'll ruin your appetite. I presume you gave him the same answer.'

He nods. 'I'm not erasing the last connection I have to Dad. It doesn't feel right.'

Liza shoos her children from the room then sits down at the other side of the counter. 'Zeke, I miss him too, both of them. But they're gone. I've had to accept that. Isn't it time you did too?'

'How can I? You know how Dad felt about us. Do you really believe he'd just wake up one morning and decide to sell top secret Foundation plans to the Outer Sector then leave us?'

'They showed us the evidence, Zeke. I didn't want to believe it either, but it was all there.'

'What if the data was falsified? What if, I don't know, he didn't die in prison and was being held somewhere else?'

'Held somewhere else? Have you heard yourself? He was an architect, Zeke. He was caught doing something illegal and was punished. End of story.'

'But there was no trial.'

'Because he was guilty.' She turns away from him and busies herself laying food out on the plates. 'You have to stop doing this to yourself. Dad wouldn't want you to waste your life. There was no big conspiracy.' She wipes her hands on a towel and looks across at him. 'Obsessing on crazy theories won't help you.'

'So I should just forget and wipe all trace of him from my life by changing my name?'

She reaches across and brushes his hair back from his face. 'It's just a name, Zeke. Besides, removing the Garvan tag might help get you a promotion. You're going to be twenty-six next month and you're still at the same level in work. How many promotions have you missed out on - three, four? Having his name isn't doing you any favours. Maybe a change will do you and your career good.'

'I can't do it, Liza.'

She smiles at him and nods. 'You're just as stubborn as he was. Just do me one favour, okay? Back off Harvey a little. He's always done right by us, and the girls love him. Please try to be civil for them if nothing else.'

He comes around the table and kisses her on the forehead. Hearing her daughters fighting outside, Liza smiles apologetically at him before hurrying from the room to separate them.

His mind continues to race on auto-pilot as he sets the table. Liza's right. The odds were stacked against their father. Maybe he was the traitor the Council said he was. But Zeke isn't convinced. Far from it. Liza spent most of her adult life away at college, only coming home on the holidays. She didn't live with him from day to day. Zeke did. He knows his father wouldn't have done the things he's accused of. Liza and Zeke were everything to him. There's no way he'd willingly turn his back on them. Not a chance.

He looks down the corridor at the ornate door of Harvey's home office. He doesn't know why, but he has a deep-seated feeling that Harvey had a hand in his father's disappearance.

Since the minute his mother introduced him to Harvey, he disliked the man. There was something he couldn't quite put his finger on, but he knew from that instant he'd never trust him. Placing the listening device under his desk had been easy enough. The man had a thing for over-the-top antique furniture with plenty of crevices for microscopic devices - especially ones routine detectors wouldn't pick up.

While he should be relieved he wasn't going mad the last few years, listening in on the conversations left him with more questions than answers.

He's heard of Admiral Leeson. The weak admiral reported directly to One. So why had he been talking to Harvey? Was Harvey somehow also working for the Council leader? He shakes his head, pushing the thought away. Harvey is pathetic. There's no way he could be connected to One.

After nearly dropping a glass for the third time, Liza kicks him out of the kitchen while she finishes getting things ready. He ruffles his niece's hair as he leaves and locks himself in the downstairs bathroom. He leans against the sink and stares at his reflection in the mirror.

Everyone says he is a clone of his father. With his brown eyes and dirty blond hair he does look like a younger version of him.

Unfortunately for his career, he also inherited his father's reputation. He swears Harvey somehow made sure Liza wasn't associated with their father's crimes. Maybe when she changed her surname after marrying Jake, a well-regarded, no nonsense security officer on one of the prison moons, the association had diluted a little. He wasn't so lucky. Not that he necessarily considered it a bad thing. He was far from ready to give up on his father's memory.

He splashes cold water on his face, but it does nothing to knock his brain out of the whirlwind it's currently spinning in. It makes no sense. He knows that. Was his father the one that designed this New Colony that Harvey was talking about? Is that what sealed his fate? He knows his dad was working on something big for the year or so before he disappeared, but he wasn't allowed to talk about it with anyone.

Zeke focuses on his reflection again. That may be the case, but something deep down in his gut, madness or not, believes the prisoner Harvey was speaking about is his father. He can't explain it and it doesn't make any sense at all, but the thought refuses to go.

He pushes upright and dries his face with the plush towel beside the sink. His sister is going to be ticked off at him for leaving, but he can't stay here and be civil with that man until he finds out the truth.

Time to do a bit of digging. If the man Harvey is talking about is his father, he doesn't have much time to find out before he loses him for good this time.

∞

ULTAR

Nova stands in the doorway and looks at the empty cell. She bends down to look at the sheets of paper sitting neatly on the floor beside a chair. The drawings are of the prototype. So, this was his cell. She sits on the bunk and frowns at the blood on the ground beside it. Thirty-Five is injured. Perhaps he is dead. That would put an end to One's plans. Without the prototype he would never get his male army.

She faces one of her team. The woman holds out a screen to Nova. 'We've searched the base. No sign of him. We found Jensen Roman and an unidentified Nomad in the tunnels. Both are dead. Thirty-Five left a message.'

Nova takes the screen and watches as the prototype leans over her fallen comrade and promises to come after them. That's good. They need him to come after them. 'There is a burial place on the surface?'

'Just outside the town centre.'

'Bury Roman and the Nomad. Bring the other body back to the ship. One will want her back on Earth.'

The woman nods and leaves Nova alone. One wants Roman's body on Earth too, but that isn't going to happen. The man stood up to the Foundation. He deserved to be honoured for that, not shot defending the Nomad leader. It hadn't been her intention to kill anyone, but that couldn't be helped now. Ultar had been his home for the last year. He should stay here.

She runs her hand over the pillow. 'Where are you?' she says quietly to herself. She closes her eyes and concentrates. The link to the rest of her team is strong, but there's nothing else. She had hoped she'd be able to feel him. Maybe his programming is too different to hers. Maybe he'll always be out of reach.

She walks away from the cell and along the corridor. The prototype's disappearance will not go down well with One. As much as she'd like to delay contacting him, there is little point. She'll have to relay the information at some stage. She enters the comms room and activates the nearest machine. As usual, One keeps her waiting, but eventually his masked face appears on the screen. 'Well? Where is he?'

'Gone.'

'What do you mean he's gone?'

Not for the first time, Nova wishes death on the man facing her. His inability to accept fact is one of his greatest weaknesses. The cyborg project is a mistake. Earth is doomed. The prototype will destroy the Council. The Outer Sector will survive. All of this is fact yet the most powerful man on Earth refuses to accept these basic truths. 'We have searched the base. He is not here.'

'He has to be there. We couldn't have linked with the other cyborg without him boosting the signal. Where is he?'

'Unknown. We've searched the entire facility and the surface. He's not here.'

'You mean you let him go.'

'He must have escaped on one of the ships moments before we got here.'

'Well that's not good enough. I need him under our control.'

'That cannot happen if I don't have him.'

'I'm well aware of that. You find him. Now! What about Roman? Did you find him?'

'No.'

'State of the art cyborg team indeed. You let a defective cyborg and a traitor escape. Find them!' He shuts down the link and leaves Nova staring at a blank screen. Her purple eye reflects off the screen as she imagines all the unpleasant things she'd like to do to One. There would be time enough for that later. First she needs to find the prototype before the Council gets their hands on him again. If that happens all is lost.

∞

EARTH SECTOR

Terra wipes her palm on her trousers as she checks the readings from her station. 'Sir, I'm picking up Foundation transmissions. We're here.'

Desyl leans forward in the command chair and looks at the view outside. Terra thinks he looks almost disappointed. Almost like he thought Foundation space would be different somehow. 'Any mention of a Nomad vessel coming through?'

She shakes her head. 'The cloak held through the Port. We're not transmitting. So far, they have no idea we're here.'

Desyl links with Ryder. 'He still with us?'

'Yes, sir. No fluctuations. Pod is keeping his vitals steady.'

Desyl breaks the link. 'That's something. Set a course for this mysterious station. No point hanging around out in the open attracting attention.'

As the ship moves away from the Port, Desyl joins Terra at comms. 'Any way of getting a message to Bray? Wouldn't mind making sure the coast is clear before we knock on their door.'

Terra shakes her head. 'He gave us rough coordinates, but nothing else. I think we'll have to wait for him to get in touch.'

'Great. So until then we're sitting ducks. Not sure I like that plan.'

'There's no Foundation activity in the area. Long range sensors show the majority of the activity in and around Earth itself. Unless we do something to attract attention, and if we move away from the Port, we should be okay.'

'I want the cloaks monitored every damn second we're out here. If they drop it'll plaster a great big fucking target on us. I've already crashed this ship once. I'd prefer to give it back to the captain in one piece this time.'

He goes back to the command chair and keeps an eye on the monitors to his left. She feels a little sorry for him. When she found herself stranded on *Ares* last year, she didn't expect to find a new friend in Gryffin's second in command. While Gryffin was busy distancing himself from her, Desyl had been appointed to look after her.

Like the other Nomad, he looks the part with his piercings, tattoos, and more weapons than she could count, but under the armour, he's one of the sweetest men she's ever met. She's seen him fight and knows he's more than capable of looking after himself, but he's also kind, thoughtful, and incredibly easy to talk to. She's spent many hours bending his ear about anything and everything. She has no doubts she would have gone more than a little stir crazy on board if not for their friendship.

Even after surviving Klay taking *Ares* and crash landing her on Ultar, Desyl still doubts his place as Gryffin's second officer. Even now he may appear relaxed, but he's chewing on his bottom lip and playing with the ring he wears on the index finger of his right hand. He'd rather be anywhere than in the captain's seat.

She turns back to her station as a message comes in. 'Sir, it's Bray. He wants to talk.'

'Go for it.'

Bray appears on the screen in front of Desyl. 'Kind of surprised to see you here.'

'Long story. We weren't left with much choice.'

Bray nods. 'I'm guessing he's in a bad way or you wouldn't have made the crossing. We have everything ready. I'll guide you in. See you in a bit.'

The screen goes blank and Terra sends the first set of coordinates to the helm.

14

Bray crosses his arms and leans against the side of a small transport in the loading dock. A few dozen crew have gathered to see the Nomad vessel arrive. Like the Hunters, everyone has heard of the Nomad, but none have ever seen her flagship.

Sayber grumbles to Bray as he looks at the gathering crowd. 'You'd swear they've never seen a ship before.'

Bray smiles to himself. He knows Sayber is put out because Gryffin's ship is getting more attention than his. Seems the rivalry will never die. 'It'll be tight in here with *Ares*.'

Sayber grunts. 'He's damn lucky his ship can fit at all.' Sayber shakes his head. 'Screw this. I'll be on *Perses* if anyone is looking for me.'

Bray opens his mouth to argue, but Sayber is already climbing the stairs to the upper level where *Perses* is moored.

'What's his problem?'

Bray glances over his shoulder at Rua. 'Sayber? Just some healthy rivalry.'

She looks up at Sayber, marching across the upper deck to his ship. 'Yeah, that looks healthy to me.'

The red light over the main bay door flashes and a siren sounds. Heath pushes through the crowd, joining Bray at the front. The ship had been cleared as it closed in on the station, but the head of security is taking no chances.

Bray hates that he smiles as *Ares* makes an appearance in the bay. The fierce purple griffin painted on her bow sneers down at everyone, her glowing purple eyes interrogating each bystander as she nears. With a grinding of heavy gears, the immense masts retract, tucking the metal sails in the top deck.

'Hate to admit but she knows how to make an entrance.'

Bray nods at Rua. 'Hate to admit it, but I agree.'

Ares swings around, her bow pointing away as her stern settles into position beside the crowd. The twin of the griffin on the front glares down at the onlookers from above the cargo doors. The damn thing matches his brother's tattoo and, like the tattoo, the artwork is incredibly realistic.

As the growl from the engines dies away, the cargo hold opens and a wide ramp lowers onto the dock. Desyl steps out of the gloomy interior of the ship and walks down the ramp, stopping in front of Bray. 'Good to see you're not dead, Commander.'

'You too.' He looks over Desyl's shoulder to the stasis pod being brought down the ramp. 'Not sure about your gift.'

'You can't say I don't care. We're going to need somewhere secure to put him. We still haven't been able to find a reason for his malfunction when he was chasing after *Alpha*. He's been staying in a cell just in case he decides to... I don't know, kill us all in our sleep or something like that.'

Bray nods towards *Alpha*. 'There's a secure med bay on her. It also has a rejuvenation pod.'

Desyl nods. 'That'll do for now. Can I have a little help with the stasis pod.'

'Desyl, where's my mother?'

Desyl's smile disappears. 'I'm sorry, Commander. I thought you knew?'

'All I know is that he's in her pod, so where is she?'

'She was deteriorating rapidly. We didn't know where you were... Roman made the decision to let her go.'

Bray clenches his jaw and pushes back the emotions that want to be released. He'll deal with Roman's decision when everyone is safely back in the Outer Sector. 'The Dixon's are waiting on *Alpha*.'

He glances down at his brother in the pod, but instead of helping to push the unit along the walkway, he walks past. 'C'mon. I'd hate for him to die in there,' Bray mutters as he walks towards the Foundation vessel in the corner.

∞

OCARRO COLONY

Milla pulls her coat tighter around her shoulders, but it does nothing to protect her from the rain. She's only been on this planet an hour and she's already done. Every stitch of clothing is soaked through - including her underwear. Her mood is far from cheery and she swears there's something crawling around in the mud under her boots.

For the third time in as many minutes she loses her footing, grabbing on to Chayse to keep her ass from landing in the mud. 'I am so done with this planet. Are we nearly there?'

Chayse checks the coordinates again and nods. 'Should be around the corner,' he shouts over the rain.

129

A few minutes later Chayse pulls her to a stop and points to the cabin ahead of them, barely visible through the rain. 'That's it.'

'You sure?'

He nods. 'That's where the coordinates lead to.'

'What the hell is in there that Gryffin sent us half way across the Sector to find?'

'Only one way to find out.' They slowly approach the cabin and stop when a tall figure steps out from the trees with a heavy rifle in his hands.

'Hello?' Chayse's greeting isn't retuned. Hidden in shadow, Milla can't make out anything except the glowing sight on the gun. Chayse takes a step closer. 'We're looking for the Blacksmith.'

The man doesn't say anything for a minute. 'That's me. Presume you've got a message for me?'

Chayse glances over at Milla. They weren't expecting that. 'Yeah.'

'Throw it over.'

'How can we be sure you're the person we're looking for?'

'Throw over the message from Gryffin or I'll shoot you and take it from you.'

'He makes a convincing argument,' Milla mutters as Chayse pulls the unit from his pocket and throws it at the man's feet.

'Stay there.'

Before either of them can reply, he disappears into the trees.

'He's nearly as chatty as Gryffin. Do you recognise him?'

Chayse shakes his head and pushes his soggy spikes back from his face. 'Hard to make out any details. Guess we'll have to wait and see what he does.'

He returns a few minutes later and gestures to the cabin. 'Get inside.' They don't immediately move. 'If I was going to kill you I would have done it when I was pointing the gun at your heads. Get inside and I'll give you answers or stay here and get wet. Your choice.'

'What do you think, Captain?'

Chayse looks around then back at the cabin. 'I want answers.'

'I'm in full agreement. After you, sir.'

They follow the blacksmith into the cabin. It's surprisingly spacious considering what they could see from the outside. As soon as the door closes, Milla can feel the warmth returning to her body. In the centre of the room, a circular pit houses a blazing fire with a cast iron pot hanging over it. Whatever is cooking inside it smells heavenly and her stomach immediately responds by growling.

Their host points to a well-worn bench against the far wall. Taking that as an invitation to sit, they both shrug out of their sodden coats and settle in front of the fire.

The man pulls off his long coat and hangs it on the back of the door. He lowers onto the bench at the far side of the fire and focuses on the flames. Milla openly stares at him. He's an impressive guy. He's got to be a few inches taller than Chayse so possibly six-foot-two. His light brown hair is long and tied up in a messy bun. His thick beard is neatly trimmed and is a shade darker than his hair. She blushes as his light blue eyes suddenly target her.

Something about this guy screams Nomad to Milla. He's got the build and along with the multiple earrings and the faint outline of tattoos showing through his shirt he's an impressive example of one.

'You're Nomad, aren't you?'

He locks those eyes on Milla again. 'How is he?'

'Gryffin?'

The man nods.

'Who are you?' Chayse asks before she can respond. Milla gets the feeling this conversation could easily consist of a series of questions with neither side willing to answer.

'He's in a bad way.' She ignores Chayse's glare at her admission. 'Now, we've come a hell of a way and would kind of like to know why Gryffin thought you could help.'

The man laughs and leans back against the wall. 'I like you. Not surprised he let you join the Nomad.'

'I'm a likeable person. Hang on. How do you know I'm Nomad? Who are you?'

'It's been a long time since I've answered that last question honestly.'

'You going to give it a shot today?' Chayse asks.

'Gryffin's asked me to, so yes.' He pulls his shirt over his head and Milla goes back to openly staring again. His broad chest is covered in tattoos.

Chayse leans forward and blows out a breath. 'That's impressive. Hold on. That's the mark of a commander? You were second in command of a Nomad ship?'

The man nods. 'I was.'

'Which ship?'

He looks in the fire again. '*Ares*.'

Milla looks sideways at him as Chayse shakes his head and sits back before leaning forward again to really look at the man again. 'How old are you?'

'Chayse!' Milla scolds. 'You can't just ask him something like that.'

The man smiles. 'It's not a problem. I'm forty-five.'

'You couldn't...' Chayse's voice trails away as he examines the man in front of them.

Their host raises a pierced eyebrow. 'You know exactly who I am. I can see it in your face. It won't make sense, but you know.'

Chayse shakes his head. 'No way. You can't be. I mean he's dead. Gryffin killed him.'

The blacksmith smirks and crosses his thick arms. 'From what I hear he killed you too. How's that working out for you?'

Milla clears her throat and waves her hand in the air. 'Eh, hello! Who exactly are we talking about?'

'There's only one Nomad who served in that position on *Ares* that fits his age. He was first officer under Rayde around the time Gryffin was found,' Chayse explains. 'His name was Creed. Thing is, Gryffin killed him when Rayde charged him as a traitor. Record states Gryffin beat him to death then sent him out the airlock.'

The blacksmith takes a deep breath and looks back at them again. 'That's what the record states because that's what Gryffin wanted the record to state. Creed is still very much alive, and I promise you, I may have been many things in my life but I was no traitor.'

∞

DIXON SPACE STATION

Terra turns in a circle, her mouth open as she tries to assimilate everything around her. She thought the med bay on *Infinity* was impressive, but *Alpha*'s makes it look like an old fashioned Ultaran set-up. 'Milla would be in heaven here. This is amazing.'

Desyl looks up from the pod. 'Yeah, let's hope it does what Bray thinks it will.'

Evie moves over to a large unit, not too dissimilar to the pod Gryffin is in. She mumbles to herself as she taps on the control panel on its side. 'Why is everyone in such a negative mood. This ship is state of the art. If this machine can't bring him back from the dead, nothing can.'

'I hope you're right.'

She points to the booth she's programming. 'Can you stop arguing with me and put him in there?' As Desyl manoeuvres the heavy pod in place, Evie looks at Bray. 'Are you going to continue holding up the wall or actually get your hands dirty?'

'We've got a room full of Foundation technicians we need to process. I should help with that.'

Desyl grabs him by the arm before he can turn away. 'Hold on. You've got Foundation technicians here? Can they not help with

Gryffin?'

Bray snorts loudly. 'I may not have too many warm feelings towards my brother, but even I wouldn't let them near him without having a chat first. What's to say they wouldn't do more harm than good? Doesn't look like it would take much to finish him off.'

Bray looks down at his brother, then to Terra before he turns and leaves the room.

Terra watches Bray as he disappears down the corridor. In her rush to get Gryffin here, she never thought about meeting with Bray again. From what just happened, he's less than happy to see her.

Evie stands beside Terra and looks at the empty corridor. 'I really hope they don't make a mess with those Foundation personnel. It would be a shame to soil this beautiful ship, wouldn't you agree?'

Terra blinks and frowns at Evie. 'Sorry?'

'Nothing dear.' She gestures to Gryffin. 'So, how long can he be out of the pod before...' Evie doesn't finish the sentence and that grates on Terra's already frazzled nerves.

Desyl scratches the side of his head as he looks over at Terra. 'A few seconds, max. When he blasted the cyborgs on Ultar, he used up his last life. Technically he's dead. His implants may be able to help get him going again—'

'But you can't activate his implants until we figure out if he's been booby trapped,' Felix says as he arrives, his hands clasped behind his back. 'What a pickle.'

'Helpful as ever, dear,' Evie says. She places a hand lovingly on the rejuvenation pod. 'This contraption will act as a stasis pod too. We'll need to transfer him quickly. Care to get that bit going so we can help this young man?'

Terra zones out as Felix and Evie spend a minute arguing over which controls to use. She just wants him out of the pod and awake again. Evie leans down to look at Gryffin, checks a few of the readings on the pod then straightens up again. Evie clicks her fingers at Desyl and Heath. 'What are you two standing around for? You really expect me to lift him in?'

Evie opens the lid and hooks some monitors to Gryffin while Desyl, Heath, and three other Nomad lift him into the rejuvenation pod. 'So, his less than reliable implants are damaging the surrounding tissue. His brain, heart, lungs, and everything else is being affected. If he's to have a chance of surviving the next few days, we need to repair the surrounding tissue, buy us some time to figure out the Foundation data and fix his implants. Did I leave anything out?'

Desyl steps aside as Evie pushes between him and the bed holding Gryffin. 'He received some sort of command from another cyborg. They could be transmitting between them. We sedated the other three as soon as we got them on *Ares*. They're in a holding cell until we deal with him.'

'Four cyborgs. And we didn't get you anything.' Felix moves over to the side of the larger pod and lowers the panel so he can get a better look. 'Can we remove any of the components?'

As much as Terra would like to say yes, it's not her call to make. 'Nothing. He wants all his implants left as they are for now. He... he's considering having them upgraded, but...' Her eyes fall on Gryffin then to the monitors showing a heartbeat only present thanks to the pod.

Ryder's blunt statement on *Ares* finally sinks in. *He's dead, Commander'*. If they turned off the power to the pod Gryffin would never wake up. Whether he had implants or not wouldn't change that simple fact. Right now, she just wants him to wake up and look at her.

'Can you stabilise his body so it's strong enough to handle the implants? Whatever happens after that is his call.'

'Of course we can do that dear,' Evie says, pushing her hat back from her forehead. 'This ingenious contraption can rebuild his body... or what's left of it. We can deal with the cybernetics later. If his body is too weak to support his implants he's dead anyway. Which he sort of is. It will buy him a little time to figure out what he wants to do.'

Terra smiles even though she's not entirely convinced about his upgrade plan. 'Thank you.'

Evie nods and turns back to the pod. She walks around the bed and stops beside Gryffin's head. 'Hmmm. Well, they say you should never meet your heroes. I guess they're right.'

'What exactly do you mean by that?' Terra asks, irritated by the woman's tone.

'Never met the man in person but I've heard a great deal about him. I have to admit I was expecting...' She leans over to examine his metal tipped stump. 'More. You appear to have left a bit of him in the Outer Sector.'

'We took it off a few weeks ago. It was pulling too much power from his body,' Desyl explains. 'We left in such a hurry we didn't have time to get it.'

'I'm sure we can sort him out with something appropriate,' Felix says as he takes a blade from a drawer and begins cutting what's left of Gryffin's clothes off.

Evie takes Terra's arm and turns her away from Gryffin. 'This process could take a few hours, dear. Might be best if you get cleaned up, have something to eat, and a catnap. You can't do anything for him right now.'

Terra pulls out of her grip. 'I don't want to leave him.'

Evie takes Terra's arm again and leads her towards the door. 'I'm going to be honest with you, dear. You can't be here for this.'

'I already said I'm not leaving him.'

'How can I put this? If we're going to help him, we have to get stuck in and I mean really stuck in.'

Terra frowns, not understanding what Evie is saying.

'We're going to take him apart,' Felix shouts from across the room. 'Try using English, Evie.'

'I was trying to be sensitive, you oaf. I apologise, dear. But Felix is right. We have to make sure he's not a risk to the station or anyone on it, and also figure out how to help him. That means opening him up and checking all his implants - external and internal. You really shouldn't be here for that bit. You understand, right?'

Terra looks over at Gryffin and nods slowly. Evie is right. She doesn't want to see him like that. 'Can you please call me—'

'The second we're done,' Evie promises. 'Big guy, can you show this young lady to the mess hall?'

Heath holds out his hand. 'I usually go by Heath. You hungry?'

'Not really, but I should eat something. Desyl, can you stay with him?'

'Sure thing.' He nods and smiles although from the look on his face, he'd much prefer to be leaving with her.

15

Leeson stands in front of One, his hands clenched firmly in front of him. One was not expecting a visit from the admiral so he doesn't rush to acknowledge him.

'Sir.'

One slowly lifts his head to look at Leeson. He cannot believe the man had the nerve to interrupt him. 'Excuse me?'

'I understand you are incredibly busy, but I really do think you will want to hear what I have to say.'

'I will be the judge of that.'

'Yes, sir.'

'Very well. You've disturbed me. What is it?'

'Sir, the prototype is in the Sector.'

One sighs and shakes his head. 'It is in the Outer Sector which is where you are going to find yourself if you don't leave immediately.'

'But, sir.' He hands a unit to One and takes a step back. One barely looks at the data, initially rejecting it as nonsense, but he sees Leeson is telling the truth. It may have lasted for less than a second, but the signal clearly shows on this side of the Port.

One stares at the data, unable to form any words. After staring at the information for a few minutes he drops the unit onto his desk. 'Has the signal reappeared?'

'No, sir. I've scanned the area several times and haven't found it again. If he's on a ship there's a strong possibility he will have moved.'

'Of course he's on a ship you fool. He's hardly out for a stroll through space.'

'Sir, there's something else. Seven knows about this. He was in the room when the alarm was raised. He is planning to discuss it at the meeting...' Leeson glances at his watch. 'At the meeting that is starting now, sir.'

One suppresses a sigh. It's far from ideal for his fellow council members to know about this issue, but there's little he can do about it now. Perhaps with them knowing he will be able to launch half a dozen ships to search the area. With their support, the prototype could be captured speedily and then repaired.

One steeples his fingers together and smiles to himself. Time to face the rest of the Council and get this search underway. With the advanced technological capabilities of the Foundation, he has no doubt the troublesome prototype would be back in restraints by the end of the day.

'Very well. Leave me. I will join you shortly.' He waits until Leeson has left then contacts Nova again. It takes the irritating cyborg a long time to respond but eventually her face shows on the screen.

'No. We have not found him yet.'

'I am well aware of that. Perhaps you have not found him because he is here.'

'He is on Earth?'

'Good gracious, no. His signal was picked up briefly around the

Port then it conveniently disappeared. I will organise a search party, but I need you to bring your team back to Earth. There's little point in you being there if he's here.'

'Just my team?'

'Yes, Nova. Just your team. I'll leave the others there to hold Ultar. Now that we have that infernal colony under our control I plan for it to stay that way.'

He shuts down the connection and stares at the information Leeson gave him. He thought the prototype had been altered to ensure he would not be able to cross the Port. One sneers to himself. That wretched Scientist couldn't get a thing right. Faulty prototype and faulty programming. It's a surprise the new models function at all.

Never mind. With the prototype and Garvan within reach of Earth, it would make modifying the two men so much easier. But first he needs to deal with this meeting. Top of his list is to shut down the Port so the prototype cannot make its escape again.

∞

DIXON SPACE STATION

Desyl glances from the monitors and instantly regrets it. Evie's fingers are a little too far inside Gryffin's leg. He clears his throat and focuses on the screens again.

Evie moves from one side of the bed to the other, her wide brimmed hat casting shadows on the table as she moves. 'Will you stand still woman. I can't see what I'm doing,' Felix snaps from the head of the table.

'I can't believe we have the infamous Gryffin here on our station! This is so exciting.'

'Calm yourself, woman,' Felix says. 'You're coming across a little crazed. Besides, I thought you said he was disappointing?'

She waves her hand at him, shooing him out of the way as she leans back over his leg. 'Now that I've had some time with him I can see there's a bit more to him. He's quite impressive, isn't he?'

'At the moment, he's a corpse. How about we bring him back before you start drooling over him.'

'I can't wait to talk to him.'

'I wouldn't get your hopes up,' Desyl says from the head of the bed. 'This is pretty much as chatty as he gets. You're lucky to get a few mumbles, shouts, or growls from him.'

Felix gently prods Gryffin's eyepiece while Heath uses the high-tech scanners to thoroughly check every inch of Gryffin's body. They haven't survived this long out of the Foundation's reach by being complacent.

Felix peers down at the damaged leg and grimaces. 'That's particularly nasty.'

Evie sucks in a breath. 'It's even worse than it looks. The infection is putting a strain on both his organic and cybernetic systems. The rejuvenation pod should help ease it, but I'm struggling to see how to help him long term. Personally, I'd recommend amputation.'

'That's what Milla has been telling him for weeks. She's our doctor,' Desyl explains.

'Found something.' Heath points to the screen on his unit. 'Tracker of some sort. It's embedded in whatever this thing behind his ear is.'

Desyl looks at the screen and frowns. 'We used to fit a monitor there. It gave us a heads up whenever he was getting... well, dangerous. Can you block the signal?'

Felix smirks. 'The station is blocked. It can transmit as much as it wants, the signal isn't going anywhere.' He frowns and looks up from the scanner. 'It probably started transmitting as soon as you came through the Port. No doubt we've got company headed our way.'

'So they know he's here,' Desyl grumbles. 'We've placed you all in danger.'

Felix brushes his concern aside. 'Our fail-safes reach beyond the walls of the station. The signal will have registered but they won't be able to get a lock on our location. Just to be on the safe side, we'll move out of the way.'

'The station can move?'

Evie nods. 'Of course it can. We routinely move around. Like us, it doesn't go very fast, but in a few hours we'll be settled in an area they've already checked.'

Felix leans over to examine the thumbnail size disc embedded in the skin behind Gryffin's left ear. 'I'd like to get this little guy out and destroyed as soon as possible but I can't.'

'Why not?'

Felix shows Desyl the scan results on the screen. 'This is the altered monitoring device, and this,' he says, tracing his finger from the device to one of the larger implants in Gryffin's head. 'This is this young man's brain. They attached it. We could possibly take it off, but the odds of doing permanent damage, well more permanent damage, is high.'

'What do you suggest?'

'I can modify one of my signal jammers. I'm sure I can attach it to this. It'll probably have to go in front of his ear instead of directly attached to what's behind his ear.'

'Could that have been the reason he wasn't able to come through the Port when we were chasing *Alpha*?'

Felix nods slowly. 'Possibly '

Evie smiles. 'Fantastic. Sort out the transmitter, Felix, while I deal with what's left of this young man's leg.'

Felix turns to glare at his wife. 'We know what we're doing, woman. We don't need you pretending you're in charge.'

Evie makes a face before returning to Gryffin's leg. Felix glances up from Gryffin's head. 'What exactly are you smiling at?'

'A few days ago we were sitting having bread without jam, I might add, saying how quiet life had become. I get the impression all these guests are going to add a little excitement to our lives over the next few days.'

∞

EARTH

Zeke easily disarms the alarm to Harvey's office and slips inside. His step-father left for work about an hour ago. Zeke was eager tear the place apart, but wanted to make sure Harvey was at the Council building before he broke in.

He pulls on a pair of gloves and closes the door behind him. The room reeks of pomp and circumstance. Harvey was never happy with what he had, continuously striving to be better than everyone else. The ornate gold gilding on every surface is probably enough to feed a family from the outskirts of the city for a year.

He pulls out the plump desk chair and sits, hating the way he sinks into the cushion. It's easily the most expensive and least comfortable chair he's ever sat on.

Zeke pulls out Harvey's personal unit and attaches a signal blocker before he powers it up. It's probably the first time Zeke has used his original training. He had been assigned to the Systems and Operations Division, but after getting in a spot of bother more than once, he had been reassigned to the Security Observation Division which involved staring at a screen looking out for possible threats on the streets of the city.

It was rare that an assigned role could be changed, but his supervisor had pulled every string available to get rid of him. Another reason for Harvey to disapprove of him. Zeke considered it well worth the move for that point alone, even though it is mind-numbingly boring.

It takes him a grand total of two and a half minutes to break through Harvey's security settings and log into the system. He starts with his step-father's personal email and finding nothing interesting there, goes to his Council email.

He stares at the blank page, shuts it down and starts again. Still nothing. 'What the hell?' Everyone has emails or message of some sort on their system. Even his three-year-old niece has emails. So why doesn't Harvey have any?

He decides to try a different route. Instead of going in through the front door, he tries a back route. 'Got you!' he exclaims when he finally finds what he was looking for - another email account hidden in the system. After trying a few more less than inventive passwords, he gets in and freezes. What he thought was an email account is actually a live video feed showing a painfully white cell.

Zeke recognises the design. It's a Foundation holding cell. This one is slightly different however. The room is bigger and, from what he can see, has been reinforced substantially. He leans closer to the screen, but he can't see anyone.

Why would Harvey be watching an empty cell? Just as he's about to cut the feed, the door of the cell opens and a man is thrown in. He rolls once and lands in a heap on the floor.

The man pushes himself to his feet and turns around, giving Zeke a clear view of a face he never thought he'd see again. His heart hammers in his chest as he watches the father he's spent years looking for, walking around a cell being monitored by Harvey.

He spends the next few minutes tracing the live feed back to its source then sits back in the uncomfortable chair as he reads the information on the screen.

Council Headquarters.

Now he's even more confused. What the hell is his father doing there? Whatever is going on, Harvey has his father less than an hour's transport ride from the house and that's all he needs to know.

As much as he doesn't want to, Zeke shuts down the feed of his father and closes the unit. He makes sure everything is as he found it with the computer then leaves the office, resetting the security system once the door is locked. He pulls off his gloves and climbs the stairs to his room. Once there he locks the door and lowers onto the end of the bed.

He knew his father was alive. Deep down he always knew it. Liza and his mother had given up, but he never had. That knowledge doesn't help him find his father or get him out. Whatever Harvey's involvement, he'd deal with him later.

He's only got one choice. He showers quickly, taking a few minutes to shave for the first time in about a week then gets dressed in his uniform. He ties his hair back and tucks the short ponytail under his hat. The Council recommended all men working on the HQ should have short hair and be clean shaven – hence Zeke's decision to have long hair and a beard. Nothing like getting on the Council and Harvey's nerves to brighten his boring life.

Not today though. If he's going to save his father, he needs to blend in. He hasn't quite figured out how he's going to save him, but he was never one for making rigid plans and sticking to them. He much preferred to wing it and see what happened. He has Harvey's access codes and will have no problem breaking into an ammunition's locker once he's inside.

After that he'll... well, he'll do whatever he has to do to get his father back. His only loyalty is to his dad. Harvey and the Foundation can go to hell for all he cares.

DIXON SPACE STATION

Bray races into the room and joins Heath and Sayber at the bank of viewscreens. 'What is it?'

Heath points to a cluster of lights in the far corner of the bottom screen. 'Foundation.'

'Don't suppose it's too much to hope they're here just for the heck of it?'

Heath leans on the console as he examines the data. 'Felix finds a tracker and they appear. Eh, no. That's no coincidence. We've been here for months and nothing. Your brother arrives and suddenly a deserted area of space is a hot target. It's him.'

Bray gives a half-hearted nod. 'You sure this place is shielded?'

Heath snorts. 'The station and everything in it is covered. The Dixon's may seem a little eccentric, but they're on the ball when it comes to security.'

Sayber frowns at the screen. 'Must be a damn powerful tracker.

Ares is shielded. I would know. I've been trying to track her down for years. Unless her captain says otherwise, the ship is invisible.'

Bray frowns. 'That doesn't make sense. Surely *Ares* and the station would have blocked any signal if he is transmitting one?'

'Nothing's a dead cert,' Sayber says.

Bray looks back at the screen and makes a face. 'How the hell did we miss this? He's been checked regularly to make sure his implants aren't doing anything they shouldn't. I'm sure if he was transmitting a signal, someone would have found it.'

'You're assuming it would be that simple,' Heath says. 'There is a small chance, if there is something nasty in him, besides his implants of course, it could have been triggered as *Ares* entered the system. If it's a Foundation signal, it could have been boosted when he got within range.'

'Well that's just great,' Sayber mutters under his breath. 'The damn man is unconscious and still giving us headaches.'

Heath glances over his shoulder at Sayber. 'Another fan, uh?'

'That scar across his neck is my doing. I'm looking forward to finishing what I started.'

Heath laughs and holds out his hand to give Sayber a hearty handshake. 'I want front row seats to that show.'

'Excuse me. You can all discuss killing my brother later. For now, we have to check the other cyborgs in case they're sending out a signal. The last thing we need is for the bad guys to knock on the door and kill us all.'

Sayber nods. 'Fair point.'

Heath holds up a hand. 'Hang on one minute. There are more cyborgs here?'

'Three more,' Bray says. 'They're locked in a cell on *Ares* until Gryffin is sorted.'

'Well this is just perfect.'

'Dante, Boone, and Trace have been rehabilitated to a certain degree. They don't have the control implant like Gryffin does.'

'What the hell does that mean?' Heath asks.

'They're the base model and Gryffin is the hi-tech version.'

'And you?'

Bray shrugs. 'I'll be sure to let you know once I figure that out.'

Heath shuts down the screen and walks to the door. 'C'mon. Better check out the rest of Gryffin's cyborg gang.'

'I'll contact Desyl and get permission to check them out.' They head towards *Ares* while they wait for Desyl to get back to them. As hypocritical as it sounds, he shares Heath's enthusiasm about having the three cyborgs on the base.

He knows little about the new models the Scientist created out of the prisoners. The few he engaged with on the New Colony had died from the modifications. The fact that three are still alive is a miracle - although he's not sure if the men feel the same way.

Desyl meets them at the bottom of the ramp with another two Nomad. Bray and Heath don't seem to be welcomed visitors. 'I got your message.'

'We need to check them out to make sure they're not transmitting.'

Desyl isn't thrilled about letting them on board, but he nods and gestures for them to follow him. He takes them to the training room and a large cell in the corner of the room.

'Weird place for a cell,' Heath mutters as he walks over to the occupants.

Desyl doesn't bother answering Heath. 'This is Trace, Boone, and Dante.'

The three men get to their feet and stand facing Heath and Bray. One look gives Bray a hint as to why they may have survived so long. They're certainly a hell of a lot healthier looking than Gryffin or any of the other cyborgs he met on the New Colony. They must be the lucky ones.

The blond one in the middle steps forward. 'I'm Boone. You're

Gryffin's brother?'

'Bray. We need to check you out. Gryffin was tampered with. We need to make sure you're safe to have here.'

Boone turns to each of his companions and they give a brief nod. As one they hold their hands out in front of them.

Desyl unlocks the door and fits a set of restraints to each man then directs them to step out of the cell. 'I'll send a Nomad security team with you.'

'My men can deal with them if anything happens,' Heath says.

Desyl puts himself between Heath and the cyborgs. 'I'm sending a team to protect these men, not defend you from them. They're under Gryffin's protection.'

'And this station is under mine,' Heath responds.

'I get that, but like I said, they're protected by Gryffin and the Nomad. I've already cleared it with Felix.'

Bray takes a step back as Heath glares at Desyl. There's going to be an impressive scrap at some stage before they're done on the station. Heath, Sayber, Rua, and Gryffin aren't used to playing nice with others. Heath may answer to Evie and Felix, but when it comes to the security of the base - it's on his shoulders. Putting four volatile people who are used to getting their own way under the same roof in enemy territory is asking for trouble. It's just a question of when the peace dissolves.

Heath clenches his jaw as he checks out each of the cyborgs standing in front of him. 'Fine. But the restraints stay on.'

Desyl smiles. 'Not a problem.'

An hour later Heath begrudgingly removes the restraints from Boone, Trace, and Dante. Like Gryffin they had the suspect programming removed and Felix deemed them safe - much to Heath's obvious objections. Evie wanted each of them to spend some time in the rejuvenation pod. They still had a way to go before they were back to full health - Boone especially. The man is trying to hide it, but he's in serious pain from whatever was done to him.

Before he realises what he's doing, Bray helps Boone into the pod and watches as he closes his eyes, the pain still etched around his eyes and mouth. Bray looks across at Gryffin, lying on a bed at the far side of the room hooked up to a life support system.

An unwelcome feeling settles in his gut. It's the same feeling he gets whenever he lets his guard down and thinks of Gryffin as anything other than the Nomad leader.

'Hey? You good?'

Bray blinks and turns to Heath. 'What?'

'You were off somewhere.'

'Yeah, sorry. I'm fine. You still need me here?'

Evie waves her hand at him. 'I can manage here. There are too many bodies cluttering the room. You go and play with your new ship.'

Bray glances at his brother, before he turns away. He's so ready to put some space between the two of them again. Life was so much simpler when he didn't know who Gryffin really was.

∞

FOUNDATION HQ

Garvan's return to consciousness is slow and painful. The worst pain he's ever experienced hits his head, sending waves of nausea through his body. An invisible heartbeat pounds in his skull, pulsing in time with the waves of nausea. Unable to control his stomach any longer, he tries to roll over, but he's still secured to the gurney. He manages to turn his head to the side just in time. The mess hits the floor and dribbles down the side of his face. He stares at the empty space where his lower right arm should be.

He has no idea how long he spent with the women in the room next door. The last few days - well, he assumes it's been a few days - has gone by in a blur of pain. If he wasn't rolled up in a ball in his cell, he was hanging by his wrists being used as a human pinata. He couldn't even escape to unconsciousness. They were pumping him with something that kept him and sleep on different planets. Lack of sleep, the beatings and no food had done the trick. He'd run out of fight.

He doesn't know when he was dropped from his chains but the landing had been far from graceful. What happened next is anyone's guess. Unlike what he heard from Bray about his procedure and Gryffin's, Garvan was given something that knocked him out. His mate wants him to suffer, but not at the expense of the damn project. Instead of derelict stations and rusted equipment, he was given five-star treatment. For that he's thankful, but not by much.

The feeble attempt to escape withers away within a few seconds. The surgery has taken everything from him, and not just in energy reserves. He can feel the screws attaching the metal to the side of his head. Every time he blinks, the skin moves, scraping against the metal and turning his stomach.

Knowing that Bray had been through a similar procedure and survived gives him a little hope. He always held some sympathy for the Hunter Commander. His implants tortured him on a daily basis.

But now he can't help but be a little jealous. Bray was lucky the Scientist had been interrupted after two implants. If Harvey's bragging is anything to go by, Garvan will have more in common with Gryffin than Bray, and that terrifies him. How the Nomad leader isn't a drooling mess in the corner of a room is beyond him.

'How are you feeling, Wade?'

He slowly turns his head to look at Harvey. 'Great. You?'

Harvey laughs and shakes his head. 'Still defiant to the end. You'll be glad to hear the implant was fitted successfully. The connectors for the prosthetic arm are in place and, so far, your body is accepting the alterations. The doctors say you need a few days to recover before we continue with the modifications. I'm loathe to give you a break, but I'd be less than happy if you died before this process is completed.'

Garvan opens his mouth to reply, but a badly timed wave of agony takes his breath away. Harvey pats him on the shoulder and the sensation turns Garvan's stomach again. 'I'm not going to die, mate. Can't kill you if I'm dead.'

'When will you cease this futile mission? You are my prisoner. This is how life is for you, Wade.' He lowers onto the metal chair placed in front of the bank of screens. Each one shows a different set of readings. Presumably they are monitoring his vitals so they can pull him back if he does decide to die.

'Will you just get this over with? Listening to you droning on and on is doing my head in. My headache is bad enough. Give me a break.'

'Very well. My associates will have a little time with you later today. Until then, I suggest you get some rest. You're going to need your strength.'

Harvey walks over to the door, then stops and turns to look back at Garvan. 'By the way. I thought you might like to know that your wife remarried after you were arrested. Both Zeke and Liza have changed their name. They have turned their back on the Garvan name for good. Do you want to know who's name they have taken?'

Garvan doesn't want to know, but that's not how this is going to play out. Harvey is in gloat mode. Nothing is going to stop him from kicking him when he's down. 'Go for it. Who's name.'

Harvey smiles serenely and holds his hands out to the side. 'Mine, Wade. I took your place as head of the family. Your children use my name.'

Whatever else Harvey prattles on about after that is lost on Garvan. The bile rises in his throat. 'You fuck.'

Harvey laughs and leaves the room, dragging his cloak behind him. Garvan barely notices the doctor hiding behind a surgical mask hovering beside the bed. Harvey destroyed his life and stepped in to take the most precious thing he has. His children.

The marriage was arranged and, while he cared for his wife, it was nothing compared to how he felt about Zeke and Liza. While he's still trying to process what Harvey said, the doctor presses a syringe to his neck and closing his eyes he does exactly as Harvey suggested.

17

Terra stares into the murky liquid in her cup. The cold coffee had done little to re-energise her. If anything, the drink hadn't settled well in her churning stomach. She's bone tired and worried sick. A plate of cold meat and vegetables sits untouched in front of her. She thought she could eat but until she knows Gryffin's okay, she can't stomach it.

A few men at the table next to her glance over then mutter to each other. She catches her reflection in the polished wall opposite her and groans. Blood smears the side of her face and arm. Her t-shirt is torn along the arm and her black leather trousers are covered in a mix of blood, dirt, and dust. She runs her hand through her hair and manages to convince most of it to stay in a loose bun. Maybe she should have found the showers before attempting food.

'Hey,'

She jumps as Desyl sits opposite her. 'Is he okay?'

Desyl smiles and massages the back of his neck. 'He's okay.'

'He's alive?'

'If he was dead I wouldn't have said he's okay.'

'What happened?'

Desyl hides a yawn behind his hand. 'Sorry. Long three hours. The Dixon's found a beacon hidden in the implant behind his ear. It's been blocked.'

'That's why the Foundation was sniffing around?'

Desyl nods. 'They gave him a good going over. There's nothing else that's going to transmit to the Foundation. We also found out something that's not sitting too well with me.'

'Oh God. What's wrong with him?'

Desyl picks up a piece of meat from her plate and chews on it for a minute. 'Well, it's not something that's wrong with him. Bray and Felix found out that the Foundation or... the Scientist hid a program in the cyborgs.'

Terra doesn't react to the pause he took before mentioning her father. She wishes there was some way of making everyone forget she's related to him. 'What sort of program?'

'Bray can give you the technical explanation, but what I can make out is they put a piece of the program in each of the cyborgs - including Gryffin. When the Foundation arrived in the Sector they were able to run it or crank it up... I don't know. Whatever they did, it allowed them to control one of the cyborgs and he dropped the defences.'

'They booby trapped them? I don't know why I'm surprised. So were the Dixon's and Bray able to remove this programming?'

Desyl nods as he helps himself to more of Terra's diner. 'They're clear now. Can't really say that's much of a comfort. We thought Gryffin was clear before. Ended up biting us in the ass.'

Terra watches as he polishes off the rest of her cold dinner. 'I can get you a fresh plate. That's been sitting there for a while.'

Desyl wipes his mouth with the back of his hand. 'Had worse over the years.' He examines her as he finishes the mouthful of cold food. 'No offence but you look... well, like crap. When's the last time you slept. Or ate?'

'I'm fine.'

Desyl laughs loudly and slumps back in the chair. 'On *Ares* the word fine can mean you've got a hole in your chest, your arm is falling off, you've got a serious concussion, and a few bullet wounds. I vaguely remember Gryffin came back from a mission a few years ago with a broken arm, dislocated shoulder, and two bullet wounds. Know that he said? 'He was fine."

'I promise I'll get some sleep in a bit. So, will Gryffin be okay?'

'The next few hours in the rejuvenation pod will sort out any of the after-effects of his stunt on Ultar.'

'And his leg?'

Desyl grimaces. 'Different story. If the machine can strengthen the tissue at all, he may have a hope of hanging on to the limb. We're keeping his implants offline for the next twelve hours or so. They put a strain on him. We want his body to concentrate on repairing itself instead of fighting with the implants.'

'What's next?'

'Bed for me.'

She smiles for the first time since she got here. 'I meant for Gryffin.'

'That's up to Bray. He's seeing if he can fix the implants. The rejuvenation pod will buy Gryffin more time, but it's not going to solve the problem. He's still in trouble.'

Terra nods. 'I know.' She blows out a long breath. 'Does Bray know Gryffin is thinking about having his implants upgraded?'

Desyl shakes his head no. 'I'm hoping after some time in the pod, he'll be stronger. Not anywhere close to where he was, but fingers crossed, he'll notice a difference. If he's feeling better, he may just forget all of it.'

'You don't believe that any more than I do. Realistically, what are the odds he'll ever be back to full health?'

'Gryffin's a fighter. He'll get through it.'

'I hope so. What about Milla and Aleena, and everyone on Ultar? What about the new cyborgs and the Foundation?'

He shrugs. 'I don't have an answer. My priority now is my captain.'

'When does Bray think he'll have some information on the implants?'

'No idea. He's not overly chatty at the moment.' Desyl smirks. 'Speaking of Bray, interesting situation you've found yourself in, isn't it?'

'What do you mean?'

Desyl rests his elbows on the table and smiles at Terra. 'Oh come on, Commander. Bray. Gryffin. You. A cosy, but highly volatile love triangle. Do I need to go on?'

Terra frowns then her eyes open wide.

'There we go, Commander. Took you a few minutes. Should I start taking bets on round two of the scrap between your men? I made a fair bit on that one a few months ago between them.'

'Desyl!'

'What? C'mon Terra, everything is as bad as it gets right now. Let me have some fun.'

Terra opens her mouth to argue, but what Desyl said about Bray and Gryffin fighting begins to sink in. 'They're okay with each other now, aren't they?'

Desyl shrugs. 'I know as much as you. Gryffin did risk himself to go after Bray. He wouldn't have done that if he had a problem. Then again, who knows what the Captain's thinking. I've given up trying to work him out years ago.'

'Yeah, but this is Gryffin and Bray. If one of them looks at the other sideways it could end in trouble.' Terra leans forward, resting her elbows on the table. 'Bray has so many unresolved issues with Gryffin. Gryffin not so much with Bray. He's not bothered that I was with Bray.' She pauses and looks over at him. 'Well, that's what he said. Do you think he really does have a problem with it?'

'You know Gryffin better than I do.'

Terra scoffs. 'Yeah, I'm very familiar with his unpredictability. Who knows what he'll do. He could kill him, Desyl.'

'Kill may be a little over the top. Seriously hurt him is a definite possibility.'

'I'm being serious.'

'Gryffin won't give a damn about the Hunter. I promise you. If he was going to do something he would have done it by now.'

'He's been locked in a cell for weeks. It could still happen.'

'Maybe. At the moment it's an awkward, but highly entertaining situation. One I'm going to enjoy watching. Once Gryffin wakes up... well, that's when the disaster part could start.' He gets up and squeezes her arm. 'On that note, I'm off to bed.'

∞

OCARRO COLONY

Milla stares across at the Blacksmith formally known as Creed, as Chayse comes to grip with what he just heard. 'As in the Creed? Rayde's First Officer when he captained *Ares*?'

'Yes. Pretty sure I was the only Creed in the group.'

'But you're dead,' Chayse repeats. 'Gryffin killed you and threw you out the airlock. Everyone knows that story. You were the first one he did that to.'

'Yeah, heard he continued the tradition he supposedly started with me.' Creed shakes his head as he looks down at his boots. 'Took him longer than I hoped to start thinking for himself.'

Milla holds up her hands. 'Excuse me, but would you care to explain how you're still alive? Kind of an important bit don't you think?'

'Well, what the stories don't say is that Rayde decided I was asking one too many questions about his treatment of Gryffin. Probably should have kept my damn mouth shut, but that's one of my flaws. Had to keep sticking my nose in. One day Rayde had enough and I found ten Nomad at my door.

'Next thing I know, I'm hanging from the ceiling in the training room facing Gryffin. I was to be Gryffin's first real test. He'd killed before, but they weren't a Nomad. Rayde wanted to see how tight his control was. Seems it wasn't as tight as he thought. Once Rayde left, Gryffin took my gag off, I gave him a few truths, and he cut me free. He was giving me the honour of going out fighting. He didn't have to. Guess he understood the way we worked, even at that stage.

'We fought and he beat me unconscious. Next thing I know I wake up in a crate of scrap metal. It didn't take me long to figure out what happened. Instead of dumping me out the airlock, he hid me in a crate. I was delivered to a merchant along with the other crates. There was a collection scheduled around the time Rayde sent him to kill me.

'I managed to get out unnoticed and made a quick exit when they docked. I spent a few years moving from colony to colony. Truth is I was terrified I'd be spotted so I didn't stick in one place for too long.'

'I don't get it,' Milla says. 'Why not just kill you? No offence.'

Creed laughs. 'None taken. I asked myself the same thing. I've kept track of Gryffin as much as I could over the years and realised I was the exception. Well, except for you, Chayse. Didn't know why until three years ago.

I was on a small colony where I'd gotten a job and was putting some credits aside. Things were going well until I go to the market and there he is. Aleena had brought Gryffin to the colony. Wanted to get more on side with the Nomad. Build up their numbers. I didn't think he recognised me but I was wrong. After work I went back to the room I was renting and he was waiting for me.

'Thought my cards were marked. I had one hand on my knife, not that it would have done a damn bit of good against him, but it made me feel better. He didn't even look at me as he said, 'I was never going to kill a Nomad just because Rayde told me to'. Then he said I looked shit. Cheeky fucker. Anyway, he treated me to a slap-up meal in my room and handed me a bag of credits. Just shy of fifty thousand. I asked him what the catch was and he said he wanted to hire me.'

'Hire you? For what?'

Creed shrugs. 'Didn't say for what at the time. Just told me to stop looking over my shoulder and start living again. Said no one was coming after me. I was safe.' He laughs and shakes his head. 'I'd been living from day to day since he kicked me off *Ares*. Can't tell you how much of a relief it was to hear I could take things easy for a while.

'He stayed for an hour or so before he headed back to the ship. He gave me a comms unit so he could get in touch if he needed to.'

'For what?' Chayse asks again.

'Like I said, no clue at the time. I'm sure you're familiar with Gryffin's fondness for explaining himself. I packed up my things and came here. Bought this place using half the funds he gave me and did exactly what he told me to do. I started living again. Found myself someone to be happy with. Things are good now. Never thought I'd be able to say that.'

'Did you hear from him again?' Milla asks as she tucks into her stew.

'From time to time. It was strange. He'd send me reports. It was like he was keeping me up to date with what was going on in the group. Didn't know why until you delivered that message.'

'So why does Gryffin want you to reveal yourself now?' Chayse asks.

Creed focuses on the fire again. He runs his hand over his beard, lost in thought for a few minutes. Eventually, Milla reaches the end of her patience. 'Ah for feck's sake. The suspense is killing me! What's his big plan.'

'According to Gryffin's message, he's just made me High Commander of the Nomad fleet.'

DIXON SPACE STATION

Terra knows she should be in bed getting some well needed rest, but she can't. There's no way she can sleep until she's seen Gryffin for herself. She nods at the pair of Nomad standing guard outside his room. 'Is it okay to go in?'

The shorter of the two opens the door for her. 'Sure thing, Commander. Desyl just checked on him. He's gone to get some shut-eye. Shouldn't you be doing the same?'

'Probably.' She closes the door behind her and looks over at Gryffin. He's barely visible under all the wires and screens, but there's one noise that reassures her. The system monitoring his heart is beeping softly in the background; slow and steady unlike her own which has been racing since the alarms went off on Ultar.

She jumps as someone places their hand on her shoulder.

'Oh dear, I'm sorry. Didn't mean to scare you.' Evie moves over to the side of Gryffin's bed and readjusts a few of the wires. 'I need to make sure he's still on track.'

'Is he okay?'

Evie nods and smiles. 'So far so good.' She tilts her head to the side as she examines Terra. 'You're going to be no good to him if you're worn out. You need to look after yourself too.'

'I know. You're not the first person to say that to me. Time is short...' She leaves the sentence unfinished.

Evie nods slowly. 'Have you been checked over yourself. You look like you've been blown up.'

'I sort of was. I'm fine though.'

'Can I suggest a shower and sleep?'

'I just need to be with him. Please. I promise I'll get some sleep in a bit.'

Evie squeezes her arm and walks away, leaving her alone with Gryffin. Terra brushes the tears from her eyes and wipes her nose. The tears won't stop coming. Part is down to exhaustion and part is down to worry. As desperate as she is to collapse onto her bed and give up the fight to stay awake, she doesn't want to be alone with her thoughts. At least if she's here with Gryffin, she won't have to worry about whether he's deteriorated while she's been asleep.

Terra shuffles closer to his head and rubs the side of his face, careful not to knock against the tube disappearing down the back of his throat, breathing for him. She doesn't know a lot about his implants, but she does know none of his organs can function without help from them. Until they can get that side of Gryffin online again, he needs the life support systems to keep him alive.

She dreads to think what would have happened if they hadn't come to the station. Gryffin would be dead. No question. He barely looks alive right now. His skin may not have the grey pallor of death, but it's not far away. She reaches out and takes his hand in hers, hoping for even the slightest increase in pressure, but there's nothing.

What the hell is she doing? It's not the first time she's asked herself that question and it probably won't be the last. Being with Gryffin is probably the most difficult thing she's ever done. What he is, who he is makes having a relationship with him nearly impossible. The longer she's with him, the more she gets to know him, the more she begins to come around to his way of thinking.

Perhaps they can never work long term. Gryffin may not even have a long term. At the moment, he can only go from day-to-day. That's no basis for a happily-ever-after. If anyone else was telling her these things, she'd advise them to get the hell out of the relationship. There's one big problem with that though. She loves him.

Terra had been in love before, or so she thought. But this is so much different. It may not make sense but she is deeply in love with him - flaws and all. He's rude, argumentative, moody, difficult to talk to, and tends to throw himself in front of a gun without a second thought to anyone else, but that's part of why she loves him.

Instead of grumbling and complaining about something, he takes care of it. He reacts. If he's angry, he's angry. Plain and simple. That's why she knows if he's spending time with her, when he's making love to her, it's real. When he looks at her like no one else exists, it's because, for him, at the moment, no one else does.

Not a lot of people see that side to him, and that makes it all the more special. He may not have ever said he loves her, but she hopes he does, in his own way. He certainly doesn't pay anyone else the same attention he pays her.

It's not like he hasn't had plenty of opportunity. Wherever he goes, Gryffin demands attention. His implants and his sheer size help him stand out in any space, but it's the other looks that initially helped the little green-eyed monster in her to creep out.

He certainly isn't aware, nor does he care, but he is incredibly attractive. He sees scars and metal where others see a breathtaking man. His touchable dark hair which used to partially hide his deep blue eye, a strong jaw that looks equally good cleanly shaved or with a few days stubble on it, and those lips take him to a whole other level of breath-taking when they break into a rare smile.

But what he's been through over the last few weeks has affected him. His broad chest has lost some of its muscle definition. His ribs are too visible, the metal plating sinking in his flesh. His strong jaw is sharper, his eye unfocused, and his hair cut short to help ease the fevers racking his body.

She hates seeing him like this. He worked so hard over the last few months to get himself back to where he was before her father took him again. Now he's pretty much back to where he started when he escaped her father a few months ago. Terra closes her eyes and leans back in the chair, not letting go of his hand. As selfish as it sounds, she doesn't know how much more she can take.

Her father started all of the pain and suffering Gryffin has endured and is still enduring. Is it too much to ask for him to get a break? For them to get a break? She would give anything to take him away from all of this. To bring him to a safe colony, somewhere no one knows who they are. Somewhere they can have a danger free, med bay free life - just the two of them.

Deep down she knows that will never happen. No matter how this ends, Gryffin will die at the helm of *Ares*. She knows that much. Whether they're together or not, he will never leave that ship. She's just kidding herself if she believes otherwise.

'Hey. It's me. I don't know if you can hear me.' She runs her thumb across his hand but there's no reaction. 'Okay, so I owe you an apology. I had no right having a go at you like I did. It's your body and your implants. I guess... I was afraid. When you mentioned upgrades I thought the worst. I thought of the Foundation and my father and what they did to you. I know that's not what you meant. I know you're just trying to figure out the best way to fix all this.'

She pauses and slides her chair closer to the head of the bed. Taking care not to dislodge the wires hooked to his ocular implant, she rests her hand on the side of his face. 'I just want you to be okay, Gryffin. Roman and Lucan are dead. I don't know where you sent Milla, Chayse, and Aleena, or if they even got away before the colony was attacked. All our friends are missing. I can't lose you too. Please, Gryffin. Don't give up. You need to keep fighting.'

∞

ULTAR

Nova sits on the bench beside the Ultaran lake and concentrates. Over time, working with and controlling her implants is getting easier. Being linked to the other thirty-six members of the team is confusing and unpleasant. After a few minutes she manages to whittle the number down to fourteen. The fourteen members of her original team. The fourteen other cyborgs who are able to, at times, override their programming.

'Have we secured the hangar?'

'Yes, Nova. The other team is still searching the village.'

'And the two ships?'

'Both are undamaged.'

'One has called me back to Earth. Thirty-Five has crossed the Port.'

'How is that possible?'

'I don't know. I need to go back. I can't find a way out of it. I need you to take the ship and leave the colony. I'll signal when it's safe to take off. It will take me a few minutes to mask the signal from the system in the control room.'

'What will you say?'

'That you perished. You will need to cut your link with the rest of us. Go to the coordinates and wait for us. If everything goes to plan, we should join you in a few weeks.'

Nova gets up and walks back towards the base. *Infinity* may have begun life as a Foundation ship, but she had received some Nomad upgrades since then. After a quick check, one of Nova's team was able to confirm she had Nomad cloaks installed. It will be those very cloaks that will help the ship to slip off Ultar undetected.

Nova steps out of the sunshine into the cool base and signals to all the cyborgs on the surface. It's not unusual for her to call a debrief such as this. She's leaving the surface so she needs to ensure everyone knows what they are doing.

She waits until everyone has gathered, pleased to see the members of her team she had told to leave are not present. 'I am returning to Earth with the remaining members of my team. One wants the rest of you to stay here. Reinforcements will arrive from Earth in a few days. Lock down the surface and do not let anything leave or land after my ship had departed. This colony is under Foundation control. Do you understand?'

'Yes, Ma'am,' they reply as one, their voices echoing in the empty base. 'Before I go I want a full inventory of weapons.'

They leave her alone in the control room. Nova waits until the door has closed before she turns to the screen behind her. She securely connects with the women on *Infinity*. 'Are you ready?'

'Yes.'

Nova keys in a few commands and the departure alarms and sensors shut down. 'Now.'

She watches on the camera as the large battleship leaves the underground hangar a few miles away from the base. Thankfully, the tremors from the ship are masked by a series of well timed, residual explosions from the downed Nomad vessel outside. *Styx* had put up a valiant fight but her demise had been met thanks to a savage attack from the other team. No Nomad had survived the landing.

More unnecessary deaths thanks to One and his ridiculous plans for dominance.

As soon as *Infinity* has left and is clear of the sensors, Nova reactivates everything. Half of her team are gone. That's something at least. All she can do is hope they can find Thirty-Five before the Foundation does.

DIXON SPACE STATION

Desyl stops at the doorway to Gryffin's room and glances down at Evie. 'How long has Terra been here?'

'Too long. The poor thing needs a proper sleep in a real bed.'

'You don't have to tell me. She's been refusing to leave his side since he malfunctioned a few weeks ago.'

Evie pushes her hat back and tries to smooth a few stray locks of wiry hair. 'She's going to run herself into the ground. He'll be up and about and she'll be in that bed instead of him.'

'I got this. Thanks for calling me. Any change with Gryffin?'

She shakes her head. 'Nope. He's stable. Until we get his implants back online we won't know if he'll wake up.'

Evie wanders away and Desyl turns to Terra and Gryffin. She's asleep on the side of the bed, one hand against Gryffin's face. Desyl slowly moves her hand out from under the wires hooked into Gryffin. Once she's untangled, he slips his arm under her legs then carefully picks her up, holding her tight against him. He's not surprised that she barely stirs. Terra was exhausted before they left Ultar. Staying up to look after Gryffin isn't going to improve that.

He stops at the door and gestures to one of the Nomad security. 'Get another team over here. I want four men on him at all times.'

'Expecting trouble, sir?'

'Our commander is being kept alive with Foundation equipment on a Foundation ship in Foundation space. Of course I'm expecting trouble.'

He makes his way from *Cronus* across the dock to *Ares* sitting at the far side of the station. One of the Nomad guards walks ahead of him and opens the door to Gryffin's quarters. Desyl lays Terra on the bed and drapes a blanket over her then sits on the chair against the wall and scrubs a hand over his face.

What a fucking mess. He can't see a happy ending for any of them. Gryffin will either die or need to have his implants upgraded. No happy ending for him either way. Terra will have to deal with his death or the fact he won't be the man she fell in love with. No happy ending for her. And he'll be left in command of a ship and a crew of Nomad. Not the ending he was hoping for either.

Serving on *Ares* under Gryffin is what he wants - not being in command of *Ares* himself. He's not a captain. There's no way he can do what Gryffin does. He's not built that way.

He might not have a choice though. Whatever happens to Gryffin, the odds are he won't stay in command of the ship. Desyl can either step up and try to be the captain the crew deserves or leave and go somewhere else. Not exactly a move that would put him in Gryffin's good books.

It's all hypothetical anyway. Desyl disobeyed Gryffin's order. He left Ultar during a fight and brought the ship to Earth. That action alone could mean he'll be kissing his career - possibly his life, goodbye.

∞

Gryffin opens his eye, blinking as he tries to get his head in gear. He frowns at the smooth white metal ceiling peppered with small lights. This isn't his cell on Ultar. He's pretty sure he's not even on Ultar. He tries to swallow, but there's something down his throat. He looks down and can just about make out a tube coming out of his mouth and trailing off somewhere to his right. Machines beep and wheeze in the background, one sounding with every beat of his heart. He tries to move but doesn't manage that either. It feels like his wrists and ankles are restrained to the bed.

He tries to pull free but his arms have other ideas. He can feel them but that's as far at the relationship goes. He opens his mouth to call for help but the damn tube blocks the pathetic whimper that comes out. He wants out of whatever this is. Now.

His messed up lungs join the party, adding to the panic by deciding to fight against whatever the tube is doing for him. Panic quickly sets in as his lungs push air out of his body at the same time the machine tries to pull it in. A shrill alarm screams in the background bringing hurried footsteps and shouting, but he doesn't hang around to see who is coming to his rescue.

When Gryffin wakes up again, he's still restrained but the tube is gone from his throat. He's also breathing so his implants must be back online.

'Lie still and I'll lift the head of the bed.'

Gryffin turns his head to the side and finds himself nose to nose with a woman in a large, bizarre looking hat. He tries to shuffle up the bed but the restraints keep him firmly in place. 'Who—' He clears his throat and tries again without the croak. 'Who the hell are you?'

'It's a pleasure to finally meet you. I'm Evie Dixon. There are plenty of ears in the room,' she whispers, looking up at the personnel working in the med bay. 'We must speak in private later.' She winks and sits beside his bed with a long, deep sigh. 'So, how are we feeling, Captain?'

'I'm on Earth?'

'Good gracious, no.' She makes a face and shudders. 'Why would you say something so horrible?'

'What do you want?'

She clasps her hands on her knees and smiles up at him. 'To, what's the best word, to ogle you.'

'What?'

'You know, to gape, stare, rubberneck. Then again, I believe gaze would better suit this situation.' She shuffles to the edge of her seat and wiggles her eyebrows at him. 'You are quite a sight, aren't you?'

'What?' he asks again.

'You can't really blame me, can you? You're a bit of a legend among us not-so-squeaky-clean folk. We've heard a great deal about you.'

Gryffin swallows deeply and considers trying to break the restraints. The strange little woman is eyeing him like he's a piece of meat.

'Evie Dixon, will you leave him alone! Can't you see you're scaring the hell out of him?'

Evie turns to face an equally strange looking man. 'Felix, don't think I won't kick you off the station if you don't watch your tongue.'

'Yeah, yeah. You should know by now I rarely listen to a word coming out of your mouth. So young man, I'm Felix Dixon, and you've met my delightful wife.' Felix ignores the glare thrown in his direction.

'Where's my ship?'

'In our hangar of course.'

'I want to talk to Desyl. Now!'

'Please.' Evie shakes a finger at him. 'Manners cost nothing, lad.

To be honest, I think we could all do with a chat. You're not meant to be awake yet.'

'What?'

She rubs her jaw. 'Interesting. Is your limited vocabulary a result of your modifications?'

Felix pushes his wife aside. 'Ignore her. What she meant to say is that we were pumping you full of sedative. It's supposed to keep you unconscious until we switch it off. Somehow, you managed to wake up in spite of all that. Twice. We figured with most of your implants off-line they wouldn't be able to neutralise the sedative we were giving you. Seems we were wrong. Or maybe it was the equipment we were using?' he mutters to himself, looking at the line of machines against the back wall, then back at Gryffin.

'Typical unreliable Foundation technology. I'm including you in that comment. It's a bloody miracle you've lasted as long as you have with all those Foundation parts on you. Have to say you surprised me by coming around so fast. You were dead.'

'I was what?'

'Dead, Captain. As in not alive. You've caused a few raised eyebrows by recovering as fast as you have.'

'Is there something wrong with me?'

'Guess that depends on your definition of wrong. There's quite a bit about you that's wrong.'

'Felix!'

'What? You're not going to tell me what they did to him is right.'

'That's not what he's asking, you bumbling oaf.'

'Fine. Leaving aside the fact you're a Foundation cyborg, then no. From what I can tell, your implants were well and truly destroying what's left of your body. Once we took them off-line, the rejuvenation pod was able to work wonders for you. Brought you back sooner than planned. Thought you'd be out of it for a few days at least. You're one tough cookie.'

'What?'

Felix shakes his head as he checks one of the screens. 'Never mind. So how are you feeling?'

'I want Desyl. Now.'

'What about Terra?' the woman asks. 'I'm sure she'd love to see you.'

'I don't want Terra. Just Desyl.'

Evie and Felix raise their eyebrows, but don't push him. Less than a minute later Desyl hurries into the room looking a little out of breath. He stands beside Gryffin's bed and straighten his shoulders. 'Sir.'

'Where the fuck are we?'

'On the Dixon space station, sir.'

'And Ultar?'

'Lost, sir.'

Gryffin clenches his jaw to stop himself from roaring at Desyl. Instead he manages to grind out a single word without taking Desyl's head off. 'How?'

'There were too many, sir. We had to—'

'Did *Ares* leave Ultar while the Foundation were still attacking? Did my ship run from a fight?'

'The colony was lost. Roman and Lucan... they were—'

'Damn it, Desyl! The Ultarans pay us to protect them. You were ordered to get *Ares* in the air and protect the colony. I didn't say you should run. Who gave the order to leave the Sector?'

'Sir, you were—'

'Who gave the fucking order!'

'Your father. Roman left a standing order. If the Foundation showed up we were to get you off the surface and away from them. No questions.'

'Are you fucking serious?'

'His main concern was making sure you were safe.'

He laughs harshly. 'You need to figure out where your loyalties lie, Desyl. You want to be on *Ares* under my command you damn well better start acting like it.'

Desyl opens his mouth to reply but closes it again as he looks at the ground. 'Yes, sir.'

'You put his orders before mine. I don't accept disobedience from my crew, Desyl. You know that.'

'I was under orders—'

'Yes you damn well were. Mine! I'll deal with you disobeying my orders when this is done. Until then you're still part of the crew. But trust me, if we were in the Outer Sector you'd be off the ship. Sayber and Klay betrayed me. Thought I could count on you.'

Desyl's face turn a sickly grey and he drops his eyes to the floor as his shoulders sag. 'Sir, I—"

'Can you get these fucking restraints off me?'

'I can't, sir. They want to run more tests to make sure everything is working as it should. They found a transmitter embedded in you.'

'The Foundation know I'm here?'

Desyl nods. 'We presume so, sir. They sent some ships to investigate. The station's been moved for safety. With any luck it's thrown them off the scent.'

'And I'm clear now?'

'Heath— sorry, Dixon's head of security, he found the transmitter in the obsolete mod behind your ear. As much as they'd take great pleasure crushing it to dust it has to stay where it is.'

Gryffin grimaces. 'Attached to something vital?'

'Your brain. It wouldn't be you if it was easy. The additional mod Felix added in front of your ear should block any transmissions that might try to escape.'

Gryffin doesn't respond, just stares at nothing in particular at the foot of his bed.

'Sir... I have something I need to tell you.'

Gryffin turns to look at him again. 'What?'

'Sir. It's Lucan. He was killed when he was bringing you out of the tunnels.'

Gryffin stares at Desyl for a few minutes, unable to get any words out. Losing Lucan is like losing a member of his command crew. He had never worked closely with the Nomad. Lucan had been put on Ultar to help Aleena and keep an eye on things for Gryffin. The only real contact they had were the weekly reports Lucan sent him. But over the last few weeks, Lucan had been a regular visitor to his cell, keeping him company when others had to work on *Ares*. He was a damn good Nomad.

Gryffin looks at the foot of his bed and finally speaks. 'Dismissed.'

'But, sir—'

'I said you're dismissed!' Desyl nods once before leaving Gryffin and his foul mood to glare at the ceiling.

He wants out of the restraints and off this ship, but, as usual, he's not the one making the decisions. What the hell is the point in him being the captain if his own crew don't have the courtesy of obeying him?

Ares has never run from a fight. Not once. Outnumbered. Out gunned. Damaged. It didn't matter. She fought. It's what they do. Running like a group of cowards, letting the Foundation take Ultar just to save his life is inexcusable. He's fucking furious at each and every Nomad on *Ares*. They let him down. Let the Ultarans down. Let the Nomad down.

Ultar was so much more than just a colony. It was the one place besides *Ares* that felt like a home to him. The Ultarans may be safe, and he's grateful for that, but knowing the Foundation have the colony is seriously pissing him off. Ultar was a refuge. It was something he had clashed with Aleena about too many times to count.

She had never refused a plea for help. Never turned away any travellers in need of a new life. It was like the heart of the Sector and now it's overrun with Foundation cyborgs.

And there's not a damn thing he can do about it. Restrained to a bed on a strange ship with a Nomad team watching him and being stared at by unknown personnel is humiliating and frustrating the hell out of him. The wires connected to his ocular implant are itching the side of his face, but that's just another thing he can't control. Commander of a fleet but he can't scratch his own face.

He closes his eye and tries to ignore the infuriating itching as he lets the anger build. Better than thinking about Roman and Lucan.

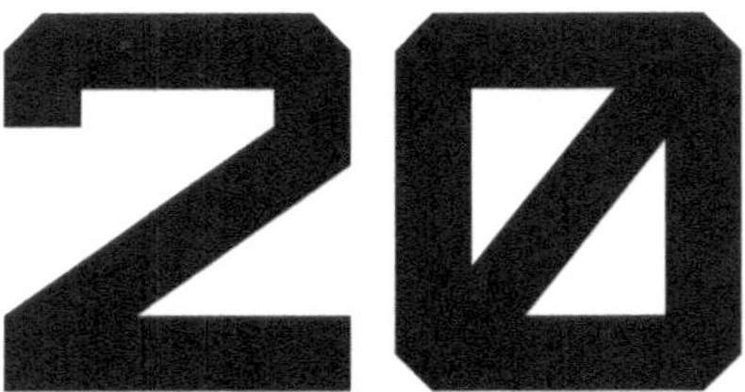

Bray sits down on his bunk and turns the chip over in his hand. All the data from the Scientist's personal files is on that chip. The computer had been found in the hold of *Alpha* - the same computer he had fought with Garvan to take when they first arrived on Earth. 'I'll get you out, Garvan. You have my word.'

He doubts there'll be any schematics or medical reports in the files. The Foundation would have made sure all that data was part of the encrypted information on the main server. The smaller unit probably just held personal files and records the Scientist made.

Even so, there might be something of use to him. Something to help him deal with what's been done to him. Maybe he entered data from other subjects and what they experienced from the same procedures? Bray doesn't know what he's looking for. He just knows he needs something to help explain what the hell is going on with his own implants before he loses his mind.

He's just grateful the Scientist was more interested in torturing people than encrypting his data. Bray drops the chip onto the desk and glares at it. The last time he accessed a file relating to the project, it literally turned his stomach. The images of his brother being tortured still haunt his dreams to this day. He doesn't have a choice but to watch it. If there's something on it that can shed light on what's happening to him, to Gryffin, he needs to watch it.

Bray scrubs his hand over his face then slips the chip in the unit and opens the file. He stares in surprise at the rows and rows of files. Information from each of the test subjects is carefully catalogued and filed away in order of subject number. He scrolls down to the bottom and his mouth goes dry.

He thought Gryffin being number thirty-five was bad enough, but according to the screen, there are another two hundred and thirty-one, and that was just up until the Scientists death. There's no telling how many the Foundation Council have added to the list.

He jumps when there's a knock on the door. 'Yeah?'

The door slides aside and his cousin Erin arrives. 'I've been let out for some fresh air. Well, air from a different ventilation unit. Fancy getting something to eat?'

Bray forces a smile on his face and shakes his head. 'Maybe later.'

She frowns at the data on the screen in front of him. 'Oh Bray. What are you doing?'

'I need to see what's in these files, Erin. There's something wrong with my implant. Maybe this happened to another subject or maybe he mentions a solution.'

'Or maybe you're just going to open the door to something you won't be able to close again. You sure you want to go there?'

He shrugs. 'To be honest, I'm not sure of anything. Whatever is in this data could help me figure out what's going on with my implants. I have to look.'

Erin pulls up a chair and tucks in beside him at the desk.

'What are you doing?'

'You really think I'm going to let you look at that alone?'

'I need to look at his files. You know that right?'

Erin nods. 'If you find anything that can help you and Daegan it'll be worth it. '

'I've seen a few of these. They're disturbing, Erin. I mean really fucking disturbing. The bastard filmed everything. '

She nods again and clasps her hands together on the desk. 'I understand. Let's get this over with.'

Bray doesn't argue. She's right. Ignoring the other test subject folders, he moves back up the screen to Gryffin's file. Dozens of video files fill the screen, but Bray focuses on the test data. If there's something of use, it will probably be there. Gryffin's original eyepiece was similar in design to his one.

He opens the very first file and scans through the data. Finding nothing of use, he moves on to the next, and the next. File number four changes things for him. Halfway down the page, he sees something that turns his stomach. His name.

'Does that say what I think it does?' Erin asks.

Bray nods. 'Subject still refusing to cooperate,' Bray reads. 'This one is...' He takes a breath and swallows. "This one is Roman's son so it is vital he suffers more than the others.' Bray rubs a hand over his face. 'Sick bastard,' he mutters under his breath. 'I know Maggie had another son. Will use his half-brother, Brayden, as incentive to comply.'

'So the Scientist knew that Daegan was Roman's son?' Erin asks.

Bray nods. 'Apparently, Daegan was targeted because he was Roman's son. The Scientist told Roman when we were in the New Colony a few months ago. He wanted payback so he thought torturing Daegan would hurt Roman. Sick fuck.'

'But he didn't tell the Foundation? Why not?'

'I'm guessing he didn't want to risk losing him. If the Foundation knew how out of control he was, they might have shut down the project. Who knows.'

He moves on to the next file. 'Initial results promising. See video file number seven.'

Erin takes his hand and squeezes it. 'Bray, you don't have to watch that.'

Bray clicks on the file. The video shows his brother chained to the wall with the familiar collar around his neck, but unlike the other video he watched a few months ago, he's relatively unhurt in this one. It must be an earlier file. Bray is instantly struck by how together Gryffin appears. His dirty cheeks are tear streaked but he faces the Scientist straight on. As soon as the man approaches, Gryffin gets to his feet and glares at him. Even at that young age, the determination and strength are clear to see.

The Scientist stops in front of Gryffin and rests his hands on his hips. 'Well Thirty-Five, are you going to cooperate today?'

'My name is Daegan.'

The Scientist sighs and shakes his head. 'Let's try that again. You are Thirty-Five.'

Instead of responding, his brother spits on the Scientist, earning him a sharp slap to the face. 'Listen to me. You can fight as long as you want but it will not change a thing. Your mother and father sold you to me. Both you and your brother, Brayden. I paid a fair price for you both.'

Gryffin's head whips up and his blue eyes darken. 'Bray's here?'

The Scientist laughs. 'Of course he is. Your parents left both of you with me. I was hoping to spare him some of this, but if you're not going to cooperate, I have no choice but to use him instead.' The Scientist turns and walks away.

'Wait!'

Bray shakes his head as the Scientist stops and slowly turns around. 'Daegan, what the hell are you doing?' Bray mutters under his breath.

The Scientist tilts his head to the side. 'Excuse me?'

'Leave him alone.'

'Why should I? Are you going to cooperate?'

Gryffin nods. 'Just leave him alone.'

The Scientist smiles and Bray wants to punch the grin from his face. 'So, what is your name?' the Scientist asks.

Gryffin pauses long enough to throw an impressive glare at his captor. 'Thirty-Five.'

Bray shouts and shoves the unit onto the bed. He gets to his feet and prowls in front of the window. He pushes his hands through his hair, grabbing two fistfuls and tugging hard as he kicks the set of drawers beside him.

'Bray! Calm down.'

He's too angry to listen to anything Erin says. Instead of calming down, Bray shouts and drives his fist against the metal wall. Erin tries to reason with him, but he's lost to the rage. Lost to the knowledge that the brother he spent a lifetime hating actually gave himself up to save him.

The Scientist's face appears on the wall in front of him and he attacks. His fist slams against the wall again and again, tearing skin and breaking bones.

He is roughly hauled away from the wall by two sets of hands. Heath wraps his arms around his chest, pinning his arms to his side as Morgan holds his head firmly in his calloused hands.

Morgan tries to get Bray to look at him but he keeps turning his face away. He just wants them all to leave him the hell alone.

'Bray! Look at me!' Morgan painfully grabs his chin and forces his head up. 'You're scaring the hell out of me, boy. What's wrong? Talk to me.'

'He said they had me too.'

Morgan frowns then follows Erin's nod to the video on the screen.

'The Scientist told Daegan they captured Bray too,' she explains.

Bray tries to break free, but Heath firmly holds his arms to his side. 'He wasn't doing what he was told so the Scientist said he'd hurt me instead. The bastard tricked him. He stopped fighting, Morgan. Gryffin just let him do it.'

'Bray—'

'He was hurt because of me, Morgan! It's my fault!'

Morgan shakes his head. 'Stop it! Don't you dare say that, Brayden. What happened to Daegan had absolutely nothing to do with you or with him. You were both kids and had no control over it.'

The energy seems to drain out of Bray. His struggles die away and he slumps against Heath. Morgan nods and Heath slowly releases Bray before leaving the room.

Bray sinks to the ground and pulls his legs up to his chest. 'I hated Daegan.' Bray laughs abruptly. 'I hated him for leaving.' He sniffs and wipes the unwanted tears from his face with the back of his hand. 'What the hell is wrong with me, Morgan?'

Morgan's knees pop as he joins his nephew on the ground and stretches his legs out in front of him. 'Your brother disappeared when you were a kid. You were bound to be angry. Hell, I was angry.'

'You were?'

Morgan nods. 'Of course. Anger is a natural reaction to losing someone. I was angry that a ten-year-old had been taken from his family. Angry that he wasn't going to be able to grow up with you. Angry that his disappearance had then taken my sister and her husband from your life. Angry that you were left an orphan.' Morgan clenches his fists. 'After hearing what happened to the two of you, I'm bloody furious. And I mean that literally. I want blood, Bray.'

'Get in line.'

'So, you said you hated him. Past tense. You feel differently now?'

Bray purses his lips and nods once. 'He did what a big brother should do. He wanted to protect me.' Bray snorts. 'I hated him for turning his back on me, as irrational as that was, but he did the opposite. He thought he was saving me. It's so bloody unfair. I just got him back and now...'

'Now what?' Erin asks.

Bray sniffs and kicks himself for the slip up. 'I wasn't going to tell you... well, not yet anyway. Gryffin's implants are failing. He's dying. He's got a couple of weeks left.'

His uncle stares at a spot on the floor for a long few minutes. 'So that's why you are so adamant you need the files. You think there's something on the data that can help him?'

Bray nods. 'Fixing Gryffin has just jumped up the urgent scale too. If the Foundation are about to unleash an army of those women, we'll need him on our side to fight with us. If we can fix Gryffin and the other cyborgs from Ultar it will help... well, a little at least.'

Morgan nods slowly. 'All right. And what about you?'

'Me?'

'Yes you. Gryffin's not the only one with implants.'

Bray wipes the rest of the irritating tears from his face and runs a hand through his hair. 'I haven't got a clue what they did to me. I thought I knew, but now...' He shrugs. 'If this is the way I am, I have to accept it. I just need to know what I am. Hell, I don't know if I'm a threat to everyone on the station. I honestly haven't got the first clue what to do next.'

Morgan glances down at his ruined hand. 'Well, my advice would be a spin in that fancy pod your brother was in. You're no good to anyone with a broken hand.'

Bray glances down at his hand and grimaces. He's done an impressive job on it.

Erin joins her father and cousin on the ground. 'It's not just you facing all of this alone. We're here for you and your crew is with you. Lean on us. Let us help you figure this out.'

'I brought this on you all. I should be the one to put it right.'

Erin squeezes his arm. 'Hey, it's not your fault, Bray. None of this is.'

'I'm with Erin,' Morgan says. 'We'll figure out a way to save you, Daegan, and Garvan. I'll be damned if I let your brother die before I get a chance to meet him.'

'I wouldn't hold your breath on having a deep and meaningful meeting with him ' He examines his torn fist. 'Morgan, I don't know if there's enough time left to go through everything on the drives and save him.'

'So, you're just going to give up trying to find a solution? The Foundation is still hurting people, hurting more family members by continuing with this horrific project. There could be something on the system that can help them all and help Daegan and you in the process. You think you have something to apologise to him for? Find a solution instead.'

Bray wipes his face again. Morgan is right. It's time the Foundation paid for everything they did to him and Gryffin. He'll start with someone on this station who was involved from the beginning of this nightmare.

∞

DIXON SPACE STATION

Terra stops by the door to the med bay on *Cronus*. She can't get herself to go inside. Desyl had given her a brief recap of his conversation with Gryffin. Even though she knew he wouldn't be happy about being brought here, she wasn't expecting that level of anger from him. She's also not keen on offering herself up to a load of abuse.

Terra rests her head against the wall and closes her eyes. A few hours of sleep in a proper bed had done wonders for her. Whatever embarrassment she felt at learning that Desyl had carried her back had quickly disappeared when she realised it was something she needed, but was too stubborn to admit. Worrying about Gryffin had been occupying every minute of her day for weeks and she'd been paying for it.

She looks over at the door and sighs. No point putting it off. Let him have his rant, get it out of his system, and then they can move on.

When she finally convinces herself to open the door, she's pleasantly surprised to see he's looking so much better than he did yesterday. The Dixon's must have put him back in the rejuvenation pod for a few hours. He still has a way to go before he's back to where he was, but the improvement is encouraging.

As she approaches his bed, he opens his eye and turns his head to look at her. His eye hardens and he clenches his jaw. It appears she's in for a less than cheery talking-down.

'Hi. How are you feeling?'

It's a ridiculous way to start the conversation, but she's desperate to buy herself even a few more seconds without having to face his wrath. Gryffin's frown deepens, but he doesn't say a word as he stares at her.

'Okay, I know what we did was wrong and that you're angry—'

'Angry? I'm fucking furious with all of you.'

Terra manages to rein herself in before she says something she shouldn't. Having discussions with Gryffin is like walking a dangerous line. He's her boyfriend, but also her captain. Makes for an interesting balancing act when they argue, especially when his default position is as captain.

'What would you have had us do? You were dead when you went in the pod. Your heart stopped. Did you really think we'd just drag your corpse on to the ship and saunter around the Sector while you slowly decomposed?'

'You think I give a damn about that? We left the colony to the

Foundation, Terra.'

She lifts her head to meet his furious gaze. 'I know, but we'll get it back, Gryffin.'

'That's it? We abandon Ultar and all you can say is I know?'

'Please don't be like this. We had to save you. Roman wanted to save his son.'

'Roman's dead, Terra. Don't bring him into this. What other ships made it off the surface?'

She takes a minute to compose herself. Hearing Gryffin speak of Roman's death so bluntly is like a blow to her stomach. 'We still haven't been able to reach anyone. Maybe we just need to give it more time. When they reach safety they'll be in touch.'

'How? We're not in the Outer Sector, Terra. We're cut off. The flagship ran from a fight then abandoned the rest of the fleet. We have no damn clue if anyone else is alive.'

'Don't think that way. We need to stay strong. We need to stay positive.'

'How the hell is staying positive going to help? My ships are missing. Ultar is under Foundation control, and my father is... dead, Terra. Lucan too. No coming back from that. Did we leave the bodies on Ultar?'

'Yes. It was too dangerous to go back for them.'

'He wasn't supposed to die like that. Shot in the back by a cyborg then left behind. It's not the way it should have gone.'

'I know, Gryffin. We need to find a way of stopping the Foundation. It's what Roman would want.'

'You're seriously going to try that one on me?'

'I just meant that we can't give up now.'

'I'm not giving up. They killed my father to get a reaction. It worked. I'm pissed off.'

'I know you are. We all are. But you have to remember, they didn't know he was your father. They killed him because he turned his back on the Foundation. The second he took *Infinity*, he put himself at the top of their most wanted list.'

'You're defending them? They shot him in the back, Terra.'

'I know and I'm not excusing that for one second. How could you even suggest that? What I'm trying to say is that... oh forget it. I'm tired and emotional and the last thing I want right now is a fight. We're all grieving. He was like a father to me too. He practically raised me after all.'

Gryffin turns to look at her. Something in his face tells her she's just said something she shouldn't have. She thinks back and closes her eyes.

His father raised her while her father tortured him. Hell of a comparison. 'Gryffin, I didn't mean that the way it sounded. I'm so sorry. I just... I don't want to lose you too. I've lost too many people I care about. I couldn't bear to lose you too.' She runs her hand up his arm but he flinches away from her touch. 'Please don't be like this. We did this for your own good. We were trying to help you.'

'That was your father's excuse too.'

Terra takes a step back, the wind knocked out of her by his comment. 'I can't believe you just compared what we did to what my father did. That's low, Gryffin. I get you're angry and fed-up and worried, but don't you dare say something like that.'

In a highly mature and possibly insubordinate move, Terra turns and hurries from the room without giving him a chance to reply. She doubts there's anything he can say to follow a comment like that. The fact that what he said is the truth doesn't help calm her as she storms away from the med bay.

21

Gryffin wakes with a shout and shuffles up the bed as much as his restraints will allow. It takes him a few seconds to remember where he is. It's been a while since he had a nightmare about the lab and had forgotten how realistic they were.

The argument with Terra isn't helping his foul mood either. He shouldn't have said what he did about her father. It was a fucking low thing to say and he has no idea where it came from.

There was no comparison between what they did and what the Scientist did. Anger, frustration, and pain had fuelled his outburst. As usual. He tries to wipe the sweat from his face with his shoulder, but he can't quite reach. 'Fuck,' he growls as he pulls against the metal restraints securing him to the bed.

'Woke up in a great mood, I see.'

He glances up at Sayber before focusing on the restraints again. 'What do you want?'

Sayber feigns hurt as he settles in the chair beside him. He rests his feet on Gryffin's bed, seemingly taking pleasure from the fact Gryffin is powerless to do anything about it. 'Came to see how my old buddy is doing.'

Gryffin rattles his restraints again. 'I'm fine.'

Sayber laughs and crosses his arms. 'I can tell. Your man is working through the data from the last set of scans. You should be out of here in a bit. Something I can't wait for, as you can imagine. Kind of getting itchy feet on this whole truce thing to be honest. It'll be nice to get back to some good old-fashioned hunting.'

'Hunting Nomad.'

Sayber shrugs as he examines his fingernails. 'Can't change who we are, deep down. Am I right?'

'Deep down you're Nomad.'

'True. Deep down perhaps I still am. Maybe that's why my failed mutiny sticks in my throat like a dry piece of meat. Can't shift it no matter how hard I try. But that's the way things played out for me. It all worked out in the end. Would have been nice if I'd managed to take your damn head off though.' He leans back in the chair and smiles. 'Seeing that scar across your neck makes me all warm and fuzzy inside.'

'How's the arm?'

Sayber lifts the badly scarred limb and wiggles his fingers. 'Fuck all use, thank you very much. Took out a few of the nerves with your knife. Had to learn to shoot with the other hand. You know, you still owe me a blood debt. It's only a matter of time, Gryffin. If the implants don't get you I sure as hell will.'

'I wasn't going in to save one person.'

'Your First Officer was asking you to help someone he cared about. She died because you wouldn't risk your precious ship.'

'She died because the station was attacked not because *Ares* didn't join the fight.'

Sayber's face reddens, before he gets control of himself. 'No point going over this again. We've been here before and it nearly killed the two of us. Our time will come.' He settles back in his seat and crosses his arms. 'So, you good to keep this best buddy thing going for a bit longer?'

'The Foundation is the priority. After that we're both fair game.'

Sayber smiles. 'I'm in complete agreement with that plan. We'd better get on with destroying the bastards so we can get back to our day jobs.'

'I hear your First Officer's been busy.'

Sayber nods. 'Your dear brother, you mean? You could say that.' In spite of having the Hunter leader in front of him, Gryffin's eye drifts close. His body is in better shape than ever, but weeks of fighting the deterioration has left him weak. 'Your brother's got balls. Taking *Cronus* from right under their nose was a brave move.'

He convinces his eyelid to lift so he can look over at Sayber again. 'The ship any good?'

Sayber looks around the room and nods. 'You should be thanking her medical facilities. State of the art. She's still throwing up a few barriers in other areas, and she cost us Garvan. Not sure it was worth it.'

'We'll get him back. What are we facing?'

Sayber passes a unit to Gryffin then winces when he remembers Gryffin's restrained. He holds it in front of him and starts the video. 'I know you've seen some of this footage, but we were able to pull the feed from a few of the cameras in the hold. Take a look for yourself.'

The image shows the interior of what looks like a cargo hold. Garvan appears on screen with a group of women. At first glance they seem normal, but when the women move closer to the camera he can make out metal arms and eyepieces like his. Garvan steps out of view and takes out some of the women leaving one left. The woman is damn strong. She'd give him a run for him money.

The video ends with Garvan and the cyborg woman falling from the ramp. Sayber drops the unit onto the bed and looks at him. 'Now I don't know about you, but she's someone I'm not looking forward to meeting.'

'How many?' Gryffin asks.

Sayber shakes his head. 'No way of knowing. Well, not without hacking the system on *Cronus* and checking the reports. No doubt there's a record of numbers somewhere on the system.'

'All the ones Bray went up against match her, strength wise?'

Sayber nods. 'You should be flattered. They replicated your design.'

Gryffin snorts. 'Right. Including me, there's four cyborgs here. Not great odds.'

'There's no way any of you could handle the new cyborgs for long. Your implants are still failing. Even if we breach the system today, it'll take weeks, months, to repair all the damage the Scientist did to you.'

'And we'd be human and no match for a group of cyborgs.'

Sayber looks strangely at him. 'What are you saying?'

Gryffin shakes his head. 'I don't know.' He looks at his former First Officer. 'I need to get off this ship, Sayber.'

'Patience. They're looking through your scans.'

'I don't want to be chained in the med bay of a Foundation ship. Chain me up on *Ares*, or on *Perses*, I don't really care as long as it's not here.' He hates the way his voice cracks at the end of the sentence. Being here like this is bringing back memories he'd prefer remain in his past.

Sayber pauses then nods as he gets what Gryffin's saying. 'Got you. Give me five minutes. I'll see what I can do.'

Gryffin looks back at the still image of the cyborg woman on the screen. These female cyborgs are a damn big issue. Without an army of men with Garvan's size and stamina, they're screwed.

He closes his eye and settles back in the bed. If they're to have any chance of surviving an encounter with the new cyborgs, he's going to need to do something drastic.

∞

DIXON SPACE STATION

Terra sits on the edge of the dock watching crew mill around the strange and mismatched collection of ships below her. She'd tried to sleep after the fight with Gryffin but being in his... their bed without him had just made things worse. She spent the next few hours sitting in his command chair staring out of *Ares* before finally making her way to the mess hall again.

If she's not thinking about Gryffin, then Milla, Chayse, and Aleena take his place. And then there's Roman and Lucan.

If she lets herself get dragged into the grief, into the pain, she doubts she'll come out again. Just when she thinks things can't get worse, something else rears its head and knocks her back again.

She feels the same as Gryffin does about leaving Ultar. By leaving on *Ares*, she had turned her back on too many people she cares about. With no way of contacting them, she doesn't even know if they are alive or dead. What if they're all gone? Like Roman? Like Lucan.

With all that going on in her head, she doesn't need to add arguing with Gryffin to her list. But that's all they seem to be doing lately. They fight, things are relatively peaceful for a day or so then they argue again.

She knew he wouldn't be thrilled with their decision to put him in the pod, but without knowing how he had been compromised, they had little choice. Typical of him to jump straight in with an attack instead of taking a few minutes to seriously think about why they made that decision. He was going to die unless they could get him help as soon as possible. Why can't he understand that?

Then to go as low as to compare what they did to him to what her—what the Scientist did to him. She doesn't know if she can forgive him for saying that. It was said out of anger and frustration, but he still must have thought it.

'You okay?'

She jumps and places a hand over her racing heart as Desyl lowers onto the floor beside her. 'Don't sneak up on me like that. I nearly went over the edge.'

'Sorry.' He looks over at her and frowns. 'What's got you looking so confused?'

Terra glances up at Desyl then back at the ships docked below her. 'Have a wild guess.'

Desyl leans back on his hands. 'Reckon I only need one. The captain's usual charm working its magic?'

Terra scoffs. 'As always. Have you spoken to him again?'

Desyl raises his eyebrows. 'Eh no. I value my life. I'm steering clear until he calls for me. I've fucked that up good. I know I did the right thing for him, but that means nothing. I disobeyed the orders of my commanding officer. Usually I'd be gone and I don't mean off the crew. After Sayber and Klay he doesn't take betrayal well. He's not going to kill me... well, I hope not. I'm probably on my last days or weeks as a Nomad though.'

'Oh, Desyl, I'm so sorry.'

'Not your fault. I made the decision to do what Roman wanted. I can deal with the punishment. '

'Seems we're both in his bad books. You know, I keep telling myself that I know him, that I have a fair idea how he'll react in certain situations. Then he has to go and do the opposite of what I thought, and I wonder if I know him at all.

'Can he not just say thank you. Just once? I mean he died, Desyl. Flat-lined in the pod. Why can't he understand that and appreciate everything that's been done to save him?'

Desyl crosses his ankles and stares at *Ares* in her berth below them. 'I like you, Terra. You know that, right?'

She looks sideways at him. 'Why do I get the feeling I'm not going to like what's coming next.'

'You need to accept you'll never get that from him. I've been on *Ares* since my mid-twenties. Gryffin was on board about eight years or so when I joined so I saw a little of his training. Apart from Rayde and Creed, who was Rayde's first officer, no one was allowed to go anywhere near him. Rayde kept him as his personal project.'

'What do you mean no one could go near him?' Desyl scratches his head and looks as if he's having second thoughts about continuing. 'Please, Desyl.'

'Rumour is Rayde figured out after a few years Gryffin could be a bonus to the Nomad and I don't mean in a good way. He trained him day and night. He'd come back from missions and be sent straight to the training room. I don't know how he survived everything Rayde put him through. He'd be pushed to work with the implant in his head instead of against it. The training sessions could be fairly brutal.'

'In what way?'

'Rayde wouldn't let him stop until he allowed the implant to take control. As part of his training, he'd put Gryffin up against prisoners. If Gryffin hesitated in killing them or showed any remorse after he finally did, Rayde would punish him.'

Terra stares out at *Ares* again. 'He told me some of the scars on his body were from Rayde.'

Desyl nods. 'He didn't hold back.'

'When did it stop?'

'I think it was still going on when Rayde handed *Ares* over to him. There are rumours it went on longer, until Gryffin was made High Commander. The story is that Gryffin finally got tired of the way Rayde was training him and stood up to him. That's probably when Gryffin's cards were marked with Rayde. Rayde lost his obedient cyborg and had to figure out a way to get him back. Or get back at him.'

'So, he escaped the hell my father put him in to end up being abused by his rescuer.'

'Hey, hold up a second. Yeah, it wasn't right what Rayde did, but he did save Gryffin. He spent years helping him. He was hours from death when Rayde found him. I just think he got greedy when he saw the potential. When you're commanding a group like the Nomad and you come across someone like Gryffin... well, he was going to take advantage.

'Anyway, whatever his reasons for doing what he did, Gryffin didn't grow up like someone on Ultar or Earth. He didn't socialise, didn't talk to people, didn't make friends. Rayde barely let him out of his room. He was alone for years in the lab then alone again on *Ares* thanks to what Rayde did. In a lot of ways, he's still that sheltered kid. But do not repeat that to anyone. I'm in enough shit as it is. Growing up, the only close relationships he had were with people who hurt him. He hasn't got a clue how to deal with anything other than that.'

Terra shivers as a cold chill settles on her skin. Desyl is right. She never thought about Gryffin's life like that. She knew what her father did to him was horrendous, but never thought about what effect the things he missed out on would have on him. How can he possibly show her love when he's never experienced it himself? The anger, the natural pull towards the fight, was beaten into him for most of his life.

The loyalty he felt to Rayde for saving him stayed with him, which is probably why he is so angry with her and Desyl when he found out they left people behind on Ultar. Those two things instilled in him by Rayde made him a formidable leader and someone who can be depended on to do everything he needs to do to keep his crew safe. Unfortunately, it didn't help her.

Gryffin may care for her. He is certainly loyal to her, but that doesn't mean he will ever know how to love her.

Desyl places a comforting hand on her shoulder. 'Hey, you okay? I didn't mean to upset you.'

'I'm glad you told me. I needed to know.'

'Probably doesn't help, but I know he has feelings for you, even if he doesn't know what they are.'

'Yeah, but is that fair on either of us? I can't keep putting pressure on him to do what I think he should. I get angry at him because he doesn't say or do what he should. But he doesn't know what he should say or do.' She lies back on the metal floor and puts her hands over her face. 'Damn it. How is this thing between us going to work?'

Desyl rests an elbow on the ground and looks down at her. 'Guess that's up to you. You need to decide what you want from him. I'm not saying he'll never be able to express how he feels. He's come a long way since meeting you. You just need to understand what you're dealing with. If what you have with him now is enough, great.'

She drops her hands to her sides and stares up at him. 'And if it's not?'

Desyl shrugs. 'Can't answer that one for you. What I do know is that he's changed a lot since he met you. That has to tell you something about how you've affected him.'

'Changed. Yeah right. He's more stubborn.'

'No seriously, Terra. He's... calmed down a little.'

'You're being serious?'

'You have to see it. He hasn't killed anyone in weeks.' Terra laughs at the smirk that spreads on Desyl's face. 'No, seriously though. He has changed. He's letting you guys in. He probably doesn't even notice he's doing it, but I can see it.

'I heard him having a conversation with Roman a few days ago. I mean a real two-sided conversation. Okay, it was Roman doing most of the talking, but Gryffin's answers went on for more than one word. He'll deny it until his last breath, but you and Roman managed to find a way through his walls. Bray not so much yet, but then again, he did nearly kill himself to stop *Alpha* going through the Port, so who knows.'

'You might be right, but I don't think he'd see that as a good thing.'

'From what I can make out, Rayde told him getting in touch with his humanity would make him weak. It'll take time to change that way of thinking. Deep down he knows it's a good thing.'

'I'm not so sure. I've lost count of the number of times he's tried to push me away because I'm someone who can be used against him.'

'Yeah, but that's just the way he thinks. You have to accept that he sees things differently thanks to Rayde and the Foundation. I think he's beginning to get that having a crew and having a family are the same thing. We just need to convince him that having people to watch his back is actually a plus.'

'Which will be difficult now. The very thing he's been saying would happen, did happen.'

Desyl nods. 'Yeah. Roman's death is going to hit him hard sooner or later. He was warming to him. Anyone could see that. Gryffin is a great leader, but I think he likes having someone to have his back. He thought Rayde did, but it was different with Roman. He was starting to like having that father figure again. Fucking shame and a waste. Gryffin will retaliate against the Foundation. You know that, right?'

'I know. I think we're going to lose him because of what they did to Roman. I'm terrified he'll revert to what feels safe and normal.'

Desyl smiles sadly and scrubs his hand over his short spikes. 'You might be right. Not sure what we can do about that. If I even look at him the wrong way right now I'm going to get my head chewed off. I'm on shaky enough ground as it is.' He gets to his feet and brushes off his trousers. 'Speaking of which, I'd better get back before he breaks his restraints and comes looking for me. I presume you're not coming.'

'I think I'll stay here for another few minutes.'

He gives her a quick smile then disappears down the stairs. Terra stares at the ceiling, looking for answers that fail to show.

She had hoped once Gryffin escaped her father's clutches he'd had a happy life. Learning what she just did sickens her. For some reason, it makes what her father did seem even more horrible. Her father's jealousy of Roman and Maggie had put their son in his twisted sights. If he had just controlled his feelings, Gryffin's life would have been so very different.

The second he took ten-year-old Daegan Sawyer from Maggie, he set in motion a series of events that changed all their lives. Daegan was the only survivor of the project. If her father had never gotten his hands on him, perhaps the project would have been ruled a complete failure and binned years ago. Daegan would have grown up on Earth with Bray, and Gryffin would never have been created.

And she would never had met him.

She drags herself to her feet and brushes off the seat of her trousers. That thought doesn't bear thinking about. No matter how difficult he is, she knows how she feels about him. She just not sure that's enough.

22

Avoca jumps to his feet as Bray bursts through his door. The Hunter flings a small computer storage unit at him and paces the room in front of Avoca.

'Brayden—'

'Watch it.'

Avoca frowns and opens his mouth to speak but Bray interrupts him. 'Watch it!'

Avoca bends down to pick up the drive and plugs it in his unit. His breath catches in his throat when he notices the name of the file. 'Bray—'

'Stop saying my name and watch the damn video.'

Avoca licks his dry lips and does as he's told. He watches in horror as the Scientist threatens a young Gryffin with his brother's safety. The video ends, leaving the room in an uneasy silence.

'How did the Scientist know about me?'

Avoca's heart races in his chest. He knows Bray knows the truth and is waiting for him to admit it. But can he say the words?

When Balfe forwarded the request from the Scientist for more information on the boy - on Gryffin - he had been told in no uncertain terms to comply. They couldn't afford any delays to the project. That's what Balfe kept stressing to him. Give the Scientist everything he needs and keep things moving. The guilt of what he'd done was part of the reason he sought out Bray when he decided to make his move. 'I told him.'

Bray kicks Avoca's chair, sending him crashing against the desk, winding him. The Commander resumes his pacing and Avoca slowly turns to face him. The man in front of him is someone he doesn't recognise. Thanks to his new ocular implant, he resembles Gryffin more than the man he has come to care for like a son.

'I had no choice.'

Bray points his finger at him. 'Don't you dare go there! There are dozens of files just like that one. You want to know what's in each one?'

'Bray, please.'

'My brother allowing himself to be hurt. Hour after hour of him quietly taking the abuse because he thought he was protecting me. He let the Scientist take his fucking hand off, Avoca. All because of you. All because you let him think I was there, on the side-line, waiting to be modified if he didn't toe the line. You're no better than the Scientist. You were holding the knife just as much as he was.

'That's why you came to Tyrat. What did you think when you saw my name? You must have recognised the surname. Or was it Daegan's name on my file? You saw more in me than just stopping whatever the Foundation was planning. You saw a chance at redemption.'

The years of being called on to do the unspeakable without argument had finally come to a head. Balfe and the other members of the group stamped all over him, threatening his career, his life, and the life of his loved ones. For what? So they could greedily take what didn't belong to them. Take the lives of innocent children, destroying countless parents' hearts when their children disappeared without a trace. It's not as if the project even worked. It's a colossal failure and always would be.

He gets to his feet and approaches the furious Hunter. 'Do you not think I hate myself? Do you not think the guilt hasn't eaten at my soul? I have allowed horrific things to be done and did nothing to stop it. Yes, I came to Tyrat to get you out for my own selfish purpose. I needed a little redemption. Just a small amount so I could perhaps sleep for an hour without nightmares.

'I recognised Daegan's name on your file, and yes, I knew at that stage I had to get you out. Do you have any idea how much I kicked myself for not getting to you sooner? A few weeks earlier and I could have gotten you and Gryffin out. I could have saved both of you from spending time in the crate.'

'Hold on. Gryffin was there the same time as me?'

'Why, yes. I assumed you knew that.'

'I knew he was at Tyrat, but I never checked his records.'

'So you don't know...'

'Don't know what?'

'Bray—'

He pulls out his gun and points it at Avoca. 'I'm at the end of my fucking patience, Avoca. What don't I know?'

'Gryffin... You and your brother were in the crates at the same time. You won a fight and were sent to the crate. He was in the cell next to yours.'

Bray's gun wavers as Avoca's words sink in. 'He was the prisoner led in while I was fighting.' He's speaking to himself, remembering his time in Tyrat out loud. 'I spoke to him. He was freaking out when they threw him in the crate. Kicking the door. Just like I had. He was there? My brother was beside me during one of the worst times in my life and I didn't know it.' He lifts his head and looks at Avoca with so much hatred. 'On the shuttle I asked you, straight out. I asked if my brother had been used in the project. You said no.'

'I couldn't tell you. It would have just clouded everything for you.'

'My brother was a few feet away from me.'

'I thought you knew about your encounter in Tyrat.'

'Well, I didn't. He probably doesn't either. Did you know when you broke me out?'

'I thought you knew.'

'I didn't know he was my brother then, did I? But you did. Why not just tell me then who he was? Why carry on with the lie? You get a kick out of making a fool out of me? Give poor little orphan Bray a second chance.'

'Absolutely not! Bray, whatever my initial reason for breaking you out of Tyrat, I grew fond of you.'

'Give me a fucking break. I was a way of getting to Gryffin. A way of trying to fix your mistake.'

'I don't blame you for not believing me. I don't deserve your trust, but I am speaking the truth. I think of you like a son, Bray. Nothing will change that.' He reaches in his pocket and pulls out a tattered piece of paper. He passes it to Bray.

'What the hell is that?'

'Open it.'

He opens the sheet and reads the list of names, spotting his brother's name near the top of the list. 'Are these all the kids they took?'

Avoca nods solemnly. 'I never forgot them, Brayden. Not one of them. I had to dispose of their belongings, falsify search party logs, report attacks on the ships that didn't happen. The Scientist may have physically taken their lives, but I am well aware I helped bury each of those children in a grave of lies. I did that and I will never be able to wipe my slate clean. All I can do is give everything I have left to make sure this ends.' He takes the page from Bray and carefully folds it along the crease before tucking it back in the pocket of his shirt.

Bray loses his fight and slumps onto the edge of the bed. He drops his head, shaking it slowly from side to side as he digests the information or tries to get a hold of his temper. Avoca hopes it's the latter, although he deserves everything Bray can do to him. Bray lifts his head and focuses his cybernetic eye on his mentor. Avoca has to look away. He's responsible for that too.

'I can only—'

'If you say apologise one more fucking time, I'm going to throw up.' Bray sits up and blows out a long breath. 'I owe you my life, but so help me I want to kill you too.'

'I deserve it. From you and your brother.'

Bray snorts as he wipes a hand over his face. 'Surprised he hasn't come looking for you yet.'

'To be honest, I've been expecting him.'

Bray pushes himself up and walks over to the door. He stops in the doorway and takes a deep breath. 'There's no redemption. Stop using me to help deal with your guilt. It ends now. We're done.'

The door silently closes behind him leaving Avoca alone. His bones suddenly feel like they can't support the weight of everything he's been carrying around for the last two decades. He collapses onto his bed and firmly clasps his trembling hands together.

He understands why Bray feels betrayed by his actions. It was only a matter of time before his involvement in the project would take everyone he cares about from his life.

First his wife and children and now the man he loves like a son. And he's got no one to blame but himself.

∞

OCARRO COLONY

Milla looks up as the door to Creed's cabin opens. A tall woman enters, shaking the rain from her blonde hair and heavy coat. 'Fucking rotten out there for a change.' She freezes when she notices Creed has company. 'Well hello. Are these people friends or do I need to shoot them?'

Creed laughs and kisses the newcomer. 'Friends.'

'That's a relief. Where are your manners? Are you going to introduce us? Although, looking at the pair of them, I'd guess they're both Nomad. Heard he'd loosened the reins and let a woman join.'

'Chayse and Milla. This is Elora Hardy.'

Chayse stares over at the blonde-haired woman. 'You're fucking kidding me. Arms dealer Hardy.'

She smirks and helps herself to a bowl of stew. 'Not quite what's written on my business cards, but yeah. I have been known to dabble from time to time.'

'And you're with Creed?'

Hardy runs her hand down the side of Creed's face then kisses him again. 'As often as I can be. This fine man is all mine.'

'How the hell did you end up together? This place isn't at the top of the spots to visit.'

Hardy nods. 'You're right there. I came here about a year ago. I'm sure you know I took a step back from the life of crime when the Foundation came to the Sector. I moved around a bit and found myself here during a particularly boring time of my life. Fuck, I missed dealing guns. My transport needed repairs and I was sent to this gorgeous beast of a man. The rest is history.

'So do you... you know...'

'We know exactly who each other are. I'm incredibly nosey. I went digging in his personal shit one day and found the comms unit Gryffin gave him.' She reaches in her pocket and holds out a Nomad comms unit 'I got one too. I knew then he had connections to the Nomad. With a bit more digging I found out who he was. I confronted him. We had an impressive row and I left.'

'For a day,' Creed says with a grin.

'Damn irresistible man. Yes. I left for a day. Haven't left again.'

'Small Sector for the two of you to find yourselves here.'

She chews thoughtfully then shrugs. 'Not so much. It's not surprising we both found each other. There aren't many places with zero Foundation or Nomad connections. We both wanted to get away. Could hardly do that somewhere we're known. So, here we are.' She sits down next to Creed and crosses her legs. 'Can I presume your leader has decided to call Creed back into the fold?'

'He wants me to be High Commander.'

Hardy stares at Creed for a few seconds then drops her bowl of stew and wraps her arms around him. 'Congratulations.'

'Thanks.'

'Damn, my dinner's in the fire.' She gets herself a new bowl and digs in again. 'I heard Gryffin isn't fairing too well.'

'I'm sorry,' Milla says, holding up a hand. 'Are you working for Gryffin too? How many more people does he have on his payroll?'

'Actually, he was on my payroll.'

'He's what?'

'A few years ago, before he was made High Commander, we did quite a bit of business together. With his brother too, although Bray and I had more of a personal relationship.'

Milla leans back in the chair and laughs loudly. 'Oh this is brilliant. You were with Bray and Gryffin?'

Hardy shakes her head. 'No. I had a few encounters with Bray, but my relationship with Gryffin was purely business. I would have got more conversation from a rock. Getting him to talk for longer than a few minutes was a bloody miracle. Anything else beyond that was out.'

Creed clears his throat and Hardy squeezes his hand. 'Down boy. We've all got a past.'

He raises his eyebrow and looks back at the fire as Milla pops another spoon of stew in her mouth. The Sawyer brothers sure know how to get around the Sector. With the plentiful supply of love interests on offer throughout the Sector, why did they continuously have to veer towards the same bloody women?

'When the Foundation arrived in the Sector,' Hardy continues, 'I decided it would be prudent to disappear for a while. I hired Gryffin to put his mark on my bar. He made sure no one took advantage while I was gone. He kept it extremely profitable for a few years until I decided to cut all ties with the place. So, back to my original question. How is he?'

'He's dying,' Chayse answers. 'He was adamant we get here as fast as we could. Guess we know why now.'

Hardy nods solemnly. 'Figured he'd be in a bad way. He wouldn't take a step back from the Nomad otherwise. Man deserves a break after everything he's been through.' She takes the empty bowls from everyone and piles them in the sink. 'I'm sure you and... sorry who are you again?' she asks, looking across at Chayse.

'Chayse, Captain of *Nemesis*.'

Hardy isn't shy about examining him from top to bottom. 'Is that so. You're the famous Chayse. I've heard a lot about you and your ship. Quite a sight if stories are to be believed. No offence, but you're a bit younger than I imagined. Good for you. Well, I'm sure you and Chayse have a bit to talk about. Leave us girls to it and head to the back room.'

Creed and Chayse do as they're told and close the door behind them. 'Hope you don't think that's rude. Thought they should have a talk in private. I'm sure Creed has a hell of a lot of questions as I'm sure you do. Fancy a beer on the porch?'

23

DIXON SPACE STATION

Avoca wipes his palms on his trousers and squeezes his eyes shut. He can think of more than a few dozen places he'd rather be right now, but this isn't about him. Well, that's what he keeps telling himself.

Past actions and decisions haunt him daily, and if he can quieten even one of the many skeletons, he'll be content. Not that he deserves even that much. Bray knows the truth and it's only right his brother does too.

Before he can talk himself out of it, he walks up to the door. The polished white metal door silently withdraws and he steps into the med bay on the station.

He doesn't know why, but the Nomad leader had been moved from *Cronus* to the station for observation. The technology on the ship is superior. It makes no sense to have relocated him. Perhaps he didn't want to be on a Foundation ship. Who could blame him?

He swallows a few times as he forces his feet to carry him across the wide expanse of the bay to a private alcove. He stops at the entrance, having serious doubts about the intelligence of this decision. The lone occupant is lying on the bed fully dressed. Numerous monitors and wires are attached to him, recording every reading from his system.

Avoca is slightly relieved to see the holster attached to his belt is empty. Gryffin turns off the report he's listening to and looks at his visitor. When recognition kicks in, his purple eye glows brightly.

'May I have a moment, Captain?' Avoca manages to ask before he has to clear his throat again.

Gryffin doesn't respond, but his look of anger is hard to misinterpret.

Avoca takes another step inside, his hands firmly clasped in front of him to stop them from twitching. Gryffin's condition may be precarious, but he is still an imposing man – only partly thanks to the modifications he had a hand in organising. 'My name is Hank Avoca. I'm... well, I was an admiral with—'

'I know who you are.'

Avoca nods, feeling more uneasy by the second. 'I was involved with the—'

'I said I know who you are,' Gryffin interrupts. He pushes himself up on the bed. Avoca can't help but stare at the metal remains of his arm. Gryffin's expression turns colder when he realises what Avoca is looking at.

Avoca takes another breath, but it does little to settle his stomach. 'I need to talk to you. I need to...' He sighs and closes his eyes, his train of thought completely lost. 'I owe you an apology.'

Gryffin swings his legs off the bed and takes a second to get his balance. He slowly walks over to Avoca. The Nomad towers over Avoca, but he manages keep his position. He tilts his head back to look up at Gryffin. 'Say that again.'

'I want to apologise. I should have done something as soon as Balfe mentioned the project to me. But I was too much of a coward. I was afraid of what would happen to me if I refused to help. I know that's no excuse, and I can never make it up to you. But I just wanted you to know I hate myself for my part in all of this. I know I can never say or do anything to begin making up for what I was a part of.'

'You walked right by me on the station when the Scientist was taking my eye out for the first time. You were with Rayde and Sayber when it was taken out again a few months ago. What's to make up for?'

Avoca's breath catches in his throat as the very scenes Gryffin mentioned enter his mind before he can stop them. Yes, he did just walk by with the rest of the participants and do nothing to stop the horrors that were taking place on the operating table. That memory is without a doubt the worst one he relived regularly.

He'd always consoled himself by saying the boy wasn't aware of what was going on. Even with everything the Scientist was doing, he was silent on the table. Knowing that, not only was he aware, but that he remembers the party being led through to watch, makes everything so much worse. 'You remember me from the station? From that long ago?'

'I remember everything. You refused to look at me. Kept your eyes turned away. First time anyway. You couldn't look away the second time.'

'I'm... I'm sorry,' he mutters. Avoca takes a deep breath and asks a question he's been dreading hearing an answer to for decades. 'What happened to the others that were with you on the station?'

'You really do want me to kill you, don't you?'

'No. No... I...' Avoca takes the list of names from his pocket and holds it in his hands. 'I kept a list. Every child I knew about. I may have been too weak to do anything about it at the time, and believe me, it's something that not even death can save me from. I care. Too little, too late, I know, but I don't know what else to do.

'I have given Bray access to every recording I made, every file I copied, the name of every participant no matter how trivial. I want to help you take them down. Yes, you and your brother believe my reasons are selfish, and they probably are. But does that matter?' He takes a step closer not caring what Gryffin does to him. He's beyond worrying about it. 'Please, Captain. I need to know. Did The Scientist... modify them too?'

Gryffin doesn't acknowledge him as he stares down at the list in Avoca's hands. After a minute of uncomfortable silence, Gryffin looks up at him. 'Yes.'

Avoca closes his eyes. A part of him had hoped Gryffin was the only survivor because he was the only one modified. He had hoped the others may have escaped before they were hurt. 'What happened to them?'

Gryffin doesn't immediately respond, just keeps his attention on the far wall. 'I killed them.'

Avoca slumps back in the chair beside him. He admits he feels a little relieved to hear Gryffin was the one to kill the other subjects. It offers a little solace to know some of the children didn't die at the Scientist hands. 'You... killed all of them?'

Gryffin looks over at him. 'He left my cage open. I took a knife off the table and slit their throats. I didn't have time to kill myself before he came back.'

Avoca feels like he's going to faint. He rubs his temple as he discretely takes a few deep breaths. He stops himself from apologising again. How can anyone apologise for that? 'You spared their suffering. It's more than I did.'

Gryffin crouches down in front of Avoca, gripping the armrest to steady himself. Avoca pushes himself against the back of the chair, feeling very much like a caged animal. 'You got it all wrong, Admiral. I was the test subject. He'd put an implant on me, test it, take it off, fix it, put it back on, and repeat the whole damn procedure until he was happy. Only then would he fit a similar implant to one of the others. Then he'd do it all again with each and every implant. Some days I'd have ten operations for one of theirs.

'You assume I killed them to save them. What if I killed them so I wouldn't have to go through any more procedures? If there was no one to fit the mods to he wouldn't have to keep using me like that.'

Avoca licks his lips. 'Whatever your reasons, he was a monster. Doing anything to stop what was going on was justified. I'm sure your companions thought the same.'

'He was your monster.' Gryffin stands up, leaning heavily on the chair. He winces as he straightens. 'Now Admiral, you have two choices.' He lifts his hand and catches a gun thrown towards him.

Avoca turns to see Bray in the doorway. He salutes Avoca then crosses his arms as he leans against the wall. Bray must have spoken to his brother while he was psyching himself up to this meeting.

Facing each of the men individually was a reason to fear for your life, but the two together... Avoca swallows and wipes his palms on his trousers. 'What choices?'

Gryffin crouches down in front of him again and takes the safety off. The metal digs into his stomach as Gryffin shoves the gun against him. 'Choice one is I kill you right now, slowly. Choice two is tell us where the ships are.'

Avoca swallows and looks over at Bray, but Gryffin applies more pressure, burying the gun deep in his gut. 'Bray? What is he talking about.'

The Hunter joins the Nomad. 'The ships the children were taken from,' he says.

'I don't understand.'

Gryffin takes over again. 'You told Bray you were in charge of getting rid of our belongings, creating search party logs, and making up attacks on the ships. What you didn't mention was what you did with the ships themselves.'

'The ships were destroyed.'

Bray shakes his head. 'You're lying again, Avoca.' He leans over the chair, putting his face in front of Avoca's. 'You see, my brother and I had a little chat about what you said to me and we both agree on something. First time for everything. You wouldn't have had to falsify attacks on the ships if the ships were actually attacked, would you?'

'Please. You don't have to do this.'

Gryffin targets Avoca with his glowing purple eye. 'My arm isn't as steady as it used to be. I get tremors.'

'The ships are gone.'

A look passes between the brothers. Gryffin's hand tightens on the weapon. 'Choice one then.'

'No! Wait!'

Gryffin flexes his fingers, readjusting his grip on the weapon. 'Location.'

Avoca closes his eyes. 'They're in the Outer Sector.'

Bray smiles. 'You'll have to narrow it down a little.'

'Giving you access to the ships won't help. I doubt any of them are still operational.'

'Let us worry about that.' Bray leans over to whisper in Avoca's ear. 'He was serious about the tremors. Wouldn't want his finger twitching just as you're about to cooperate. Bullet to the stomach...' He sucks in a breath. 'I've seen it in Tyrat. Seriously painful and slow way to go. And I very much doubt he's going to let any medical staff in here to help you. I'll leave and he'll watch you die. Just like you watched him on the station.'

'Very well. I'll give you the coordinates.'

Instead of removing the gun, Gryffin pushes the metal tip of his damaged arm under Avoca's chin, tilting his head up. One of the connectors tears his flesh, drawing blood. 'Bray doesn't want me to kill you. That's the only reason you're still breathing. It's a one-time favour though. You keep out of my way. Understood?'

'Yes.'

Gryffin gets to his feet and Avoca releases a long breath. Bray takes the gun and slips it back in his holster as the Nomad limps back to the bed and sits down, wincing as he rubs his leg. Bray grabs Avoca by the arm and hauls him off the chair. He shoves him towards the door, pausing in the doorway to look back at Gryffin. 'You good?'

Gryffin drags himself up the bed and closes his eye. 'Yeah. Get the coordinates.'

Bray pushes Avoca down the corridor towards the meeting room and forces him into a chair. 'There's no need for any of this.'

'You want redemption, you'll do as you're told.' He slides a portable unit along the table. 'Coordinates.'

'Bray—'

'What the hell is so special about these ships? Why are you protecting them like this?'

'I want this to end as much as you do, but those ships are not the way to do it. People died on those vessels. A lot of innocent lives were lost when they removed the children for the project.

'I strongly believe they should be left and no one should have access to them. If anything, they should have been destroyed. The ship Gryffin was on is there too. Do you really think he wants to see it again?'

'You don't get to make that decision. If we're going to have any chance in hell of taking down the Foundation we'll need more firepower. If even one of those relics fires up, we'll be better off than we are now. Write down the coordinates or I swear I'll drag you back to Gryffin so he can get some of the revenge he deserves.'

Avoca takes a deep breath then pulls the unit towards him.

∞

Bray stops by the door to the engine room on *Ares* and watches Gryffin pulling wires and cables from under one of the units. His brother had left the med bay on the station after the chat with Avoca. Bray is surprised they'd managed to convince him to stay there as long as they had.

He takes the two memory chips from his pocket and stares at them. One has all the details for the hidden ships. The other has Gryffin's files from the Scientist's computer.

'You got the coordinates?'

Bray looks at Gryffin who has stopped destroying the unit. 'What?'

'The coordinates. Avoca give you the ships?'

Bray holds out the chip. 'Yeah. It's all on this. Can I ask you something?'

'If I say no you're just going to ask me anyway so get on with it.'

'Do you really remember your time with the Scientist?' The question pops out without any thought or build up, surprising Gryffin.

His brother stares over at him. 'What?'

'You heard me.'

'No.'

'I don't believe you. That's not what you told Avoca.'

Gryffin reaches under the unit and tears out another cable. It doesn't look like he's going to answer. Bray steps into the room, leans back against the unit, and crosses his ankles. 'You see, I know you have a near perfect memory and it has nothing to do with your implants. You were there for five years and again for ten months. You must remember something.'

Gryffin slams his fist against the unit, denting the surface. 'Enough!'

'I'm not trying to upset you, really. I just need to know.'

Gryffin slides under the unit with a handful of cables. He checks the connectors and plugs the new cables in to the unit. 'What happened is none of your business. It's no one's business.'

Bray takes the memory chip out of his pocket and throws it at Gryffin's feet. 'I got into the personal files on the Scientist's system. It doesn't have anything about the new mods the Foundation are using, but it does have all the details on the procedures he carried out years ago. That chip has all the data from your file. Every procedure, every component... every reaction is noted in there.'

Gryffin sits up and stares at the small chip at his feet for a minute before looking up at Bray. 'You watched it?'

It's an accusation more than a question but Bray nods anyway. 'I thought there might be something in it that could help with my implants.' Bray scratches the skin beside the metal on his face and takes a deep breath. 'I saw him use the threat of hurting me to make you more compliant. You refused to answer to your designation so he said he'd work on me instead. You stopped him and did what you were told.'

Gryffin reaches over and picks up the chip but doesn't say anything.

'Did he make you think he had me the whole time?'

Gryffin turns the chip over in his hand. 'What do you want?'

'I want to thank you.'

'For what?'

'For what you did. For changing my mind about you.'

'This where we hug?'

'I'm being serious, Gryffin. I get some of what was done to you. I'm not comparing your experience—'

'This conversation is done.'

'I need to say this to you.'

'And I don't need to hear it.'

Bray pushes off the unit and shoves Gryffin in the chest. 'What's your problem? For once can you try to let your human side out? You're surrounded by people who, for reasons I can't figure out, actually give a damn about you.'

'I never asked—'

'You don't have to ask. For fuck's sake, it's like talking to a child sometimes.' Bray shakes his head when he realises what he said. Gryffin doesn't know how to deal with the people in his life, but that's not entirely his fault. People skills weren't on the curriculum with the Scientist. 'We care about you, okay, in spite of the way you constantly try to push us away.'

Gryffin frowns but doesn't respond.

'Forget it. I don't have time to explain this to you.' He rubs his forehead. 'I should have just said thank you and left it at that. The Dixon's said you're up for connecting to *Cronus* tomorrow. See if you can break her open.'

Gryffin shrugs. 'Worth a shot. I've never hooked to something that size but I might be able to get in.'

'I suppose I better go and get things ready then. Wouldn't want to fry your brain by mistake when you hook up to *Cronus*.' Bray turns around and heads to the door, regretting ever starting this conversation.

'I didn't remember your name.'

Bray stops in his tracks and slowly turns to face his brother.

Gryffin crosses his arms as he leans against the unit. 'Like you said, I've got a near perfect memory of everything since I woke up in that place, some from before.' He frowns and clears his throat. 'I didn't know the woman in the stasis pod was our mother. I remember her, but not what she looked like.'

'You remember Mum - from before I mean?'

'It's more flashes of memories instead of individual people.'

'Like what?'

Gryffin takes a deep breath while Bray gives him some time to respond. He can tell Gryffin is far from happy about the conversation, but if he's willing to talk about it, Bray is going to listen. He didn't know Gryffin had any memories of his past life at all.

'A meal on a beach. You got lost.'

Bray is speechless for a few seconds. 'Yeah. I didn't want to go home so I hid behind a transport. Mum went crazy. You found me a few minutes later and brought me back. You always looked out for me. Do you remember anything else?'

'Yeah. Lots of screaming when the transport was attacked then waking up in a cage. You want more memories?'

Bray drops his arms to his sides as his body turns cold. He wipes a hand over his face, nods then leaves the room.

His brother sacrificed himself to save him. After hating him for so many years Bray doesn't feel comforted by the actions. Instead it just makes his own actions seem sickeningly harsh.

24

Bray lies back on the couch and looks up at the stars. The small platform at the top of the station is the perfect place to escape everything going on below him. The giant form of *Cronus* sits below him with *Ares*, *Perses*, and *Lir* circling her. Having the main ships from each group this close to Earth is something he never thought would happen.

He squeezes his eyes shut. The headache is going to drive him crazy. How Gryffin deals with it every day of his life is beyond him. He's going to catch a few minutes to himself then go back to *Cronus*. Gryffin is going to hook up to the ship in a few hours. It's a procedure that could kill him, but without him trying it could take months to break into her.

Gryffin had sent the coordinates of the ships to a contact he has in the Outer Sector. In true Gryffin style, he hadn't been forthcoming with a name or even a location. By giving the coordinates of the ships to Gryffin, Bray had helped increase the fleet of the enemy. No doubt Sayber would kick his ass for that. To hell with it. There's nothing to say any of the ships would power up after sitting in a hangar for so long.

Dealing with Avoca and his part in this mess would have to wait until they had time. Right now, all he wants is to get Garvan out and fix whatever is wrong with his own head.

'I apologise. I didn't know anyone was up here.'

Bray opens his eyes and turns over. Rua is already walking back down the spiral stairs to the deck below. 'Wait! I'm leaving now anyway.'

She slowly climbs back up and steps onto the platform. He swings his legs around to give her room to sit down. Rua takes the seat furthest from him, looking anything but comfortable as she perches on the edge with her hands on her knees.

Bray places an arm behind his head and gazes out the skylight.

Rua tilts her head, trying to see what has caught his attention. 'Is something wrong?'

He turns his head towards her. 'Wrong? Why?'

'You're frowning.'

He forces his face to relax. 'Bad day. I'm sorely tempted to get on *Perses* and get the hell away from here at top speed. When the hell did life get so damn complicated? Sorry, ignore me.'

He hears the couch rustle as she shuffles closer to him. 'What good would running away do? The cyborgs would still exist. The Foundation would still be in power, and the Outer Sector would still be at risk.'

He laughs to himself. 'Yeah, I know. Just a nice thought.' He rubs his hand over his face, wincing when he accidentally bumps against the implant. 'I'm just pissed at everything right now.'

'Gryffin anywhere on that list?'

He glances over at her before focusing on the stars again. 'Always.

It's getting pretty boring.'

'Do you mean thinking about him or people assuming you're thinking about him?'

'Irritatingly, both.' He scrubs a hand over his face, hissing when he puts pressure on his implant again. 'Damn it. Why do I keep forgetting that's there?' He slams his hand back on the seat. 'For years I've hated him. Well, not Gryffin exactly, but I hated my brother.'

'I'm confused.'

'I only found out Gryffin was my brother last year.'

'Ah.'

'I just found out that he did something years ago to protect me, but that was as my brother, not Gryffin. That gesture was by someone who doesn't technically exist anymore. I'm a Hunter and he's a Nomad. That's what I should be thinking about. That one gesture shouldn't be clouding the core truth. It's just so irritating.

'The whole damn Sector revolves around Gryffin and his precious Nomad. I get that he's... well, that he's in a bad way and it's important to the wellbeing of the damn universe and all that live in it that he gets better, but just for once, I'd like to have a conversation or even a lone independent thought without my brother popping up. I'm tired of thinking about him. Oh shut up, Bray. I'm starting to piss myself off now.'

Rua doesn't say anything as she looks at him. Bray risks a glance at her and frowns. 'What the hell are you smirking at?'

'Are you done?'

'What?'

'I didn't want to interrupt while you were wallowing in self-pity.'

'Self-pity? I am not—'

'Yes you are. You've had a hard time. I'm torn up for you. There. Feel better now? How the hell did the Hunters exist longer than a week? There's too many emotions clouding everything you do.'

Bray can't help but smile as he turns to face her. 'You know how to make a guy feel better, you know that?'

She shrugs. 'Feeling sorry for yourself is a waste of time. Changes nothing. It won't pay for food, fuel, or weapons.'

Bray smiles. 'I guess you're right.' He shifts around to look at her and props his head up on his hand. 'I never said thank you.'

She tucks a loose lock of hair behind her ear. 'For what?'

'For risking your ship and crew. For coming here to help.'

She looks away from him, back to the darkness outside. 'I had nothing else planned at the time.'

'Yeah, well, I still appreciate it. You barely know me and Garvan. It was a big risk coming here to get us.'

'I know enough about you to know it was worth it.' She turns her head to look at him. 'Besides, having you on our side won't hurt.'

'You mean because I'm Gryffin's brother?'

'You brought it up that time.' She shakes her head. 'No, as you said, the Sector doesn't revolve around him. Having a Hunter Commander in our debt will be useful someday.'

He grins. 'Fair enough. How do you think things will play out once we take care of the Foundation?'

She shrugs and looks back at the stars. 'I can't see the alliances holding out. Gut feeling is the Nomad will step in as the main group.' She meets his eyes again. 'Unless of course the Rogues or Hunters can stop them.'

Bray now sees where his debt to the Rogue Captain might be called in. 'Sounds like things could get interesting.'

'Perhaps.'

Bray's reply is smothered as she pins him to the seat, her body covering his as she kisses him. His initial surprise quickly disappears. He runs his hand through her hair, unleashing it from its braid. He pulls off her vest and removes her bra then sits up so she can deal with his t-shirt.

Bray tries to flip them over but Rua shoves him back down and takes control again. He hisses as her nails tear at his chest, the pain adding another level to the intensity of her attack. It's more than clear she wants to take charge and he can't find a reason to argue.

Rua shoves his trousers and boxers down to his knees then stands up and pushes her leather trousers down her long legs. Her lean body is that of a fighter. Tight muscles line her powerful legs and trim stomach. Numerous scars pepper her torso and legs, but as far as Bray is concerned they only add to her appearance.

Leaving her trousers around her ankles, Rua straddles him, taking him deep inside her without pausing. Bray gasps at the sudden pressure but Rua doesn't give him a chance to recover. She digs her nails in his wrists as she holds his arms over his head. Rua fiercely kisses him, adding a few nips of her teeth as her tongue explores every inch of his mouth. She moves down to his neck, kissing and biting the skin behind his ear all the while keeping a mind-blowing pace on top of him.

'Oh fuck, Rua.'

'What's the matter Commander? Too rough for you?' She pulls his earlobe between her teeth.

'Goddammit! I didn't say that.'

Her strong fingers hold him down. He's going to be black and blue if he survives, but he couldn't give a damn. He feels the pressure building in his balls, but she's not ready for this to end.

Rua slows and groans as she slides him in and out of her, driving him crazy. She smiles down at him and it does nothing to calm him. She playing with him and enjoying every minute of it. 'I'm the superior officer here. You don't come until I say.'

'Rua—'

She digs her fingers in his jaw and forces him to look at her. 'What was that?'

'Yes, ma'am.'

Rua smiles and runs her hand down his chest, tracing his tattoo with her fingers. 'Smart man. I haven't had a man in too damn long. I'm going to enjoy this. Leave your hands over your head.'

Her fingers twist his nipples as she increases her pace. The mix of the intense pleasure with flashes of pain is driving him crazy and he's not alone. Rua rides him even faster, burying him deep inside her as she slams her hips against his.

Rua screams against his shoulder, her fingers squeezing his wrists as her orgasm works through her. He struggles to hold back, desperate to hang on until she tells him otherwise.

'Now Commander.'

He doesn't need to be told twice. Bray's own release hits and Rua stifles his shout by covering his mouth with her hand. She goes limp on top of him, her body trembling as she takes fast, deep breaths.

Rua slowly rolls off him and lies with her arm over her face. Bray's whole body is on fire. He manages to lift his head and sees angry red welts running through the black lines of his chest tattoo. He drops his head back and blows out a long breath. 'Wow.'

He grimaces at the stupidity of his comment, but Rua doesn't seem to have noticed. He rolls to his side and props his head up on his hand. 'You okay?'

Rua turns her head and looks at him from under her arm. Her red hair lies in a tangled mess on the couch around her. 'You have no idea how much I needed that.'

'Glad I could help.'

'That you did, Commander.' She smiles at him and runs her nails down his chest. 'Being on a ship full of woman has definite disadvantages.'

'Try being on a ship with a crew of men.'

He sucks in a breath as she takes him in her hand, squeezing him gently. 'Ready for more?'

'You serious?'

Rua smirks. 'Oh I'm very serious, Commander. I have a lot of lost time to make up for.'

∞

DIXON SPACE STATION

Bray groans and rolls over. Every inch of his body aches. His chest is raw and stinging, his dick is throbbing, and his throat is sore. He can't remember ever feeling so good. Rua is like no one he's ever been with before. She didn't hold back and certainly wasn't gentle with him. Not that he's complaining. He's never been with someone who took complete control like she did and he's beginning to think he could get used to it.

Not overly keen on being caught by Evie or Felix, Bray had convinced Rua to come back to his room. He'd lost track of how many times they'd been with each other over the last ten hours. Making up for lost time was an understatement. Rua was unstoppable.

He reaches out but there's no sign of Rua. He rolls onto his front and rubs his eyes, trying to convince them to open fully, but like the rest of him, they're less than enthusiastic. After a bit of persuasion his vision clears as his artificial eyes come online and he smiles when he sees Rua sitting on the end of the chair, pulling her boots on. Her long hair is loose and trailing over her shoulder. She's dressed again, her tight vest and leather trousers not doing much to hide the powerful fighters body underneath.

'Hey.'

The large scar on her face moves slightly as she clenches her jaw. Her cold green eyes bore into him but she doesn't say a word. Bray pushes onto his elbows and rubs his eyes again. 'Something wrong?'

'About what we did last night.'

Bray frowns at her. He's got a bad feeling about where this is going. 'What about it?'

'It never happened, got it?'

'Did I do something wrong? You took the lead. I thought it was what you wanted?'

'It was a mistake.'

Bray is irritated with himself for the flash of hurt at her words. First Terra and now Rua. 'Right. What the fuck was all that last night then?'

She closes the distance between them and, before he can react, pushes him to his back and straddles him. The tip of her large blade digs in his neck just above his Adam's apple. Her fierce eyes glare accusingly at him. 'It didn't happen.'

He swallows, wincing as the blade nicks his skin. 'I get it okay. You can get the fucking knife away from me.'

She presses the blade close to his skin. 'Say it didn't happen.'

'Fine, whatever, just leave my head where it is.'

She stares down at him then shoves him away as she stands up. Without a backward glance, she disappears out the door. Bray lies on his back and rests his head on his arm. Damn women are driving him crazy. Why the hell can't they make their mind up?

First Terra wanted him, then she wanted Gryffin and now Rua is following her example. It's not like he has the same level of feelings for Rua as he did for Terra, but there's still something there. She's unlike any woman he's ever met.

The colonists he was with from time to time were great, but Rua is in another league entirely. She's stubborn, rude, cold, and more than a little intimidating. Not the best first impression, but it's a shield. There is more to her and he's itching to find out what that is.

He rubs the raw skin on his neck and frowns at the blood on his fingers. Looks like he'll have to learn to live without knowing anything else about her. It's either that or lose his head.

DIXON SPACE STATION

Bray crouches down in front of his brother as Gryffin pulls off his top and opens the connectors on his chest implant.

'I'm not so sure this is such a good idea, Gryffin.'

'The Dixon woman said it was your idea.'

Bray rubs his forehead and sighs loudly. 'Yeah I know, but maybe it's too soon. You're still not back to full strength yet and your implants are, for want of a better word, shit.'

'Thank you,' Terra says, interrupting their conversation. 'Couldn't agree more - on all points. He died a few days ago or has everyone forgotten? He's not well enough to connect to an entire ship. This is a really bad idea.'

'I'm fine. Can we just get this over and done with?'

'This is serious, Gryffin,' Terra says.

He slides onto the bed and leans forward, resting his arms on his legs. 'I know it's serious. We need to access the files.'

'We need to keep you in one piece.'

He holds out his hand. 'Cable.'

'Gryffin—'

'Terra, I'm doing this so stop arguing. All the cyborg files are buried in *Cronus*' system. The access to the Foundation comms can be made through her. We need to open her up.'

She sighs and crosses her arms. 'Fine.'

Bray looks from Terra to Gryffin and back again before slowly holding out the cable to him. Gryffin opens the port on the side of his ocular implant and plugs the cable in. Once he's happy about the connection he lies back on the bed and looks up at the ceiling. Bray glances at Terra briefly then hooks the monitors to Gryffin's chest. The Dixon's burst into the room mid argument as usual and stop when they see what Bray is doing.

'You weren't going to start without us, were you?' Felix asks.

'Of course not,' Terra interrupts. 'No one is starting anything until every available monitor in this place is attached to him.'

'I'll help,' Evie offers, hurrying across the room to grab some of the cables from the table. Before Gryffin can argue, Evie is in front of him getting up close and personal with his chest implant. Terra stuffs her hands in her pockets to stop herself from fidgeting.

She's far from happy about this as anyone could be. Overloading his implants is the least of her worries. If he can't keep control while hooked up, the link could kill him. 'How long will you need to be connected?'

Gryffin shrugs. 'I won't know until I'm in. A few hours. Maybe longer.'

She takes a deep breath and nods slowly. 'How will we know if there's a problem?'

Evie wiggles a cable between her thumb and forefinger. 'That's where these little beauties come in.' She attaches the cable to one of the fine metal needles then targets one of the minute ports on his chest plate and slowly pushes the needle in.

Gryffin flinches as it passes through the implant into his body.

'The probes will give us a clear picture of what the link is doing to his implants and his body.' Felix taps the metal on his chest. 'This is quite ingenious.'

'And truly horrible, of course,' Evie adds as she throws an exasperated look at her husband.

'Yes, yes of course. But you can't deny the complexity of the design. Each of these little ports gives you direct access to every inch of his body. Every component, every connection, it's all linked to this implant.'

Gryffin lifts his head and glares at Felix.

Evie pats him on the chest. 'Lie down and mind your own business.'

Gryffin opens his mouth to reply, but reconsiders and lies back on the bed.

Terra quietly watches from beside his bed as Bray and the Dixon's pepper his implants with cables and monitors. Twenty minutes later his implants are barely visible under all the machinery.

Evie stands at the foot of the bed and places her hands on her hips. 'Right, well I think that's all the monitors we have here. We're ready to go. You okay, Gryffin?'

'Yes.'

Bray picks up a monitor and stands next to Gryffin's bed. 'Okay, just take it slow. If you feel anything is off let me know immediately.'

'I know what I'm doing. Can we just get this over with?'

Bray shakes his head and turns away from the bed. 'You're good to go whenever you're ready.'

Terra leans over the bed and runs her hand over the side of his face. 'You be careful, okay. Please.'

'See you in a bit.' Gryffin closes his eye and a few seconds later, his body jolts on the table. Evie holds Terra's arm, stopping her from going near him.

'He's okay. Readings are fluctuating, but still well within normal levels.'

'Why is his body trembling like that?'

'He's just linking to the system. He's doing fine.' Terra paces beside the bed until Evie glares at her. 'Would you kindly refrain from making a dent in the floor. Sit down.'

'Sorry. How is he?'

'Do you see me flapping around the room shouting at people?'

'No.'

'Then he's fine. Sit down and stop distracting the people who are doing their best to keep him alive.'

Terra collapses back in the chair and wrings her hands together. She hates watching him like this. She knows it's a great talent, but would rather he wasn't hooking his brain up to a large battleship.

Felix crouches down in front of her. 'You can't do anything here. Probably best you go. Someone will get you when he's done.'

Terra stares up at him. 'I'm not going anywhere until—'

'Yeah, yeah, yeah,' Felix adds. 'We get the message. Not until he's all right. Listen, he could be in there for half an hour or five hours. No offence but you'll drive all of us a little crazy if you stay here staring at him. He can't twitch without us knowing about it.' He ushers Terra to her feet and turns her to face the door. 'Go before I call Heath in here to remove you. I promise your cyborg is in good hands.'

With one long lingering look, Terra slowly shuffles from the room. She wanders through the station back to the familiar dim corridors of *Ares*. Once alone in the room she shares with Gryffin, she lowers onto the bed and lies back to stare at the ceiling. She can't shake the sinking feeling of dread that's been growing over the last few days.

She loves Gryffin. She's never been more sure of anything, but she's struggling with the ever increasing bag of issues his implants bring to the relationship. She'd never admit it to him, but a part of her was hoping this trip to Earth would help deal with some of those issues. Being able to reverse some of the work would be an amazing thing. She'd like to believe she feels that way because it would help Gryffin, but in truth the guilt is eating her up. Her father's involvement in the project has soured their relationship and Terra fears she'll never be able to fix it.

Every time she looks at his face, she can see her father fitting the implant around his eye. Knowing her father hurt him so horribly for years and took pleasure from it, sickens her. She's tried hard to force the images from her head, but Gryffin only has his implants because of her father. He was cruelly torn from a loving family and thrown in a living hell because of her father. There's no escaping that fact no matter how much she wishes otherwise.

She rolls onto her side, burying her face in the pillow. What if she can't get beyond this? What if she can't be with Gryffin without thinking about what happened to him? She wants his implants removed, but is that for his benefit or hers? She closes her eyes and takes a deep breath. She hopes she can figure this out before she ruins things and loses him forever.

∞

DIXON SPACE STATION

'He's done it!' Felix exclaims. 'We're in.'

Bray opens his eyes and drops his feet from the chair in front of him. He didn't realise he'd dozed off. 'What?'

Felix taps on the screen in his hand and passes it to Bray. 'He's somehow managed to crack the passcodes. We have access to everything.' Felix laughs and slaps Gryffin on the shoulder. 'Good lad.'

Bray scrolls through the data on the screen. The master files from *Cronus* are listed, giving them Foundation level access to everything.

This is better than they could have hoped for. 'I thought he'd try to access some of the systems - not everything. How long as he been under for?'

'Four hours. It appears the Foundation had one set of master codes for the ship. Once he cracked them, the rest of the systems were a doddle.'

'Time to wake him up then.'

Felix shakes his head. 'That's not down to us. If we unhook him from the system we risk shrivelling his brain, or short-circuiting it, or—'

'Okay,' Bray replies a little louder than necessary. 'I get it. So we just wait?'

Felix nods. 'All we can do. He's done this kind of thing before, right?'

'Yes, but—'

'Then we leave him to it. I'm getting myself some of that jam before my darling wife has it all. Would you like anything?'

Bray shakes his head as he settles back in the chair. A few minutes later he hears footsteps approaching. 'That was quick.'

'What was?'

He turns to face Rua. 'Sorry. Thought you were Felix. This isn't the best time.'

Rua ignores him and sits in a chair opposite the bed. 'Feeling sorry for yourself again?'

Bray looks back at her. 'Seriously? The last time we were alone you threatened to slice my neck open. I don't know what your problem is, but I'm not in the mood for games. My bother just connected with a fucking battleship. Can you wait until I know whether he's going to wake up before you have another go at me?'

'You really have a low opinion of me if you think any of this is a game to me.' She leans forward, resting her arms on her legs. Her green eyes bore into him as she glares at him. 'I heard your brother was in a potentially life threatening situation so I came to see how he is doing.'

'Yeah I get it. Don't worry. Everyone's concerned about the Nomad leader.'

He sees Rua rise to her feet but doesn't have time to brace for her fist. The blow sends him to the ground as he lands unceremoniously on his side with the chair on top of him. Rua crouches over him, pressing her knee to his chest to hold him down.

'What the hell are you doing?'

'Shut up and listen. The Foundation could be building a shiny new cyborg army and, at the moment, we have no way to stop any of it. Feeling sorry for yourself isn't going to do anyone any good. I thought better of you, Bray. Self-pity doesn't suit you. I suggest you quit wallowing and get your head back on the big picture.'

He tries to push her off him but the Rogue is surprisingly strong. 'What do you suggest? What would the Rogue's do? Please enlighten me.'

She leans forward, putting more pressure on his chest. 'For starters talk to Gryffin when he wakes up. Put your anger aside. You need to work with him. You have the leader of the Hunters and the leader of the Nomad on this base. Sit down together, plan how to get Garvan out, and what to do with the cyborg information now that you have it.'

'So you're saying we should break into the Foundation HQ and get Garvan?'

'Yes.'

'Yeah, sure, it's that easy.'

She pushes off him and sits down again. 'This is the time to take the Foundation out. You're not alone, Bray. *Ares* is here. You've got *Perses*. And you've got *Lir* too.'

He looks back at her. 'You? Why would the Rogue's get involved in this mess?'

She shrugs and looks away from him. 'This mess could seriously endanger all of us. There will never be a better time to try. Erin and Avoca know the building. Use that knowledge to our advantage.'

'There's no way I'm involving Erin again.'

'Have you asked her what she wants? From what I've heard, she likes Garvan. She probably wants to get him out as much as you do.'

'As much as I want to get him out, I'm not going to sacrifice my cousin for Garvan.'

'It's not your choice. Believe me, if she feels anything for him she will go to Earth to get him out. What you want won't come into consideration.'

'What the hell do you know about my cousin? You've barely met her.'

She smiles sadly. 'True, but I know family is important, Bray. You and Gryffin are so angry you're missing the point.'

'Which it what exactly?'

'Neither of you have realised you're not angry with each other. He's angry about what happened to him. And who can blame him? All that anger is eating him up and leaps out at anyone who looks at him sideways. As for you — you're angry that the Foundation took your family from you.

'It also doesn't help that you think Gryffin took Terra from you. She was in love with him. He died. He came back. She wanted to be with him. Can you honestly say you wouldn't have done the same? Be angry at her and not him about that. He didn't do anything wrong.' A few minutes go by before she speaks again. 'I had a family once. A pretty amazing family actually.'

Bray looks at her, but her eyes are somewhere else, somewhere in the past. He wants to ask what happened but stays quiet.

She tightens her hands in fists then releases them again, wiping her palms on her trousers. 'Raiders came to our village. I was seventeen and my brother was twenty. My parents tried to stop him from fighting with the other men in the village.'

She smiles and looks down at her hands. 'He was a stubborn fool. Thought he could protect us. They barely looked in his direction as they shot him. One bullet was all it took for my life to change.' She clicks her fingers. 'Just like that. My father raced out to him, but joined him in the dirt. My mother died protecting me. In the space of two minutes, I'd lost everyone I'd ever given a damn about.'

Bray opens his mouth to say something, anything, but can't find the right words.

'They took me and any women left alive back to their ship. After spending a few hours celebrating a successful raid with stolen ale and food, the Captain decided to check out his new pets.' She laughs harshly and shakes her head. 'He was so drunk, one of his men had to help him stagger to my cell. I was dragged out and brought to his room.'

She stops and gets lost in her memories for a moment. 'I'll never forgot the stench as he loomed over me. I reacted and kneed him where it hurt. It was a foolish move. The door was locked and I had nowhere to go, but it felt damn good. Unfortunately, the drink helped dull the pain. He grabbed my hair and threw me on to the floor. He pulled his knife out and...' she glances over at Bray, pointing to the large scar that runs down her face. 'Once he was finished he held the knife to my throat as he...'

She takes a shuddering breath and wraps her arms around herself. Bray feels sick as the realisation of what she endured hits him. He feels the anger boiling inside him.

'Anyway, afterwards, he was so happy with himself, he forgot that he hadn't disarmed. I grabbed the gun from his belt and shot him between the eyes. After I shot him in the dick of course.'

Bray winces and squirms in his chair at the thought. No less than the bastard deserved though. 'How did you get off the ship?'

'I made my way back to the cells and let the others out. It didn't take much to overpower the rest of the crew. By the time their drunken brains realised what was happening they were either dead or restrained. Three of the prisoners were crew from a transport the raiders had attacked the day before. With their help, we brought the ship back home.'

She smiles sadly at Bray. 'It was too late. The raiders had done a good job making sure there were no survivors. So, with nowhere else to go, we decided to stay on the ship. See if we could find somewhere else to live. I'm not sure how it happened but I became the leader of our mismatched group.

'We spent every free minute learning about the ship from the transport crew. The men taught us how to effectively run the vessel ourselves, and after we dropped them back at their world, I was made Captain and the rest is history.'

She meets his eyes again and Bray notices the sadness in the dark green depths. He now understands why she needed to be the one in control and why she was so hostile with him after their night together.

'I didn't tell you that so you'd look at me with pity. I told you that for two reasons. Firstly, to explain why I acted the way I did with you. I...' She sighs and looks at the wall. 'It's been a long time since someone has drawn my interest as much as you do.' She looks over at him again. 'I don't want what happened to be a one off. But I can't promise I won't—'

'Try to kill me after?' Bray finishes.

A small smile plays on her lips. 'Trust will take time. I know you're different, Bray, but past experiences are hard to forget.'

'Hey, I've got a few trust issues myself, believe me. But I'd like to try getting over them. I guess, if you want, we could maybe help each other. Small steps together?'

'Small steps.'

'And the second reason you told me?'

'Yes, the second reason. That's pretty simple.' She nods up at the prone body of Gryffin, lying on the bed above them. 'I'd give anything for my brother to come back from the dead. To have the chance to talk to him again, even for a few minutes. You have what I would give anything to have. Don't waste it.'

∞

DIXON SPACE STATION

Gryffin slowly and painfully breaks the link to the Foundation ship. He has no idea how long he was hooked up, but judging by the gut-wrenching pain that's working through his stomach, it was a few hours. He jumps as a hand brushes his chest.

'Sorry,' Bray says. 'Just unhooking a monitor. You okay?'

Gryffin's only response is to lunge to the side and vomit on the floor.

'I'd say that's a no,' Evie mutters from the head of the bed. 'Is there more of the same coming our way?'

Gryffin nods once, instantly regretting the action. His brain feels like it's too large for his skull. He clutches his head in his hand to keep the top of his skull in place.

He hears someone running towards the room, then a few seconds later soft hands run through his hair. Terra kisses him gently on the forehead. 'Hey, how do you feel?'

'His stomach is a little volatile,' Evie says. 'Probably best to stay away from that end.'

'Has the hook-up caused any issues?'

'So far so good,' Bray says from somewhere behind him. 'But it was a big strain on his system. I'm going to take these readings to Felix to see what he says.' Bray pauses for a moment and squeezes Gryffin on the arm. 'Good job.'

Gryffin nods once. He doesn't trust his stomach right now. He's hooked to computers many times, but never to anything as big or complex as *Cronus*. The bizarre out of body feeling mixed with a severe case of food poisoning topped off with the sensation of being in a free dive on a plummeting ship is making him damn glad he didn't eat much today.

His facial implant is pulsing like it's got its own heartbeat and who knows when his vision will come back online. He concentrates on Terra's hand resting on top of his. Her touch is keeping him from getting sucked to the painful blackness.

He can handle his stomach not behaving. He can handle the blades piercing his skull. It's the blindness that gets him every time. The Scientist had taken days, weeks... sometimes even months to fix his eyes after he messed them up. That time, alone in the dark, was the most terrifying of his years on the station.

He pulls his hand out from under Terra's then grips her hand tightly in his. She squeezes back and he feels her lean over him.

'What can I do?'

'Stay,' is all he manages to say before he leans over the bed again. He retches a few times, but doesn't have the energy to lie back down. Terra helps him back on to the pillow and places something cool on his head.

'Thank you for your help,' Terra says. 'But I can take it from here.' Gryffin hears footsteps fading and the side of the bed tilts as she climbs up beside him. 'Everyone's gone. Roll over.'

'My stomach.'

'I'm all prepared. Just do as you're told and roll over.'

It takes him a few attempts but with her help he manages to roll over and rest his head on her chest.

'Thanks.'

'For what?'

'Getting rid of everyone.'

She runs her hands up and down his arm. 'Don't be silly. Seriously though, are you all right? You're grey.'

'I feel like shit. My head and stomach are spinning in opposite directions. I hate not being able to see.' He swallows and pauses as his stomach flips before he gets a hold on it again. 'Terra. About what I said. About your father.'

She wraps her arm around him and holds him close. 'It doesn't matter.'

He groans and curls against her as a wave of pain hits.

'I've got you. Just close your eyes and try to relax. I have one of your father's books here. He let me borrow it a few weeks ago. With everything that was going on I didn't get a chance to start it. Can I read it to you?'

'It's not one of those romance ones is it?'

She laughs, jostling his head and his unhappy brain. 'No it's not. It's called Treasure Island. It's about pirates and hidden treasure. Think you can handle that?'

'Yes.' He'd listen to anything she read if it distracts him from whatever his body is doing. If he didn't know better, he'd swear the artificial gravity on the ship had failed. The out of body feeling is throwing him. He's not sure which way is up.

He buries his fingers in the mattress so he doesn't fall off the bed. The nausea isn't new. He always got it after he hooked up to a system, but this is taking it to a whole new level.

He clenches his jaw and focuses on Terra's voice as she reads to him. It's either that or he was going to disgrace himself by freaking out and screaming.

∞

OCARRO COLONY

Milla sits on the wooden bench on the porch and watches the rain collecting in already more than ample puddles in the mud. 'What in the world convinced you to settle here?'

Hardy laughs and rests her feet on the railing running around the deck. 'It's bloody miserable, isn't it? But that's part of its charm. Who in their right mind would voluntarily come here? If you're looking for somewhere to disappear, this pile of mud is the perfect spot.' She smiles and gestures behind her. 'Besides, Creed is here. I'll take a bit of mud if it means I get him too.'

Milla may not get the attraction of the colony, but she understands what Hardy means. She left a comfortable Foundation life to join the Nomad so she could be with Chayse. It didn't really matter where they were as long as they were together. 'So, how do you feel about Creed rejoining the Nomad?'

Hardy takes a sip from her bottle and smiles at Milla. 'Couldn't be happier for him. I love that man to death, but he doesn't belong here. Never has. No matter what they say, I fully believe there are some Nomad born into their roles. Gryffin obviously tops that list. You cut that man open and I swear you would find the word NOMAD going right through the centre of him. Creed is just like him in that regard.

'When Rayde sent Gryffin to kill him, he may not have stopped his heart from beating but he killed him nonetheless. Not being a Nomad has destroyed a part of him.'

Milla wraps her coat around her. 'Being a Nomad is something they take seriously, isn't it?'

Hardy nods as she flicks a scary looking bug from her leg. 'That's an understatement. I didn't know him when he was a Nomad, but when he talks about it you can tell how much it meant to him. Every single night he comes out here and raises a glass to the stars. He belongs up there.'

'But taking over the Nomad fleet when things are so... bloody shite.

You must be worried about that.'

'Of course I am. I know there's a strong chance he won't come out the other side of this, but there's no way I'm going to stop him. Gryffin has given him exactly what he never thought he'd have again. If he makes it out the other side in one piece - fantastic. And if he doesn't... Well, I'll know he died doing something he was born to do. Besides, I wouldn't write him off just yet. You've got to remember something.'

'What?'

'Who the hell do you think taught Gryffin to fight? Creed can more than take care of himself. Speaking of Gryffin. Cards on the table. How bad is he?'

Milla takes a drink of her beer before she answers. 'He's running out of time. And I don't mean months, it's weeks at the most. His implants are killing him. It's horrible to watch, Hardy. He's just lying on a cot in a cell. On a good day he's conscious for a few hours. On a bad day I have to keep checking to make sure he's still with us.'

'And his woman? How's she fairing?'

'How do you think? The man she loves is dying in front of her eyes. He wants to be released to *Ares* so he can die without her there to witness the whole thing. The entire situation is depressing as hell.'

'Sounds that way. So what's the big plan here?'

'I don't know. I'm assuming Gryffin told Creed what it is.'

'Indeed he did,' Creed says as he and Chayse join them on the porch. He sits down beside Hardy and drapes his arm across her shoulders. 'Seems I'm hitching a ride off this rock. You too Hardy if you're game.'

'Try to stop me.'

'I don't suppose he gave you anything else to go on?' Milla asks.

'Bits. First thing we got to do is find out what ships we have at our disposal. Chayse, we need to prioritise repairing long-distance comms on your ship. Once we know who's still out there, we can regroup and see if we can get a hold of Gryffin. Ultar is off limits. The

Foundation won't have packed up and left. Now they have the colony, they'll be keen to hang on to it until they get everything they can from it. We'll need to find somewhere uninhabited to get our shit sorted.'

'We have the leader of Ultar onboard. She should know of a planet we can hold up on.'

'Sounds good. So, you two head back to *Nemesis* and make a list of exactly what you need. I want the ship ready to go in ten hours. Hardy, you should be able to source what they're missing.'

'Of course.'

'Okay. We'll meet back here in an hour. Got it?' Chayse and Milla nod. Creed pushes to his feet and runs a hand over his hair. 'That felt strange. Long time since I've given orders. Think I could get used to that again.'

'It suited you, babe.'

He grins at Hardy as he opens the gate leading from the porch. 'Why thank you. Now, Chayse and Milla, your new High Commander just gave you an order. How about you both stop drinking my beer and move.'

26

Gryffin barely suppresses a growl as he examines the specimens in the containment cells. Even the cells on *Alpha* or *Cronus* or whatever the hell the ship is called, are ridiculously lavish. The cells on *Ares* consist of a bare cot, somewhere to take a piss, and not a lot else. The prisoners in front of him had been living in better accommodation than his quarters on *Ares*. The monstrous ship has twenty cells so each of the technicians has their own room. What a fucking joke.

The men and women were unlucky enough to have been on *Alpha* when Bray stole her. Bad luck for the technicians - good luck for them. Well, as long as they were willing to help out. Or could be persuaded to help. Or threatened to help. Gryffin really doesn't care which tactic works. If the technicians could earn their keep they'd stay breathing a little longer. If not, he'd have no issue killing the lot of them, but he doubts that'll be an option he'll be allowed to pick.

They'll either be sent back to Earth or have to spend the rest of their lives in the cells on the station or *Cronus*. Killing them might be the better option.

He walks past each cell, examining the occupants. To look at them you'd never suspect they could do the horrors he knows they're capable of. Were they even aware of the damage they've done? Do they give a damn? Probably not. They wouldn't be part of the team if they had any reservations about the outcome of the project.

His left eye twitches and his vision swims in and out of focus. Hooking up to *Cronus* had taken its toll on him more than he thought it would. He was meant to have a chat with the prisoners twelve hours ago, but instead of only lasting a few short hours, the blindness caused by the link had stretched on for just under eleven hours.

He'd never admit it, but he was terrified it would be a permanent issue. Now he just has to deal with everything else linking up had caused. His eyesight is more temperamental than usual, he's struggling to keep himself upright, and the odds of him being able to eat anything for the rest of the week are slim to none.

But he accessed the system so it was worth it. Or will be if Bray and the Dixon's can find anything of use. Finally his eyesight decides to settle on its usual slightly out of focus vision, distorting the features of the personnel. Not a bad thing. He'd prefer not to remember their faces. 'Can they hear us?'

Bray shakes his head. 'Not until we want them to.'

'You really think they'll talk?'

Bray pauses as he looks at the personnel. 'No clue, but if they do they'll knock months off our plan. Plus, they deserve a bit of one-on-one time with the infamous prototype.'

Gryffin glares over at his brother. The way he feels right now he's going to be a massive disappointment. He's going to have to make this quick and brutal.

'What?' Bray asks. 'It's the least they deserve. They knew what they were getting themselves in to when they joined the project.'

'You think they had a choice?'

'Does that make a difference?'

'No.'

Gryffin takes a step closer to the cells and the Foundation personnel shrink further in the corner. Using their knowledge to help build a program to disarm the cyborgs is a good plan, it's just not one he likes. Or even remotely wants to consider. He doesn't want anything to do with them.

'So, how do you want to play this?' Bray asks.

'Keep shooting them until they agree to work with us.' He nods at the third cell from the left. The man had glared at him when he walked past. 'That one first.'

Bray unlocks the door and Gryffin steps inside. He grabs the man by the neck and carries him out, dropping him on the floor in full view of the other cells. He crouches down in front of him. 'Turn on the sound to the cells.' He waits until Bray nods at him before he speaks again. 'You know who I am?'

The man nods quickly. 'Yes.'

'You know about cyborg programming.'

It's a statement rather than a question, but the man answers anyway. 'You won't get away with this.' His voice is shaky but there's a trace of Foundation arrogance underneath.

Gryffin ignores him and takes the computer console from Bray. He throws it at the man who fumbles to catch it. 'There's a dummy program loaded on that. Tell me what it does.'

'What?'

Gryffin leans closer, his nose almost touching the doctor's. 'Tell me what it does.'

'The Foundation will come for us. You'll be returned to the lab you were created in.'

Gryffin responds by pulling his gun from its holster and shooting the man in the head. He steps over the body and faces the remaining prisoners, each one frozen in silence as they stare at the body of their colleague.

Gryffin wipes the man's blood on his arm, smearing it rather than removing it. The body of their colleague mixed with his glowing purple eye and the smeared blood is doing more than any verbal threats could.

'Who's next?'

Less than half an hour later, Gryffin and Bray step out of the cells with four Foundation personnel shuffling along between them. Desyl and Terra frown as they get closer. 'What happened to the others?' Terra asks.

'I'll talk to you in a minute.'

She comes closer, then notices the blood on his arm. 'Please tell me you didn't.'

'Not now, Terra.'

'What did you do to them?'

Gryffin gestures for Desyl to take his place then grabs Terra by the arm and drags her away from the group. 'What the hell is your problem?'

'You can't kill whenever it takes your fancy. There are rules.'

He shakes his head as he blows out a loud breath. 'Rules? You see the Foundation playing by the rules?'

'So we stoop to their level, is that it? We're not murderers.'

'I am.'

Terra licks her lips and looks away from him. 'Do you really think killing their colleagues in front of them might have brought about their sudden cooperation?'

'Give me a little credit, Terra. I only killed one of them.' He points down the corridor where Desyl led the prisoners away. 'They willingly helped create cyborgs. They did that because they're loyal to the Foundation. Empty threats wouldn't have done a thing. I had to give them incentive to open their damn mouths and talk.'

'You didn't kill them all?'

'No, I didn't. I killed one and roughed a few of them up a little. I don't care about them enough to put them out of their misery. I'm going to keep them locked up wondering what I'm going to do to them, how long they have left to breathe, or how many fingers I'll tear off. Imagination can be a better punishment than anything else I might want to do to them.'

'Sorry. I just don't want us to lose sight of ourselves in all this. The Foundation will stoop to all new lows, we shouldn't do the same. You don't need to resort to violence.'

Those blurred lines rear their heads again which doesn't help his mood. He's not used to people arguing with him. Until *Infinity* arrived in the Sector, his orders were followed without question. All the conversations and questions and discussions are making him irritable - especially when they involve Terra in any way. Being in a relationship with her means he can't just give her an order and not expect her to have something to say about it. He's learning things don't work that way.

'Have you had your fucking eyes shut the whole time you've been on *Ares*?'

'What do you mean?'

'I'm a Nomad. I'll do whatever the hell I have to do to protect my ship and my crew. I don't have limits or a conscience. You have no idea how much I want to go back in that room and put a bullet in each and every one of those... things. I want to see the life drain out of their eyes and know I was the one to end it. If you don't get that, *Ares* isn't the ship for you.'

She takes a step back and swallows. He knows he's scaring her, but right now that's what he wants. She needs to stop seeing the good in everyone and everything. The Foundation sure as hell won't be looking at things that way. She needs to understand and accept that.

'So I have to condone murder or leave *Ares*?'

'I want you to understand how things work on my ship, Terra. You want to stay on *Ares* - great. But if you're on my ship I can't have you getting on my case when I do my job.'

'Right.'

She stuffs her hands in her pockets, something she does when she's upset. A part of him feels a little bad for doing that to her, but she needs to know how things work.

'Whatever we have between us, it needs to stay private. You can't have it both ways. If you want to be treated like a member of the crew you can't undermine me. I don't know how things work in the Foundation, but that's not going to fly with me. I've killed people for disobeying me. The ship comes first.'

'But everyone knows we're together. It's not going to undermine you or your authority.'

'How the hell is questioning me in front of my crew and prisoners not undermining me and my authority?'

Terra clamps her mouth shut and looks away from him.

'Exactly. I don't give a damn that everyone knows we're together. This is about chain of command and following orders. Plain and simple. When we're around my crew, I'm your Captain - nothing more. I don't tolerate being questioned. Understood?'

Terra straightens and pushes her shoulders back. 'Yes, sir. Of course.'

He wants to retaliate to her snapped response, but he can't find the energy right now. She's angry at him and will have to stay that way until he recovers from the link. 'Liaise with the Dixon's. Get some people over from *Ares* to help go through the data.'

'Yes, sir.' She salutes sharply and turns on her heal, storming away from him. Gryffin leans against the wall and watches as she hurries down the corridor. Desyl slowly wanders over and stands beside him.

'Everything okay, sir?'

Gryffin shrugs. 'Sometimes I think things were easier when we didn't allow women on board.'

Desyl grins. 'Maybe, but life would be pretty boring, right?'

'I wouldn't mind some boring.'

'C'mon, sir. Let's go threaten some Foundation personnel. That'll cheer you up.'

∞

NEMESIS

Milla knocks on the door and Aleena looks up from her console. 'Sorry. Am I disturbing you?'

Aleena shakes her head. 'I just reached out to Damon. He is a close friend who runs the colony Gryffin set up as a rendezvous point. It appears most of the fleet has arrived.'

Milla joins Aleena at the unit and asks the question she needs to ask but is afraid to. 'What ships haven't made an appearance yet?'

'*Ares, Epsilon, Styx*... and *Infinity*.'

Milla knows Roman wouldn't have left the surface if his son was still there. There's also no way they would have hung around long after *Ares* left. So either *Ares* didn't leave which means Gryffin didn't leave. Or *Ares* left but Roman, Lucan, and Vance didn't.

The two Nomad vessels were tasked with watching *Ares*' back. If *Ares* left they would have too... unless they were taken down while covering her.

By the look on Aleena's face she's thinking the same thing. Something has happened. Something bad. 'I presume you've tried to raise them on comms.'

'There is no response. I understand they could be out of range, but I have an unsettling feeling about this, Milla.'

'Yeah. Me too. Hang on.' She walks away from Aleena as her comms unit sounds. 'Hey sexy.'

Chayse sighs loudly. 'How about you try calling me captain while I'm standing on the command deck in front of about half a dozen crew.'

She grimaces to herself. 'Ah. Right. Got it. Sorry, Captain.'

'I need you and Aleena up here.'

They walk in silence to the command deck, each one still thinking about the missing ships, missing friends, and missing lovers.

Milla's mood instantly brightens when she sees Chayse at the comms station. He smiles across at her and she knows he has good news.

'What is it?'

'We just received a message from Gryffin.'

Creed plays the message and Gryffin appears on the screen. Milla is amazed how well he looks. The last time she saw him he was withering away. There was no muscle on his bones and his skin was pale and pasty. He's still got a way to go before he's back to how he was when she first met him, but the improvement is incredible.

'He looks terrible,' Creed mutters to himself.

'Actually,' Chayse says. 'He's a hell of a lot better than he was. Believe me, this is a definite plus.'

Creed sucks in a breath. 'Right. Well, let's see what he's got to say for himself.'

'Not sure when or if this will get to you. I'm hoping it will. If it doesn't we're all kind of screwed.'

'Cheery way to start a message,' Milla says.

'*Ares*, *Perses*, and *Lir* are with the Dixon's. We got some intel from Avoca. He gave us the location of a hangar of ships. The ships are connected with the project. Seems the Foundation didn't destroy any of the transports they attacked. They just took the personnel and stored the ships.

'It's Creed's call, but if you wanted to check it out and see what you could get up and running it would help. Beating the Foundation is going to be about strength in numbers. I've given you the coordinates for the hangar and any intel we could find out. Get the ships and make your way back towards the Port. We should be able to talk once you're closer.'

Then the screen goes blank.

'No how are you or any word on the other ships.'

Chayse sits down and pulls up the coordinates Gryffin sent through. 'C'mon, Milla. It's Gryffin. That message was probably the longest one I've ever had from him.'

Creed pulls up another seat and crosses his arms. 'Is there any way of letting him know we got the message?'

'Not yet,' Chayse says as he scans through the data Gryffin sent. 'But that could change. According to this, the hangar is manned. They're bound to have a comms system that can send messages to Earth. Once we have access to that, we can easily contact Gryffin.'

'So does our esteemed leader even know we're in one piece?'

Chayse glances over his shoulder to Creed. 'He's not our leader anymore.'

Milla grins apologetically at Creed. 'Sorry about that. It'll take some getting used to.'

'Not a problem. I still think you're talking about Gryffin too.'

'He knows the ship is still transmitting, but that doesn't mean any of us are still alive,' Chayse says as he continues to read the data.

'So for all he knows we could be a pair of attractive corpses together forever in death.' Milla looks up to see Creed and Chayse both wearing strange expressions. 'What? I was trying to be poetic.'

'You were being weird and a little creepy,' Chayse says.

Creed nods. 'I've got to agree with Chayse. Weird and creepy.'

She waves her hand in front of them. 'Focus gentlemen,' she says trying to take the attention off herself. 'So are we going shopping for some new ships?'

Creed stares at the screen and scratches his jaw. 'Fuck it. I could do with my own ship. Don't reckon you'd fancy having the High Commander hitching a ride with you for the foreseeable future.'

Chayse clearly doesn't know the right way to respond so he just looks at Creed.

'Relax, Captain. I want my own ship, and no, I have no intention of stealing yours. Set a course for the coordinates. Aleena, I don't suppose you've had any luck with your friend?'

She shakes her head. '*Infinity*, *Styx*, and *Epsilon* are still unaccounted for. The ships that have arrived are being repaired as best they can with the supplies they have. Damon is happy for the colonists to remain there for safety until the Foundation issue is dealt with. He will notify me when the ships are ready for launch.'

Creed nods and gets up to join Chayse. Milla sits down beside Aleena and squeezes her hand. She doesn't bother offering her any empty platitudes. There's no point. They both know the odds of the three missing ships arriving in one piece is slim at best.

∞

DIXON SPACE STATION

'I heard the little motivational speech you gave Terra,' Evie says as soon as Gryffin steps inside the med bay. 'Why were you so hard on her? She's only saying those things because she cares about you.'

'It's got nothing to do with you.'

'Oh, that's where you're wrong, dear. You can glare at me all you want, but I'm going to say my piece.' He turns to leave but she steps in front of him. 'You're going to have to physically move me.'

Even though he's tempted to swat the irritating woman aside, he thinks better of it. 'You call me here to check my implants or for a talk?'

'Bit of both I suppose.'

'What do you want?'

'I want you to admit you're afraid.'

'Of you?'

She waves his comment aside. 'Not of me you silly man, although that would be quite a feather in my cap, wouldn't it? No, I mean you're afraid of losing her.'

'No, I'm not.'

Evie laughs, pushing her wide brimmed hat back from her forehead. 'You can deny it as much as you want, but I can see the truth in your eyes.' She frowns at the floor. 'Well, I can see it in your eye. That robotic one is impossible to read. Anyway, it would probably save everyone a lot of time and arguments if you just admitted you love her.'

Gryffin doesn't have a reply for that. Terra tells him a lot that she loves him. He's never said it to her and he knows it's getting to Terra. He'd tell her if he knew... but he doesn't.

Evie must see something in his expression because she clasps her hands in front of her and nods slowly. 'You don't know, do you?'

'You done yet?'

She takes a step closer and leans back to look up at him. 'You poor thing. What happened in your past to keep you and your emotions so far from each other?'

'My past is none of your damn business. And neither is my relationship with Terra.'

'True, but when I see two people on a destructive path, it's hard to keep my nose out of their business. You need to figure out what that girl means to you before it's too late.'

'She can't keep questioning me. If any of my crew did it, they'd only do it once.'

'Well I have a feeling that may have been the last time she attempts that. I doubt she'd be eager to have you put her back in her place like that again.'

'How I deal with my crew is my business.'

'That is true, but from what I have heard, she's not a full member of your crew yet. Nor is she a Nomad. She was born on Earth under Foundation rule.'

'So was I.'

Evie nods slowly and looks at the ground. 'Grew up there. Their rules, their regulations are embedded in her. Have been since she was old enough to understand them. Her principles are very different from yours. From ours even. She wants the Foundation taken down just as much as we do, but in a very different way.'

'There's only one way. The leaders of the Council have to die.'

'We know that, but I doubt she'll agree so easily. She wants this to end, but not by killing left, right, and centre. I imagine she will want a peaceful finish if at all possible. You may need to meet in the middle somewhere.'

'How can there be a middle between not killing them and killing them?'

She scratches her head and readjusts her hat as she shrugs. 'Don't know. You probably should figure it out before it's too late though.'

'Thanks,' he replies sarcastically.

'And speaking of too late, when are you going to let the real you out?'

'The real me?'

'You're not going to try to convince me that this person in front of me is The Gryffin I've heard so much about? After all the work you've done for us I know you're holding back for some reason. Don't get me wrong, you look intimidating to a certain extent, but you're missing the fire in your belly. Or it's been extinguished, not sure what happened.

'All I know is that it's not there anymore and it sure as hell should be.' She sucks in a breath and covers her mouth. 'I trust you won't tell Felix about my little slip up. I try to keep this base as civilised as I can.'

'I don't understand you.'

She smiles widely and rests her hands on her hips. 'I'll take that as a compliment. I'm not trying to be cruel or kick you when you're down. I just know there's a lot more to you than you're letting show right now.'

'You want me to go on a rampage?'

'Not on my station. But it could help with taking down the Foundation. I understand that you have perhaps mellowed thanks to Terra's influence, and that's an achievement in itself. However, mellow is not what's needed right now. Don't be afraid to use who you are in the fight against the bad guys.'

'You're telling me to embrace the cyborg side? I snapped the neck of the last person who told me to do that.'

She jumps from foot to foot as she claps. 'Wehey! That's exactly what I'm talking about. Let that side out again. And no, I am not saying to embrace it and ignore the man. I'm saying use it. Use it against the people who hurt you. Use it against the people who are still doing this to other innocents. Use their weapon against them. Use their weapon to destroy them. Captain, I have no idea what it must be like to live as you do. No idea what it must be like to have parts of myself replaced as if they meant nothing.'

'You trying to get in my head?'

'No, Gryffin. I am trying to be serious with you if you'll allow me.'

'Do I have a choice?'

'No. I am trying to say that... I am sorry for what you've been through. I shudder when I allow myself to think about the procedures. I am also a little embarrassed to admit I didn't allow myself to think about it. Meeting you has raised a question with me. I was wondering, Captain how do you see yourself?'

'What the hell are you talking about?'

'Human or perhaps less than human?'

Gryffin licks his lips, unwilling to even go there with her. He hasn't gone there with anyone.

'I consider you human. Perhaps before I met you I didn't. But I've changed my perception. You are absolutely human, Gryffin. Modified, yes, but still very much human.'

'Why are you telling me this?'

'I believe you may need to hear it. You have feelings, Gryffin. Feelings you need to respect and acknowledge. You are not a machine. I may be incorrect, and please do not feel like you have to correct me, but I suspect you may think of yourself as less than human because of your modifications.'

He doesn't respond. There's enough going on in his head without pulling himself into a conversation like this.

'In one of your chatty moods I see. That's quite a skill, Captain. Can you teach my dear husband how to not argue back when I'm giving him advise?'

'What do you want?'

'I know you're facing a difficult decision. I suppose I'm just saying that you yourself are an important factor in this decision. Your feelings are an important factor. Whatever decision you make, don't forget that.'

'You're saying I should have my implants upgraded?'

Evie shrugs and stuffs her hands in the pockets of her skirt. 'No one can make that decision except for you, Captain. What I can say is that if you do decide to go that way, we will be able to facilitate you.'

'You can finish me?'

'You're hardly unfinished right now. Apart from your obvious lack of an arm of course.'

'You know what I mean.'

She pauses then nods. 'Yes, I do and yes we can. My dear husband and I examined your scan data in detail. We can stabilise the control implant with the help of some upgrades. It would override certain areas of your brain, however. In layman's terms your personality - as delightful as it is - could be pushed aside.'

'Temporarily or permanently?'

'When it comes to the brain who knows anything for sure. I think that if this is an option you are considering, it would be best to presume it will be permanent. Anything other than that will be a bonus.'

He thought as much. When he was used to attack Ultar he was under control of the implant. He fucking hated it. He remembers everything he did but couldn't stop it. 'Can you create a kill switch?'

Evie frowns at him. 'If you believe that is necessary, yes. We can make sure there is one in place. Are you saying you're seriously thinking about this?'

'Yes, but I want there to be something in place if it goes wrong. The last thing you need is four hostile cyborgs on your station.'

She nods solemnly, the usual mischievous grin wiped from her face. 'Very well. Leave it with us. If you decide to go down this path, we'll make sure everything is ready.'

'Keep it to yourself for now. I'll tell her once I know for sure.' Evie nods and strolls out of the room. Is he seriously considering doing this? Death is a preferable option, but that's not going to help the Nomad. Staying alive and fighting for them - that's all he has left.

27

Terra straightens her shoulders and clears her throat as she approaches Bray. She spotted him seconds too late to make a convincing escape. The Hunter stops at the top of the stairs and looks over at her.

'Hi Bray.'

He turns away from her without acknowledging her. 'The silent treatment. Really? You've been taking lessons from your infuriating brother.'

'What do you want, Terra?'

'I just wanted to talk to you. We haven't had a chance to speak properly since *Ares* arrived. Things got a little crazy on Ultar after...'

'After you told me you loved my brother and not me? I'm fine.'

'Please, Bray. I don't want things to be awkward between us. Or between you and Gryffin.'

'You dumped me for my brother! How could things be anything

but awkward? I'll work with you, but that's it. And as for Gryffin, my relationship with my brother has nothing to do with you.'

He pushes past but she follows him. 'I don't want to leave things like that.'

He stops suddenly, startling her. 'I don't give a damn what you want. What is it with you, huh? You always think it's about you.' He winces and turns his head away.

'What's wrong?'

Bray wipes a smear of blood from his eye and blinks a few times. 'Your father's handy work.'

'Bray—'

'Don't, Terra. I've got bigger problems at the moment than having you on the same station as me. It's done, Terra. I don't have a problem with you or with Gryffin because of you. The only thing on all our minds should be how to get Garvan out and stop the Foundation. There's no time to worry about you and how you feel.'

'I didn't mean to—'

'Why are you even bothering with this?' he interrupts. 'You should be worrying about Gryffin and how the hell we're going to save him. He is your main priority after all.'

Bray storms away leaving Terra feeling like he punched her in the gut. She knew he'd be less than friendly with her but she never thought he'd be outright aggressive.

She wanders back down the corridor and away from Bray. As she walks, the realisation of what she just did hits her. Bray is right. There are so many more important things to be concerned with other than a failed relationship. What was she thinking even bringing it up? Bray just found his family and lost his best friend on top of everything her father did to him. That conversation with her was the last thing he needed.

She grabs onto the nearest door frame as her stomach rolls and she has to fight to keep it under control. Her father has too much to answer for. His jealous revenge turned to madness and is still hurting people to this day. His legacy will haunt her until she dies and no matter what happens, Gryffin and Bray will never fully recover from what he did. She honestly doesn't know how either of them can stomach looking at her.

Instead of walking towards the med bay, she turns back on herself again. She needs some time alone on *Ares*. She stumbles to a stop when she hears a scream coming from the corridor ahead of her.

Bray's scream.

She races around the corner and finds Bray lying on the floor with his head in his hands. She drops to her knees beside him, trying to pry his hands away, but he won't let go.

'Bray! Can you hear me?'

His only response it to throw his head back, hitting if off the ground as he roars in pain. Blood drips from his ears and the corner of his left eye. She brushes her hand against his implant and hisses as it burns her. Terra looks at the small crowd gathered behind her.

'Stop standing there! Get help! Now!'

∞

DIXON SPACE STATION

Sayber rests his hands on the edge of Bray's bed and takes a deep breath. Bray is finally resting. He never wants to hear screams like that again. The last time he saw something like that was when he saved Gryffin's life after the Nomad attacked his ship. Seeing his enemy covered in blood, writhing in pain on the floor was an unsettling experience that will stay with him.

Evie throws the pressure syringe on the counter then pulls off her hat to run a hand through her wiry hair, further releasing the messy locks. 'That should knock him out for a few hours.'

'Thanks, I don't think he could have coped for much longer,' Sayber says.

'What happened?' Rua asks. The Rogue had arrived at the scene of Bray's incident a few minutes after Terra, and, unlike the Commander, she has refused to leave.

'I'm still trying to figure it out.'

'Is it his eye?' Morgan asks. 'He's been struggling with it since he got to the Sector.'

Sayber glares over his shoulder at him. 'Struggling how?'

'He didn't say much, but it's clear he's been in pain. On the journey from Earth it was bleeding... you know, from under the metal. He tried to hide it.' Morgan rubs a hand over his face and curses. 'I was too focused on Erin to give it a second thought.'

Sayber snorts. 'Wouldn't have done any good. His arm could be falling off and he'd never say a word. Damn stubborn fool. Just like his brother.'

Erin bursts through the door, freezing when she sees Bray. 'Is he...?'

Sayber shakes his head. 'No, he's alive. Something's wrong with his eye or the implant around it.' Before she can ask any more questions, Sayber turns to Evie. 'Any ideas?'

She takes a scanner off the counter and moves Bray's head so the implant is facing up. Sayber's stomach churns when he sees blood oozing from around the implant to cover the left side of Bray's face. Evie wipes some of the blood away, but it keeps coming.

'What the hell is wrong with him?' he asks a little louder than he intended.

'Patience.' Evie spends the next few minutes examining Bray. After what feels like a lifetime, she straightens. 'What colour are his eyes?'

'Brown,' Rua answers immediately, surprising everyone. Seems the Rogue and Bray have got up close and personal at some stage. 'His eyes are brown.'

Evie nods. 'Interesting.'

Sayber opens his mouth to give the woman a verbal kick, but she raises her hand and wiggles her finger at him. 'It's interesting because he now has blue eyes.'

'Eyes don't just change colour,' Morgan says.

'True. Organic eyes don't just change colour... but cybernetic ones can.'

'You've lost me.'

Evie smiles sweetly at Sayber. 'Not a difficult task from what I can tell. I'll explain in simple terms. Brayden's eyes are artificial. Well... not fully artificial. His right eye is organic with cybernetics inside it. His left eye has more in common with my scanner than a human eye. From what I can tell, the cybernetics have only just come online.'

'How is that possible?' Sayber asks.

She shrugs. 'How would I know? I didn't design the implants. Perhaps it was working, but only reached fully operating status now. I imagine the sensation would have been painful. Poor mite probably felt like his head was being split open.'

Erin takes Bray's hand. 'His eyes changed colour when we were taking *Alpha*. They must have changed back again.'

'Whatever's going on with him may have been taking a bit of time to adjust.'

'Is he going to be okay?' Erin asks.

'Again with the questions,' Evie says. 'Is the eyepiece the only modification he has?'

Sayber shakes his head. 'Chest too.'

He helps Evie pull Bray's t-shirt up and steps back to give her room. After less than a minute she shakes her head. 'Well, seems he's taking after his brother. It's operational.'

'In what way?' Morgan asks.

'His heart rate is being controlled.'

'Damn it!' Sayber shouts, kicking the wall beside him. 'He's had them for a year. Why would this happen now? This can't be a coincidence.'

'Shocking thought, but I actually agree with you.'

Sayber bares his teeth at the small woman. 'Thanks,' he replies sarcastically.

She walks around the table and pats him on the arm. 'You're welcome, dear. I think it would be best if I give him a thorough examination. Get Felix in here. I'll call you when we're finished.'

'I'm staying.'

She shakes her head at Sayber. 'You are most certainly not staying.' She points to Rua. 'She can keep an eye on Bray. Go now.' She ushers them all from the room and the door shuts in his face. Sayber rests his forehead against the metal and closes his eyes. He jumps slightly when he feels a hand on his shoulder.

Morgan smiles apologetically at him. 'You look like you could do with a drink.'

'You read my mind.'

∞

FOUNDATION HQ

Garvan's heart races, threatening to burst out of his chest when the door to the lab hisses open. He clenches his fist, digging his fingernails in the palm of his remaining hand. He barely notices the pain. He's about to lose his brain to a machine. Pain is going to be a constant in his life in a few minutes.

He tries to slow his breathing as he listens, but the mystery guest remains silent. It definitely can't be Harvey. That man couldn't stop gloating if his life depended on it. He turns to look towards the door, but he can't move his head far thanks to the strap around his neck. He licks his dry lips and waits.

A few seconds later a guard moves into his line of vision. The guard is new. Very new if the expression of confusion mixed with a dollop of horror on his face is anything to go by. 'You want something or just like what you see?'

The frown deepens and the guard takes another step towards the gurney. He tilts his head to the side and looks down at Garvan. Instead of saying anything, he shakes his head then lifts the gun in his hand, slowly at first then faster as the door opens again. He dives out of view. Garvan doesn't know what's happening and he really couldn't care less.

He hears two of the doctors entering the room, muttering to each other. No doubt about what piece to take off his body next. One of the doctors steps up to him and pulls the side of the bed out. Garvan's restrained arm moves out with the edge of the bed, giving the doctor clear access to what's left of his limb. He swallows the rising bile and focuses on the ceiling, willing his brain to get with the program and knock him out.

The doctor freezes then crumples to the ground. He hears a dull thud to this left as another body hits the ground. The guard appears again and pulls a blade from his jacket. He grips Garvan's arm and slips the tip of the blade in the flesh on the underside of his arm.

Garvan hisses and the guard digs around for a few seconds before he pulls the knife out. He picks up the tiny Foundation transmitter from the tip of the blade, places it on the counter beside him and crushes it under his gun. He returns to the table and fumbles with the locks. Once Garvan is free, the guard disappears from view again.

'Get up.'

Garvan would like nothing more than to comply, but even moving his eyes is a struggle. He turns his head to the side, and watches in confusion as the guard secures the doctors to a unit with sets of restraints. He tucks his gun in his waistband and faces the table again.

'You have to get up.'

He rolls on to his side and, after three failed attempts, balances on the edge of the bed. He squeezes his eyes shut as his head pounds. He barely manages not to disgrace himself all over the floor. He looks up as the guard takes his arm and helps him off the table. He supports Garvan's weight as he adjusts to being upright again. Ignoring the painful protests from his abused body, he puts one foot in front of the other, but progress is slow and painful.

The guard props him against the wall then opens the door, checking both sides of the corridor. 'We're good. Time to go.'

Garvan shakes his head to try and clear his vision. 'Be right with you.'

The guard stands in front of him and keeps checking the corridor to either side. 'I know you're in pain, but you have to help me get you out of here. I can't carry you.'

Garvan nods. 'I hear you.' Everything tilts, but he manages to stay upright as the man ducks under his arm and leads him out to the corridor. The guard lowers Garvan to the floor outside the maintenance lift as one of the cyborgs comes around the corner. The man fires at her, hitting her in the arm.

'Target her eye.' The guard does as Garvan says and the next round takes her down. 'There'll be more coming.'

Garvan is guided through the endless maze of tunnels, and again, finds himself completely lost. It takes him a good five minutes to realise he's not being taken to the lab.

The guard takes him to a large underground parking lot and directs him over to a maintenance transport sitting in a corner. Before he can ask what the hell is going on, the side door opens and he is unceremoniously shoved inside.

The guard opens a large crate labelled LAUNDRY. 'Get inside.'

'What?'

'If you want to get out of here in one piece, get in there and keep quiet.'

Garvan looks from the guard to the crate and back again. 'A laundry truck? You're seriously breaking me out in the back of a laundry truck?'

'Do you want to get out or not?'

Garvan shrugs. 'Last time it was a garbage truck. Guess this is a step up.' He climbs inside and shuffles down so the guard can close the lid.

The transport starts and Garvan spends the next who knows how long being thrown around the inside of the crate like a damn rag doll. Anything that didn't hurt before, hurts now and he may have picked up a case of claustrophobia on the way.

The transport eventually comes to a stop and the lid is taken off the crate. Garvan pulls himself over the side and unceremoniously lands on the floor of the transport. He lies on his back breathing in fresh air as he tries to convince his stomach and his pitiful last meal to stay friends. After a few deep breaths, they come to a slightly uneasy truce and he sits up.

The guard is sitting on a fence beside the transport, staring at him with a confused look on his face. Garvan wants to get up and get the hell out of here, but he barely has the energy to stay awake let alone stand. He sits on the cold metal floor and looks around the forested area outside the transport.

Tall trees line a narrow track winding through the forest. He immediately thinks of Ultar. He didn't realise such an unspoilt area still existed on Foundation Earth. He breathes in the earthy tones surrounding him and can't help but smile. The trees sway in the gentle breeze and the birds fill the air with their song. It's heaven after where he's just been.

He looks back at the guard, but half of his face is hidden under the shadow of his cap. 'Didn't know—' he stops as a coughing fit wracks his body. He winces, squeezing his eyes shut as the pounding returns. 'I didn't... know the Foundation took prisoners on field trips. Not that

I'm ungrateful, just wondering what exactly is going on here.'

The guard slowly takes off his cap, showing Garvan his face. A name instantly comes out even though he knows it makes no sense to say it. 'Zeke?'

A small smile tugs on the man's lips and he nods slowly. 'Hey, Dad.'

DIXON SPACE STATION

Bray feels too big for his body. He doesn't have a better way to describe it. The pain has dulled, but it's still there. A band of pressure squeezes his eyes and around the back of his head. He doesn't even attempt to open his eyes. He's quite happy in the dark.

He gingerly lifts his arm off the bed and moves his hand up his chest. His fingers brush against the plate on his bare chest and he bites back the groan of pain. He swears there's a weight thumping against the plate, keeping perfect time with his heartbeat.

'You okay?'

Bray inwardly groans at the sound of Gryffin's voice. 'What do you want?'

Leather creaks as the Nomad moves to his left. 'Terra told me to stay until you woke up. Wasn't worth arguing with her.'

Bray laughs, instantly wishing he hadn't. He licks his dry lips and takes deep breaths to calm the thumping in his head. On top of everything else, something must have crawled in his mouth and died while he was asleep. 'Yeah well you can go. I'm fine.'

Gryffin actually has the nerve to laugh at his comment. 'That's my line. Whether you like it or not, I can help you. Open your mouth. I've got some water.'

Even though he wants his brother to leave, he wants the water more. Bray greedily sucks the liquid through the straw before rolling onto his back again. 'Damn it. What's wrong with me?'

He hears Gryffin take a long, deep breath and instantly knows he's in trouble. 'Your implants have come online. Technically, you're an operational cyborg. The Dixon woman examined you when you were out. The mods the Scientist gave you were dormant, not obsolete. Don't know why, but they've come to life. Your left eye is artificial, but it's a damn good copy. Far more hi-tech than mine. Until the mechanics turned on, it looked real. Your other eye is like mine too - real outside with components inside.'

Gryffin's words echo in Bray's head. His worst nightmare has come true. 'What else?' he whispers.

'Chest plate is on too. It's regulating and supporting your heart. The Dixon's don't have anything that can help remove or undo it at the moment.'

'So, you're saying I just have to suck it up?' Bray replies sarcastically.

'Yes.'

Bray pushes up to his elbows, groans in pain, then flops back on the bed. 'I can't just accept what was done to me and move on.'

'You have to. Nothing you can do to change it. Believe me.'

'I'm not human anymore, Gryffin. That's a fucking big deal.'

Gryffin silently watches him for a minute. 'You don't think you're human now?'

'Of course not. Well, not fully.'

'Right. I've got a hell of a lot more components than you do. What the fuck does that make me?'

Bray turns away from him. All the answer he needs.

,'Stop feeling sorry for yourself, Bray. You've got two state-of-the-art eyes. If you'd stop whining and open them, you'd realise it's not that bad. Open your eyes.' Bray instinctively squeezes them shut. 'Damn it, Bray. You're worse than useless if you can't even open your eyes. You're a Hunter. Start acting like it.'

'This has nothing to do with being a Hunter! I'm a cyborg. I didn't ask for any of this. I just want to be myself again.'

'If you're looking for a hug you're talking to the wrong person.' The edge of the bed tips as Gryffin leans on it. 'You're no good to the Hunters if you're lying in a bed. Open your eyes!'

'Leave me the hell alone!'

Gryffin's hand clamps around his neck, cutting off his air supply. He leans on Bray, pushing him back in to the bed. 'You either open your eyes or I'll keep squeezing 'till your neck snaps. Your choice.'

Bray ignores the band of pain spreading across his chest and forces his lids up. He blinks, trying to clear his vision. Images swim and tilt as his new eyes assault his brain with information. He slams a hand against his left eye and the sensation slows to a more bearable level. Everything looks clearer, more defined, like he's looking at the world through a high-resolution lens.

Gryffin's face appears in front of him and he releases Bray from his grip. 'Well?'

Bray rams his fist in Gryffin's jaw, but the damn man barely flinches. Acting as if the punch never happened, Gryffin pulls Bray's hand from his eye. Bray curses and tears his hand from Gryffin's grip to cover his eye as the stomach churning sensation hits him again. He breathes through his nose and swallows deeply. 'Can't do the left eye. It's too...'

'Weird?'

Bray nods, regretting the movement as soon as he makes it.

Gryffin sits down in the chair and massages the skin above his metal covered stump. 'Your brain will learn to deal with your eye.' He taps the side of his ocular implant. 'It was maybe a week or so until I got the hang of this.'

How his brother can talk about his implants like he's talking about a ship report he doesn't know. 'Great. Something to look forward to.'

Gryffin leans forward, bringing himself closer to Bray. 'Look at my eye.'

'I'm not in the mood—'

'Will you just shut up with your complaining and look at it?'

Bray sighs and focuses on Gryffin's robotic eye. 'You want me to compliment your eyes or something?'

Gryffin sighs and glares at Bray. When he looks at Gryffin's eye he sees the inner workings spinning slowly. 'What are you doing?'

'It'll take getting used to, but you'll be able to zoom in and out. Everything else is the same as a normal eye. You'll just have to train yourself to use it.'

'Let me guess — after a while I won't even notice it's not real, right.'

'No. But it's what you've got.' He gets up and throws a shirt at Bray. 'You can't get Garvan back if you're wallowing in bed. As much as I don't want to say it, we need to work together to tear them apart. That means you getting your shit together. You're a cyborg. That stopped being a big deal months ago. We're all over the damn place now.'

He holds his hand out. Bray stares down at Gryffin's outstretched hand and wonders if his vision is messed up more than he thought. Gryffin doesn't touch people unless absolutely necessary. Offering his hand to anyone, let alone a Hunter, is one hell of a shock.

Bray squints as he tries to focus on Gryffin's hand. His vision clears and Bray can make out details he never noticed before. Small scars and scratches in the palm of Gryffin's hand, tiny cracks in the leather cuff wrapped around his wrist, tool marks from whatever was used to fix the rivets holding the cuff in place. He can see it all like he's looking at it magnified.

'Useful isn't it.'

Bray accepts Gryffin's gesture and takes his hand. Gryffin pulls him out of bed but the room tilts, forcing him back against the edge of the bed so he doesn't fall on his ass.

'It's no good if I can't stand up without everything spinning.'

'Won't last. Just got to force your body to deal with it.' Gryffin sits back down on the chair and stretches his legs out. 'What the hell you waiting for. Walk.'

'What if I fall on my ass?'

'Get up and go again. I'll stay in case you knock yourself out when you fall. I'm not going to hold your fucking hand though.'

'You'd make a great motivational speaker, you know that?'

'You had no control over what was done to you. None of us did. This part you have control over. The implants are painful. Nothing you can do about that. The only thing you can do is put one fucking foot in front of the other and force your body to deal with the mods. It's what I've done for over two decades.'

Bray doesn't want to think about having operational implants for two days let alone two decades. Gryffin has a point though which doesn't help his mood. If he can deal with dozens of implants for as long as he has, Bray can deal with his two.

Bray opens his eyes again, swallowing to keep his stomach from showing him up, then puts on foot in front of the other.

∞

ARES

Gryffin sits in his command chair and leans back against the worn leather. From his seat he watches Heath's men working in the cargo hold of *Cronus*. The larger ship may be more sophisticated, more powerful than *Ares*, but he wouldn't swap. Tried and tested is better than new and unproven. Kind of like his mods and those of the new cyborgs. And now Bray's implants.

It shouldn't bother him that Bray's implants came online, but it does. Whether it's the fact there's another cyborg or because he's his brother, he doesn't know. It's probably the former.

He looks down at his stump and pulls the casing off the end. Still to this day, the sight of the crude connectors sticking out of what's left of his arm turns his stomach. He forces himself to keep looking. Forces himself to relive how he lost the limb in the first place.

It's time he stops fooling himself. Since the minute Rayde found him, he's been living a lie, pretending to be something he's not, and all it's done is prolong the agony for himself and those around him. The creature the Scientist created out of the remains of Daegan Sawyer was meant to be an emotionless cyborg.

When Rayde saved him, he threw that thing to a world it was never meant to be part of. Even if they do manage to take off the implants and rebuild his body, it's still a lie. Those body parts are no different to the implants. They would be made in a lab and fitted to him. The ones he was born with are gone forever.

He massages his thigh as a dart of pain shoots up his rotting leg. As much as he doesn't want to admit it, his leg needs to go too. It's beyond saving. Gryffin runs his hand down the worn leather arm of the command chair. He knows the decision he's come to is the right one, but he's not looking forward to the upcoming conversations as a result.

He hears Terra coming a few minutes before she arrives on the command deck. She stops in front of him and leans against the railing. 'You wanted to see me, Captain.'

Great start. She's still angry at him. Then again, maybe it's better to tell her while she's already pissed off at him.

She frowns at him when he doesn't respond. 'You okay?'

Gryffin wants to get up and hold her. He'd give his other arm to have one more night with her, to feel her soft skin, to taste her, to look in her eyes as she moans his name and tears at his back with her nails. But that's in the past. No matter how much he wants her, she won't want him. Not after the upcoming chat.

She crouches down in front of him and squeezes his leg. 'Hey, you're worrying me. What's wrong? Are you feeling okay?'

He focuses on the wall behind her head and forces the words out. 'I'm having my mods upgraded. It's the only way we have any chance of getting near the Foundation, let alone of taking them down. If the upgrade works, there's a chance I might be able to control the Foundation cyborgs too.'

She gets to her feet and takes a step back from him. 'Right.'

'Felix and Evie can do it. They have the equipment here.'

'So you've spoken to them?'

'Yes.'

'Right. Can I ask what exactly you're planning to have done?'

'The plan is to fix my arm and leg, upgrade my chest implant, fit a new ocular implant, and some other small bits and pieces.' He's not going to mention anything about his leg. There's a slim chance the Dixon's will be able to fix it. Very slim. Non-existent odds, but it's best she doesn't know ahead of time.

'So that's that. The decision is made?'

Gryffin gets up and has to hold on to the back of his chair as his leg complains. 'I don't want to live like this anymore.'

'But you want to live with more mods?'

'I don't want that either, but at least that way I'll be good for something.'

She hurries over to him and grabs a fistful of his shirt. 'You're good for something now. You don't need to do this to help defeat the Foundation. '

He wipes the tears from her face, hating that he's the reason they're there in the first place. 'I want what's left of my life to mean something. I want to do this. I want to help.'

He steps back from her. 'I've been on borrowed time since Rayde found me. The implant in my head should have killed me years ago. I need to finish this. I need to have a hand in fighting the Foundation before...' he stops himself a little too late.

'Before you die.'

'Yes. You're not an idiot, Terra. Can you honestly look at me and say I'm okay?'

Terra turns away from him which is all the answer he needs. Gryffin takes her chin in his hand and tilts her face towards his. 'I'd hate myself if I was in a stasis pod waiting on the off chance I could be put back together while everyone I give a damn about is killed by the people who did this to me in the first place.'

Terra wipes her hand across her face and sniffs. She nods a few times then looks back at him. 'And what about *Ares*?'

'Until I come out the other side I won't know if I'll be able to captain her. Desyl's going to have to take over.'

'Have you told him about any of this?'

'Not yet. I'm going to make an announcement, but I wanted to speak to you and Desyl first. I've also stepped down as High Commander.'

'You have? Who have you appointed?'

'Creed. I worked with him years ago. He was Rayde's first officer, but he's a good one. Rayde sent me to kill him years ago as part of my training. I pretended to and got him off the ship instead. He should be on *Nemesis* with Chayse and Milla.'

'So you sent them to get him when Ultar was attacked? You've been planning this for a while.'

He shakes his head. 'Not the upgrade part. I needed to make plans for my successor either way. Creed was the obvious choice. He's a good Nomad and nothing like Rayde. He'll keep the group heading in the right direction.'

She nods again and the silence between them remains unbroken for a few minutes. Even though his leg is killing him, Gryffin stays where he is, unwilling to disturb Terra and her thoughts.

Eventually she steps up and wraps her arms around him. Surprised, Gryffin hugs her back. Maybe she will be able to accept his decision after all.

'When is this planned for?'

'The Dixon's want me to have another few sessions in the rejuvenation pod before they do anything. The plan is to work on us in two days.'

'Us?'

'Boone, Trace, and Dante are going to have work done too. If we're going up against the new cyborgs, we all need to be improved. Boone has a wife and kid in the Sector. He wants to be able to finish this so he can go back to them and get some of his life back.'

'And what about the control implant? Do the Dixon's have any idea what it will do to you?'

'There's a strong chance it will take over. Anything less is a bonus apparently.'

She nods slowly. 'One way deal then.'

'Yeah. Until I get the upgrades they won't know for sure.' His leg decides it's had enough and he drops back in his chair and stretches it out in front of him.

'You okay?'

'Fucking leg is agony. Terra, you've got to understand I'm heading towards a shit decision either way. They bought me some time but I've only got a few days before I'll have to either be put in a stasis pod, get the upgrades, or turn off my implants. Out of those three I'll go for the upgrades.'

'Days? I thought the rejuvenation pod helped?'

'It made me strong and repaired my body but it can't help the implants that are attacking my body. They're what's killing me.'

Terra leans against the railings and hugs her arms to her chest. Keeping his emotions out of this isn't working. Terra's hurting and it's down to him. The damn blurred lines are kicking his ass again. Gryffin, Captain of *Ares* knows it's the right decision. But the Gryffin who is with Terra has serious doubts. Unfortunately, that's the side of himself he has to ignore, as much as it's going to hurt himself and hurt Terra.

'Okay.'

He frowns across at her. 'Okay what?'

'I understand why you think you have to go this way. I love you, Gryffin. I always will. But if you're looking for my blessing, I don't think I can give it to you.'

Looks like his first instinct was bang on. 'What are you saying?'

She grips the railing behind her and shrugs. 'I don't know. I... I honestly don't know, Gryffin. I want the Foundation gone as much as you do, but you're asking too much. You really want me to stand by and watch as the man I love allows himself to have more implants put on him, to have his head cut open and metal put inside, to have someone else control what he does? How can you honestly expect me to be okay with that?'

'I don't want this to happen any more than you do, but I can't see another option.'

'I know.' She smiles and steps over to him. 'I just need a little time to process all this. Is that okay?'

'Yes.'

She leans down and kisses him briefly on the cheek before hurrying out of the room. Gryffin stares down the corridor long after her footsteps have disappeared. He gets the horrible feeling that marked the start of the end for them.

∞

DIXON SPACE STATION

Terra fills her cup with coffee from the dispenser and wanders over to a table at the edge of the room. Feeling someone looking at her, she glances around the room, coming to a stop when she meets Evie's eyes. Terra smiles at the woman and goes back to her drink. A few seconds later, she lifts her head to find the woman looking at her again. Evie slowly gets to her feet and walks over to Terra's table. She settles in the seat opposite her and clasps her hands together.

After a long silence, Terra frowns at her. 'Is something wrong?'

Evie examines her nails as she shrugs. 'Not wrong as such, but I do believe there is a problem.'

'Are you going to share your thoughts with me or just leave that comment out there?'

'You and him.'

'I'm sorry?'

'You and your cyborg friend.'

'He has a name you know.'

She waves the comment away. 'Names and me don't get on well.' She takes a long breath as she removes her hat. 'You're a sweet girl, Terra.'

Terra crosses her arms then uncrosses them when she realises she's being defensive. She wraps her hands around the cup instead. 'But?'

'He needs to have these modifications done. You have to accept that.'

'I'm sorry, but my relationship with Gryffin has nothing to do with you. What I accept or don't accept isn't your concern.'

'Perhaps, but I'm going to have my say. You and Gryffin will never end the way you want it to. He can never be what you want him to be. You need to accept that or you're both in for a long and miserable life.'

Terra pushes her chair back and stands up. 'I don't have time for this.'

'Your problems won't flutter to nothingness if he allows us to reverse the modifications. You will always be completely incompatible.'

Terra drops onto the chair again and leans over the table. She tries to keep her voice low so she doesn't attract any more attention from the other crew in the mess hall. 'You have no idea about our relationship so I'd appreciate if you kept your opinions to yourself.'

Evie smirks which rubs Terra up the wrong way. 'True, but any fool can see what you want. Just like any fool can see he is incapable of giving it to you.'

Finally giving in, Terra leans back and raises her eyebrows. 'Which is what exactly?'

'A companion for life. Someone you can grow old with. Someone you can settle down with. Someone you can perhaps have a family with.'

Terra swallows once, hating that a small hollow has opened up in her chest at Evie's words. She's had similar thoughts over the last few months but is not going to admit that to Evie. 'We've only been together a few months. None of that has been mentioned or even thought about.' She hopes Evie doesn't see through the lie. 'Besides, no one knows what it will be like for him once the Foundation are dealt with.'

'Ah, but that's not what I'm talking about. The fact he's a cyborg is an issue, but not one that can't be remedied in some way. I'm referring to the other issue.'

'Which is what exactly.'

'He's a Nomad, dear.'

'I'm aware of that.'

'Yes, but are you aware of what the Nomad are? At their core, I mean. Felix and I have been around the block quite a few times. In all our years, in all our dealings, bar the Foundation, the Nomad are the ones to watch out for. Your boyfriend may trade from time to time, but that adjustment to their MO is relatively new.

'Gryffin is solely responsible for a lot of people losing their lives. Yes, some deserved it, but most did nothing except stand up to defend what was theirs. Rayde used Gryffin to brush those people aside, and from what I've heard, he was effective... and brutal. When he was given command of his ship he continued along that path until he made the decision to raid Ultar.

'I'm not saying this to discredit him. He has done a lot of good and he is changing the way the Nomad operate, but I am not convinced as to the longevity of his current path. If we are successful and manage to dislodge the Foundation, there will be a power vacuum in this Sector. That will affect the Outer Sector and all the groups operating there. They may be forced to return to past means of operating to survive. Can you honestly sit there and tell me he won't revert to what is a big part of who he is?'

'If he has no choice—'

'Oh sweetie, you love him, but don't let your feelings cloud the truth from you. It's not fair on either of you. I don't know a lot about his past but I know some of what he went through. Truly nasty business and something that would have a resounding effect on his nature.

'If that wasn't bad enough, Rayde was a horrible creature who, by all accounts, treated Gryffin badly. Violence is at his core, Terra. I'm not saying for one minute that he'd hurt you physically, but you have to accept living with someone like that long term isn't a pleasant prospect.'

Terra opens her mouth to defend Gryffin, but Evie holds up her hand.

'I'm not finished. He also has a bounty on his head on quite a few worlds. Even those who are still loyal to him would not welcome him settling there. His life started on that hulking ship of his and I assure you, it will end there too.'

'Are you finished?'

Evie shakes her head. 'Not quite. I also believe that as soon as the Foundation are taken out of the equation, Sayber will kill Gryffin or Gryffin will kill Sayber. Perhaps they will kill each other. Once they make their move, the groups will retaliate. The current uneasiness between the Nomad and Hunters will be nothing compared to the war that will break out with the death of one or both of the leaders.

'They may have many flaws but the loyalty the groups show to Gryffin and Sayber is impressive. Neither side will back down until the other is destroyed. Perhaps Gryffin and Bray will go up against each other. New divisions will tear the current groups apart. Friends will side with Sayber, or Gryffin, or Bray, or Aleena. Perhaps some will stay on the station with us. Maybe align with the Rogues, who will most likely tie themselves to the Hunters.'

'What exactly is your point, Evie? I may come across as a naive Foundation officer, but I've spent enough time on *Ares* to have a fair idea how things work. I know Sayber and Gryffin will face each other sooner or later. Gryffin and Bray too. But what he's decided to do to himself has nothing to do with all that. Whether he's dead or alive, the Hunters and Nomad will fight. I may be hoping against all odds that doesn't happen, but the rift is there and I can't see that going away.

'Gryffin getting his mods upgraded isn't going to change any of that so don't try to muddy the waters by bringing it up. What you're doing is trying to justify your part in this plan of his. Trying to justify the fact you're going to help him mutilate himself.'

Evie snorts loudly. 'I am not trying to justify anything. I don't need to. Besides, would you rather he carried out the work himself or that the process is done in a sterile environment in a state-of-the-art facility?'

'I'd rather nothing was being done to him full stop.'

'Terra, he is doing this because he feels there is no other option. Given the information we have at hand, I have to agree this is the best option we have. We are fighting cyborgs, Terra. He is the original functioning cyborg. We would be completely crazy to contemplate fighting without Gryffin.'

'He can fight without being modified.'

'No, Terra. He can't. The poor fellow can barely walk without support. How exactly would you envision that fight playing out? Because I can see a slaughter with Gryffin falling within the first three and a half minutes. And that's being optimistic.'

'I can't agree with what he's planning.'

'Then you will lose him. You are in love with a Nomad cyborg, Terra. If you cannot accept that perhaps the kindest thing for both of you would be to walk away from him. If he's to have even the slightest chance of surviving what we're about to put him through, he needs to be focused. If he drops his guard at all, the programming will take advantage and then it's bye-bye Gryffin.

'Support him or walk away, Terra. There are no other options.'

29

The door opens in front of Bray and he steps inside the darkened room. Since getting the sensitive ocular implant, Bray understands why Gryffin favours the shadows. He hates to admit it, but Gryffin was right. Using the new eyepiece was becoming easier. The pain is lessening. Either that or he's getting used to it. Whatever the reason, he'll take it. There's not a lot else he can do.

He lets his night vision kick in and scans the room. Gryffin is sitting in the chair at the far side of the room, one elbow resting on the edge of the large window overlooking the cargo hold below. Even in the gloom, the Nomad appears more sombre than usual. 'Implants okay?'

'Still dizzy every now and again, but I'm getting the hang of my eye.' Bray sits down beside him and watches the personnel below working on the ships. 'So, what do you want to talk to me about?'

'I need your help to bring me up to spec.'

'Spec? What spec?' Gryffin raises an eyebrow and Bray nods slowly. 'Ah. Heard you were thinking about having mods done. I hoped it was a bad joke.'

Gryffin rests his head against the wall and looks across at Bray. 'All my life I've been running from the Foundation and from what I am. I can't keep doing that.'

Gryffin focuses on the wall opposite them again.

'*Ares*, this whole captain thing, whatever I have or had, with Terra... it's all fake. I've been playing at having a normal life since Rayde found me. Under it all, I am what I am. Nothing me or anyone else does will ever change that. I need to be finished. I need to be what they designed me to be.'

Bray pushes a hand through his hair as he turns away from Gryffin for a moment. 'What about the control implant? If we give you more mods, we'll have to activate it. There's a strong chance you won't be you after that.'

'What does it matter?'

'It matters a hell of a lot.'

'We don't have a choice. They're not going to stop until they kill all of us. Killing Roman and Lucan was only the start. They're picking us off one at a time, but I can't do a damn thing about it if I'm falling apart. I have two choices. I either sit in a pod here, waiting to see if you and the Dixon's can figure out a way to fix me, or I have more mods done, and take down the Foundation.'

Gryffin leans forward and rests his arm on his legs. 'I'm not an idiot, Bray. I know you're months away from being able to help me. That's time I don't have.'

'You don't know that for sure. You got us into the system. We just need time to go through all the data. Martyring yourself isn't the answer.'

'I'm not doing that. I'm giving you the weapon you need to get this done.'

'What about Terra? She can't be on board with this.'

'I think we might be finished.'

'Shit.' Bray thought he'd be happy to hear those words, but nothing about this conversation is making him feel good. 'I know what the mods are like. You really expect me to put anyone, no matter how much of a pain in the ass they are, through that?'

'The file you found on the computer — the one with me accepting my designation. I remember that.'

Bray looks at his brother. 'You do?'

He meets Bray's eyes again, the centre of his purple eye glowing menacingly. 'I remember every second in that place. I've no regrets about what I did to save you. I'd do anything to stop even one person from going through what I did. That's why I have to do this. You have to understand that.'

Bray does. Even after minimal time on the Scientist's table, he knows how his brother feels. That doesn't mean he's on board with anyone, even Gryffin, having any more procedures. 'So I'm guessing the Dixon's are already on your side.'

'Yeah, but you have a better understanding of the implants. We need your help.'

Bray buries his head in his hands then looks back at Gryffin. 'I can't tell you how much I hate you for asking this of me.'

'These new cyborgs only exist because I do.' He beats a fist against the side of his head, making Bray jump. 'This thing in my head is the only way to stop this from happening over and over and over again. You know that.'

For the first time in a few days, Bray looks at Gryffin's now blue eye. 'You know more about my implants than anyone else on the station. This doesn't happen without you. I need your help to do this, Bray.' Gryffin takes a deep breath. 'I need my brother.'

Bray frowns as he looks at him. Gryffin saying he needs him and calling him brother in the same sentence? He must be hearing things.

'Excuse me?'

'There's no way in hell you're getting me to say that again. Will you help or not?'

Bray opens his mouth to speak, but his implant interrupts. He sucks in a breath as his eyesight flickers, sending the room in a visual spin. He presses his palm to his eyepiece, tasting blood as he bites the inside of his cheek. A few minutes later the pain subsides and he takes a long shaky breath.

He slowly opens his eyes and is surprised to see Gryffin crouched in front of him. 'You good?'

Bray nods. 'Just giving me a bit of a kick. How can you even consider more of this?'

'I'd get a hundred more implants if it means all this stops.'

Bray wants to argue with his logic but it's hard to when he completely agrees. 'Damn you.' Bray takes a deep breath and nods once. 'Have I mentioned how much I hate you?'

'Once or twice.' Gryffin's smile throws Bray straight into his past. For the first time since he found out the truth about who Gryffin is, he looks like the Daegan from the countless photographs covering every available surface in his old house. Instead of a forced smirk, he's getting a real smile and for some reason that just makes what he's agreed to so much worse.

∞

DIXON SPACE STATION

Erin watches Bray and Gryffin leave the room and go their separate ways. Whatever they were talking about it was far from light-hearted. Both men look as if they have the weight of the world on their shoulders.

She waits a minute then takes a deep breath before following the

Nomad leader down the corridor and around the corner. She catches up with him just outside the med bay.

'Captain, can I talk to you for a minute?'

Gryffin stops and looks over his shoulder briefly before turning away. She grabs his arm as he walks away from her. Gryffin glares down at her hand then back at her. 'You've got one chance to let go before I break your fucking arm.'

She drops her hand. 'I need to talk to you. In private or in the med bay. I don't care where, but I am going to talk to you.'

His purple eye zooms in on her but she doesn't flinch away. 'I'm in a fucking shit mood. Back off.'

'I'm saying my piece here in the corridor or in private, but I'm not backing off.'

'Fine.' Erin follows him into the med bay, determined to have her say whether in front of a room full of medical personnel or not but Gryffin clearly wants privacy. 'I need the room. Now!'

The personnel, a mix of Nomad and Dixon staff, decide not to push him. They leave what they're doing and in less than a minute have gone to the adjoining room. Gryffin turns to face her and crosses his arms.

Erin relaxes slightly at his posture. If he's on the defensive already, she's got the upper hand. 'Thank—'

'What do you want?' he interrupts.

'You know who I am?'

'Yes.'

'I was kind of hoping you'd say no to that. Not sure what I did to deserve all this hostility. We're family.'

Gryffin doesn't respond, just stands in the centre of the room with his arms crossed. Erin pauses as she composes herself. Bray was right. Gryffin is without a doubt the most infuriating man to try and have a conversation with.

The Daegan she remembers from her childhood was always

talking, joking, and laughing. She looks up at his face and an invisible hand squeezes her throat. Gryffin isn't Daegan. Not anymore. Her fun-loving cousin was torn apart and Gryffin is what's left after the Scientist and the Nomad were done with him.

'My father, Morgan. He's struggling with everything that's happening.' She lowers onto the edge of the nearest bed, but Gryffin remains motionless in front of her. 'He lost both his nephews and his sister in the space of a few years. Now you and Bray are back and he found out what that Scientist guy did to Maggie... I know he has so many questions only you can answer.'

Gryffin drops his arms to his side and scowls at her. 'No.'

'I'm asking for you to spend five minutes with him. Just answer a few questions. Clear up a few things for him about his sister... and about you.'

Gryffin shakes his head and walks towards the door.

'Daegan.'

He stops in his tracks and spins around faster than she thought possible. 'Forget that fucking name,' he growls.

She stands up, and storms over to him. 'No. That's your name. To us you're still Daegan. I'm sorry if, for whatever reason that makes you angry, or irritated, or whatever. Denying who you are isn't helping anyone. Whether you like it or not, you have a family and we care about you. We love you, Daegan.'

'I'm not denying who I am. My name is Gryffin, Captain of *Ares* and Former High Commander of the Nomad. That's my full title and apart from Captain or sir, that's all I answer to. You and your father need to get that. Daegan died on that transport. You can't get answers from a corpse.'

She laughs humourlessly. 'That's not the way it works. You're standing in front of me. You honestly expect me not to ask you questions, not to be curious about what happened to you, about where you've been all these years? You may not remember me or the rest of our family, or you may not want to remember, but we were all close. You and Bray were like brothers to me. We used to spend a lot of time together.'

His fist clenches tightly as his eye glows. 'Stop talking.'

'You don't scare or intimidate me. In my Foundation position I've heard a lot about you. The Nomad, *Ares*, and her captain were detailed in a lot of security reports over the last few weeks. I get why people are intimidated by you, but it won't work on me.

'I remember you pushing me on my swing and trying to steal my lunch if I wasn't eating fast enough.' She takes her personal unit from her pocket and holds it towards him. 'This is us with Shayla, my mother. Look at the picture!'

Gryffin glances down at it and frowns. Erin flicks to the next photo - this one of just Shayla. Something in his expression rings alarm bells. He recognises her. She's positive of it. 'You know her, don't you?'

'We're done.' He storms through the door, leaving her staring after him.

∞

NEMESIS

Milla logs the details from Creed's results and puts the unit down. 'Well, you're in tip-top condition, High Commander. Wow, that sounds strange. Sorry, I didn't mean that in a bad way. It's just Gryffin's always been the High Commander... well, as long as I've known him.'

'Sounds strange to me too.' He pulls on his shirt and brushes his hair back in a ponytail. 'So, you okay about all this?'

Milla sits on the edge of her desk and shuts the computer down. 'About you? Of course. I trust Gryffin. If he wants you to take over

289

then you must be the right Nomad for the job. Well, unless you're thinking of reversing his woman allowed rule.'

Creed laughs and shakes his head. 'Absolutely not. Hardy would kick my ass. He did the right thing when he scrapped that rule. Rayde kept the Nomad in the dark for too long.'

'Was he really as bad as I've heard? Rayde I mean.'

'It's a hard one to explain. When the Nomad began, they had to fight fucking hard to be taken seriously. The way they attacked, the ruthlessness, the ferocity - it was all to make a point. When Rayde moved up the ranks he kept it up. Then Gryffin arrived and he passed the tradition on. There wasn't any room for weakness. Gryffin struggled so much adapting to being away from the station where we found him. I'm not excusing it for a fucking second, but Rayde raised him the only way he knew how.

'I remember going to check on him after one of his training sessions. Rayde had made him kill a prisoner with his bare hands then locked him back in his room. It was a few years after he'd joined the ship. Gryffin was sitting on the floor, covered in blood, shaking.' Creed flashes her a tight smile. 'No surprise Gryffin ended up the way he did.'

'Wow. Between that and selling out Gryffin to the Foundation I'm not surprised Gryffin killed him the way he did.'

He sighs and clasps his hands together on his knees. 'I loved being a Nomad from the second I stepped on board *Ares*, but Rayde slowly picked apart everything that was good in the group. We were never law abiding by any stretch. We weren't thugs though. Not at first anyway. Can't say I'm broken hearted Gryffin snapped his neck.'

'So you were on board when Gryffin was found?'

Creed looks up at Milla and blows out a long breath. 'Yeah. I was with Rayde when we found the station. We were on our way back to *Ares* when Rayde found him. Never will forget that place. No matter how much I try and believe me, I've tried damn hard. It's always there unless I have one too many ales,' he adds with a flat laugh.

'What was it—'

'Best you don't finish that sentence, Milla.'

'Why not?'

'Because I'd have to tell you, so I'm begging you not to ask. I may remember, but putting it in to words... well, best you don't ask, please.'

'Of course. Sorry for prying.'

Creed shakes his head and rubs his hands on his legs. 'You weren't prying. There aren't many still around who were on the station, but believe me, some things should stay in the past. Besides, if we don't sort out this Foundation mess, we could be finding more stations like that. Don't know about you but I'm not so keen on that happening.'

He pulls out his comms unit and reads the message. 'That's Chayse. We're here. Let's go see what toys the Foundation have for us.'

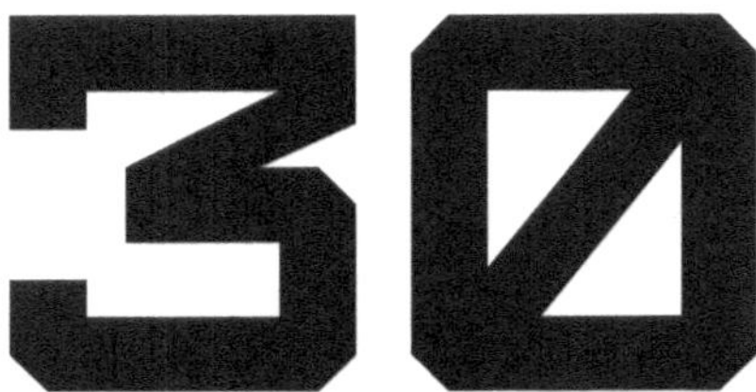

DIXON SPACE STATION

Gryffin steps into the office to face two very surprised Dixons. The couple stop their conversation and stare at him. 'Captain?'

'We need to talk. In private.'

Felix gestures to the couch opposite them. 'We were wondering when you'd want to meet one-on-one. Have a seat.'

Gryffin sits on the large leather couch as Evie busies herself with the drink dispenser behind the twin desks. While she's making drinks, Felix rests his feet on his desk and scrutinises Gryffin. 'So, young man. From the brief conversations we've had with your crew, can we assume they do not know of our past interactions?'

'No. I kept that between us. They don't need to know. Still don't.'

Evie smiles as she passes a mug of steaming tea to Felix. She offers one to Gryffin, but he refuses. Evie takes a sip and rests the cup on her knee. 'We are in full agreement, aren't we dear?'

'Too right we are,' Felix answers. 'Like you, we like to keep the different sides of our business separate. Keeps things simple.'

Evie nods and brings the tea to her lips again. 'I must say, Captain. You are far from what I imagined after our numerous conversations. I thought you'd be a lot older. You must be in your late twenties, early thirties at the most.'

'You don't strike me as the ruthless handler types either. Guess we're both disappointed.'

'Disappointed is not a word we'd use to describe our dealings with you, Captain,' Felix says as he crosses his arms. 'You are without a doubt the best mercenary we've had the pleasure to work with. You've made us a lot of money. And I believe working with us helped fund a new battleship. A pretty impressive one if all accounts are accurate. So why all the secrecy from your side? Why not tell the crew where you were getting the credits from?'

'They knew I was doing some clean-up work. I just didn't mention the details. That's the whole point, isn't it?'

'Very true.' The Dixon's fall silent as they look at him. 'So, Captain. Why the meeting? Not that we aren't happy to discuss work with you, but something tells me you are troubled.'

Gryffin readjusts his leg as he gets his thoughts in order. Working with the Dixon's over the years had helped get *Nemesis* off the ground and put food on their plates. Trading and protecting the colonies was the main income for the Nomad, but when there's a battleship to fund, he needed to go down a different path.

A contact had put him in touch with the Dixon's and he started working for them on the side. They never met in person, just relayed the target through a series of convoluted channels and the Nomad got a healthy cut of the fee. He had only taken about a dozen jobs through them, but had always found them reliable. Seeing them in the flesh, he still can't match the couple he was dealing with to the couple sitting in front of him.

'Do you want us to line up some work for you?' Felix asks, looking slightly concerned at the idea.

'I can't do a job right now.'

Evie laughs and shakes her head. 'Oh good gracious boy. That's a relief and one impressive understatement. I dare say even I'd be able to escape your clutches if you came after me like you are now. After we upgrade you however... well, that's a different story.'

Gryffin doesn't bother commenting on that, He'd prefer not to think about how he could be used to kill people once he's been upgraded. 'I need to speak to you about a job from a few years ago. Reliant-Five transport.'

Felix holds up a finger silencing him as he taps on the desk in front of him. A few seconds later the file for the job appears on a glass screen suspended to the side of the room. They both take a few seconds to familiarise themselves with the details.

'I remember this one,' Evie mutters as she reads. 'One of our contacts heard about a shipment of weapons that was winging its way to a Foundation outpost close to the border. We got in touch and you were able to intercept the transport. The job was a success as I remember. Then again, I believe all your jobs were successful.'

'I killed three people on the transport.'

'Yes, unfortunate, but you wouldn't have killed them unless you had no other option.'

'Can you call up the Foundation file for Morgan Richards. Family members.'

Felix raises his eyebrow but does as requested. An image of Morgan, Erin, and a woman fills the screen. 'Morgan, Shayla, and Erin Richards. Shayla is deceased. Died in a...' Felix and Evie read the rest of the report then flick back to the data from the Reliant-Five job. Felix mutters under his breath as he calls up more information.

A list of the fatalities from the attack on the transport appears next, and the Dixon's both freeze. It takes a few seconds for Felix's fingers to come back to life again. He lines up the data side-by-side and curses loudly.

'Captain, you killed your aunt. And we paid you to do it.'

∞

ARES

Terra wanders through *Ares* in a daze. She doesn't want to go back to the station and risk another helpful chat with Evie, but she doesn't really want to be here either. *Ares* is a maze of corridors, but she'd bump into Gryffin sooner or later. The way she's feeling right now, later would be preferable.

She kicks a doorway before stepping through to the adjoining corridor. *Ares* is her home. She can't imagine being anywhere else, but that's because Gryffin's here. Once he is upgraded who knows what condition he'll be in. She seriously doubts they'll be sharing a room let alone a bed.

She climbs the stairs to the upper command deck as quietly as she can. The one thing about this ship is that it's noisy. Every footstep echoes, every movement sends groans and creaks through her metalwork no matter how quiet Terra tries to be. At the top of the stairs Terra breathes a sigh of relief. No sign of Gryffin. Instead, Desyl is working on the bank of units at the front of the deck, muttering to himself.

'Hey. Do you have a minute?'

Desyl glances up at Terra then shakes his head before focusing on the screen in front of him again. 'Not now, sorry. I've got loads to get through.'

Terra stops beside him and examines the station he is intently staring at. 'Weapons check?'

He nods. 'No point attacking Earth with handguns. We need everything working.'

She leans against the railing and silently watches him. He's always been one to get deep in his work, but this is a bit much. It's blatantly obvious he's avoiding making eye contact with her. 'Okay, what's he said to you?'

'Sorry?'

'Desyl, I'm not an idiot. If you concentrate on that reading much longer you'll give yourself a nose bleed. What did Gryffin say to you?'

He sighs and looks across at her. 'He didn't say anything to me. I just don't think there's any point going over it.'

'Excuse me?'

'I know you, Terra. I know you want to talk about his decision, but it's a done deal. Now, I really have to finish this. He needs me to help look for parts in a bit.'

Terra chews her bottom lip as she clamps her hands around the railing. 'So you're just going to ignore the issue and keep your mouth shut?'

Desyl doesn't respond, turning his attention back to the console again.

'He's going ahead with this and you're refusing to talk to me about it. I thought you were my friend?'

Desyl sighs and rests his hands on the screen as he turns his head towards her. 'Low blow, Terra. I am your friend, but this is different.'

'How is it different?'

'Look, I get this isn't what any of us want, Gryffin included.' He points a finger at her dismissive expression. 'Gryffin too. You have to see that. We all know how he feels about his implants. You really think he'd consider getting more work done if there was another way? There is no other option, Terra. Can't you see that?' Desyl scrubs his hand over his hair and shakes his head. 'He's dying, Terra. Let him go out fighting. He deserves that much at least.'

'I get that, okay. That doesn't mean I have to be happy about it. I wasn't expecting to lose my boyfriend and my friend because of it.'

Desyl slams his hand down on the screen, startling her. 'He's my Captain, Terra and I'll follow his orders no matter what. I'm already on my last fucking life with him. There's no way I'm going to disrespect him again. If he wants to be upgraded, I'll help him. No questions. No arguments. No discussions. I'm certainly not going to talk about his decision with anyone other than him. It's his fucking body.'

Desyl closes his eyes and takes a deep breath before looking at her again. 'I care about you, Terra. You know that, right? I'm closer to you than anyone else on this ship. I wish I could help you, I really do, but I'm a Nomad. That will always have to come first. I'm sorry.'

∞

DIXON SPACE STATION

'Will you calm down, woman. This is no time for hysterics.'

Evie waves her hat wildly at her husband. 'I am far from hysterical. I'm— I don't know what I am. All I know is that her family are on board this station. And we killed her!'

'We did no such thing.' Felix glances over his shoulder at Gryffin. 'He did.'

'Oh like that makes the slightest difference. Do you honestly believe Bray will just shrug and leave it at that?'

'You're forgetting one thing - we didn't pay him to kill her. We paid him to get the shipment. Killing her was on him.'

Gryffin pushes to his feet and approaches the couple. 'Shut up!'

They stop and turn to face him. Evie crosses her arms as she does her best to stare him down. 'Oh, I'm sorry, but this is a bit of a problem for us. Without wishing to diminish what you do, Bray is rather adept at—'

'Killing people,' Felix finishes.

'Yes, thank you, dear.'

'I'd argue that Gryffin is better.'

'You really want to have a which brother is the better hitman contest?'

Felix shrugs. 'I'm just making a point.'

Evie glares at him then focuses on Gryffin again. 'Bray is on our station. Do you realise what he'll do to us if he finds out?'

Gryffin stares at the couple as he tries to keep his growing irritation at bay. If he'd met these two before he started dealing with them, he doubts he would have taken any work from them. They're crazier than he'd heard. 'You planning on telling him?'

'Are you out of your mind? Of course not!'

'What's the problem then? Erase the data and any backups.'

Evie squashes the hat back on her head. 'You really think it's that easy? These things have a way of getting out. They always do. And guess who he'll target once it does come out?'

'All that matters is that it doesn't come out until this truce with the Hunters is done. After that it doesn't matter. If he finds out, Bray isn't going to come after you. I'll be the one in his sights.'

'But he's your brother? Surely he wouldn't—'

'He's a Hunter and I'm a Nomad. Of course he would. Just like I would if I had the right motivation. Bury the data and move on.'

They both nod but look as happy about the prospect of a confrontation with a pissed off Bray as he is.

Gryffin leaves them to deal with the data and makes his way back to *Ares* and the safety of the training room. His body is clearly telling him he needs to beat something. He grabs one of the sparring sticks from the stand against the wall and walks to the centre of the room.

Gryffin rolls his shoulders as he tests the weight of the sparring stick in his hand. Training with one hand is going to make the session more interesting. He may not have started to fight yet but even being here, on his own two feet, feels comforting. He missed this more than he realised.

The newly repaired drone begins its attack and Gryffin counters. It takes him a few minutes to get back in the flow again, ignoring the protesting from unused muscles as he continues to move.

He told the Dixon's the uncovered information isn't important. That was a lie. Having the people hiding them in Foundation space freaking out and second guessing themselves would have been a disaster for everyone. At least this way, they would hopefully relax, thinking their part in Shayla's death would never come to the surface.

He's not so sure though. They were right. Things always have a way of coming out. If Bray ever learned the truth, he'd kill the three of them. He's sure of it.

He grunts as the drone's stick embeds itself in his side, momentarily winding him. Instead of finishing him off, the drone backs away, giving him time to get himself together. 'Pause program.' The drone lowers its arms and comes to a stop. Gryffin opens a panel at the side of its head and pulls out the chip containing the safety protocol. Training with one of these things is only effective if the threat is real. A tap to the ribs isn't enough incentive to fight back with any enthusiasm.

He'd killed his aunt.

The thought hits him like a blow from the drone. Why the hell did another family member have to enter his life in the worst way possible? Since the Nomad rescued him, he'd taken his fair share of lives. Hell, he'd taken a few people's fair share of lives. None of those gave him restless nights. Why is he even giving this one a second thought?

It's the damn family thing again. He never spoke to the woman. Until the moment he put a bullet in her head, he'd never seen her before... well, not that he remembers. Now he can't get her face out of his mind.

He curses and throws the stick at the drone before he remembers he's removed the safety protocol. The drone takes its chance and targets the side of Gryffin's head with its stick. Gryffin curses as it makes contact with his ocular implant, disrupting the connection.

His artificial vision shuts down leaving him with his less than reliable human eyesight. He blinks a few times, trying to clear the picture in front of him but gives up. Without the mechanics, he's as good as blind.

Focusing on the dark block of shadow in front of him he rams his boot in what he hopes is the drone and not the wall. Something large and metal crashes to the floor so he rolls to the side and kicks out again. This time his boot embeds in wiring instead of metal. With a grind of gears, the drone falls silent. Gryffin pulls his foot out of the machine and lies back on the ground to catch his breath.

He runs his fingers along his ocular implant and pulls the casing off. One of the wires is hanging free, knocked out of its connector by the drone... and his stupidity. With a hell of a lot of difficulty, he finally reunites the wire and connector, bringing his eye back online.

He pushes onto his elbow and frowns. The drone is for the scrap heap. It was a one in a hundred shot, but his kick hit the processor on the back of the drone's head at just the right angle. He's not going to be popular with the crew. The drone was only brought back into service a few days ago.

He flops back against the floor and looks up at the fans spinning nosily in the ceiling until his comms unit brings him out of his trance.

'What?'

'Sir, it's Boone. You told me to contact you when we were ready to look for parts.'

'I'll be there in a minute.'

Gryffin rolls onto his feet and hobbles towards the door. First thing on his list of parts to find is a new leg. He's done with this one.

31

Creed stands facing the vast view screen at the front of the command deck and smiles to himself. From a cursory glance you'd assume the moon was just that - a small moon with nothing exciting or remotely interesting about it. But they know different.

Thanks to Avoca's intel they know the moon is hollow. Whether a natural occurrence or artificially created he doesn't know. Doesn't care either. All he knows is that the unassuming moon is full of ships just waiting to be claimed.

The ship Gryffin was taken from as a child could be in there. Milla found the ship's designation when she poked in Gryffin's Foundation record. He's under orders from Gryffin to destroy that ship. He doesn't want it to be used no matter what. That's something Creed can fully understand.

'Any activity?'

'Nothing to worry about,' Chayse reports. 'There's a small control station on the surface. Looks like a mining substation.'

'But we all know that's not the case. Any life signs?'

'Ten. We have to assume they'll raise the alarm as soon as a Nomad battleship appears in their orbit.'

'That's why we won't be going in. I think there's a way of getting close without them giving HQ the heads up.' He looks sideways at Milla and Hardy. 'Fancy stretching your legs?'

Hardy grins as she cracks her knuckles. 'You know me so well. You want them dead or incapacitated?'

'Try for incapacitated, but if that doesn't work do what you have to. The main thing is stopping any transmissions from leaving that moon.'

'Got it, babe.' She kisses him long and hard then crooks a finger at Milla. 'Let's go have some fun.'

Chayse waits until they've left the deck before he walks over to Creed. 'You sure it's safe to send them without backup?'

Creed laughs and nods towards the retreating women. 'Hardy's reputation is founded. She's trained with me every single day and has kicked my ass as much as I've kicked hers. As for Milla, I've read her file. Gryffin sent it to me as soon as he made her a Nomad. He's seriously impressed with her. She's more than capable of doing this. Don't get me wrong, I'd prefer to go there myself, but having two women arrive on their doorstep will appear to be less of a threat than a group of Nomad.'

'I kind of wish I could see what Hardy and Milla are going to do.'

Creed shakes his head as he looks back at the view screen. 'Oh I'm with you there, Chayse. I almost feel sorry for the Foundation personnel.'

∞

EARTH

Garvan grips the side of the transport and pulls himself upright. His son hurries over and helps him prop himself up. Garvan carefully examines the young man in front of him.

'Well, I'll be damned.' He rests his head against the side of the door, overwhelmed by the rush of emotions. 'It's really you, Zeke.'

His son nods and his eyes turn dark as he examines the metal covered elbow and each and every bruise, cut, and sore on his father. 'Damn it, Dad. You been hitting the steroids while you've been dead?'

Garvan laughs. The reaction is odd, but it feels good. 'Survival of the fittest, Zeke. Not that I'm not incredibly grateful, but what exactly are you doing? How did you find me? How did you get me out? I thought you were told I was dead?'

'It's a long story and I'm not sure this is the best place for a catch-up.'

He gets up and leans against the transport to examine the nav unit. 'It took a little longer than I planned to get you out. Traffic will be building up around the city walls. I'm not sure if we can get to Liza's holiday house without being spotted.'

'How is your sister?'

'Catch-up later. Right now being caught seems like a more likely end to the day, and I'd prefer to avoid that.'

'I know somewhere we can go. It'll be deserted and has a shielded safe room.'

Zeke frowns as he looks over his shoulder at his father. 'You haven't been hiding out there since you left?'

'I wish.' He quickly gives Zeke the coordinates and crouches back on the floor in the cargo hold while Zeke turns the transport around and out of the woods.

It takes them less than an hour to get to Morgan's farm. Zeke ditches the transport in a shed on the same building site Garvan and Bray had passed through on their first visit to the farm.

They hide in a prickly hedgerow running the length of the main field as they watch the property for a few minutes.

'What is this place, Dad?'

Garvan wipes the sweat from his brow. He's beyond exhausted and desperately needs to lie down before he falls on his ass. 'It belongs to a friend.'

'It looks empty.'

Garvan nods. 'If things went to plan, they should be a hell of a way from here.' He gestures to the range of outbuildings at the back of the property. 'There's a shelter under the barn on the left. It's shielded so we should be safe enough.'

'What are we waiting for? After you old man.'

Garvan rolls his eyes at the comment. Moving quickly and silently, Garvan crosses the stretch of grass separating the house from the first of the barns. He flattens his body against the side of the building and peers around the corner.

He doubts the Foundation would be keeping an eye on the farm but taking a few minutes to be sure won't hurt any of them. Once he's sure they're alone, Garvan gestures at Zeke. A few seconds later his son is beside him.

'Which barn?'

Garvan points to the larger of the buildings. 'The access is at the back of that one.' He squints as he examines the sky. Can't see any drones in the area. Ready to make a dash for it?'

As he finishes the sentence, he hears the familiar buzzing sound nearing their location. 'Damn it. Guess I spoke too soon.'

'If they get here before we're hidden, we're screwed.'

'You don't say? It's now or never. On my mark. Go.'

Garvan aims for the barn and makes a run for it, ignoring the protests from his battered body. Zeke reaches the door before him and lifts the large metal bolt. Garvan bursts through and Zeke secures the door behind him. Garvan keys in the code to unlock the door, then ushers Zeke underground before he drops the cover and collapses onto the stairs.

'You okay, Dad?'

He smiles. 'Just enjoying a day in the countryside with my son.' He groans and tries to push himself to his feet, but whatever small reserve of energy he had is well and truly exhausted after all the exertion.

Zeke whistles as he looks around the room. 'Not bad. So, why were your mates hiding?'

'Usual reason people hide. They didn't fancy living under Foundation rules.'

'Don't suppose you have a plan beyond hiding under the floor?'

Garvan rests his head against the step. He can't remember ever being this tired before. The only plan he's interested in is the one that involves him sleeping for a week. He pries his eyes open, startled when he sees Zeke looking down at him.

'Don't sneak up on an old guy like that. You trying to kill me?'

'Sorry. You don't look so good. C'mon.' He holds out his hand waiting until Garvan grabs it firmly before helping him to his feet. He carefully supports his father as he makes his way over to the couch and lowers him on to it. Zeke crouches down in front of him. 'Can I get you anything?'

'A new head would be just swell. Or a new arm. I've lost a bit of mine.' Garvan attempts a laugh but it comes out as a cough. 'I'm good, son. Forty winks and I'll be right as rain. Grab me a cover from one of the beds.'

He waits until Zeke disappears in Bray's old room then slowly rolls onto his back to keep pressure off his various bruises. He bites back the curse of pain and squeezes his eyes shut as he slowly rests his arm on his chest. He feels a soft cover being laid over him and opens his eyes even though it's a fight. 'Thanks. Nice and cosy now.'

Zeke kneels on the floor in front of him and holds out a glass of water and some painkillers. 'Found these in the bathroom. How bad is the pain?'

'It smarts a little.'

'Stop it. Tell me the truth.'

'Hurts like hell.'

'Where?'

'Honestly? Everywhere, but mainly my head and arm.'

'What happened to you, Dad? Where have you been?'

He wants to sleep, needs to sleep, but he'd stay awake for days if it means spending that time getting to know his son again. He's only been with Zeke for a few hours and he's already impressed with how he turned out. From his appearance it's clear he's not entirely playing by the Foundation's strict rules and he couldn't be more proud.

He spends the next forty minutes telling Zeke everything that happened since he left for work all those years ago. More than once he has to stop to talk Zeke down.

His son had a fiery temper. Always did. Barely a week went by without getting a summons to the school. If Zeke wasn't fighting, he was talking back to his teachers, and that's if he even bothered to show up in the first place. He just didn't take instruction well. Garvan has no doubt, if allowed, Zeke would have stormed the HQ and put a bullet in Harvey without a plan or backup.

'So, what do we do now? We can't hide out here forever.'

'I need a few hours kip to clear my head. You should do the same. We're safe enough here.'

'I'll do an inventory. Be good to see how long we can stay here before starvation forces us out.'

Garvan nods, but quickly loses the fight to stay awake.

32

Milla has never been more terrified and completely excited in her life. It'll take an hour to get to the moon from where *Nemesis* is hiding so there's plenty of time to work out a plan. It's not the most detailed of plans but it doesn't need to be. They're keeping it simple.

Before leaving *Nemesis*, Hardy had done a little creative destruction of one of the engines on the transport. Nothing serious, but enough that an error would show up if the station on the moon had sensors in place. They needed a reason to land and a damaged ship fit the bill perfectly. Then it would just be a case of accessing the main control room and making sure everyone was incapacitated.

Easy.

Hardy smiles over at her as she guides the transport towards the moon. 'Look at your little face. You're all excited aren't you?'

'I'm a Foundation doctor. Doing stuff like this wasn't on the curriculum.'

'That's what you get for attaching yourself to a Nomad. Never a dull moment. You've got a good one with Chayse. It's great to see new blood coming to the group and shaking things up.'

'From the stories I've heard, it was well overdue. Gryffin's made some drastic changes over the years.'

Hardy nods. 'Absolutely. Problem is, the old Nomad group didn't take to change well.' She snorts. 'That's a bit of an understatement. You didn't agree with the way things were being done and you got the same treatment Creed did - without the still being alive to tell the tale part. Then again, it's not that different to the way the Foundation runs things.'

Milla can't argue with that. How many people ended up in Tyrat because they had the nerve to disagree with the Foundation? She's worked a little with Boone, Trace, and Dante. The three men had done nothing remotely unlawful, yet each had been torn from their lives like they didn't matter. Just like what had happened all those years ago when the Foundation took children for the project. Children like Gryffin.

'It's strange. I grew up on Foundation Earth. I knew things weren't right, but I never gave it much thought.'

'Because that's what you were conditioned to do,' Hardy says. 'The Foundation are experts at making people accept what they do. It's how they stay in control. Anyone who steps out of line finds themselves in Tyrat. Not exactly incentive for speaking out.'

'I guess you're right. I know what they did to Gryffin and the others is inexcusable, but I honestly can't see them paying for any of it. Things may change, but all those families won't get retribution.'

'How many kids were involved?'

Milla taps her fingers on her knee as she tries to hazard a guess. 'It's hard to put a number on it. It's well in the hundreds in any case. Then there's all the men the Scientist took from Tyrat and modified. Only three survived but there must have been dozens more.'

'And now there's these new ladies with attitude.'

'Yep. I have no idea how many of them there are.'

Hardy turns to look at her and her smile chills Milla. 'Oh there'll be retribution, Milla. Are you really going to sit there and tell me that not even one of those poor souls didn't have someone who'd be willing to step up and get a piece of revenge?

'You're talking about hundreds of innocent lives. If each of those people had even one relative or loved one, that's a lot of hurt, a lot of pain, and a lot of anger. If Gryffin doesn't manage to take the Foundation down for what they did to him, I sure as hell guarantee at least one of those family members will.'

Milla nods and looks back out the front of the transport. Hardy is right of course. Too many lives were affected directly and indirectly by the Foundation and Project Conscript. Someone will make them pay. She just hopes Gryffin hangs around long enough to get his piece of revenge. He absolutely deserves it.

'Right. We're within comms range. Time to go all damsel in distress.' She shudders as she hits the distress button. 'I'm going to need to kick some serious ass to make up for that.'

After a quick vid check to make sure they are actually two damsels and not a group of armed men, they are allowed to land in the small hanger in the facility. Hardy and Milla stand at the door and wave at the three personnel who come to greet them. A rather unfit looking man with thinning hair and a ridiculously styled moustache greets them.

'Well, well, well. Aren't you both a sight for sore eyes. What can we do for you?'

Hardy smiles sweetly and points to the engine, still spewing smoke after her tampering. 'We're having engine trouble. I don't suppose you can help us out?'

His smile shows a missing front tooth and Milla has to force herself to keep smiling. Clearly the Foundation didn't think anyone would come near the moon. They hadn't given a lot of thought to the personnel. One by one, the men drop as Hardy takes them out before Milla even gets a chance to even pull her weapon. 'Thanks for sharing.'

Hardy grins as she climbs off the ramp and examines the men. 'Sorry. I get a little carried away when it comes to shooting people.'

Milla looks at the unconscious men. 'Yeah. I can see.' She grabs the restraints from the transport and secures the men while Hardy relieves them of their weapons.

They move to the door and on the count of three, Hardy opens it. The corridor outside is empty and with a lone door at the far end, there won't be any wrong turns to make.

Hardy nods to the security screen mounted above the door. 'As soon as we step outside this room, we'll give whoever is inside a top to toe view of us. Might be best to keep up with the whole sweet and innocent thing.'

They hide their guns behind their backs and stroll up to the door, trying to appear as innocent as they can.

Milla waves at the screen and the door slides back. Hardy directs her gun at the man. 'You fancy taking this one?'

'Really?'

'Why not? Go for it.'

The man opens his mouth to interject in their to and fro, but Milla stuns him in the chest and he falls wordlessly to the ground. The other men sitting at the table, stuffing their faces with cold meat and bread fall onto their lunch as Milla and Hardy knock them out.

'That was a little disappointing,' Hardy says as she rests her hands on her hips. 'The Foundation are supposed to be this superpower. These guys were a complete let down. I didn't even work up a sweat.'

They restrain everyone and Milla opens the door to the far side of the room. Her arms drop to her sides as she steps onto the platform. 'Eh, Hardy.'

She joins Milla at the door. 'Fuck me. That's a lot of ships.'

They had been expecting maybe a dozen or so ships, but there's easily two or three times that many hidden in the cavern. The vessels are squeezed in every available space. The Foundation hadn't planned on ever accessing or using the vessels again. There's no boarding ramps or access platforms.

'I can't see a lot of these getting in the air again.'

Milla nods. 'Gryffin was taken twenty-five years ago. I'd say a lot of these have been laid up here nearly as long. Where exactly are we supposed to start?'

'Not our call. Let's make sure this place is secure and get the guys down here. We've only got enough pilots for maybe six or so ships. We just got to see which ones will take the least amount of work to fly.'

∞

DIXON SPACE STATION

'This is ridiculous. Have I said that to you?'

Bray glances up at Sayber. 'Once or twice.'

Sayber pulls out another drawer and places it on the table. 'I mean, I know he has a few screws loose - no offence - but this is downright certifiable.'

'He's got a point. It's a plan.'

'You're not behind this damn stupid idea?' Desyl asks from the other side.

Bray concentrates on looking through the box in front of him. The last thing he wants is to hear the objections to the plan in stereo. 'Of course I'm not but we either help him or he'll get out the solder and start sticking things on himself. You know what he's like.'

'Stubborn. Still don't like it,' Desyl mutters as he pulls a large unit open and empties the contents on the floor.

Bray nods. 'Couldn't agree more.' He holds up a component and examines it, before putting it back in the box. The implant store on *Cronus* is vast and contains everything a cyborg could possibly need to spruce themselves up. The problem is, without having examined all the files, they're still in the dark about what a lot of the parts do.

'Is this of use?' Bray looks up as one of the cyborgs undergoing the procedure with Gryffin hands him a component. Boone was the first to show signs of his old self which just made what they were willing to do to themselves even harder to deal with.

The man had served in Tyrat as many of the others had. His crime of theft had been entirely fabricated. He'd been torn from his wife and daughter and thrown in hell. Then to add insult to injury, he finds himself on the Scientist's table being modified.

Just like everyone else, his arm and eye have been replaced, but Gryffin is still the only one with the aggressive control implant in his brain. The others will follow orders, but unlike Gryffin, the orders can't be altered or modified in any way.

Once programmed, the male cyborgs will just keep fighting for their sole goal until they stop functioning. Unfortunately, as much as he would have liked to claim Boone and the others as potential Hunter recruits, the part of their programming that still worked, linked them to Gryffin.

Bray takes the component and checks it. 'That's perfect, Boone. Can you stick it with the others?'

The last two hours have been spent cataloguing and checking all the components, putting aside anything that could be of use. He hates to admit it, but the new ability to magnify something by just looking at it is coming in handy.

'How are you doing?' Gryffin asks as he limps in. Bray frowns as he gets to his feet. 'Do you need the brace back on your leg?'

'It's fine. You have any luck?'

Bray doesn't bother pushing the issue. It won't get either of them anywhere. He points over to the large table at the far side of the room. The surface looks like something out of the Scientist's lab - only without the blood. An eerie procession of ocular implants, together with the bionic eye attached is circling the end of the table.

'We've managed to get enough familiar pieces together to do most of what you want. You'll each get a new ocular implant and have the casing on your face replaced as well as some upgrades to your arms.'

'Weapons?'

Bray nods. 'That's the plan. You're going to need the most work. Along with your eye, your chest implant will need some serious upgrading to deal with the added strain on your system. The others are newer so they can handle a little more without much upgrading.' Bray pauses as what he's saying sinks in. Gryffin leans over to catch his attention. 'You good?'

'Me? Great. Couldn't be better,' he replies sarcastically.

'Focus on what you have to do.'

'That easy, huh?' Gryffin shrugs which doesn't help Bray much either way. 'As I was saying, we're on track. Boone managed to find the last piece we need for your chest implant so we're pretty much good to go.'

'When can you start?'

'I want to sit down with the Dixon's for a few hours. I need to get this straight in my head before I start doing anything to any of you. I'll also need to run a set of scans on the four of you to make sure everything is up to date.'

'Whatever you need to get this done.'

'I'll let you know when we're ready to run the scans.'

Gryffin nods and limps over to the table holding the vast array of components. As he stares at his new parts, his face changes. If Bray hadn't been watching him he would have missed it. He's not sure if it was dread or fear, but it was there briefly before Gryffin hid it again.

∞

FOUNDATION SHIPYARD

Creed stops at the top of the balcony and blows out a long breath. When Gryffin sent the message about the ships he was expecting there to be a few - not ten times that. He swallows, but the lump remains lodged in the back of his throat. All those lives lost so the Foundation could create cyborgs. It doesn't bear thinking about, let alone picturing. Which is what he's doing right now.

'Hey. You good?'

He smiles at Hardy and nods. 'Yeah. I'm fine. A few days ago I was wading through mud and sweating over a furnace. I wasn't expecting any of this.'

She runs her hand up his arm. 'Keep your head on the bigger picture. Don't let your head go there.'

'I know. So, where the hell do we start?'

She points to the far side of the makeshift hangar. 'I'm guessing we target the ships nearer the door first. Keep fingers, toes, and everything else crossed that the operational ships aren't buried at the back.'

'While you and Milla were down here we ran through the records of everyone on *Nemesis* and *Dannan*. Turns out we're better off than we thought. We've got eleven personnel capable of flying a ship. Depending on the size of some of these we may have more.'

Hardy leans on the railing beside him and looks around the cavern. 'What's the name of the ship Gryffin was on?'

'*Astral Six*. It's a small transport. No weapons systems.'

'Easy target.'

Creed nods. 'Easier still when their attackers were told where to find them. Anyway, I promised him I'll destroy the ship.'

'Okay. You organise the teams. I'll have a look for it.'

Creed steps back in the control room and walks past the bound and gagged Foundation personnel. 'Time's getting on. Chayse, set the teams loose. Start at the far end of the cavern and work back. Life support and engines are the priority. Weapons would be a bonus, but as long as it flies we can use it. Hardy will look for Gryffin's ship. Have you got the cloaks up and running?'

Chayse nods. 'Yes, sir. We've extended the cloaks on *Nemesis*. It should take another few ships.'

'Great. So once you find something that works, move it out to *Nemesis*. Clear a bit of space inside. How about comms?'

Baila pulls herself out from under the bank of units. 'It'll take about thirty minutes to rework this but after that we'll be able to boost our signal. You can have a chat with the delightful Gryffin in real time.'

'Sounds good.' He steps aside and gestures to the door. 'Time to increase our fleet.'

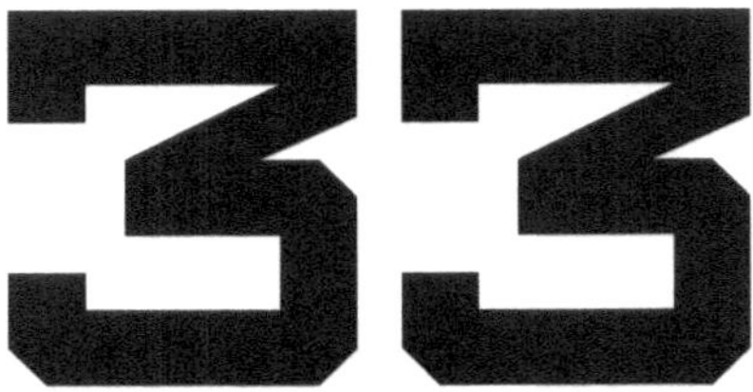

EARTH

Garvan accepts the steaming drink from Zeke with a smile. He sips the scalding liquid, his eyes rolling closed as the warmth works its way down his body.

'You okay, Dad? You've got a ridiculous smile on your face.'

'Tea, Zeke. Couldn't stand the stuff until right now. This very second marks the start of a beautiful relationship between me and this beverage.'

'What the hell are you talking about?'

'After drinking slightly warm water since I was taken, this is pure heaven. What the hell do they put in the water on this planet? I never remember it tasting... well, tasting at all. But it's got this...' He makes a face and wrinkles his nose. 'It's got this sort of soapy aftertaste.'

Zeke shrugs. 'Never noticed it myself.'

'Yeah, well, you've been drinking the stuff for years. Trust me. It's beyond terrible. Now the stuff on Ultar. That's water.'

Garvan looks away as his son scrutinises him. He hasn't had the courage to take a peek at himself in the mirror. The parts of his body that aren't pounding in time to his heartbeat are downright painful. Talking to Zeke is the only thing keeping him from screaming. His thoughts want to wander back to the lab, but he's got a firm grip on them for now.

'Dad? Hey, you with me?'

Garvan frowns at Zeke and blinks. 'Sorry. What was that?'

'How are you feeling today?'

Garvan nods. 'Not too bad all things considered. Still got an angry cyborg with a pick axe trying to get out the side of my head, but other than that I'm just grand.'

Zeke laughs. 'Yeah, right.' He picks a bag off the floor and empties the contents on the table in front of them. An assortment of bottles housing colourful tablets spill out. As well as the drugs, there's a few packets of food and some clothes.

Garvan picks up a container and examines the details printed on the side. 'Morgan Richards. You've been to the house?'

'Don't worry. I waited until the drone had done its flyby. Don't look at me like that. We needed supplies.' He throws a clean shirt at him. 'And maybe a change of clothes. Foundation escaped prisoner attire doesn't quite suit you or help us stay inconspicuous.'

He gets up and fills a glass with water, looks at the drink, then remembering what his father said, empties it down the sink. 'Take a painkiller. You look like you need it.' Zeke sits down next to his father and examines him as he swallows the medication. 'What is that thing on the side of your head meant to do?'

Garvan grimaces as the hot tea burns the roof of his mouth. 'They didn't exactly sit me down and go through the details. All I know from Gryffin and Bray is that it connects with something inside.'

'Like your brain?'

He shrugs. 'Beats me, son. All I know is that I'd prefer it wasn't there.'

'Can your friends remove it?'

'I can't tell you how much I hope so. From what I've heard, Gryffin has had the implants for a hell of a long time. Doubt he would have left it there so long if it could be removed. Until I talk to him I won't know what my future holds. Don't suppose you have a ship buried somewhere?'

Zeke shakes his head. 'Getting you out was as far as my plan went. I didn't have much time to think about anything else. Listen, I've been thinking about what you said earlier. Are you sure Harvey is One?'

Garvan laughs then takes a mouthful of tea. 'Oh I'm sure. C'mon, prancing around in those damn ridiculous robes full of self-importance. Damn surprised no one else has put two and two together.'

'Yeah, just can't see the power bit. He jumps if I look at him the wrong way.'

'Didn't get on, huh?'

'I'm going to limit it to a simple no. After finding out what he did to you I want him dead.'

'Get in line. Harvey is weak, you're right there. Problem is, that robe and mask give him the power he craves. Wearing that stuff he's strong, he's powerful, he rules the planet.'

'With the other Council members.'

Garvan snorts. 'You and I both know that One has the final say unless the others all disagree. From what I've heard about them, independent thought ain't high on the list of job requirements. Listen, can I ask you something?'

'Shoot.'

'Did you change your last name, after I... left.'

'You didn't leave. You were taken. And no, of course not. I'm still Zeke Garvan. Why?'

'No reason.'

Zeke lowers his glass to the table with a thump. 'That bastard told you I changed my name, didn't he?'

'It might have been mentioned in conversation.'

'He tried to get me to change my name a few days ago. Must have been wanting to get one over on you while he could gloat.'

'Yeah, sounds about right. Got to say though, why didn't you? Not that I'm complaining. Having the same name as a traitor can't have helped you.'

'You know that would've been more of a reason to keep it. Besides, it's my name. No way I was going to believe any of the lies they spread about you so there was no reason to change my name.'

'Music to my ears.'

'So, I don't suppose you have any idea where your friends were going? Do you know the name of the people they were meeting?'

Garvan shakes his head. 'Bray talks a lot. Can't say I listen to everything he says. It's a bit hit and miss. I think he mentioned a couple that helped Avoca get him out of Tyrat. Dawson or Davis or—'

'Dixon?'

Garvan clicks his fingers. 'That's it. Dixon. See I knew I was listening. Any idea how to get a hold of these Dixon's?'

Zeke shakes his head. 'I was hoping it wasn't them. They're as off the grid as you can get. They live somewhere on the outer edges of the Foundation right under the Foundation's nose. They've escaped capture so long because they are impossible to find. This isn't good.'

'You're telling me. Don't suppose you know of anyone who would have some slightly shady connections?'

Zeke shakes his head then stops suddenly.

'What?'

'Liza.'

'Your sister? Something you're not telling me about her?'

'No. Her husband, Jake, works for the security services on the nearest penal colony. If anyone has shady connections it'll be him.'

Zeke pauses then smiles widely. 'Yeah, Jake may be able to help us. So, you fancy meeting Liza?'

'Not going to say no. Besides, might not be a bad idea to get her away from Harvey.'

'There's no way he could pin your escape on me.'

'Not saying he would, but I'm not where he left me. That'll raise alarms. Best we have her under our protection.'

∞

NEMESIS

Aleena sits in front of the console and turns it on. This is not the first time she has been contacted by Gryffin over the years. She has lost count of the conversations they have had while she was on Ultar and he was on *Ares*. For some reason, this request is different.

Since she received the message, her stomach has been in a knot. Gryffin may be a dear friend, but he has never contacted her without a valid reason. Idle chats were not something the Nomad captain did.

She clears her throat and keys in the code to reach him. When she left Ultar so abruptly, she had not had a chance to say goodbye to him. In truth, she did not expect to see him again.

Their relationship was volatile at times, but since he first arrived on Ultar and held a gun to her head, he had been an important part of her life. She still does not quite know how they turned that hostile initial contact into a trade partnership, and then a deep friendship.

Over the years, she has seen him at his best and at his worst. She nursed him back to health after Sayber tried to kill him. He had been at his lowest and had contemplated ending his life.

Then Terra arrived and the change had been noticeable. More friendships had been formed and those he tried to push away refused to go, giving him support he never had before.

Including his father. Someone she has fallen deeply in love with. Someone, she fears, she will not see again.

When Gryffin appears on the screen she realises her fears are well founded. 'He is dead,' she says before she can stop herself.

Gryffin nods once but does not say anything.

'How?'

'He took a bullet meant for me. He died saving me. Aleena, Lucan's dead too.'

She closes her eyes and lowers her chin to her chest. Gryffin does not offer empty words of support. There is little point.

She knows Gryffin well enough to be certain he bears a great deal of guilt for what happened to both Roman and Lucan. The relationship between Roman and Gryffin was new to both of them, but over the last few weeks she had seen it grow. It should not have come to an end so abruptly.

She looks up at the screen and is surprised by his expression. She had expected him to be angry, but instead she can see such deep sadness.

'I'm sorry, Aleena. I tried... I told him to go. But he wouldn't.'

'This is not your fault, Gryffin. He gave his life to save his son. He would have no regrets. I am certain of that.'

He nods and slumps back in the chair. 'We had to leave their bodies on Ultar. I can't even bring him to you so you can bury him.'

Her tears break free at his words. She glances up at him and sees he has moved closer to the screen. He places his hand against the side of the screen and she mirrors his actions, resting her palm against his as the grief takes her over.

Gryffin does not end the transmission. Instead he stays with her, his presence on the screen offering a little comfort as she cries.

34

Gryffin splashes icy water on his face and glares up at his reflection in the cracked mirror. The hours in the rejuvenation pod have done their bit. He looks a lot better than he did a few weeks ago. His pale, gaunt face has filled out again, the black ring has gone from under his eye, and he's managing to put some weight back on. He's still not as big as he was, but he doesn't look like a walking corpse anymore.

The call with Aleena lasted well over an hour but he's not complaining. She's been a big part of his life for years. He wasn't going to tell her Roman was dead and then disconnect the comms.

Being with her like that had actually helped him a little. Since he woke up on the station, he hadn't had time to think about what happened to Roman. Not properly anyway. He'd focused on the anger, on the need for revenge, but not the fact his father was dead.

They hadn't spoken much after she broke down and he's grateful for that. Talking about what happened over and over isn't something he wants to do. Killing more of the cyborgs responsible for his death is a different story.

He didn't mention what he's about to do either. Aleena had enough to deal with without worrying about him getting more mods. Losing Terra is bad enough without adding Aleena to the list. And probably Chayse. If he thinks about it too much, he can come up with a list of people who would be less than thrilled about his plan.

He knows he's making the right decision, but that doesn't help ease the pain of possibly losing Terra. He knew she'd be furious at his decision, but he wasn't prepared for her to pull away from him like she had.

Everything that's happened is because of him. Roman, Lucan, Bray, Aleena, Chayse... and now Terra. The list of people he's hurt is growing by the day. Having people he gives a damn about has ramped up his guilt levels when something goes wrong.

Life was so much easier when it was just him, his crew, and his ship. A father, a brother, a partner, and now these new family members... He never wanted any of it, but somehow it crept up on him.

Of all the new and unwelcome relationships, Terra was the one that really blind-sided him. A Foundation officer and a Nomad Captain shouldn't work, and for the most part it didn't. He tried to push her away, tried to put his feelings for her down to a malfunction, but it was a big lie. Since he'd stepped in to save her life two years ago, she'd changed his.

He'd lost track of the amount of out of character decisions he'd made since that day. Telling her his name. Meeting with her again. Sleeping with her. Somehow, she became a part of his life. She was the first thing he thought of when he woke up. She was the thing that kept him relatively sane when the Scientist held him prisoner for ten long months. Thinking of her had distracted him from the horrors of that place.

She saved him.

Evie is right. Terra had helped to calm him. Helped to bring out a part of himself he didn't know existed. His humanity. The Scientist had torn it out of him in the lab. Then Rayde had taken care of whatever was left over the years. But she had seen what he thought he'd lost a long time ago.

He walks over to their bed and picks up the t-shirt Terra left on the covers. It's one of his, but for reasons he can't figure out, she insisted on wearing it. He holds it up to his face and closes his eye as he breathes in her scent. It's a scent that, until this moment, he didn't realise was a part of his life. Just as she had become. He lowers the shirt and looks around his room. Their room.

There are reminders of Terra everywhere. Her clothes take up most of his small wardrobe. The once empty shelves have small trinkets from different colonies she had visited with him. Her drawing pad is open on his desk, pencils scattered on top of the paper.

He sits on the chair and pulls the paper closer. Each page has another drawing of him. Page after page after page. Every now and again she sketched a landscape, but for the most part it was him.

Gryffin stops at a page with two hands on it - his old metal hand holding her much smaller one. He traces his finger along her hand on the paper and the empty feeling in his gut gets so much worse.

He runs his fingers over the scar on his upper chest. Terra's bullet had left the permanent mark on his skin the first time they met. He has too many scars on his body to count, each one a reminder of an event in his life he'd prefer to forget - except that one.

She changed his life the moment she shot him. That one bullet had led him to his past and brought Roman, Bray, and Terra into his messed-up life.

He went from being alone, from barely surviving, to having her in his life and wanting a future. Just a pity it hasn't worked out like that. Gryffin looks around their room, looks at her clothes and the trinkets then back to the drawing.

The empty feeling in his gut and tightness in his throat come back as he looks at their hands on the page in front of him. He frowns as a thought suddenly hits him. The strange feelings he's been getting lately aren't down to malfunctions. They come when he thinks about Terra. It's her.

Does he love her? Is that what these feelings are?

Gryffin laughs and scrubs his hand over his face as the truth sinks in. He loves her. He loves Terra. Then his smile fades as something else hits him. He's felt like this for a while. For months. Does that mean he's loved her for months? All that time she was telling him how she felt and he gave her nothing back.

He didn't recognise what he was feeling and there's damn all he can do about it now. He wants to tell her how he feels. He needs to tell her, but it's too late for that. She'd just think he was saying it to get her to stay with him. The moment has passed and he has to live with that.

The Foundation has taken so damn much from him, but forcing him to make this decision - to choose between more mods or a short, but happy life with Terra is too much. This whole thing started when they decided to pluck innocent people from their happy lives and do whatever the hell they wanted with them. Enough is enough.

He goes back to the bathroom to collect his shirt from beside the sink. He doesn't want to leave his quarters. As soon as he steps outside, his life is going to change forever. He knows it's not going to be the same as when the Scientist worked on him, but he's still dreading it.

He splashes his face again, watching as the water trickles off his hand. He looks up and wipes a droplet of blood from his nose. He can't even get five minutes alone with his thoughts without his body telling him he's done for.

He wipes his nose again, making sure he's not going to drip blood all over Evie's station, then pushes back from the sink. Time to get to get this over with.

He opens his door and stops in his tracks. Terra is standing at the bottom of the steps to their quarters. Her eyes are red and puffy, and her arms are wrapped around her chest.

'I couldn't let you go... If something happened...' she stops talking and leaps up the three steps, throwing her arms around his neck. He lifts her off the ground and buries his face in her hair.

'Terra—'

'No talking, Gryffin. Please. Just be with me.'

He doesn't need to be asked twice. He backs up and closes the door behind them.

∞

EARTH

The bowl Liza was holding shatters on the floor, scattering pieces across the room. She stares at Garvan, her brows raised as she takes a step forward. 'Dad? Is that really you?'

Garvan smiles but doesn't make a move towards her. He wants to give her space to process everything that's happening. 'Hey honey. It's me.'

She stops in front of him and reaches out with a shaking hand to touch his face. 'Wow. You look a little... different.'

'It's a long story. One that I don't have time for right now.'

'What's wrong? Why don't you have time?'

Zeke pulls out one of the chairs from the breakfast bar and gestures for Garvan to sit. He lowers onto it and sighs in relief.

'What happened to you, Dad? Are you in pain?'

Garvan hopes his smile puts her at ease, but one look at her face and he knows he's failed. 'Just a little tired, love.' He reaches out his hand, hoping that she'll come to him. Liza doesn't leave him waiting for long. She embraces him, crying softly against his shoulder. 'Hey, it's okay.'

'We were told you were dead. How is that okay?'

'I need you to get a hold of Jake,' Zeke interrupts.

'Jake? Why?'

'We need to find some people and Jake is our best bet.'

Liza looks from her father to her brother and back again. 'What are you two up to?'

'Nothing.'

She places her hands on her hips and stares at the two men. Zeke finally blows out a breath. 'Fine. We're joining in a rebellion against the Foundation and need help finding someone who can put us in touch with a big group of rebels in the Sector. One of whom is a cyborg.'

Garvan holds up two fingers. 'Actually at least two are cyborgs.'

Zeke nods. 'Sorry. At least two cyborgs. Well, is it three now?' he asks waving his hand at Garvan's mods.

'Fair enough. I guess it is.'

'Oh, and Harvey is One on the Council and is behind the whole thing. Including having Dad arrested after falsifying charges against him.'

Liza stares at them again for a few minutes before shaking her head. 'There's no way you two could have made that up.' She leans against the counter and purses her lips as she examines them both. 'Damn it anyway. Fine!'

'Really, love? The last thing I want is to land your family in trouble.'

'Dad, you, Zeke, Jake, and the girls are my family. But are you sure about Harvey? I mean him being One. I just can't see it. He's not exactly... He's just so...weak.'

Garvan nods. 'Sorry, love. Hard to believe I know, but he's One.'

Liza slams her hand down on the table. 'Fucker is out of this family as far as I'm concerned. I'm sorely tempted to show him exactly how pissed off I am.'

'As much as I'd give anything to see that, you have to stay quiet for now. If he gets a whiff you're involved he could hurt you. Actually, scrap that. You need to come with us.'

'To the prison?'

'No. We can drop you at the Morgan farm on the way. Can you pack a few things for you, Jake, and the girls?'

Liza stares at her father, then nods solemnly. 'Of course. Give me a few minutes.'

Zeke waits until she's out of earshot before he speaks again. 'You really think Harvey would do something to her to get to you?'

'I'm not willing to take that chance. He cut my damn arm off. I wouldn't put anything past the bastard. Go help your sister pack for the girls. I don't want to freak them out.'

Liza hurries back to the room and passes Garvan her personal unit. 'It's a secure link. I've told Jake who you are.'

Garvan smiles his thanks and looks down at the screen. He'd seen pictures of Jake in the hallway on the way in. The young man's hard green eyes examine him like he's a new inmate being sized up.

His blond hair and beard are cut short and from what he can see of Jake's upper body, he wouldn't want to go up against him one-on-one. Most of the prison guards at Tyrat had kept control through fear and intimidation. He has no doubts Jake would be able to do it with pure brute force. 'Hi Jake. Nice to meet you.'

'I'd prefer if our first introduction didn't involve looking for criminals or forcing my family into hiding.'

Garvan grimaces. 'Not how I would have planned it either. Sorry about that.'

'Yeah, I'll bet. Are you sure the location you're taking them to is secure?'

'Absolutely.'

'It better be, Wade. This is my family you're messing with. Can't say I give a damn about you, but I'd kill for them.'

Garvan nods. He hears Jake's unspoken threat loud and clear. 'You can trust me.'

Jake laughs. 'We'll see about that. Our next door neighbours are away for a few days. We've got the code for their house so we can keep an eye on it for them. They have a second transport in the garage. Code is 875645. No one will be looking for it so you should be able to move around without anyone checking you out. I'd like to be able to give it back to them at some stage so please try not to destroy it.'

'Thank you. Now for the other help.'

'I've heard of the Dixon's but most of the stories involve how off-grid they are. I think there's one or two inmates I can persuade to help me, but I can't promise anything. I'm off shift in two hours. Doesn't give me a lot of time.'

'I appreciate anything you can do to help.'

'Where will you be?'

'We're hiding out at a friend's farm. I don't know how long we'll be off the radar for though. I'm not someone they want wandering around.'

Jake sighs and rubs his forehead. 'Okay. I'll meet you there. Tell Liza to leave it for two hours then send the coordinates to my personal comms unit.'

'Will do.'

'I've told Liza to empty the gun safe in our room. I've got twelve unregistered weapons and ammunition. I'm hoping you won't need them, but better prepared than screwed.'

'Hold on? You have unregistered weapons?'

'I'm a security guard in a Foundation prison. I don't go around with my eyes closed and my fucking fingers in my ears. I know the Foundation is corrupt. Why do you think I'm not putting my foot down and telling you to fuck off and leave my family on Earth? If you have a way of getting them off that damn planet I'm not going to stop you. Keep them safe, Wade. I mean it. I'll be coming to the farm armed and I swear the first bullet will be for you if anything happens to them.'

Jake kills the connection and Garvan blows out a long breath. Wasn't quite how he imagined his first chat with his son-in-law would go, but so far he likes the guy.

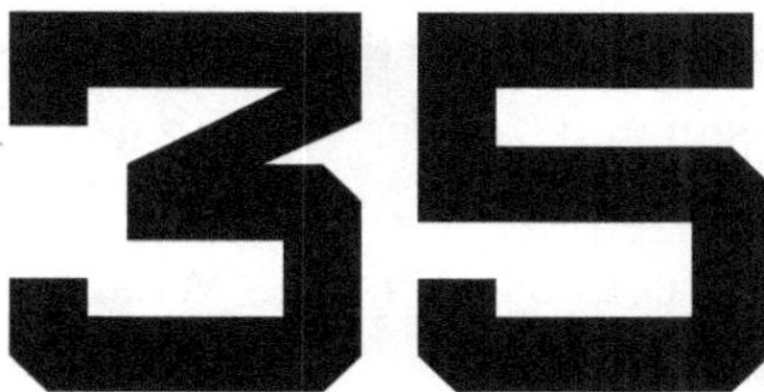

FOUNDATION SHIPYARD

Creed pulls himself out from under the console and curses as he shoves the wires aside. 'No bringing this one back.'

Baila contacts the rest of the team checking the other systems on the ship and tells them to move on. 'Thought we'd get more than we are.'

Baila has a point. They've been at this for two hours and so far only two ships have joined *Nemesis* outside. Everything else either needs a new engine or a new hull. Neither of which they have time to deal with. If they had a year to rebuild the ships they'd be laughing.

'Creed.'

He taps his comms unit. 'You find it, Hardy?'

'I got it. It's at the back and is fairly beat up, but the name is clear.'

'Is there any way of getting it out?'

'Don't know how, but the engines are still operational. I should be able to manoeuvre it out. Creed, there's still personal belongings in the rooms. What do you want to do with all the items?' Hardy asks.

Destroying the ship is one thing. Destroying belongings of all those children that died is something entirely different. The families deserve to get those things back. 'How many rooms are we talking about?'

'About twenty on this ship. All the belongings have names on them. This room was Mason and Troy's. The one next door was assigned to Ellis and Daegan. It's all kid stuff, Creed.'

'Hang on.' Creed contacts Chayse. 'What was Gryffin's name. I mean before he was taken.'

'Daegan Sawyer.'

'I thought so. Hardy, Daegan is Gryffin.'

'Fuck. I never thought of Gryffin before he was... well, Gryffin. Seeing his stuff here like this is not sitting well with me.'

'Dammit. Okay. Change of plans. Leave the ship where it is. There are too many ghosts here. We're going to take this base too. I'm not giving the Foundation a chance to destroy all this evidence. Join with the other teams. We can sort out the rest of the ships once we've dealt with the Foundation.'

He meets Baila on the loading ramp and she sprays a thick red X on the back. Chayse steps out from behind the ship beside them and shakes his head. 'This one's dead.'

'Same here,' Creed mutters. 'Listen, I've decided to keep this place under Nomad control. Give us time to deal with the rest of the ships at a later stage - if any of us are still alive of course.'

'Gryffin's ship?'

'We'll leave it for now. His stuff is still on board.'

Chayse's face drops and he looks away for a moment. 'Better keep going.'

Creed lets him get back to work and turns in the opposite direction. He runs his hand over the hull of another ship. 'Well, let's see if you're going to cooperate.'

∞

ARES

Gryffin twists Terra's dark hair around his hand as he crushes his mouth to hers. She moans and bites his bottom lip. Not able to hold back, he rips her shirt open, scattering buttons all over the floor, but he doesn't care. All he can think about is getting her undressed as fast as possible. He needs all of her. He needs to feel every part of her body, needs to taste her, needs to be in her, on her, under her.

He pulls down her trousers and stands on the material so she can step out. Gryffin tears her underwear off her body and takes a step back to look at her.

It doesn't matter how many times he sees her naked she still manages to knock him on his ass. Terra blushes as she tries to cover herself, but he gently holds her wrist. 'I want to look at you. Every damn bit.'

Her long dark hair hangs over her shoulder in stark contrast to her pale, smooth, flawless skin. Skin he needs to be all over, right now. He lowers to his knees and licks, sucks and kisses his way down her breasts, along her side and across her tight stomach. She moans softly and grabs his hair when he slowly moves further down her body.

He slips a finger inside, followed by a second. Terra writhes against his hand, pushing his fingers deeper inside her. He looks up at her, the expression of lust on her face tipping him over the edge.

He keeps his fingers inside her as he rises to his feet and pushes his tongue in her mouth again. She scratches her short nails along the skin against his chest implant, sending fireworks up his spine. 'Goddammit, Terra,' he grinds out through clenched teeth. She writhes against his hand as he increases the speed, squeezing his hand tightly between her thighs.

She looks at him through hooded eyes with a smile on her face as she moves her hand down further. He growls as she finds her target, holding him tightly through his leathers as she continues to move on his hand. She pushes his trousers down his legs and strokes him while she kisses along the scar on his throat, nipping playfully at the skin. He groans as she rubs her hand along his length. 'Gryffin,' she gasps.

He licks his lips and pushes harder against her hand. 'Yeah?'

'I want you inside me. Now.'

Hell, he doesn't have to be told twice. He lifts her on to his desk and pushes his trousers down his hips. She wraps her legs around him as he slips inside her, before groaning as her body grips him tightly. She digs her fingers in the back of his shoulders and throws her head back against the wall as he slowly fills her. 'Gryffin.'

He braces himself against the desk, slightly off balance thanks to his missing arm. Terra drags her nails down the edge of his chest implant sending jolts of pleasure through him. She mutters his name as she tightens her legs around his waist.

He could listen to her saying his name forever. His name never held much meaning for him - it was just the designation Rayde had given him, but the way she says it, with him inside her, drives him crazy.

Terra has a way of making simple things like his name mean so much more. It makes him want to do things he would never have considered before. She bites her bottom lip and breathes faster. Not wanting her to come yet, he forces himself to slow down.

'Gryffin, please!'

'Look at me,' he growls.

She digs her nails in his back. 'Gryffin... don't stop.'

'I said look at me,' he commands. 'I want to see your face.'

Terra raises her head and he locks eyes with her as he moves again, increasing his pace, diving deeper. He hisses in pain as her nails dig in his flesh.

In response, he slams in to her faster and faster until she screams out his name. Her body squeezes him tightly as the waves of her orgasm ripple through her. He follows her a few seconds later and his body tenses as his release hits him.

He stays inside her as a few final tremors work through her body. She blows out a breath before smiling lazily at him. 'How about we try the shower next?' She kisses him again, slow and deep. He pulls away to catch his breath and playfully nips at her neck as he grinds against her.

He slowly pulls out of her and carries her over to the bed. He gently lays her on it then collapses beside her. Terra rolls over and rests her head on his chest, tracing her fingers along the black lines of his tattoo. 'Shower now?

He lifts his head to look at her again. Damn, she's stunning, with her dark hair falling over her shoulders, her red, slightly swollen lips turned up to a small satisfied smirk and those green eyes that bring out his human side.

He knows what she's doing. She's trying to delay things, but, as much as he'd love to take her in the shower, he's out of time. 'They're waiting for me.'

She continues to trace the lines of his tattoo, as her body tenses. 'I know.'

'Why did you come to see me? Not that I'm complaining, I just want to know.'

She rests her chin on her hand and looks up at him. 'I know you have to do this, but I'm terrified about what's going to be done to you. About how you'll be after. We've been through so much together, Gryffin. What's happening... you're reacting to the situation we're being put in by the Foundation. They're doing this to us. I'd give anything to change your mind, but I know I'd be wasting my breath.'

'Terra—'

'No, let me finish. You're doing what you have to do. I understand that. I'm not happy about it, but I understand.'

'Am I going to lose you?'

She wipes a tear from her cheek and looks away from him. 'I want to say no, but I don't know, Gryffin. I've seen you twice after you've had more work done and you weren't you afterwards. What if deep down you won't be my Gryffin anymore? What if you're more like what he...' She shuts her eyes and shakes her head.

It hits Gryffin like she punched him in the gut. 'What your father designed me to be.' She nods, but keeps her eyes closed. How the hell had he not thought of that? No wonder she's tempted to run from him as fast as she can. 'This coming up because of the mods or has it been there all along?'

'Ever since I found out the Scientist was my father I haven't been able to get the images out of my head.'

'What images?'

'Him working on you. Him hurting you. Enjoying the pain and torment he was causing you. I thought I'd be able to ignore them or they'd lessen in time, but it's not going away. If anything, the shame and guilt I feel knowing what he did to you is only getting worse. It's absolutely not your fault and I hate what it's doing to us. But I don't know if I can be with you while I feel this way. It's not fair to either of us.'

Gryffin nods. He understands what she's saying. Realising how he feels about her came a few hours too late to help them. But there's no way he's going to tell her now. It wouldn't help either of them. All it will do is make things so much worse. He doesn't want her to be with him just because he's finally figured out how he feels. 'You should have said something sooner.'

She takes his hand and squeezes it. 'It really just hit me when you told me what you're planning. I meant it when I told you I have no problem with your implants.' She runs her finger along the edge of his ocular implant. 'You have to believe that.'

'I know. If the Foundation hadn't created this army of theirs I'd ditch the plan, get the work undone as much as I can, then disappear on *Ares* with you. But if there's the smallest chance the Foundation will make more cyborgs I can't do that.'

The comms unit beside his bed sounds. As one, they turn to look at it. 'Damn it. I have to go.'

She nods, but doesn't say anything. He sits up and rubs his hand over his face before heading for the shower. He stops as he gets to the door. 'I could use some company.'

'What about Bray?'

'I want you in the shower with me, not my brother.'

'That's not what I meant.'

'I know.' He walks over to her, lifts her off the bed and takes her to the shower. 'They can wait another few minutes.'

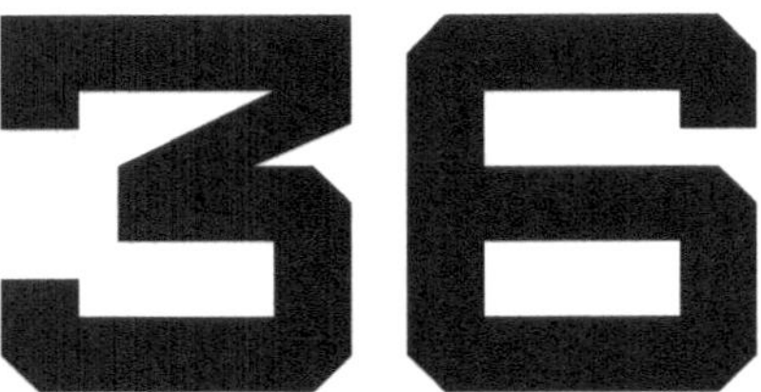

DIXON SPACE STATION

Gryffin takes Terra's hand and pulls her aside as they near the med bay. He opens his mouth to speak, then sighs and closes it again. He rests his hand against the wall, pining her against the wall with his towering body. 'I don't know what to say.'

'That makes two of us. After everything we've been through, neither of us can escape fate.'

'I'm still glad you shot me on the station. No regrets.'

Terra laughs in spite of the gravity of the situation. 'Are you so sure about that? I've brought you nothing but trouble.'

He pulls down his t-shirt and places her hand over the scar left by her bullet. 'Like I said. No regrets about anything. Understood?'

'No regrets.' She squeezes his arm and he winces in pain. 'What's wrong?'

'Nothing.'

She pushes his sleeve up to get a better look. Blood is weeping from the casing covering the tip of his arm. 'That doesn't look like nothing.'

'The Dixon woman checked it. One of the connectors is broken. It's digging in me. It'll be fixed with everything else.'

Terra swallows and forces a smile on her face. She can't stand watching him deteriorating in front of her. Every day something else seems to go wrong with him.

She pulls the red bandanna from her hair and ties it around the wound on his arm. 'Can't have you dripping blood all over Evie's floor. You'd never hear the end of it.' She looks back up at him and her breath catches in her throat. This is probably going to be the last time she's with him. The real Gryffin. Her Gryffin.

He bends down and kisses her, long and hard and deep. He rests his forehead against hers and squeezes her hand. 'I love you, Terra.'

She hears the words and knows it was Gryffin's voice, but her brain can't link the voice with the words. Terra lifts her head and meets his eyes. 'What did you say?'

Gryffin looks her straight in the eyes. 'I love you.'

Terra has no control over the smile that breaks out. 'You do?'

He nods and brushes her hair back from her face. 'Yes. I should have told you weeks ago, but I didn't know what it was. I only realised today what I was feeling. Bad timing I know, but I love you and you deserve to know how I feel.'

She wraps her arms around him and hugs him close. Terra's lost count of the number of times she'd hoped and wished for him to say those words to her, but actually hearing them from him is so much better than she could have imagined. He holds her for a few minutes then she feels him move away from her.

'I better go.' She nods, unable to trust her words to come out without the accompanying tears. That's the last thing he needs right now. He walks towards the door, only letting go of her hand at the last second. Gryffin turns around to look at her again. 'I love you.'

'I love you, too.'

As the doors close behind him, Terra is aware of someone standing a little down the corridor. She turns around to see Rua silently watching her. As if aware of the exact second Terra is going to break, Rua rushes over and awkwardly takes her in her arms. 'You're coming with me.'

'I want to stay out here.'

Rua forcefully turns her in the opposite direction. 'Come to *Lir*. I have numerous comms units that could do with attention. Take your mind off what's going on in there.'

Terra nods and allows herself to be led away from Gryffin.

∞

DIXON SPACE STATION

'Are you okay, dear?'

Desyl lifts his head from the sink and wipes his mouth on his sleeve. He looks over his shoulder at Evie and attempts a smile. 'Oh yeah. Just great.'

Evie sits on the edge of the bath and hands him a glass of water. 'Forgive my bluntness but you look like... well, shit, if you don't mind me saying.'

He takes a long drink then wipes his mouth on his arm. 'Cheers. I feel like shit.'

'You did very well.'

'I've been there while Gryffin's been worked on in the past, but knowing he was awake and in pain through the whole thing was a big incentive never to do it again.' He laughs harshly as he runs a hand over his close-cropped hair. 'At least those times we were helping him. Now... we've hurt him and taken something from him. Something he may never get back and I don't just mean his leg. I'm meant to have his back, Evie. How could I have let this happen?'

'Firstly, they all volunteered. You didn't force them to do this. The Foundation did in a roundabout way. Secondly, he's your leader. From what I know of the Nomad, disobeying a direct order is a bit of a no-no.'

He leans on the door-jamb and rests his forehead against his raised arm. He blows out a long breath as he peers inside the room beyond. Some of the Dixon's personnel are helping to make the men as comfortable as possible after their procedures. 'He's not my leader anymore. Not my captain either. I should have pulled rank and stopped this from happening.'

'Perhaps you could have, but how would that have helped anyone? This needed to happen.'

He wipes a hand over his face and watches the Dixon personnel hook Dante, Boone, and Trace up to dozens of monitors. Gryffin was still in the rejuvenation pod having his dozens of wounds healed.

With the help of the Foundation files and the implant stores on board, they added everything Bray and Gryffin wanted. Retinal implants have given each of them perfect night vision as well as the ability to increase magnification when needed.

Together with neuro-pharmaceuticals, their concentration level has increased. Neural interfaces have been fitted to the men linking them to each other. The plan is for the team to work as a single unit without the need to give vocal instructions. Gryffin is still the only one able to hook directly with a computer, but being able to communicate telepathically with the team will be a definite bonus.

At that moment, Gryffin's bed is wheeled back in. Each of the men had been heavily sedated but, as usual, Gryffin's implants fought to neutralise it as fast as they were pumping it into him. His friend had felt everything they were doing to him. His extraordinary pain threshold helped him during the procedure but because Desyl knew this, every time the Captain winced or grunted Desyl knew he was in a serious amount of pain.

As well as having the same work done as the other cyborgs, Gryffin needed a little extra work. With no other viable option, his leg had been removed. It was going to happen sooner or later anyway. Desyl fully believes it was only a matter of time before it decided to detach itself from the rest of his body out of spite. His new arm was attached but they were giving his body time to adjust to the new connectors before the artificial leg was attached.

His bed is slotted in place against the wall and the bile rises up Desyl's throat when he sees the new ocular implant. Watching that being fitted was the worst part for Desyl and for Gryffin. The Scientist had made a right mess of the process initially, like he did with all the implants.

To make sure the upgraded parts worked as they should, Gryffin needed extensive work done to his eye socket. No amount of sedative had kept him under once they started poking around there and no amount of ale would help Desyl forget his friend's roars of pain. It had been a relief when they were finally able to fit the new eyepiece in place.

Desyl closes his eyes and curses himself. Two years ago he was just another member of the crew. Following orders and trying not to get on the wrong side of Gryffin. Now, he's acting Captain of the flagship after letting his captain - his friend, go through hell again.

This isn't what he signed up for. Chayse was the one Gryffin earmarked to take over the Nomad. He got the new ship and the hand-picked personnel to help him. What does Desyl have? A shit-load of inexperience and self-doubt mixed with a generous helping of not-having-a-clue-what-he's-doing.

'He has faith in you.' Evie squeezes his shoulder, startling him.

'What?'

'You look like the weight of the world is on your shoulders. Gryffin has faith. Trust that.'

Desyl rests his head on his hand as he looks down at the strange little woman. 'You in my head or something?'

She smiles. 'Not too difficult to get in there.'

He looks back at Gryffin. 'Cheers.'

'I didn't mean that as an insult. It's not too hard to figure out where your head is. I don't know much about that impossibly rude man out there, but I have figured out one thing. *Ares* and her crew are his world. By deciding to do what he has is a pretty hefty compliment to you.'

'How'd you figure that out? His head is on the Foundation and revenge. He barely gave *Ares* and the Nomad a thought.'

'Exactly.' Evie rolls her eyes when Desyl shoots her an irritated look. 'Oh come now, Commander. You just proved my point. He trusted that you have it under control. I have no doubt he gave the ship and crew a great deal of thought and came to the same conclusion I have.'

'And what's that?'

'That he has nothing to worry about. He knows you've got their best interests at heart.'

He opens his mouth to argue, but she reaches up and places her fingers over his lips. 'Best not to argue with logic, dear boy. Just go with it.' She nods towards Gryffin. 'I think your former captain would like a word.'

Desyl wipes a hand over his face and looks back at Evie. 'What am I supposed to say to him? This is Terra's job.'

'Yes, well one problem at a time, dear. I have a horrible feeling it may be easier to sort out the Foundation than those two. As for right now, he's your friend. Just be there for him. Get him through this so he can end the blasted project once and for all.'

Desyl takes a deep breath, wipes his mouth on his sleeve again, then walks over to Gryffin. He's focusing on the empty space where his right leg should be. Desyl gives him a minute to get used to his new body. If his face is anything to go by, Gryffin isn't taking it too well. After a long silence, the captain pulls his attention from the bandaged stump to Desyl.

'How are you, sir?'

'I'm fine.'

His voice is weak and hoarse from all the screaming as they pulled him apart. They're no better than Terra's sadistic father. 'I was here for the whole thing, sir. There's no way in hell you're fine.'

'I feel fucking terrible. That better?'

Desyl shrugs. 'Hell if I know. How's the pain level?'

'It's there. How are the others?'

'The same. Listen, I'm sorry—'

'Stop.'

'But Gryffin—'

He pushes onto his elbow and stares at him with a bloodshot eye. 'I said stop. Thank you for helping me. Now I don't have to kick you out the airlock.'

'That makes me feel so much better.'

Gryffin smiles and closes his eye. 'When will Bray and the Dixon man finish the programming?'

'In a few hours. We want to give you as long as possible to recover before we activate the new components and link all of you together. Your... your new prosthetic arm and leg are being adjusted to fit you. You're larger and heavier than they were designed for. Like your arm, the connectors have been embedded in the... in what's left of your leg. Thanks to—'

Desyl clears his throat again. Talking so bluntly about Gryffin's loss of his leg and fitting of a mechanical one is difficult, especially with Gryffin staring at him. 'Thanks to the store of components on *Cronus*, your chest implant has been upgraded to accept the leg. We'll be able to fit that at the same time.'

'Have everything ready in two hours.'

'Sir, you all need more time.'

'We don't have more time. I'll give them two hours.'

'You're a real pain in the butt, sir. Fine. I'll tell them two hours. Try to get some rest before then. You're going to need to be as strong as possible.'

'Where's Terra?'

'Rua took her to *Lir*. She thought it would be best to get her as far from the bay as possible. You know, in case she heard anything. Do you want me to get her?'

'No. Where's the bandanna from my arm?'

Desyl looks around and finally finds it sticking out of one of the bins. He holds it up to Gryffin. 'You want me to give it back?'

'Tie it around my arm where it was.'

Desyl shrugs and does as he's told. 'Get some rest, sir.'

'I need to talk to Sayber.'

'You need to rest, sir.'

'Get Sayber in here now. I need to talk to him. Alone.'

Desyl nods to a Nomad standing guard and the man leaves to make the call. 'Is there something wrong. I mean, something else wrong?'

'Nothing to do with you, Desyl. Your priority is *Ares*.' He pushes himself up the bed, wincing in pain as he settles back in the bed. 'I need you to stay focused on the ship.'

Desyl nods, but Gryffin grips his arm, squeezing it firmly. His clear blue eye bores into him with an intensity that leaves him cold. 'Whatever happens to me, the Nomad will need you, Creed, and Chayse to keep them together. You're key to their survival. Understood?'

Desyl licks his dry lips. 'Yes, sir.'

Gryffin drops his arm and flops back on the bed as Sayber saunters in. 'You called?'

'Give us a minute, Desyl.'

He nods at Sayber as he passes, making sure the door to the room is firmly closed behind him. Whatever the hell that was, it's done nothing to put him at ease. If anything, Gryffin's words and the secret meeting with Sayber leaves a bad taste in his mouth.

He stifles a yawn and rubs his aching eyes. He's probably over-thinking everything. Gryffin's been through hell and they still don't know if he'll be a fit leader after all the modifications. Of course the Captain wants to make sure Desyl is up to the challenge.

That still doesn't explain the meeting with Sayber though. There's not a lot he can do about it. The only thing he can do is make sure the Nomad are ready to fight alongside the modified Gryffin.

37

Gryffin stares over at the far wall as too many hands touch him. Those two hours had gone by too fast. He ignores the pull of wires and connectors on his skin as monitors are fitted and implants checked. He's exhausted and can barely think straight thanks to the pain. If someone came in and offered to knock him out he'd let them, even if it meant a whack to the head.

He looks at what's left of his body. Now his entire leg is gone it's probably an even split between his cybernetics and original body. Maybe the odds have tipped in favour of the metal. Whatever the ratio he'd rather not know. As long as everything works as it should it's worth it.

As much as he's dreading the whole procedure, he wants his arm and leg attached. He's done being helpless on a bed in a Foundation ship. Not being able to defend himself is nearly more unsettling than what's about to happen. If Sayber decided to try taking his head off again, there's fuck all he could do to stop him.

'Eh hello!'

Felix weaves his hand in Gryffin's face. 'Are you listening or am I talking to myself?'

'What?'

'As I was saying, to myself clearly, you'll be linked to Boone, Trace, and Dante. You should, if this works of course, be able to relay orders to them.'

Evie pulls a very rough schematic onto the screen on the far wall. 'If the neural link works we should be able to relay orders to you without being in comms reach, then you should be able to issue them to the others in the group. If we get this right, there's also a chance you'll be able to override the leadership protocol in the cyborgs on Earth, but that's the absolute best case scenario. At the moment, taking them out of commission is the priority.'

Bray examines the data on the screen and nods to himself. 'It should work, but there's a lot of factors we haven't taken into consideration, starting with the one big glaringly obvious one. Who's going to be relaying orders to you? It's going to have to be someone trustworthy. It's a damn big ask.'

Gryffin silently stares at Desyl. Evie rests her head in her hands and mirrors Gryffin's expression. Desyl suddenly gets what they're thinking and vigorously shakes his head. 'No. Not a chance in hell.'

'Can I get a minute with Desyl?' Gryffin waits until everyone is out of earshot before he speaks again. 'You're the only one who can do it.'

'A few days ago you were threatening to kick me off the ship. You can't just drop this on me and expect me to agree.'

Gryffin pushes up the bed and makes the mistake of looking down at where his leg used to be. He couldn't care less about the rest of the implants, but he wants his prosthetic leg fitted. 'I was angry at what you did. Still am, but I don't trust anyone else with this. It needs to be a Nomad in control of me. It needs to be you.'

'This is a big ask, sir.'

'It's just Gryffin now. If anything I should be calling you 'sir'.'

Desyl curses and rubs his eyes. 'This is all wrong. It shouldn't be like this.'

'Yeah, well it is. I want it to be you, Desyl, but I'm not going to order you.'

Desyl sits on the edge of the bed opposite Gryffin and crosses his arms. Gryffin leaves *Ares*' new captain to his thoughts. Fuck knows he's landed him with enough to think about.

Desyl was far from happy about being given command of *Ares* without adding this to the mix. But it's that very reluctance that proves to Gryffin he made the right decision. He knows there are Nomad on board *Ares* who would have jumped at the chance to command her, unlike Desyl.

Desyl underestimated himself. Always has. He doesn't realise how much of a natural Nomad he is. Rayde would have called him a weak leader. Desyl wasn't feared. He wasn't cruel. He's so similar to Creed in that way. Creed wasn't feared, but he was respected.

Rayde tried hard to prove to Gryffin that in order to succeed you had to be feared. But that's not how it works. Respect was a far better motivator than fear. Gryffin hopes that after making some of the changes he did, he'd earned the respect of his crew over the years.

Desyl looks up at him and shakes his head. 'Fuck.'

'That a yes or no?'

'It's a fuck. How exactly do you see this working? Me controlling you I mean.'

'I'll be a member of the crew like everyone else. You give me orders just like everyone else.'

'It's not that simple, sir. Gryffin. Fuck.'

'It is.'

'But you're my friend.'

'What?'

'You heard me.' Desyl pushes off the bed and paces the room. 'Having to help stick those things on you. In you. That was bad enough. I can't give you an order you won't be able to disobey.'

'It's no different to what I did as captain. Don't make this different.'

'It's so different! How can you not see that?' Desyl curses and wipes a hand over his face. 'The kill switch.'

'What about it?'

'You got them to fit a program that'll kill you all if you get out of control. Do you want me to control that too?'

'Yes.'

'Oh great. How the fuck did I get myself into this? You were threatening to kill me a few days ago and now you want me to be able to kill you with one simple command. I can't, Gryffin. No way.'

Gryffin closes his eye and drops his head back against the pillow. He knew Desyl wouldn't be thrilled about this idea but he wasn't expecting any of this. 'I can remember the face of every single Ultaran I killed when Rayde and the Foundation had control of me.'

Desyl stops pacing and looks over at him. 'I'm begging you, Desyl. I need you to make sure that doesn't happen again. I don't want to be used to kill people I know. Not again. Please, Desyl.'

Desyl crosses his arms and looks down at his boots for a good five minutes without saying a word.

'Okay. I'll do it.'

'Thank you, sir.'

Desyl groans and shakes his head. 'Yeah, that's just all wrong. My first order as your Captain is to forbid you from calling me sir. I'm Desyl and you're Gryffin. No sir or captain or anything else. Just our names.'

Gryffin smirks. 'Understood.'

Desyl calls the others back in. 'So, it looks like I'll be controlling Gryffin.'

Felix nods. 'Of course you will. Not sure what took you so long to agree. Anyway, we probably should get this show on the road.' Felix moves away from the bank of screens and stands beside Gryffin's bed. 'Okay, we'll get Gryffin's implants up and running first then bring the others online.'

Gryffin resists the urge to tell him to get a move on. He'd welcome the pain receptor blocker right now. The pain is only getting worse and he's not sure how much longer he can control it.

Bray picks up a cable and stands over his brother. 'We'll hook you up and load the programming. While we're doing that, we'll attach your new leg and arm then get the rest of the implants up and running.'

He pauses and twists the cable between his fingers. 'The program block we fitted to you a few months ago can't be removed so we had to add a device to counteract our block. There was no way of linking you with the others without it. Because of that, we don't know how much control you'll have once we load this. Hopefully you'll be able to keep it in hand, but there's a chance you'll be pushed behind the programming.'

'Understood. Hook me up.'

Gryffin turns away from Bray to focus on the ceiling. Ignoring the twisting in his gut, he tries to think about anything but what's going to happen. Being modified was the right decision. He has no doubts about that.

The part that's scaring him is whether, once the program is loaded, he'll be able to think for himself. He accepts Desyl will be able to give him orders and he'll more than likely be forced to follow them, but he also hopes he'll have a little independent thought.

The other big fear is whether they'll be able to undo the work again. Deep down he knows there's a chance this will be the start of the end for him. A one-way trip that finishes with the loss of his humanity. But if it means stopping the Foundation, it's a sacrifice he'll gladly make.

He winces as the connector is pushed into his ocular implant. Hands gently pull the bandage off the remains of his leg and probe the new connectors. Gryffin makes the mistake of glancing down. He's actually pleasantly surprised.

Unlike when his arm was removed, the wound is clean. The new connectors have been fitted neatly to his flesh with care. It still sickens him that he had to sacrifice this part of himself, but the Dixon's and their team have treated him with a level of respect he isn't used to.

Evie smiles as she looks up at him. 'Well, Captain— Sorry, Gryffin. Your leg has healed beautifully. The connectors are in place and we're ready to fit your prosthetic, if you're ready.'

He nods and Felix appears behind her with his new leg. The dull metal is sleek and clean looking. Even though they had to modify it to fit his body, it looks like it was specially made for him.

'Now, as you can see we tried to keep it the same shape as your old leg. Once you have your uniform and boots on, no one will be able to tell the difference. If you can lie back for me, I'll lift your leg up.'

He does as he's told and holds his breath as her hands slip under the neat stump to raise it off the bed. Fully expecting the usual searing pain that accompanied fitting his arm, he is pleasantly surprised when all he feels is a strange pull on his limb before she places it back on the bed. 'Looks good. How does that feel?'

Gryffin lifts his head and stares at his new leg. If he hadn't seen it there he wouldn't have believe it was attached.

'You look confused. Is something wrong?'

'It didn't hurt.'

Evie smiles at him. 'That's good to know.'

'But my arm always hurt?'

Her smiles fades. 'Usually, those in the medical profession try to reduce your pain as much as possible. I believe the last person who worked on you to this extent had a very different objective.'

His arm is fitted with the same absence of pain. In the past, he'd always avoided taking his arm off, no matter how sore the connectors became. Leaving it on and suffering through the discomfort had been a better option than taking the arm off and refitting it again. If this first fitting is anything to go by, he'll be able to give his body a break from the prosthetics more often.

Desyl's face looms over him. 'Last chance.'

Gryffin attempts a weak smile, but it has little effect on him. 'Do it.'

Desyl nods and steps back giving Bray space at the head of the bed. Gryffin focuses on the ceiling again as his brother starts activating the implants and loading the program. The pain hits him like a thousand knifes piercing his flesh over and over. His breath catches in his throat, the scream caught, desperate to be released.

He arches off the bed as the pain escalates to a whole new level for him. The flesh around the new components burns as his body fights against the invasion. He thought he was prepared for the procedure, thought having them fitted would be the worst part, but he was seriously mistaken.

He doesn't know if it's the new pain receptors kicking in or the new programming, but he welcomes whatever it is that sends him to blissful darkness.

∞

ARES

'Are you going to talk to him?'

Terra keeps stuffing clothes in the bag lying on Gryffin's bed. Or Desyl's bed now. Whoever owns the room isn't her concern. Leaving the ship as fast as she can is. 'What exactly would you like me to talk to him about?'

'Terra.'

She throws a pile of clothes on the bed and turns her attention to anywhere but his face. For someone who's meant to be a heartless mercenary, Desyl can manipulate anyone with one look. 'Don't you dare 'Terra' me. I'm out of things to say to him.'

'Damn it, Terra. I care about you. Please don't be like this.'

'Yeah, well tough. I needed my friend a few days ago and you made your feelings perfectly clear.'

'Terra—'

'No, Desyl! What is it with you Nomad? You lay down the law in black and white. Leave no room for discussion or allowing someone else to get their point across. Then, when you change your mind, you think a simple 'I'm sorry' or 'please' will undo everything. It doesn't work that way.'

'I know I hurt your feelings.' He sighs and rests his hands on his hips. 'I was between a rock and a... well, a Gryffin. One word from him and I'd be off the crew. I'd lose my job, my home, and my family. He didn't want you to know about his leg because he cares about—'

'Don't go there! If that's how he shows he cares, we've got a serious problem.' She closes the bag and grabs a box so she can pack her art supplies. 'He told me he loves me.'

'Are you serious?'

'Do you have any idea how long I've been waiting for him to say that to me? Two years, Desyl. Two years hoping he felt the same about me. Hoping that one day he'd wake up and realise that he loves me.

'When he said it to me, I just stared at him. I couldn't believe he'd actually said the words. But then he goes and does this? He should have told me it was something he was considering.'

He scratches the back of his head and looks away from her. 'Yeah. I get that. I've told you how things work for him.'

'I am painfully aware how things work for him. Believe me. He cut off his leg, Desyl. Without mentioning it to me. His leg!'

'I get that, but you know why he did it. It was beyond saving.'

'I understand that. All I'm saying is that you shouldn't have been the one to tell me. It should have been Gryffin.' She throws the drawing pad in the box and her stomach clenches when she sees a drawing of Gryffin. 'I'm almost afraid to ask, but who's holding his reins, huh? Who is controlling him?'

His face drops and he looks away from her. Terra shakes her head and takes a step back. 'I don't believe it. You? Well this couldn't have worked out better for you. You get *Ares* and Gryffin under your control.'

She knows she's taken quite a few steps too far, but the words are out and there's no taking them back. She didn't mean what she said, but that's not going to change anything. She risks a quick look at Desyl and swallows.

In the space of a few seconds, he's transformed from her friend to a pissed off captain. His brown eyes are cold and any trace of emotion has gone from his face. He doesn't even look angry and that's more than a little unsettling. She's not used to seeing this side of him.

Desyl slowly walks over to her, stopping right in front of her. His tattooed arms are down by his side, but the muscles are strained. He may not look angry, but she has absolutely pushed him too far. Terra resists taking a step back.

Until that moment, she hadn't realised how big Desyl actually is. 'The only reason I'm not personally kicking you off my ship right now is because I promised Gryffin I'd have your back. You're a friend, Terra, but don't you dare suggest I'm happy about anything that's happening. I thought you knew me better than that by now.'

'I know and I'm sorry. I didn't mean—'

'Do you want to be a Nomad?'

'I don't know. I'm not sure I can be on the same ship as—'

'Until you sign off *Ares* you're under my command. You can stay on *Ares*, I can transfer you to another Nomad ship, or you can leave the group. Let me know by the end of tomorrow what you want.

Whatever you decide, you will be under our protection. I keep my word.'

He turns around and stops at the open door as something in the corridor gets his attention instead.

'What is it?'

'Gryffin.'

Terra's stomach drops. She doesn't want to look, but her body has other ideas. She slowly turns and gasps when she sees Gryffin standing at the top of the stairs leading up to their quarters with two Nomad security just behind him.

'What... what's he doing here?'

'Wants to see you.'

'What am I supposed to do?'

'Try talking to him. And don't have a go at him about his leg. I mean it, Terra. It's done. He needs to focus on keeping control of himself. That's far more important.'

Terra turns back to Gryffin as Desyl quickly makes his exit, nodding at the Nomad security as he passes. She knows she has to say something, to acknowledge Gryffin in some way, but she doesn't know what to do.

A part of her wants to run over to him and throw her arms around him. But she's scared. She's scared to drop the small semblance of a wall she's been desperately trying to build around her heart since he went to surgery.

Even in the gloomy corridors of *Ares* she can see the modifications on his face and arm. His repaired, glowing purple artificial eye zooms in on her as he patiently waits for a reaction from her. Or perhaps permission to come closer.

Terra takes a deep breath and nods at Gryffin. Her heart beats in time to his footsteps. A part of her wants to run, to get as far from him as possible. To shut and lock the door before he gets too close. She watches in morbid fascination as he limps towards her, clearly still getting used to his new leg.

Gryffin steps through the doorway but, to her relief, programs it to remain open. He stops in front of her and drops his head to meet her eyes. She forces herself to look up at him.

She doesn't know what she was expecting. A dozen scenarios raced through her head since he first mentioned his plan to her, but she never expected this. The person in front of her still looks like Gryffin, even with the new modifications.

'Hi.' Her croaked greeting catches in her throat. His artificial eye spins as it focuses on her. The time crawls by, and with each passing second Terra's relief begins to fade away. She swallows deeply, hoping that someone... anyone will come and save her from this awkwardness.

Gryffin takes a step closer and she resists taking a step back. She hates that he is making her feel slightly nervous. An invisible hand wraps around her throat, constricting her air supply. 'Do you remember me?'

He pauses as he examines her, his robotic eye spinning one way and then the other. 'You're scared of me.'

She swallows and shakes her head, trying to convince him that he's mistaken even though she's not convinced herself. She doesn't know the man in front of her. Not anymore. For the most part he looks the same. If Desyl hadn't told her about his leg, she wouldn't have guessed it was a prosthetic. 'Of course not.'

His robotic eye continues its strange dance so she focuses on his right eye instead. Somehow, knowing that their friends had given him his new eye makes it so much worse. Knowing that their friends had taken more of his humanity from him is too much to think about.

He looks down at the pile of her things on the floor. 'You're leaving?'

'This is Desyl's room now. I'm going to move to the station until we know what's going on...'

'With us?'

'Yeah. We don't know which quarters you want. Or we want. I guess you'll be in the med bay for a few days.'

'Yes.'

'Is everything— Are you okay? Are you in pain?'

'No.'

'Good. That's good.' She steps back suddenly feeling like the walls of their room— His room— Desyl's room, are folding in on themselves. 'I better get back to it.'

He nods and frowns ever so slightly. Something about his expression reminds her of the old Gryffin, but it's gone as fast as it appeared. Without another word, he turns and leaves the room.

Terra's legs collapse from under her and she drops to the ground in a heap as she sobs.

38

EARTH

One paces his office, wearing a track in the plush carpet. His ornate mask is on the floor against the far wall. He used it to smash the view screen on his desk before sending it across the room.

That bastard Garvan is gone. A drugged prisoner who had just come out of a rather invasive surgery had picked himself up and walked out of the Council building without anyone seeing him. Quite impressive if not for the fact that, yet again, Garvan had managed to fuck him over.

Why didn't he just kill him? One bullet. One strike. One blow. Whatever the means, he could have taken care of this irritation once and for all. Now, not only had he lost Garvan, but the prototype has also vanished.

He rights his overturned chair and checks the broken screen. No new messages. He leans back in the chair and laughs over and over again.

It's all falling apart. The cyborg program was supposed to create obedience. Each of the participants should have been totally loyal to him and him alone. If the rest of the Council find out that their most expensive asset had yet again evaded capture, and that the female prototype has a serious attitude problem, his career would be cut short.

He can't shake the niggling feeling that Nova has somehow managed to align herself with Thirty-Five. Something about her tone before she left Earth troubled him. But it makes little to no sense. This Gryffin or whatever he was calling himself had never met Nova. The two cyborgs had never crossed paths. He's sure of that. Could something in their programming be drawing them to each other?

He sincerely hopes not. He has no doubts whatsoever he wouldn't survive an encounter from Gryffin and Nova. If the two ever united it would spell the end to the project once and for all.

One groans as a message comes in from Leeson. He's being called to an emergency Council meeting. Perfect timing as usual. His colleagues will be looking for an update on the situation on Ultar. If he had his way, he would destroy the planet once and for all. Once less thing to worry about.

∞

DIXON SPACE STATION

Bray stops at the door to the med bay on *Cronus*. He looks through the glass door and swallows hard to quell the increasing nausea which has a firm grip of his stomach.

Three beds are lined up against the far wall. Each bed is occupied by one of the cyborgs from Ultar. The fourth bed placed at the far side of the room holds Gryffin. For security purposes, they are all restrained to the beds and their implants are being closely monitored.

Gryffin more so than the others.

Their mother's face comes to his mind and he closes his eyes as the nausea twists his insides again. His mother would never forgive him for his part in the procedure. He would never forgive himself.

In the last few days, for the first time since learning about Gryffin's identity, he felt as if he had his brother back. Working with Gryffin to get the coordinates of the ships from Avoca was something he would never forget. He actually enjoyed the experience although Avoca would probably have a different opinion.

He opens the door and checks on the three newer cyborgs first. He had accessed their records earlier. Each man is roughly the same age as Bray with the exception of Boone who is closer to Gryffin's age. The Foundation had sent them to Tyrat for ridiculous reasons. Such as they had with Garvan. They had all lost their lives, wives, families, and children so they could take part in an experiment against their will.

Instead of using the faulty control implant, the Foundation had resorted to old-fashioned brainwashing to force the cyborgs to do their will. The men had suffered as a result and still showed the scars physically, but more so psychologically.

Their time on Ultar had helped undo some of the damage, but they would never fully regain everything they'd lost. That's probably why they were so willing to sacrifice everything they had left for payback. Hell, he can't blame them.

He smiles at Felix as he stops at the foot of the first bed. 'How are they doing?'

Felix nods as he checks the readings on one of the monitors. 'Surprisingly well considering what we did to the poor fellows. Dante and Trace are recovering well. They've had two sessions in the rejuvenation pod which has done wonders for them. Boone however is taking a little longer to get over the work. According to his record, the Foundation sent him back to Tyrat after he was altered. Guards used him as a 'how to deal with unruly prisoners' training tool. They didn't hold back. He was beaten to a pulp repeatedly. They used a rejuvenation pod to heal him them sent him back out there.'

'Fuck. Will he recover?'

'He should. His body has been through a lot before we ever laid a finger on him. I'm hoping he'll be fine in a few hours.'

Bray nods then turns towards his brother. 'And him?'

'I'd love to know how the hell that boy keeps going. He should be... well, dead would probably be the word I'd use. Truly baffling. Anyway, his original implants are working with the new ones. The wounds have healed, but he's different. Kind of like he's there, but not there.' He shrugs. 'Who the hell knows? I'm too old for all this. He's awake so go and see how he is for yourself.'

Gryffin glances up at him as he gets near the bed before he goes back to staring at something fascinating on the far wall. He looks worn out and more than a little beaten. Not a good thing for someone trying to hang on to control of a chip in their head.

Bray checks the various monitors seeing that Felix was right. Gryffin is doing extremely well considering. He unlocks the heavy restraints pinning Gryffin's arms and legs to the bed. The Nomad frowns and looks at Bray as he sits on the chair beside the bed and clasps his hands together. 'How do you feel?'

Gryffin frowns but doesn't respond.

'I don't know how you're doing it, but you've got a firm grip on the mods we made. Have to admit I'm a little impressed. Thought the procedures would kill you. The readings show the implant in your brain is working, but I can also see it's not running you.'

'Not yet.' Gryffin turns to look at him. 'It's fighting. I won't be able to hold it off for long.'

Bray nods. 'The link between you, Boone, Dante, and Trace is working. Can you connect with them?'

'Yes. The problem is not connecting. They're in my head all the time.'

'I'll see if there's something I can do about that.'

'Leave it. It's working. You mess with it and you could damage the link.'

He's right. The last thing they need is to give themselves more work trying to fix something they damaged.

'You tired?'

Gryffin shakes his head. 'Too much going on in my head. Don't think I'll be able to sleep.'

'Yeah. You and me both. C'mon. Let's get you up and about for a bit. You need to get the hang of that leg. You're no good if you have to slowly limp after the enemy.'

∞

NEMESIS

Creed stands on the command deck of *Nemesis* and rests his hands on the railing surrounding the upper deck. In front of *Nemesis* are their spoils. It's not exactly a fleet worth shouting about, but it's better than nothing which is what they started with.

A total of eight ships had been moved from the cavern. It's less than he was hoping for, but they could easily have spent the next few months sorting through everything in the cavern. The eight ships they picked were mid-range cruisers and thankfully, each one had weapons.

He filled Gryffin in on how the mission went including the fact he had taken control of the facility. Gryffin had been quite vocal on the point. 'Fine.' One word. Nice and simple.

Creed had laughed loudly when the message came in. Seems some things never change.

He had expected a little discussion when Gryffin found out the ship he was on is still in one piece, but the one word answer had covered everything.

Creed wraps his arm around Hardy's shoulder and kisses the top of her head. 'You'll need to pinch me.' He yelps when she pinches his side. 'Okay, thanks. You didn't have to do it so hard.'

'You know me, babe. Don't do things by halves. So, you picked your one yet?'

Creed points to the third ship from the left. 'She's not the newest and certainly not the largest.'

'But she's the fastest.'

'Got it. What do you reckon?'

Hardy examines the ship for a few minutes before nodding approvingly. 'Ah sure why not. With a bit of a Nomad face-lift she'll look the part. So, you got a name for her?'

'*Talos*.'

'*Talos* it is. The High Commander has a ship. What's next?'

Creed takes her in his arms again and looks out at his new ship. A few days ago he was wading through the cold puddles on Ocarro. Now he's High Commander of a group he was branded a traitor in and has just got himself a ship.

When Gryffin ambushed him in his room, he had thought his life was over. Gryffin's parting words that day had stuck with him. He never told Hardy what he said. Never told anyone. Gryffin told him he would command the Nomad one day. Creed had laughed at him, straight in Gryffin's face. He's not laughing anymore.

'I guess I better learn how to pilot the damn thing. How long until we're ready to head off to the colony? I'd like to leave the civilians somewhere safe ASAP.'

'Aleena has cleared it with her friend,' Hardy replies. 'He's ready to offer us somewhere to hide whenever we're ready. It's an old mining colony. The majority of it is underground, but we should be able to fit most of the ships in their hangar. Anything else will have to stay under *Nemesis*' shield.'

'Great. I'll let Gryffin know what's going on.'

'You think he'll come back?' she asks.

'Hard to say. We'll either get the ships ready and meet them over there or he'll come back and we'll assess our options in a little more safety. He wants to get this Garvan guy back first.'

Hardy holds out her hand. 'Well, High Commander. How about we leave Chayse to his ship and get you on your own?'

Gryffin keeps his eyes away from anyone he passes as he walks with Bray through the station. He wasn't welcomed here with open arms in the first place. Even he could tell the station personnel had been wary of him, but this is a whole other level of distrust. They're looking at him differently. Now there's a little fear in their eyes. He doesn't doubt he deserves it.

He never thought he'd be back where he was when he met Terra, but, for the first time in months, his body looks like it used to. He'd never been vain. There wasn't a lot to be vain about when it came to how he looks. Scars, metal, and screws. Not something that deserves a second look unless it was to stare in horror.

Since the Scientist took him again last year, his body had felt weak. He never fully recovered from his time in the lab. His body had taken non-stop abuse for ten months and struggled to recover. Until now.

He'd spent too many hours in the rejuvenation pod to count, but it had done the trick. His body was back where it was before his implants started failing. For the first time in months, his chest implant is flush with his rebuilt muscles instead of sinking into him. His body feels strong. It's his mind he's struggling with.

There's too much going on in there and he's having a hell of a time keeping a hold on himself in all the noise. He knows he keeps drifting off and each time it happens, it's getting harder to come back.

Going to see Terra yesterday had been one of the most fucked up ideas he'd had for a while. The second her eyes met his, he knew he should have stayed away. But he needed to see her. It was selfish and all he'd done is make things so much worse for her and for himself.

After he left their room last night he'd been taken back to *Cronus* for monitoring. The hours when he should have been resting and recovering from the procedures were spent staring at a ceiling panel lost in his own thoughts.

He missed her. They may not have been sleeping in the same room as each other since he was moved to the cell, but he knew she was only a call away if he needed her. He'd wanted to call her. Ask her to spend some time with him, but after the fucked-up meeting with her, he didn't want to put pressure on her.

There was also a part of him that was afraid to sleep, even if she was there, in case the implant forced control while he wasn't able to do anything about it. If he loses control to it, he's gone, and he doubts he'd be able to get himself back this time. So, he'd forced himself to stay awake.

To pass the time he had examined the new implants on his body, getting a feel for how they work and what they do. Surprisingly, the biggest adjustment is his new arm. Having a heavy, lump of metal attached after being without anything for so long is going to take a bit of getting used to. The added weight of the weapon on the side of the limb increased the pull on his connectors. He's just grateful he isn't able to feel the pain from the modifications.

'Gryffin?'

He looks up to see Bray and Felix are standing in front of him with strange expressions on their faces. He had been walking the corridors with Bray, trying to get used to his new leg. Now he's outside the meeting room and Felix is here and he has no idea how he got here. 'What?'

Felix crosses his arms as he frowns at Gryffin. 'You zoned out again. Are we boring you?'

'What?'

Felix waves a hand at him. 'Never mind. We better keep an eye on that,' he says to Bray, completely ignoring Gryffin. 'It might be something to do with the link to the others or maybe the control implant. If he does that out in the field he could get the lot of you killed. He can't go daydreaming mid-fight. Anyway, I need the two of you inside for a minute.'

Gryffin follows them into the meeting room. Evie and Heath stop fighting amongst themselves when they notice they have company. 'Oh. You brought him.'

Felix glares at his wife who shrugs and focuses on Gryffin again. 'How are you feeling?'

'Fine.'

Evie points a finger at him. 'That 'fine' nonsense isn't going to work. We need to know how you are. How you really are.'

'My head is killing me and I can't concentrate.'

Evie ushers him to the nearest chair and directs him to sit. 'Well, that's not great now, is it? You probably need to rest.'

'I don't need to rest. I need to get used to the mods. If I don't, I'm no good to you.'

Evie pulls a chair closer to his and sits down beside him. She reaches out and squeezes his arm briefly before focusing on the small handheld unit on her lap. Even without being able to read, he knows it's got data from his scans on it.

'So,' Felix says, getting the conversation back on track. 'We've just got a puzzling transmission,' Felix explains.

'Stop trying to be mysterious, dear. It doesn't suit you.'

Felix glares at his wife. 'I was not trying to be mysterious. The transmission is downright odd. Take a read for yourself.'

'Dinner's on the table, jackass, and it's getting cold.'

Bray laughs and pumps his fist in the air.

Evie leans over to her husband. 'I swear all these Outer Sector folk are a few spoons of jam short of a decent sandwich.'

'It's Garvan,' Bray explains.

'You sure?' Felix asks.

'It's the jackass bit.'

'I don't follow.'

'He made a comment on Earth about me being called after the noise a jackass makes. You know, braying.' Much to Bray's obvious annoyance, and Gryffin's confusion, the Dixon's find the comment hilarious. 'Yes, I know, it's funny. You can stop laughing now.

'Can't blame us,' Evie says. 'It is funny.'

'Thanks. How the hell did he get out?'

As one the Dixon's shrug. 'Why are you asking us?' Felix replies. 'Do you know where he is?'

'He must be at Morgan's farm. There's a bunker hidden under the floor in one of the barns. It's shielded from Foundation scanners. He'll be safe there for the moment, but we need to get him out.'

'Can you get a ship to Earth?'

The Dixon's look over at Gryffin like they forgot he was there. 'You're not planning on going there, are you? It'll take time before you're ready to be set loose.'

'You need me if you're going to the HQ. I should stay off the Foundation radar until then. Dante can go. He's recovered better than the rest of us.'

'I agree,' Bray says. 'There's a chance the Foundation cyborgs could pick up on Gryffin if he gets too close. We don't want to give them a chance to alter their design before we can use him. Dante is a good choice.'

'So we need to send a team who won't stand out. I'd suggest Heath, Bray, Rua, and Terra with Dante.'

Gryffin looks across at Evie. 'What?'

'They'll need Heath to pilot through the defences. He's done it countless times. Bray is still officially dead so there's no problem sending him. Rua is obvious. That woman is scary. Terra is officially dead too. A four-person team with a cyborg bodyguard should be sufficient.'

Gryffin desperately wants to argue about sending Terra, but he has no authority. Creed commands the Nomad and Desyl the crew of *Ares*. Whether Terra still considered herself a member of the crew or not doesn't matter. He's nothing anymore. Not High Commander or Captain - just Gryffin. It should be Desyl in this meeting, not him.

His new position is nearly as hard to deal with as the mods. He's not used to being... whatever he is. It's like he's gone back in time to when he was first brought to the Nomad. Rayde had kept him isolated, not letting him be part of the crew. He was nothing until Rayde realised he could be used to hurt people.

Twenty years on and he's back in the same place, instead this time he's done it to himself.

∞

Terra looks up from the training drone and grimaces when she sees Evie smirking at her. 'Oh please leave me alone. You told me so. I get it, okay. I don't need to hear it all over again. I'm having a crappy enough day.'

'That's not why I'm here, I assure you.' Evie settles onto the bench and sits on her hands. 'So, what exactly are you doing?'

Terra turns the drone's head around to look at Evie. The old woman snorts when she sees the crude red scar across its face. 'Childish I know. I just wanted to hit something and the real Gryffin wouldn't appreciate it if I targeted him.'

'So, you're going to hide down here and beat a fake Gryffin. I have to agree it is a little childish, but highly amusing.'

'What else would you have me do? If I was back on Ultar I'd have Milla to talk to about all this, but I don't even know if she's alive. Desyl isn't talking to me. Worse, he pulled rank on me which he's never done before. Roman is dead. I got Lucan killed because I hesitated. Ultar is under Foundation control. Gryffin has done exactly what my father wanted and had more mods fitted. And I've never felt more alone or more lost in my life. I feel like I'm losing my mind.'

Evie gathers Terra in her arms as the tears break free from their dam.

'I haven't got a clue what to do, Evie.'

Evie stands up and examines Terra with a critical eye. 'Well, firstly, you're going to use the facilities over there and clean up your face. You look a sight.' She turns Terra around and grunts. 'I have no idea what that thing you're wearing was in a past life, but you really should do it a favour and give it a decent send off.'

Terra holds out her arms. 'I wear this when I'm doing work on *Ares*. The shafts on that ship are freezing.'

'That may well be the case, but you look like the peppermint I fished out from behind Felix's desk last week. Okay, so we'll sort you out and then you are going to accompany me to the meeting.'

'With Gryffin?'

'With everyone. We've just got a transmission from Earth. It appears Garvan is alive and got out of the HQ all on his lonesome. Heaven knows how. Anyway, we're heading over to Earth to pick him up.'

'Evie—'

'No, Terra. You will be at the meeting and we will need your help to stop the blasted Foundation in their tracks. You are as key to that as he is you stubborn fool. Now, get cleaned up. Garvan is waiting and I suggest we get to him before the Foundation tracks him down.

EARTH

The Council meeting comes to an end and Seven leaves his seat, exiting the room through the door that leads to his private dressing room. To keep the identity of the Council secret, they each leave by a separate door to avoid any interaction.

He locks the door and pulls off the ornate mask, placing it carefully on the dressing table before he does something stupid like drop it to the ground and stamp on it until it shatters. He runs a hand through his dark hair, pushing the jaw length locks back in place after being stuffed under the heavy hood of his cloak.

Reaching for the jug of ice water, he fills a glass and takes a deep drink. Being wrapped in the stifling mask and cloak for the last hour and a half has left him thirsty and in desperate need of a cooling shower. Whoever decided cloaks and masks would be a good idea needs to wear the getup for ten minutes.

He drops down onto the leather chair and stretches his legs out in front of him as he sips the icy water. He pulls off the ring with his designation engraved in it and throws it against the far wall. On the table opposite him, the mask stares blankly back at him. He raises his glass. 'To the Foundation and all who suffer because of it.' He shakes his head and empties the glass.

He detests everything that fucking mask, ring, and ridiculous designation represents. Everything the Foundation represents.

Not that his real name gives him a warm fuzzy feeling either. He hates both names equally. As only heir to the well regarded Admiral Balfe, Treyton Balfe's future on Foundation Earth was safe. His father died a hero, a damn legend. Selflessly giving his life to protect Earth from the lawless inhabitants of the Outer Sector.

It's a fucking joke. His father died because he was a disgusting human being who tortured people for no good reason. Trey only hopes his death was painful. It's no less than his father deserved. The only legacy his father left Trey was all his files on Project Conscript. As one of the founding members, his dear father had copies of every single file ever made.

He picks up the ring, slipping it in his pocket. As the days go by, he's finding it increasingly difficult to bite his tongue during the arduous meetings with his fellow Council members. At thirty-seven years old, he's pretty sure he's the youngest member of the group. He may not be able to see their faces, but it doesn't take a genius to figure that bit out. Their archaic ideas and thinking process confirms that.

This path the current One is taking the group on is insane to say the very least. Over the last few days, it's become clear One is focused on his prisoner, losing grip of whatever semblance of reality he may have had. Although he doubts there was much there to begin with. It did make his week to learn that the prisoner had escaped.

For some reason, One was adamant they send every available unit out to search the surface for him. Thankfully, the rest of the Council agreed with Trey. They'd send one team and that's it. Whatever the issue between One and the prisoner, it had nothing to do with the other Council members.

Trey never aspired to the position of One, but after everything the current and preceding occupants of that role have been involved in, it's high time someone young with fresh ideas takes the lead. Foundation Earth is on borrowed time and cyborgs are certainly not the answer to a happy, healthy future.

He gets to his feet and wanders along deserted corridors to the lift, and down to the ground floor. Without his mask, he blends in with everyone else working in the facility. He makes his way to the garage and over to his transport. He starts the engine and programs the transport to take him home.

Once securely locked inside his lavish apartment, he strips out of his Foundation uniform, donning workout clothes, then spends the next hour in his gym, working the frustration out of his system.

Training is one of the few things which helped calm him, helped keep the anger at bay. And he's damn good at it. He's damn good at everything he does. Not that his father ever thought that.

He wipes sweat from his brow with his arm, and lunges at the training drone again. Nothing he ever did pleased his father. Too busy with anything else, his father never had much time for his son. The most interaction he got was when he didn't quite meet expectations. The beatings were swift and brutal, designed to show his son exactly how much of a disappointment he was.

Trey attacks again. He hates what his father did to him. Hated every bruise, every cracked and broken rib. Hated that his father's vast fortune helped to cover up his injuries, paying off doctors to treat him without putting anything on his record.

His father's complete disappointment in him had helped in an unexpected way. Trey's constant attempts to please someone who couldn't be pleased meant he pushed himself above and beyond what he probably would have had he been blessed with a half-way decent father.

With the way things are on Earth, that can only help him. He shuts off the drone and takes a drink of water. Pity his dear dad's dead. He'd give anything to see his face as his own son destroys his precious legacy one implant at a time.

∞

EARTH

Garvan leans on the sink in the small bathroom and watches water drip off his hand. Liza and Zeke were getting dinner ready for his granddaughters.

If only everyone could take to change so easily as kids could. Hiding out under the floor of an old barn was the most exciting thing that's happened to the girls. It's a big adventure and one they're loving every minute of. Garvan would like to think Harvey wouldn't have laid a finger on Liza or her girls had they stayed behind, but he wasn't willing to take that chance. Neither was Jake if he was so eager to get them off Earth.

He looks down at what's left of his arm. The pain killers he's popping like fucking candy are helping, but they won't miraculously grow him a new limb. He's going to end up with something like Gryffin's arm. As long as he can use it to kill Harvey he doesn't care if they attached a fork to his arm.

He dries his face and runs a hand through his hair, trying to rearrange the messier-than-usual spikes. Jake should be here in a few minutes. He'd like to make a slightly better second impression on his son-in-law. Jake's threat to kill him if anything happened to Liza and the girls was genuine. He doesn't doubt that for a second.

At least Jake was able to get the information on the Dixon's they desperately needed. He'd also sent a message to Bray that the Hunter should understand without giving away their location to anyone who may intercept it. If he's to get his family off Earth they'd need help from the Dixon's. The transports they have access to on Earth are surface crafts. Even if they did have a long-distance ship, getting through the security around Earth would be nearly impossible.

Garvan looks at the door as someone knocks. 'Dad? Jake's here.'

He opens the door and smiles at Zeke. 'Fingers crossed he doesn't kill me.'

'His family is safe. You should be okay, I think.'

'Yeah. That's filled me with oodles of confidence. Thanks.' He hears the transport land in the bay above their hideout before the engine shuts down. Zeke goes up to greet him and a few minutes later re-joins them with Jake. The girls run over to their father as he crouches down to hug them both. Jake kisses Liza then walks over to Garvan.

His initial impressions of Jake had been accurate. Even though Garvan is a little taller, the way Jake holds himself tells Garvan he's not used to being intimidated or pushed around. If the Foundation had more guards like Jake at Tyrat, it would have been a very different place.

'I need to talk to you. Alone.'

'No problem.' Garvan shows him to the main bedroom and sits on the end of the bed. 'Nice to meet you.'

'They're on the way.'

There go the pleasantries. 'Sorry?'

'Your friends.' He holds out his personal unit. 'Make sure you've got enough grub for everyone. Presume that means there's a few coming to get you.'

'Wow. I wasn't expecting them to come here. I thought they'd help us from afar.'

'You have the guns I told you to bring?'

Clearly Jake isn't a fan of small talk. 'They're in the pantry. Liza wanted to keep them away from the girls. Are you expecting trouble?'

Jake laughs and scratches his head. 'Of course I am. However good the Dixon's are, the Foundation will know they're here. They will come. You know that right?'

Garvan nods tiredly. He's in no way fit enough for a gunfight. Hell, even throwing dirty looks would wipe him out the way he feels right now.

Jake looks down at his arm. 'I've heard about the project. Never fully believed it though. I probably didn't want to believe it.'

'Have to admit I wish it was all made up too. Guess we're both out of luck. I know you're less than thrilled with me bringing all this to your door, but you have my word I will die before I let anything happen to Liza, Zeke, or the girls.'

Jake studies him for a long time before he nods. 'I know. How about we get everyone ready to move out so we can get the fuck off this planet? I'd prefer to leave the second your friends arrive.'

DIXON SPACE STATION

Terra zones out as the meeting continues. Against her will, her eyes move up to rest on Gryffin again. He's not looking at her. He's not looking at anyone - just staring at the screen on the table in front of him. The more she sees of him, the more the differences jump out at her. Evie's words play round and round in her head, mocking her and her plans for the future.

She's loathed to admit the eccentric woman may be speaking the truth, but she can't ignore what's right in front of her. Over their months together, she had thought he was changing, but that wasn't the case. He never truly veered away from the Gryffin she originally met.

When she first met him on the station a few years ago, he had a firm grasp on his emotions. Rayde had made sure of that. But over time, his humanity had seeped through the cracks.

His tone had changed. His mannerisms had softened. He smiled more. Even went so far as to laugh every now and again, although those times were reserved only for her. His abrupt, gruff monosyllabic grunts had extended to full sentences and even conversations from time to time. Bit by bit, the harsh exterior had been stripped away to allow the man out. To allow Daegan out. Now she fears all traces of Daegan are gone forever.

But does it go deeper than that? His implants had never bothered her, but now they're so much more visible. And there's more of them. She had never thought of him as anything other than human, but the term cyborg keeps coming to her mind since he mentioned getting mods. That's what he is, isn't it? Man and machine combined. How much of Gryffin is machine after yesterday? Does it matter?

'Commander Rush!'

Desyl's rough voice has the desired effect, jarring her out of her thoughts in the worst possible way. Terra blinks a few times as all the faces around the table turn to look at her. 'What?'

Desyl frowns. 'That the way you address a superior officer?'

Terra bites the inside of her cheek to stop a snide remark from helping to embarrass her further. 'I apologise, sir.'

His eyes narrow but he doesn't comment on her tone. 'You still a Nomad?'

The awkward silence drags on as all eyes target her. She looks over at Gryffin and he slowly lifts his head and smiles at her. It's a brief smile but definitely a smile, and that gives her a little comfort.

She smiles back then addresses Desyl again. 'Yes, sir. I'm still a Nomad.'

'Fine. You'll be going to the surface.'

Terra stares down the table at him as his words sink in. Then she looks at Gryffin. If she hadn't believed the mods had changed him before, she does now. In all the time she's known him, Gryffin has done everything he can to keep her safe and on *Ares*. Every single time she had stepped off the ship it had been after a heated argument where she had to remind him she could look after herself. The fact he's silently staring at her, then nods once, is so out of character.

'Me?'

'You got a problem following orders, Commander?'

Seems Desyl is enjoying publicly throwing his command in her face. 'Of course not, sir.'

Evie takes over, diffusing the hostility between Terra and Desyl. Her stupid remark earlier had effectively ruined their friendship. And she can't blame him. She had no right saying what she did.

'So that's Dante, Terra, Bray, Rua, and Heath going on an outing to Earth. I want you all armed to the teeth and prepared for anything.' Evie pushes her hat back on her head, dislodging an unruly lock of hair. 'We've been keeping an eye on Foundation transmissions and, so far, there's been no mention of Morgan's farm, but that could change.'

Heath stands up and gestures to the other members of his team. 'Let's get prepped. I want to leave in thirty minutes.'

Terra glances over her shoulder at two of the most important people in her life. Desyl's cold eyes meets hers briefly before he turns away and examines some data Felix hands him. Gryffin on the other hand locks eyes with her and doesn't turn away. He's not happy about her going to the surface. She can tell that much from his eyes.

She slowly follows after Heath. Maybe once this mission is done, she'll have to give her long term plans a serious rethink. If she can't sort things out with Desyl, there's no way she's going to consider staying on *Ares*. What that means for Gryffin and her is anyone's guess. Right now, getting Garvan back is the priority. She'll worry about her place with the Nomad when she returns.

'Terra.'

She turns to see Gryffin standing outside the meeting room door. Heath gestures down the corridor. 'I'll give you a few minutes.'

Gryffin doesn't move until Heath disappears around the corner, then slowly approaches her. He looks down at her but remains silent for a minute. When he does finally speak, his voice sounds less confident than usual. 'Be careful down there.'

Terra can't help but smile at his words. When he hadn't spoken up during the meeting she thought he may not have been bothered about her going to Earth. 'I promise I'll be careful. We'll get Garvan then leave.'

He nods once then slowly reaches out with his flesh hand to take hers, squeezing it gently. 'I don't want you to go. You have to go, but I don't want you to.'

'You don't know how relieved I am to hear you say that.'

'Why?'

'Because you've never wanted me to put myself in dangerous situations. If you didn't have a problem with this, I'd be worried. I thought the mods might have, I don't know, changed that part of you.'

'That would be the last part of me that would change.'

She hugs him close to her, and after a brief pause, he wraps his arms around her. He's different since he had the modifications done, but perhaps more of her Gryffin survived than she first thought. She does know one thing. Pressed against his chest, breathing in his scent, listening to the steady beat of his heart, she knows without a doubt that she still loves him.

He kisses the top of her head and she can't stop the tears that escape. This is just a reprieve before the real test. If he can't keep control of the implant in his head, he will be lost to her forever.

Gryffin moves back from her and frowns. 'Why are you crying?'

'I'm scared, Gryffin.'

'About going to Earth?'

'No. About what's going to happen to us.'

'I am too.'

'You are?'

'Of course. I love you, Terra. I don't want to lose you because of what I am.'

'What you are?'

He pauses and looks down the corridor for a moment. 'I'm a cyborg, Terra. I don't think I've ever called myself that out loud, but it's what I am.'

She places her hand on the side of his face and smiles at him. 'Hey, that's never been a problem for me. My problem is with who did this to you, not the actual implants. My father did horrible things to you and so many other people. I just... I hate that part of it, Gryffin. But I promise you, I have never seen you as anything other than human. I mean that.'

He smiles and rests his head against her forehead. 'You better go.'

'I know. I promise I'll be careful. I'll see you in a few hours.'

'I do love you, Terra. The extra implants haven't changed that.'

'And I love you too.' She gives him a quick kiss on the lips then turns away and hurries down the corridor after Heath.

When she gets back from Earth she needs to sit down with Gryffin and figure out where they go from here. If anywhere. A lot still depends on the control implant in his head. At the end of the day, that's the part that will decide for both of them.

∞

EARTH

One looks at the report on his screen and a chill settles over him. Jake. That ungrateful, backstabbing bastard has betrayed him. There's no other explanation why his son-in-law would be asking questions about the infernal Dixon's.

Everyone knows what those two irritating people do. Their very existence is damaging to the Foundation. People like that give the populace the belief that they can also defy the Foundation and the

Council. That is not something One wishes to encourage. Quite the opposite in fact.

He leans back in his chair and stares at Jake's file. One is too late. He doesn't know how, but Garvan got to Liza who in turn brought her husband in to help reunite Wade with his friends.

One shakes his head and laughs to himself. He's been a fool. Zeke must have gotten his father out. The brat must have found out he was holding his father. So, after all he's done to Wade, his old friend has come out on top yet again.

He grinds his teeth together as he slowly shuts down the screen. Well, if that's the way they want to play, he is more than capable of joining in. He contacts Nova and waits as she takes her sweet time reporting to his office.

The cyborg has been in isolation since she returned from the Outer Sector with the others. Arriving back with only half her team, no prototype, and no Roman, had been more than a little irritating. Clearly she had malfunctioned in some way. There's no other explanation for such a colossal failure. Spending hours being thoroughly examined one piece at a time may have convinced her not to fail him again.

She enters his office without knocking, but he has bigger issues at the moment. She stands in front of him and looks at the wall above his head. She used to look him in the eye. Maybe her visit to the med bay had finally put some manners on her. 'What took you so long?'

'I had to wait while my arm was fitted again.'

He grunts and activates his screen. He turns it around so she can see the picture of Jake from his Foundation file. 'This man is married to my step-daughter. It appears he is a traitor. I believe he is working with an escaped convict Wade Garvan. I want you to kill them both.'

She examines the photo then looks up at him. 'Kill them?'

'Of course. Traitors to the Foundation must be killed.' He pulls up another file and shows it to her. 'This is a farm owned by the father of a former member of the security team. She conveniently disappeared after *Alpha* was stolen. She was involved. I have no doubts about that. The farm is empty, or it was last time we checked. I believe that is where Wade is hiding with Jake. Go there. Take as many cyborgs as you want. Kill these two and any others you find with them. They are a direct threat to the Foundation. Do you understand me?'

She frowns a little then nods. 'Yes, sir.'

'Good. Liaise with Leeson. He'll make sure you have enough personnel with you.' She nods again and turns to the door. 'Oh, and Nova.'

She stops and looks over her shoulder at him. 'Let me down again and what you've just been through will pale in comparison to what I will do to you.'

'Yes, sir.'

42

Heath brings the transport closer to Morgan's farm and lands in a forested area about a mile from the residence. Terra checks the screen in front of her. 'I can't pick up anything suspicious. We're clear at the moment.'

Bray opens the hatch and looks over at Dante. 'Don't suppose you're picking up anything?'

Dante tilts his head to the side and the inner workings of his ocular implant spin. 'No. I can usually feel Trace and Boone when I'm near them, Gryffin too. But there's nothing.'

'Doesn't mean they're not out there,' Bray says. 'You may only be able to pick up on your own group.'

Rua checks her gun then stands up. 'You heard them. We're clear right now. Why are we sitting here? Where's the house?'

Bray points through the trees. 'That way. We should probably leave the transport here. We don't want to attract attention by landing right on their doorstep.'

'Okay,' Heath says. 'Let's head out.' Bray waits until everyone is out of the shuttle then seals the door and activates the signal blockers the Dixon's installed. Hopefully the ship will stay out of everyone's sights. The last thing they need is to get back and find the place surrounded by Foundation personnel.

With Dante taking the lead, they move towards the old farmhouse, keeping to the trees lining the edge of the field. Bray follows at the back using his new eyes to scan their surroundings. He hates to admit it, but the ability to zoom in and out is pretty damn useful.

They get to the barn without any problems and Terra and Heath cover the surrounding area while Bray keys in the code to open the floor. Dante, Rua and Bray stand over the entrance as the floor retracts to uncover someone he didn't think he'd ever see again. Bray smirks as Garvan grins up at him from the bottom of the stairs.

'Hello mate.'

Bray's smile falters when he notices what the Foundation did to his friend. 'Fuck, Garvan.'

'Hey, I'm fine and dandy. Could do with a lift though if you've got room. Foundation hospitality isn't to my liking.' A tall blond-haired man joins them at the stairs. 'Bray, this is my son-in-law, Jake. He was able to get the message to you.'

'Nice to meet you, Bray, but we've got a problem.'

Bray takes a deep breath. 'What is it?'

'Just got a heads up from a mate at work. We could have trouble heading our way. One of my superiors took a little too much interest in what I was looking into on the system. I— Damn it, I knocked him out. I should have killed him and hid the body, but I didn't. He's screaming bloody murder now. Not saying they'll track us here, but who knows.' He holds out a destroyed Foundation transmitter. 'I dug this out of my arm just in case.'

'By destroying that you'll have put yourself on the wanted list.'

Jake shrugs at Bray. 'Who the hell cares about that? We're in the shit as it is. Can't see how the level of shit makes a difference at this stage.'

'We left the transport in the forest behind the barn. How many are coming with us?'

'Six including me,' Garvan responds. 'Two of those are my granddaughters. I'd prefer if we kept things relatively light-hearted with them if possible. No need to scare the hell out of them if we can help it.'

Liza, Jake, Zeke, and the two children grab their things and follow Garvan out of the barn.

'Shit.'

Bray turns to look at Dante.

'Excuse me?'

The cyborg tilts his head to the side. 'They're here.'

'Who's here?'

Dante pauses then looks at Bray. 'I can feel them. There are cyborgs here.' He turns to the road leading to the farm. 'Coming in from there.' He points to the left of the house. 'There too. Don't think they can pick up on me but I don't know for sure.'

'Damn it. Time to pick up the pace.' Without letting on they're up to their necks in a world of trouble, Liza and Jake gather the kids in their arms and hurry after Heath. Dante takes the lead again, guiding them away from any possible company hiding out in the trees while Bray covers the rear with Terra and Rua.

After a few minutes Dante stops the group and turns to Bray. 'They're gaining on us.'

'Fuck. Okay. Dante, you get them back to the ship and make sure you keep them safe. I'll run interference.'

'Not alone you're not,' Jake says as he joins them. 'I'm trained. Dante and Zeke too. Let Heath take Liza, Wade, and the girls back to the ship. The rest of us can deal with our guests.'

Bray isn't keen on getting anyone else involved but Jake has a point. Bar Liza and the girls, everyone here is more than capable of handling themselves in a fight. 'Heath be ready to take off as soon as we're clear.'

Heath nods and guides the others back towards the ship while Bray turns back the way they came. 'Time to see what these new cyborgs are made of.'

∞

DIXON SPACE STATION

'Will you please sit down? You're making me dizzy.'

Gryffin barely suppresses a growl as he continues to stalk across the command centre floor. Whatever reply Erin was planning disappears when he glares at her.

Felix steps in front of him, blocking his path. 'Sit, please before you damage that new leg of yours.'

He drops into the nearest chair and clenches his fists together, cracking the knuckles of his flesh hand with his metal one. 'I should be down there.'

Erin pulls up a chair next to him, ignoring or not noticing the look he gives her. 'You had no choice but to sit this one out. It was risky enough sending Bray. You really think the Foundation wouldn't have your face programmed in every monitor, every droid, every security system on the surface? You'd set off a worldwide alarm as soon as you stepped foot down there.'

'I know that!' he snaps. Just because he knows Erin has a point, doesn't make it any easier to accept.

'Okay, so just relax and trust they know what they're doing.'

Gryffin swallows his less than pleasant reply and focuses on the screen opposite him. He's never been good sitting around while his

389

people left the ship, but this is so much worse. If anything happens to her he'll tear the whole fucking planet apart.

He hisses as the control implant gives his head an intense kick. He can't keep it at bay and worry about Terra at the same time. The mods dulled the pain in the rest of his body, but nothing can help the one in his head.

He buries his head in his hands as it gets worse. Might be better if he stopped fighting and just gave in to the damn thing.

Someone grabs his hand so he reacts, wrapping his own hand around their neck. It takes longer than it should for his brain to register he's choking Erin. He drops his hand and she slumps to the ground gasping for breath.

'What the hell was that?' Felix asks as he helps Erin to her feet.

Gryffin looks at Erin. 'I didn't plan to do that.'

She rolls her eyes. 'Oh, that's okay then. Makes me feel so much better.'

'Fighting the programming isn't working.'

'So what do you suggest?' Felix asks.

'Maybe I need to just let it take over.'

Felix shakes his head and pulls over a chair so he can sit down opposite him. 'I get that is probably the easier option right now, but think long term. The best thing for you is to keep a firm hold on that control implant for as long as you can. More chance of getting all these implants off you afterwards that way.'

'I keep zoning out. My reactions are slower than usual, not faster. The programming and my brain are confusing the fuck out of each other. It really hurts too.'

Erin sits back on the chair and rubs her neck. 'This isn't right. Surely he shouldn't be in pain. Can he not just let it take over then you undo it all when we're done.'

Felix shakes his head. 'If your cousin lets it take over there's a fair chance we won't be able to get him back.'

'Get him back?'

'I'm going to put this in simple terms to save time. If that control implant takes him over, there's a fairly high chance you'll never speak to Gryffin again. You can also kiss goodbye to Daegan, if there's any of him left in there. He'll be Thirty-Five forever. A programmable cyborg with an unimaginative designation just like all the others.'

Erin turns to look at Gryffin. 'Is this true?'

'Yes.'

'Then why the hell would you do this?' She points her finger at Felix. 'You said he'd be getting some of his cybernetics upgraded. You failed to mention losing him forever.'

'Don't you wave that finger at me. This was his decision,' Felix replies. 'If it makes a difference, neither Bray nor Gryffin were entirely on board with the plan.'

'No, it doesn't make a damn bit of difference. You still went ahead with it. Are you all out of your minds?'

Evie takes off her hat and waves it in the air. 'Would you all just shut up. It's done. No point making anyone feel worse by going on and on about it. And no one is making any decisions about anyone else's brain until we get that team back from Earth.

'Now I suggest anyone who wants to keep breathing gives Gryffin a clear berth. Gryffin, you keep a firm grip on yourself and for goodness sake, don't attempt to strangle anyone else or you'll have to be restrained. Felix, get back over here and keep an eye on these screens.'

He can feel Erin staring at him long after Evie and Felix have gone back to the bank of screens. 'What?'

'Why would you do this to yourself knowing it could be a one-way thing? I don't get it.'

'You don't have to get it. It has nothing to do with you.'

Erin laughs harshly. 'Yeah. I forgot. We mean nothing to you.'

He gives her the look that usually has people backing away from him, but it has no effect on her. Stubborn woman.

'Glaring at me now? Really? Maybe there is more of Daegan left under all that than I thought. You gave me that look a lot when we were kids.'

Gryffin stands up again. He needs to get away from Erin. Needs her to stop talking to him. Thinking about what he did to her mother on top of everything else isn't going to do him any favours. But Erin isn't done. She follows him across the room and puts herself in front of him again.

'You can't keep walking away from me. You're going to have to talk to all of us at some stage.'

'No. This is the last time I'm saying this to you. Daegan is dead. There's nothing left of him.'

'Is that what you really believe? Cause I don't. Once all the cybernetics are removed—'

'I'll be Daegan again? Is that what you think? I'll be human again. Part of your family.'

Her face drops and she shakes her head. 'No. That's not what I meant. It's just... I don't want this for you, Gryffin. I hate seeing you like this.'

He takes a step back from her as the pain in his head ramps up. 'Get the fuck away from me.'

Gryffin doesn't know if it was his tone, or his expression, or the fact he was clenching both fists tightly, but she gets the hint and walks away. He's having a hard enough time dealing with his new mods without every fucking person on the station questioning what he did.

He leans against the table in the centre of the room and watches the Dixon's as they mutter to themselves at the console. If he wasn't watching them so intently he would have missed the look that passes between them.

'What?'

They look over their shoulders at him then back at each other before Felix spins his chair around. 'Heath has just sent a message. The team has met with heavy resistance. The farm is surrounded by cyborgs.'

'How heavy?'

'A few dozen.'

Gryffin looks at the screen, not understanding any of the words. That's too many for the team to deal with. They need help. Terra needs help. She needs him.

'I'm going to Earth.'

EARTH

Terra peers out from behind the barn and targets another cyborg. They'd managed to get back as far as the farm before the met with the cyborgs. At least if they engaged with them here, it would keep them away from the transport until Heath can get Garvan and his family safely onboard.

Rua fires from beside her and takes another cyborg down.

'A few more shots like that would be great,' Terra says as she ducks behind the barn again.

The Rogue smiles as she continues to fire. The woman seems to thrive in battle. Terra targets the next cyborg and takes her down with a clean shot to the optic. Rua curses as a round slams into her shoulder. She switches her gun to her other hand and continues firing without pausing.

The Dixon's transport appears above the trees. Heath leans out the hatch, his gun in his hands. His shots pepper the ground behind the cyborgs, temporarily distracting them.

'Terra!'

'Bit busy here, Bray,' Terra shouts in her radio

'Get inside the house and go upstairs. There's a window in the spare room. It opens to the roof. Heath will be able to pick you up from there.'

Terra glances over at Rua then back at the house. There's a good stretch of open ground between them and the house. Jake and Zeke appear from the side of the building.

'We've got you covered,' Zeke says.

She peers out the barn and spots Bray crouched down behind a large drinker in the corner of the adjacent shed. 'Okay Rua. Plenty of cover. Let's make a run for it.'

Keeping low, they burst out of the barn, the sound of accompanying gunfire helping to spur them on. Without stopping Rua barrels into the backdoor of the house. They race upstairs, both pausing at the top when they hear heavy footsteps behind them. Terra lowers her gun when she sees Bray charging up the stairs followed by Jake and Zeke.

Bray pushes past them and opens the door at the side of the corridor. They follow him inside the attic as he opens the window.

Bray gestures for Rua and Terra to climb out. 'Keep low and to the left. There are four old chimney stacks. You can take cover between them until Heath is clear.'

Terra climbs out and carefully makes her way around the side of the roof. The tiles are old and covered in moss which doesn't give her much grip. She crouches between the old stacks and Rua joins her a moment later.

Unfortunately, the cyborgs on the ground notice their attempted escape and target Bray. Terra peers over the edge and smiles when she sees a tall figure methodically working his way through the cyborgs on the ground.

Dante's attack is savage. Each strike is meant to kill and it does. Using his knife and gun, Dante targets the ocular implant on each of the women, leaving a path of bodies behind him.

She shields her eyes as Heath brings the transport down to collect them. Garvan reaches out of the door and grabs Rua's hand, pulling her in the transport first.

Terra ducks behind one of the chimney stacks as the cyborgs spot her and decide she's an easy target. Bray and Rua lay down cover fire as she makes a dash for the transport again. Garvan reaches out for Terra's hand but then things take a serious turn against her.

Her foot finds an unsecured tile and before she can compensate, she loses her balance and slides towards the edge of the roof.

∞

EARTH

Gryffin gets to his feet as the transport nears the farm. Even from this distance he can feel the other cyborgs. And there's a hell of lot more than he thought there would be.

When he suggested that he should go to Earth with Trace and Boone, he'd been expecting an argument. Instead, Erin had offered to pilot the Dixon's other shielded transport.

Felix and Evie didn't argue either. Felix had fitted each of them with a block that should prevent the other cyborgs from getting into their heads. In theory. The last thing they want is to have the three of them fighting for the opposition as soon as they land.

Erin points out the window and Gryffin leans over to see what's caught her attention.

'Fuck', he mutters as he gets a proper look at what's facing them.

'There must be dozens of them.'

At the very least. The main farm building is surrounded as is the house. 'The others must be trapped in the buildings. No way out.'

'So what's the plan?'

He looks over his shoulder at Boone and Trace, but the two men are already on their feet, checking their weapons. 'Get a little lower and open the hatch.'

'I don't think there's anywhere I can land.'

'We don't need you to land. We can jump.'

'Are you kidding me. It's too high.'

'Just open the hatch.'

She does as he tells her and drops the back hatch. Gryffin, Trace and Boone walk to the edge and look down at the group gathered under the transport. The women are focused on his team in the transport. Might give the others a chance to break free.

They drop from the back, landing on the ground in the middle of the group. Gryffin, Trace, and Boone stand back-to-back, facing the circle of Foundation cyborgs. He hears a few of them muttering the word prototype. Seems his reputation precedes him.

'*No holding back*,' Gryffin says in his head to the others as the circle of cyborgs tightens around them. '*Dante?*'

'*Yes, sir. I'm by the main house. Terra is on the roof.*'

'*Stick with her. Keep her safe.*'

'*Will do.*'

Instinct or programming or a mixture of the two kicks in as the first women get close enough to deal with. Like a well-oiled machine, Gryffin, Boone, and Trace attack.

Gryffin is one hell of a fighter, but being linked to Boone and Trace brings that skill up a level. He can see what they're doing even though he's not looking at them. Every move either man makes, every kill, it all registers with him.

They've all been hit. The three of them are bleeding, but the pain isn't registering. The only thing on their minds is taking out their targets.

EARTH

Bray stares in horror over the edge of the roof and relaxes when he sees Dante lower a very much alive Terra to the ground. He watches Dante as he grabs Terra by the arm and pulls her towards the relative safety of the trees.

'She good?'

Bray nods at Garvan. 'Dante has her.'

'Well fuck me!' Garvan says as he leans out of the transport. 'Looks like big brother has arrived.'

Bray looks where Garvan is pointing and can't quite believe what he's seeing. Gryffin, Trace, and Boone are in the centre of a group of cyborgs. Three against a dozen or so isn't great odds, but that's not stopping Gryffin and his team.

Bray is mesmerised watching them. Every single blow is hitting home with deadly accuracy. They're actually holding their own. More importantly, they're keeping the majority of the cyborgs occupied.

'What are you doing standing there?' Garvan shouts at him. 'Get your fucking arse on the ship.'

Bray's eye zooms in on a blonde-haired cyborg climbing through the window, taking her out of the equation with one shot.

Bray leaps onto the ship moments before Heath pulls away. 'What about Dante and Terra?'

'They're on their own for a minute. No way to land.'

Bray wipes his face and looks over at Rua. She's holding a bandage to her arm, stemming the flow of blood. 'You okay?'

'Clean shot. Went right through.'

Bray reloads his gun and looks out the door at his childhood home. The place is peppered with bullet holes. They'd underestimated how much the Foundation wanted them out of the way.

There must be at least twenty cyborgs lying dead around the farm grounds. The Foundation was willing to risk a lot of credits to get them. A lot of innocent women have just died for no reason. At least they weren't living with the modifications any longer.

'Dante? You read me?' Bray asks.

'Yes.'

'You both okay?'

'Terra is ahead of me. I had to hang back. I've got company. I'm trying to keep them away from Terra.'

'Where is she?'

'Heading back towards our initial landing site. Pick her up from there.'

Bray relays the information to Heath and peers out the door, watching Gryffin and the others fighting the remaining cyborgs.

∞

EARTH

Nova stands in the shadows of the trees and watches Gryffin and the other two men fight. One talks a lot. It was easy to believe quite a bit of what he said was utter nonsense. But perhaps when it comes to the prototype, he is correct to fear him.

Nova has never seen a team work so efficiently together. They duck and dive around each other, avoiding blows and dodging kicks. She would be proud to fight alongside him.

But she can't.

If even one of the cyborgs loyal to One saw her help in any way, One would find out she's malfunctioning. That she's defective. If that happens, she'll be taken apart again.

The pain receptors may mask the effects of the last few days, but they had been turned off while the doctors examined her. One's punishment for letting Gryffin escape had been brutal. And excruciating. He wanted to show her that defying him was not an option.

All he had done was prove to her that she must be defiant. Gryffin has done nothing but defy the Foundation. He's survived. He's thriving.

Gryffin pauses as a round hits his arm, then returns fire, taking down his attacker.

She continues to watch Gryffin and his team as a message comes through her comms. Another team is in pursuit of two people. She looks around her and spots the dark-haired woman and her cyborg protector racing through the trees.

It's Gryffin's woman. Nova looks over at Gryffin again and smiles. Soon. She just needs to wait a little longer, then she can fight side-by-side with him.

Until then, saving his woman will definitely help put her in his favour. It's going to be hard enough to get him to trust her. Might as well start with this gesture.

Nova draws her weapon and sprints through the forest after the woman.

∞

EARTH

Terra races through the trees, trying to put a bit of distance between the house full of cyborgs and herself. She can hear Bray and Dante shouting in her ear, directing her towards somewhere they can pick her up.

Dante can feel the other cyborgs and is keeping her clear of them. She pushes through the undergrowth, making her way back to the clearing where they'd hidden the transport when they first arrived.

'Terra! Company dead ahead. Go left.'

She doesn't question Dante's instructions, using a tree to shove herself to the left without breaking her momentum.

'Faster, Terra. There's a cyborg coming after you.'

'Where are you?' She forces her legs to move her through the forest. She risks a quick look behind her. 'Shit.'

'What is it?'

'I can see her, Dante.'

'I'm coming. I need you to veer left again. Another two ahead of you.'

Terra does as she's told. 'Dante.'

No reply. 'Heath? Bray? Anyone hear me?'

Nothing but static. Damn cyborgs must be blocking the transmission. She skids to a stop as a tall black-haired cyborg steps out from behind a tree and smiles at her. Terra tenses as another joins the first one. Where the hell is Dante?

She flinches as the second cyborg shoots the black-haired one in the ocular implant. The first cyborg turns to face her and Terra recognises her. It's the cyborg Garvan fought on *Alpha* before Bray stole her.

'You need to go that way,' she says, pointing behind her. 'I've cleared the way for you.'

'What?'

'Go that way. Now! More will come for you and I won't be able to take them all down. Run!'

Terra doesn't need to be told twice. She weaves through the trees, smiling in relief when she hears a transport overhead. She follows the sound and bursts into a small clearing, skidding to a stop when she sees the transport. It's not their transport.

The hatch opens and a dark-haired man steps out. He holds his hands up in front of him. 'Hi. You look like you need a lift.'

'Who the hell are you?'

'A friend,' he replies before pulling out his gun and shooting something behind her. She spins and watches as a cyborg drops to the ground. 'We have to go.'

'My friends—'

'Your friends aren't here right now. We're surrounded and they're under orders to take you alive. They think they can use you to get to him.'

'What?'

'You know who I mean.' He curses and launches himself at her, knocking her to the ground as a hole appears in the tree where her head was a second ago. He gets up and pulls her to her feet. 'Sorry about that.'

She tries her comms again but there's still nothing.

'They knocked out my comms too. You need to come with me. I can keep you safe.'

'I need to find my friends.'

He curses and reloads. 'You want to tell that to those cyborgs?'

Terra has no interest in going with this man, but he takes the decision out of her hands. He grabs her arm and presses a pressure syringe to her skin. 'I'm sorry about this, but if we stay here and argue we're both dead.' He throws her over his shoulder and races back to his transport, but Terra is already asleep.

Gryffin wipes blood from his eye and faces the woman who threw the lucky punch. She smiles at him, the knife in her hands coated in blood. 'Thirty-Five.'

He really fucking hates that designation. Gryffin looks at his opponent and knows he's going to have a job taking her down. She's tall and well-built, but that's not what's bothering him. It's the look in her eye.

He's seen it so many times when he fought new recruits on *Ares*. It's over-confidence. He saw it in recruits who thought they could play up to the crowd by taking the captain down. Earn themselves a reputation from the start. No recruit had ever taken him down, but a hell of a lot had tried.

This cyborg is going to do the same. For some fucked-up reason, she wants the glory of being the one to destroy him.

Gryffin ducks, dodging her initial attack but her blade swings around as it passes, tearing through the back of his t-shirt into his flesh. His warm blood pours down his back but he can't feel the pain.

She smiles as she turns the blade in her hand. 'You're no match for me. I'll take you a piece at a time if I have to.'

Gryffin isn't interested in having a chat. She lunges at him again, her thick arms swinging for his chest. Gryffin grabs her arm, twisting it sharply, breaking her elbow, but she doesn't slow down.

With her arm now useless, she kicks out, catching him in the side of the leg. Her metal arm strikes his stomach temporarily winding him. Gryffin takes a breath, trying to get back in control of the fight, but she doesn't give him the chance.

She barrels into him, driving them both to the rough stone yard. Gryffin tries to dislodge her, but she wraps her legs around his leg, locking them together. Her blade moves towards his face, but a blow to her broken elbow changes her mind.

She screams at him in frustration then drives the blade into his flesh arm, burying the metal through his lower arm and into the compact stone surface of the yard.

Her metal fingers grip the edges of his ocular implant and she smiles at him, her teeth coloured with blood.

Gryffin grabs her wrist, trying to stop her from tearing the implant out of his skull. She snarls down at him, dripping blood from her mouth onto his face.

There's something seriously wrong with her programming. None of the others had fought like this. He can feel her metal fingers digging into his face. If he doesn't do something, the crazed bitch will remove half his face.

There's only one thing he can do, and it's going to completely fuck up his flesh arm. In one quick movement, Gryffin lifts his arm off the ground. Skin and muscle tear as the hilt of the knife passes through his arm, leaving an impressive hole.

Without pausing he slams his fist against her ocular implant knocking her unconscious. He kicks her off him and is about to put a bullet in her head when he picks up something from Dante.

He's lost Terra.

∞

EARTH

Jake comes out of the cockpit with a heavy rope. He passes one end to Bray and gestures to the support on the side of the door. 'Fix it around there. Time to go fishing.'

Jake throws the rest of the rope out the door as they near Dante, sprinting across the field. Without stopping, Dante leaps at the rope and Jake gives Heath the thumbs up. The transport lifts above the trees and away from the farm as Bray and Jake pull Dante inside the transport.

The cyborg collapses on the deck and smiles. 'Thanks for the lift. Thought you might leave me behind.'

'Not a chance,' Bray replies. 'You saved our necks down there, Dante. Cheers.'

He brushes the comment away. 'It's why you brought me along for the ride. Kind of felt good to give a little back. Fucking hate cyborgs.' He winks and grins, then his smile drops. 'Where's Terra?'

'Gone.'

'Gone where?'

'We don't know. Her comms unit is offline and we've searched the area, but can't find her. We were hoping you know what happened.'

Dante focuses on the bulkhead and frowns. 'A team of cyborgs was closing in on her. They were taken down. I thought it was you.'

Bray shakes his head. 'So someone took out the cyborg team

and saved her?'

'I can only see up until the team was killed. I've got no connection to them after that.'

Heath looks over his shoulder to Bray. 'What's the plan, Commander?'

'Does Erin have Gryffin and the others?'

Heath nods. 'They're at the original landing site.'

'Does Gryffin know about Terra?' Bray asks Dante, hoping he says no, but one look at the man's face tells him otherwise. Dante's eyes are squeezed shut and his fists clenched on his knee. You okay, Dante?'

'Gryffin. He knows and he's angry. As in seriously fucked off.'

Bray leans back against the side of the transport feeling the eyes of everyone on board turned towards him. That's something to look forward to. 'Okay. Heath, better rendezvous with the others. Get this over and done with.'

Garvan lowers onto the bench beside him and nudges him in the side. 'There's nothing you could have done differently. You know that.'

'Yeah and you really believe he's going to see it that way? He's going to kill me.'

∞

EARTH

Gryffin sits at the back of the transport just staring ahead of him. Boone and Trace hold position to either side. They're sticking close to make sure he doesn't kill anyone. Thanks to the link between them he knows they're more than willing to take him down if he steps out of line.

The way he feels right now they could be doing just that in the next few seconds. His emotions may be under control thanks to the implant, but that doesn't mean he won't kill someone. Emotions never bothered him when he killed. He wouldn't have been as good at it if they did.

Blood pools on the seat beside him but he couldn't give a damn about it. The three of them are a mess. Boone's arm is broken and he was shot in the chest and the leg. Trace's ocular implant is damaged and he has an impressive compound fracture to his leg. He's lucky he survived being thrown against the side of the stone farmhouse. It could have killed him instead of just breaking his leg.

Gryffin looks down at his arm and grimaces. The wound from removing the knife the way he did has left a gaping hole in his arm. He's done a hell of a lot of damage. Punching that cyborg was the last straw for it. He hasn't been able to move it since he hit her.

Gryffin glances up as Bray's transport lands beside theirs. He desperately wants to tear the door off the ship to get to anyone with answers. Fuck knows how, but he stays where he is. Maybe the control implant and the programming are helping to keep him from going berserk.

Bray walks over to him, making sure to keep at a safe distance.

Gryffin holds himself back for another few seconds before he speaks. 'What happened to her?'

Bray runs a hand through his hair. 'We were trying to get back on the transport. A group of cyborgs came up behind us. We got separated. There were so many of them, Gryffin. We looked for her, but we couldn't find her.'

One second Gryffin is sitting on the bench a few feet from his brother and the next he's pointing his gun at Bray's head. Less than a second after he targets Bray, Trace and Boone target him.

'Put it down, sir.'

Trace's voice sounds in his head as clear as if he'd spoken the words.

'You shoot him and it will start a war with the Hunters. We've got enough on our plate without adding to it.'

'He lost Terra.'

'And we'll get her back,' Boone says as he gently presses the tip of his gun to the side of Gryffin's head. *'He's a Hunter. Not worth getting yourself killed over.'*

Gryffin slowly lowers his arm, followed by Boone and Trace who holster their weapons again.

Bray swallows and licks his lips. 'What the hell was that?'

'Trace and Boone just saved your life.' Gryffin looks over Bray's shoulder to Dante. He winces as Dante shares what happened after Terra fell from the roof. His stomach objects as images fly in front of his vision. Just before he throws up, the assault slows down.

Gryffin pauses and looks at the ground as he tries to sort out the images in his head. As useful as it is to be able to communicate with the others, it's sickening, confusing, and he hates it.

'Someone helped her. They shot the cyborgs.' Gryffin looks up at Bray again. 'The Foundation can't have her. They wouldn't shoot one of their cyborgs. There's no reason for them to do that.'

Bray nods in agreement. 'You got a point there. Listen, I don't want to call it, but we need to go.'

'Not without her.'

'We're on Earth, Gryffin. We've barely survived their cyborg attack. The three of you are barely functioning. If we stay here we'll all die.'

'I'm not leaving her here.'

'You don't have a choice, Gryffin.'

Heath and another guy Gryffin doesn't recognise join Bray as they pull out stun guns.

They fire at Gryffin and his team and they fall to the ground. Gryffin forces his eye open and sees Dante being given the same treatment by Erin.

Bray crouches down in front of him. 'I'm sorry, Gryffin, but we have to go.' He fires again and everything goes black.

EARTH

Terra groans and slowly opens her eyes. She freezes and looks around the room. This isn't the station. It's not *Cronus* either. Or *Ares*. She pushes up to her elbows as the door to the room opens. A tall, dark-haired man enters and closes the door behind him.

The sleeves of his white shirt are rolled up to show thick arms. His brown leather trousers fit his tall form well and scream of wealth. He smiles at her showing perfect white teeth. Whoever he is, he's eye-catching. Almost like an untarnished version of Gryffin. She kicks herself for the unfair comparison. Most of Gryffin's tarnishes are thanks to her cruel father.

'Terra, right?'

His deep voice is kind. He instantly makes her feel at ease even though the situation dictates otherwise. 'Where am I?'

'Earth. Would you like to answer my question now?'

'I thought it was rhetorical.'

He laughs. 'I'll give you that one. So, Terra. I know you probably have a dozen questions so I'll do what I can to answer them. First, my name is Treyton Balfe, or Trey.'

He grimaces. 'Yeah, I see my name rings a few alarm bells for you. Yes, my father was the infamous Admiral Balfe. Believe me, I have the same feelings towards my dear father as you do. He was a bastard every single day of his life and I can never thank whoever finally killed him, enough. I can only hope it was a slow and excruciatingly painful death.'

'Do you honestly expect me to believe a word you're saying?'

'Honestly, no. But I'm hoping I'm wrong. I'm hoping you'll see I'm telling the truth. You hungry? How about I get you something to eat and I'll explain everything.'

He walks over to the door and opens it. Outside, Terra can see an open plan living room with a well equipped kitchen overlooking a manicured roof terrace. She follows Trey to the living room and looks around the stunning room as he busies himself in the kitchen. 'You have a beautiful home.'

'House. Not a home. It's somewhere to sleep and work out. Nothing else. If I didn't have to live in the city to be close to the HQ I'd be quite happy to get myself somewhere small as far from here as possible.'

He smiles as he pushes a plate of pasta across the counter towards her. He picks up a fork and spears a few pieces, popping them in his mouth. 'Not too bad. And not poisoned or drugged or anything. Just in case you were wondering.'

He winks at her and gestures to the chair. 'Go on. You eat and I'll talk. You'll need your strength if you're going to take down the Foundation.'

∞

DIXON SPACE STATION

Garvan accepts Zeke's help to stand then slowly makes his way out of the transport and onto the space station. He glances down at his arm and a heavy ache forms in his chest. For the first time since his arm was removed, the realisation sets in. He wasn't expecting to leave parts of himself on Earth, but he shouldn't really complain. He's alive and that's better than he thought he'd get from his end of the deal.

'Are you okay, Dad?'

'Never better, Zeke. Just tired.'

'C'mon old man. Let's get you sorted.'

Garvan smiles as the hatch opens on the other transport and Erin steps onto the dock.

He may have rejected her out-of-the-blue kiss weeks ago after they first arrived on Earth, but that doesn't mean he isn't interested. He'd been caught off guard and thoughts of his family had clouded the situation.

Seeing her again makes him all the more positive he likes her. Even taking in to account her scary cyborg cousins.

She waves at him, then drops her hand - presumably when she sees the harsh implants and missing arm. As the Dixon's personnel crowd around the transport, he loses sight of her. 'Can you give me a sec, Zeke?'

Garvan extracts himself from the crowd and hobbles over to where he saw Erin last. He spots her at the far end of the corridor walking away from him.

'Hold up, Erin.'

She turns around then hurries over to him. 'What are you doing? You need to take it easy.'

He rests against the wall and holds up his hand as he catches his breath. 'Give me a sec. Damn I feel old. I need to say something to you.'

'Can it not wait until you've had medical attention?'

'No. I've waited long enough. I'm saying it now so please shut up. Using up valuable energy reserves here. I'd prefer not to fall on my ass until I'm done.'

She smiles and gestures for him to continue.

'Cheers. First off, last time I saw you, you were on the floor of the Foundation ship. Are you okay?'

She laughs at his question. 'Me? Have you looked at yourself recently? I'm fine, Garvan.'

'That's good. And I'll be fine and dandy in no time. I hope.'

'I hope so too. I was worried about you.'

'I was worried about me too if I'm being honest.' He winces and rubs the side of his face.

'You really should go to the med bay.'

'In a minute. I need to ask you something and I'm damn well going to do it before I fall on my ass. This has been on my mind since... well since it happened. Okay, here goes.

'In the barn you did something and I reacted the total fucking opposite of what I should have. I don't suppose it's too late to... I don't know, maybe react differently?'

She frowns then her eyes open wide and she looks up at him. 'You mean when I tried to kiss you?'

He nods. 'I know I'm looking a little dishevelled and well—' He holds up his metal tipped arm. 'And I know bits are missing but fuck it. I like you, Erin. So I'm asking if it's too late to maybe go back in time a little and maybe react differently? It would mean you trying to kiss me again though. So, have I completely missed my chance or—'

'No, it's not too late.' She smiles and shrugs. 'It would never be too late for you.'

'That's a fucking relief. Thought I might have messed this up.'

Erin stands on her tip-toes and kisses him. Instead of pushing her away like he stupidly did the last time, Garvan wraps his arm around her and pulls her closer. Erin cups the side of his face and he grunts as she brushes against the metal.

'I'm sorry. Are you okay?'

'Just getting used to my new bits and bobs.'

'I think it's time I get you to the med bay. I don't need you keeling over on me. I fully plan to pick this up later. When you're up for it of course.'

'Yes, Ma'am.'

DIXON SPACE STATION

Bray stands beside the four beds in the med bay and scratches his head. Stunning his brother and the rest of the team wasn't what he wanted to do. Far from it, but he was out of options and out of time. Not that Gryffin will see it that way.

Evie moves away from the head of Gryffin's bed and removes her gloves. 'I think I need a jam sandwich after all that.'

'Are they okay?'

She removes her hat, attempts to fix her hair, then pushes the hat back on. 'I don't see why not. We've removed any rounds they brought back as souvenirs, repaired the many cuts and gaping wounds. They've each had some time in the rejuvenation pod so all broken bones are sorted. A bit of rest should see them all right.'

'What about Gryffin's arm?'

'He'll need another session in the pod in a few hours but it will heal. Did he tell you how he did it? He pulled a knife clean through it.

The wrong way. I mean the handle.' She shudders and looks back at Gryffin again. 'Daft fool. Did the trick though so I guess it was worth it.'

Evie turns to face him again and smiles widely. 'So, young Bray. I'd say that was a fairly effective test, wouldn't you? They worked exceptionally well as a team and remained upright even with all their injuries. Well, remained upright until you stunned them all.'

'Yeah, thanks for reminding me. I've got that to look forward to when he wakes up.'

'He understands.'

Bray laughs at that comment. 'Is that right? You a mind reader now?'

'No. He told me.'

'He did? When?'

'He woke up for a short while about an hour ago. We were all set for him to go a little crazy, but he was remarkably subdued. He asked if everyone got back okay bar Terra. I said yes, and he just nodded.'

'How do you get that he understands from a nod.'

'How else would you take that? He nodded in agreement. Don't you think?'

Bray shrugs and Evie takes that as her que to leave. She wanders into the next room so Bray sits on the chair beside Gryffin's bed and stretches his stiff muscles.

Maybe Evie is right. Maybe that nod is him accepting that leaving Terra was the only option at the time. Gryffin wasn't an idiot when it came to things like this. He wouldn't have held on to command of *Ares* if he thought with his heart instead of his head.

It also doesn't mean that he's happy about leaving people behind. None of them are. As soon as possible, they will go back and get Terra.

∞

EARTH

Terra tucks into her delicious meal while Trey leans against the sink. 'You see, growing up my dear father had more important things to do than spend time with me. I was raised by a long line of women paid to look after me. He was too busy with Project Conscript.

'It's funny, Gryffin and I have more in common than you may think. We both lost our childhoods to the project. Not the same I know. Not by a long shot, but it took that innocence from both of us.'

'You seem to have done well out of it. I can't imagine how much a place like this would cost.'

Trey nods. 'True, but that's all down to dear Dad. When he died I was left everything. All of it is blood money though.'

'Did you know about Project Conscript?'

He nods and smiles sadly. 'I found out about the project and all those innocent lives they stole about ten years ago. My father was never overly inventive with passwords. Add in one bored and ignored son with too much time on his hands and it didn't take long to figure out why he had been so preoccupied.

'I told him that I knew what he was doing and he had to stop, but he didn't care. He told me to keep quiet or I would have an accident.' Trey laughs harshly and shakes his head. 'I did what I was told. So, instead of fighting him I trained, worked hard, made sure I was appointed to the Council using slightly unconventional means, but I couldn't do what needed to be done unless I was sitting among the rot.'

He pushes off the sink and approaches Terra. 'You have no reason to believe me, but I can help you destroy them. I'm a member of the Council. Seven to be exact.' He laughs and shakes his head. 'I mean seriously, how many brain cells were needed to come up with those designations?'

Terra looks over at him again. She wasn't expecting him to say he's a Council member. She liked to think she was a good judge of character, but this is Balfe's son. Conscript wouldn't exist if not for Balfe's involvement. Then Gryffin wouldn't exist either. Rewriting the past erases Gryffin from existence. Not something she wanted to even think about.

'Anyway, I'm well placed in the group. I have support from the majority of the Council. There are those still in One's pockets, but his grip is lessening. There's only so many times he can lose a valuable asset like Gryffin before it's going to spell the end for him.'

'Why would you help us? What do you want out of this?'

'I want an end to the production line One has built. I want an end to any more cyborgs. Hopefully the ones already modified can be reverted back to the way they were, but if not, they don't deserve to live as pawns for the Council.'

He disappears in a side room and comes back in with a comms unit. 'I know about the Dixon's. Don't ask how. I may or may not have a few shady connections. If I'm going to take the Council down I need to have connections all over the place. If you send them a message, something generic that the Foundation won't be able to decipher, they'll pick it up and we can go from there.'

Terra looks down at the unit. She doesn't have a way of getting in touch with the station directly. But that doesn't mean he can't use whatever message she leaves as a way of luring them out into the open.

'I get you trust me as far as you can throw me. All I'm suggesting is you leave them a message so they know you're alive and well. If they want to respond it's on them. The Dixon's have been around for so long because they're careful. There's no way you sending them a message can hurt them in any way. With your comms knowledge you know that as well as anyone.'

He's right. She has no doubts the Dixon's will have fail-safes in place to ensure they can't be traced back to the station. She needs to send them a message. She needs them to know she's safe and well. She needs Gryffin to know.

She types out a quick message and sends it to the nearest comms station. Fingers crossed the Dixon's will pick it up.

Garvan pushes up the bed when he hears a knock on the door. He frowns when he sees Gryffin standing in the doorway. 'Captain?'

'You good to talk?'

'Sure.'

Garvan quietly watches as Gryffin limps past his bed and slowly lowers in the chair next to it. 'You okay after what happened on Earth? Heard you took a bit of a beating.'

'I'm fine.'

'Bray said you'd had more work done, but I got to say, I didn't believe it till now. Speaking from experience, that must have hurt. Are you okay? I mean after all the work.'

He's not surprised when Gryffin doesn't answer. 'Evie said your son got you out before they connected the implant to your brain.'

'Impeccable timing. Never been so glad to be reunited with my boy.' He adjusts the pillow under his arm, trying to ease some of the pain.

The connectors below his elbow had been checked by Bray and the Dixon's. Thankfully, they had been fitted with a hell of a lot more care than Gryffin's had been. The wound is clean and free from infection.

They took a sample so they can grow a new arm for him, but it'll take a few months to organise and even then it may not be a viable option. Until then, he would prefer to have an arm of sorts so he told them to leave the metal connectors. Hopefully, he'll be fitted for a robotic arm later today from the stores on *Cronus*.

'Listen Gryffin. I'm sorry about Terra. She was only on the surface because of me.'

'Not your fault. She wasn't taken by the cyborgs. Not sure if that's a good or a bad thing.'

'Yeah, Bray said you can communicate with the other cyborgs. Are you picking up on what Dante saw or something he picked up on from one of the other cyborgs?'

Gryffin shakes his head. 'Both, I think. I don't know what I'm getting. It's taking time to sort through. But she's safe. Or she was. Whoever took her was gentle with her.' Gryffin frowns and stops talking. Garvan can't tell if he's thinking or seeing something or picking up on something. Whatever he's doing, he's not here with Garvan.

'Gryffin?'

He looks back up at him again. 'Any useful intel you can give?'

'Well, they've rebuilt the lab. They've even got the delightfully sadistic ladies working on the mods. They've hit back, Gryffin. Taking the ship didn't slow them down for long.'

'What did they do to you?'

'They tenderised me like a prize cut of meat for a few days. When my mate was satisfied I was messed up enough, they strapped me down and gave me the worst damn headache of my life.'

Garvan tries to laugh, but it sticks in his throat. 'We need to stop them, Gryffin. I've got this thing on my face and left my arm in their lost property box. I got off light. What they did to those women, to Bray, to you... it's not right, Captain. Sorry, Gryffin. Going to take time to get used to calling you Gryffin instead of Captain.'

'How many cyborgs are there?'

Garvan blows out a breath. 'I counted at least fifteen. That's only the ones who came to bring me to and from the lab. Can't say how many more there are elsewhere.'

'I accessed the system on the ship Bray stole. It's got some details on the mods. Anything useful you can tell me? Anything that might help take them down?'

Garvan focuses on his feet as he thinks back to his time on Earth. 'The only thing I can think of you've already figured out. They didn't talk to each other. It was like they were talking up here,' he says as he taps the side of his head. 'They were definitely communicating with each other. They'd look at each other then one of them would act. Like she had received instructions, but they sure as hell weren't verbal. Is this a new thing you can do or has it always been there?'

'It's fairly new. One of the cyborgs from the New Colony connected with me before he died.'

'Before he died? Jeez, it's still happening then.'

'We're all flawed. Boone, Trace, and Dante have been getting problems with their implants too. Nothing major, but they based all the designs off me. Not a great starting point.'

Gryffin gets to his feet and steps out of the room. He returns a few seconds later with an artificial arm. 'Lucky for you, they were able to improve some parts. You're getting a slimmed down version of mine.'

Garvan stares at the arm with a mixture of regret and excitement which confuses the hell out of him. No point regretting what happened to him. He'll never be reunited with his arm. It's gone and he has to get used to it. On the plus side, the arm Gryffin has in his hand is not a bad looking replacement. It's obviously metal but instead of having the bulky tubing and wiring Gryffin's does, it's sleek and pretty neat looking. 'Don't tell me you have arm envy, Captain.'

Gryffin smirks. 'Mine has a built-in gun. Yours doesn't. You ready?'

'Nothing else planned at the moment.' He'd rather not try it right now, but it's probably best to get it over and done with. In truth, he's terrified about having the thing connected to him. After where he's just been the idea of having any more metal attached to him isn't something he's overly keen on.

He lifts his arm up and watches in morbid fascination as Gryffin lines up the connectors. Everything clicks in place and Garvan winces as a strange pressure pulls at his elbow. 'Yeah, that feels fucking weird.'

'It'll take a while to get used to it. Leave it on for a few hours if you can.'

Garvan smiles as his new metal thumb twitches. 'Ha! I did that.'

Gryffin ruefully shakes his head and leans back in his chair. 'You're dealing with this better than Bray did.'

'Yeah, well, I've had my fair share of shit thrown at me over the years. Not saying I won't fall to pieces about what happened at some stage, but I got a debt to repay first. And I don't mean the warm and fuzzy kind.'

'One.'

'One. Fucker is on borrowed time, Gryffin. I promise you that.'

Gryffin rests his head on his hand but doesn't say anything for a few minutes. 'When we go back to Earth it's going to be a one-way trip for some of us. The odds aren't in our favour. Even if I can link with the other cyborgs and can control them, I don't think it's a fight we can win.'

'Probably not. It's one we've got to fight though.' Garvan holds up his new arm. 'We owe it to ourselves. We've got to put a stop to this, Gryffin. Not saying I fancy bidding my life farewell just yet. Hell, I didn't survive all that fun Harvey put me through just to lie back and die, but if I got to die I want it to be while I'm screwing with the Foundation and this fucking project.'

He pauses and closely examines the Nomad. He looks beaten, worn down, and exhausted. Terra's disappearance following so close after losing Roman is the last thing he needs. 'I'm sorry about Roman. Bray told me what happened.'

Gryffin nods, but doesn't look at him.

'Have you heard anything from the rest of the fleet?'

Gryffin frowns and stares at something on the floor. The Nomad clenches his jaw as he concentrates on a remarkably uninteresting patch of floor.

'Gryffin?'

He looks back at Garvan and the frown deepens. 'What?'

'You went a little... strange there for a minute. You good?'

He taps the side of his head. 'It wants me to back off. Wants me to stop fighting it.'

Garvan is far from an expert but you don't have to be one to see Gryffin is struggling to keep control of whatever the hell is in his head.

'I asked if you'd heard from the fleet.'

'Yes. The High Commander is sending a group to Ultar to keep an eye on what the Foundation are up to. The rest will wait on the other side of the Port until we're ready.'

'So you're launching a full scale attack?'

'Not a lot left to lose at this stage. I'm done fucking around. We'll hit Ultar and Earth at the same time.'

Garvan frowns as something Gryffin said registers with him. 'Hang on. I thought you were the High Commander?'

'I stepped down. I'm barely keeping a hold on myself. The Nomad need someone solid in place. Creed was born for the role. I worked with him years ago and trust him.' Gryffin finally looks up at him. 'He'll give as good as he gets.' He pushes to his feet and winces as he puts weight on his new leg. 'I'll let you rest.'

Garvan shuffles up the bed as he tries to figure out how to broach this next subject with Gryffin. 'I don't quite know how to say this, but I think I'm going to be possibly dating Erin.'

Gryffin leans on the back of the chair to keep his balance. 'Right.'

'Is that a problem?'

'Why the hell would it be? I couldn't care less who either of you are with. None of my business.'

'Okay. That's a relief.'

'Why? You think I was going to kick the shit out of you?'

'Got to admit it crossed my mind.'

Gryffin frowns for a minute before he speaks again. 'If Bray and Sayber hadn't got to you first and brought you to the Hunters, I would have tried to recruit you myself. I've never done that before. Usually new recruits come to us, not the other way around. Erin could do worse.

'Get some rest. If you want a piece of One you've got a lot of work to do. You need help getting to grips with any of your implants let me know.'

He smiles briefly then leaves the room and a stunned Garvan behind.

∞

DIXON SPACE STATION

Gryffin comes awake with a shout to find someone looming over him. He scrambles up the bed, desperate to get away. 'It's okay, sir. It's Boone. Calm down, sir.'

Gryffin winces as the lights come on and he finally sees Boone and not the Scientist beside him. Trace and Dante are on the beds opposite him, each with the same expression on their faces as Boone. 'You saw all that?'

Boone nods. 'We tried to block it, but we couldn't.'

Gryffin lies back on the bed and puts his hands over his face. Dealing with the nightmares alone is bad enough. Having Trace, Boone, and Dante in his head with him, experiencing everything he did, that's so much worse.

Boone nods over his shoulder and Dante and Trace leave the room. Not that it will do much good, but at least he won't have to look at them.

'I don't want to talk about it, Boone so don't even go there.'

'We all have memories we wish we didn't have. Only a matter of time before I show you some of the fun I had at the hands of the Scientist. Same goes for Dante and Trace. Doubt any of us will want to talk about it afterwards.'

Gryffin nods, relieved that Boone isn't going to try to get him to open up. Not that he needs to. Having Boone in his head rules out the need to talk about anything. Of the three cyborgs left alive from the New Colony, Boone is the one he's had most contact with. He's an impressive fighter and Gryffin can easily see him at the helm of his own ship in a few years. If he survives the next few weeks that is. 'You have family?'

Boone nods and smiles widely. 'A wife and daughter. They live on Aura One. It's a small farming colony. Not exactly Ultar, but it was my home.'

'Do you remember them? I mean remember your life with them?'

'I know it's not what you want me to say, but no. Each day I'm remembering more about them, but I don't remember me with them. It's hard to explain. Whatever the Foundation did to me... it blocked them from my memory. I can't remember the things I want to remember and can't forget all the horrors I'd give anything to forget.'

'Yeah. I get that.'

'Is the control implant getting stronger?'

'Yes. I've got it for now. How do you deal with...' He scrubs a hand over his face as he tries to figure out what the hell he wants to say. 'When something happens to them.'

Boone sits on the side of the bed and massages the connector on his arm. 'Having people you care about is an amazing thing, sir, but it's also painful when something goes wrong. You just have to hope the good outweighs the bad.' He pauses and glares at his mechanical arm. 'The Foundation took those good times from my memory, but I still know they existed. I can still feel them even if I can't remember them.'

'I don't want to forget her.'

'You might, Gryffin.' Boone pulls a locket out from under his t-shirt and shows Gryffin the picture of his family. 'Evie got this off the system for me. I forgot them for a while, sir. I may have forgotten them, but they still remember me. Someone out there remembers what we had. They have memories of the good times they had with me. I'm hoping my head will sort itself out one day but if not... well, at least they have those memories. They're not lost forever.

'We just have to hang on another few days, sir. After that, we'll either be dead and the people we care about will be safe or we'll be alive and, hopefully, will be able to put things right with them.' He smiles and holds up his mechanical arm. 'Hell, we may even be able to kiss goodbye to all these implants.'

'You really believe that? About the implants I mean.'

'No. I believe there's a chance we can stop the production of any more cyborgs, but whatever happens, we're cyborgs for the rest of our lives. No coming back from what was done to us. Just hope my wife and daughter can accept that. I'm not the same person anymore.'

Boone just put in words exactly how he feels. There is no coming back for any of them. As soon as they were put on the table and the first component fitted, they lost a large piece of their humanity.

Boone looks around as Bray steps in the room. 'You both okay?'

Gryffin nods. 'Yeah. Something wrong?'

Bray grins widely as he shakes his head. 'Quite the opposite actually. We just got a transmission from Terra.'

Boone reads the transmission to Gryffin again in his head. *'I'm safe. Don't lose my bandanna.'*

Gryffin looks down at the red bandanna tied around his right bicep. No way he's going to lose that.

Felix points to the screen at the head of the room. 'We've managed to get a few messages to and from Terra since that one. She's on Earth. Poor girl. But she's very much alive and well. I think we're happy enough to go with a quick video call.'

Evie nods as she examines the data. 'We can send the transmission through a few dozen stations to mask it, but I agree. We'll be safe enough.'

Gryffin stares at the screen and a wave of relief hits him when Terra's face appears. The relief dies away when he spots someone behind her.

'Am I glad to see you all.'

Her eyes go to Gryffin, but he can't stop looking at the man behind her. Terra points over her shoulder to the person holding Gryffin's attention. 'This is Treyton Balfe. Don't worry he's on our side,' she adds quickly. 'He's no fan of his father or the project. He saved me from the cyborgs and is keeping me hidden.'

'Where?' Gryffin doesn't realise he's spoken until everyone turns to look at him.

'I probably shouldn't say where exactly. I don't want the Foundation to pick up on anything.'

Gryffin clenches his fists as Trey leans over her shoulder and smiles at them.

'Don't sir.' He hears Boone's voice in his head. So much for the implant dulling his emotions. If Boone can pick up on his anger it's not doing a great job.

'Time isn't on our side,' Trey says as he leans close to Terra. Too fucking close. 'I don't have the luxury of trying to convince you how much I hated my father. I'm on the Council and I want to help you kill or replace or whatever you want to do to the other members. The Foundation is rotten and I'm on board for changing that. By working together we can all get what we want. An end to the corrupt Foundation and to the cyborg project.'

Trey smiles down at Terra which pushes Gryffin's grip on the control implant to its limits. 'If Trey can help I think we'd be crazy not to use him,' Terra says. 'He knows all the access points in the building. He knows the security numbers. Hell, he has all the information we need.'

Bray looks over at Gryffin, but Gryffin can't stop staring at Trey. He has the irrational need to break his neck and he can't explain why.

'Just breathe, sir.'

'Get the fuck out of my head, Boone.'

Bray frowns at Gryffin. He must have caught the surprise on Boone's face at his internal reply. Bray turns his attention back to

Trey and Terra. 'Give us some time to talk about this. Can you keep Terra safe for the moment?'

Trey leans on the counter behind him and crosses his arms. 'I have Council duties to attend to, but she should be safe enough here. If I get wind of anything I'll get her out. I promise. It's in my best interests to keep on your good side. If anything happens to her I'm fully aware of what will happen to me.'

He meets Gryffin's eyes and the bastard has the nerve to smile at him.

'You can get me on this channel,' Terra says, wrapping up the conversation. 'I'll see you all soon, okay.'

Gryffin knows he should look at her, but the fucker is still smiling over her shoulder. Just before the transmission ends, Trey winks.

Sayber speaks for the first time since Gryffin entered the room. 'We need to regroup back in the Outer Sector.'

Evie and Felix stop their muttering and look over at him. 'You want to leave?'

'Not leave. I said regroup. The Hunters are still on for taking down the Foundation, but we can't do it with *Perses* alone. If we're going to attack, it needs to be a coordinated fight from both sides of the Port.'

Desyl leans back in his chair and plays with the ring on his finger. 'He's right. We need to go back. Find out how many ships we've got. Then make an informed, focused attack. If we go in with a few ships, the Foundation will swat us away, taking out the flagship of each of the major groups. It could destroy us before we get the chance to show them exactly how dangerous we are.'

Sayber slaps his hand against the table and laughs. 'You know what Gryffin? I like this one. He's got a fire in his belly.'

Gryffin ignores him. 'We trust Trey?'

Evie puts herself between Gryffin and the blank view screen he still staring at. 'You go back with Desyl to the Outer Sector. Gather your Nomad and come back here with your teeth bared and claws out.

We'll wait until it's safe then send Heath back to Earth to get Terra.'

'I can't leave her.' The damn words pop out again without any thought from him.

'Everyone out!' Evie commands. After a brief pause, Gryffin and Evie are left alone in the room. 'Now you listen to me young man. You are not leaving her, do you hear me? What you are doing is making sure everything is in place to finish this. She's doing the same. I saw that wink he threw at you. Ignore Balfe Junior. Focus on the fact we have a Council member willing to help our cause. Focus on the fact he saved Terra. I promise you we will bring her back to the station ASAP. You know you can trust me, Gryffin.'

'I don't trust him.'

'I'm with you there. Hell, Felix and I would have been dead years ago if we threw trust around. He's yet to earn it, but he might.' She sits down beside him and adjusts her floppy hat. 'Listen to me very carefully. You went through these mods to destroy the Foundation and Project Conscript. You sacrificed so much over the years, Gryffin. Too much. You're so close to getting your revenge. Don't let Mr. Perfect Hair throw you off your game.'

'Hair? What?'

'Never mind.' She takes his metal hand in hers. 'End this. Go and meet with Creed and the others then come back to kick some ass. I, for one, cannot wait to see the mighty Nomad in action.'

∞

DIXON SPACE STATION

Gryffin stands beside Desyl on the command deck as *Ares* leaves the safety of the Dixon's Space Station. A deep pit opens in his stomach the further they move away from it and from Earth. The implant is keeping him calm enough, but inside he's as far from calm as he can be. Boone, Trace, and Dante are standing behind him and he can feel their unease.

It's not the only unease he can feel. His crew— Desyl's crew are uneasy about his new and improved self. More than once, he's felt someone looking at him and the others. He's gone from being their captain to an untested cyborg weapon.

He pushes that thought from his head, but not before Boone, Trace, and Dante pick up on it. They're picking up on the same tension on the command deck.

Desyl sighs as he pushes off the railing and looks over his shoulder at the command chair.

'You're going to have to sit in it,' Gryffin says.

Desyl crosses his arms and glares at the chair like it's an armed enemy ready to launch an attack. 'Every time I've sat in that damn thing something goes wrong.'

'You're the captain. You can't stand forever. Sit in the fucking chair, Desyl.'

Desyl sighs again and walks over to the command chair, staring at it for another few seconds before he turns and slowly lowers onto the worn leather. 'Now what?'

'Your call, Captain.'

'Don't do that to me, Gryffin. I need you to help me. I get why you stepped back and I get why I'm sitting here. Sort of. But I can't do this alone. I need your help.'

Gryffin walks over to Desyl and crouches down in front of him. At least his leg and the rest of his body have come to a bit of a truce. 'No you don't. I picked you for a reason. I know you have what it takes to be captain. Your crew is the best group of Nomad in the fleet. Have you decided on a second yet?'

'No. Not yet.'

'Wait until we meet with rest of the fleet. You can always take from another ship if you want. I'm sure the new High Commander won't mind.'

'Yeah. Okay.' Desyl's face drops a little and he looks away from Gryffin. 'I hate saying this, but we'll be heading through the Port in a bit. I suppose we should get you four secured just in case.'

Gryffin gets to his feet. 'You got this Desyl.'

Ares' new captain nods unconvincingly as Gryffin leaves the command deck with the other cyborgs. They go to four spare crew quarters and the Nomad security teams waiting for them. Gryffin faces the small cot in his new quarters and stares at the wall opposite as his wrists are secured in front of him.

The Dixon's had run countless checks on each of them, but they're not taking any chances. They could have missed something in his programming that'll be triggered when he goes through the Port. He'd prefer to be restrained than risk any Nomad lives.

His restraints are fixed to a thick chain embedded in the wall and he's left alone. Gryffin sits on the cot as the door closes and is locked. Gryffin spends the next few minutes just breathing, trying to keep control of himself and the building need to break the restraints and ram the door out of the wall.

He goes through different scenarios in his head. Different ways he's going to tear the Foundation apart. Different ways he's going to fight the female cyborgs, but it doesn't work. His mind wants him to focus on Terra and the fact he's leaving her alone on Earth with Balfe's son.

'She's safe. He saved her life.'

Saying the words aloud does nothing to calm him. If anything, knowing someone else had to step in to save her is like a kick to the gut. It should have been him. Fuck that. She shouldn't have needed to be saved in the first place. Getting the mods may be the way to protect the Nomad and take down the Foundation, but all it's done is put up a wall between himself and Terra.

Even though he wants nothing more than to kick the shit out of the door, he forces himself to lie down on the cot. Boone and the others are silent. They're leaving him to wallow in self-pity and he's grateful for the peace.

He looks down at his new mechanical arm, locked in the heavy restraint. It was a mistake. Getting his mods upgraded was a mistake. But it's too late to do anything about it.

He thought he could live with the mods and fight the control implant. Thought he'd be able to keep hold of himself in all the noise. But it's too difficult. Knowing what he threw away is slowly eating away at him.

Terra is the only person he's ever loved and he turned his back on her to do this to himself. Now she's on Earth with that man and he's back in restraints. Alone again.

He rolls over and buries his head in the thin pillow. As soon as he's met with Creed and Aleena he'll stop fighting. It's better for everyone if he just lets the implant take him over.

He did this to fight the Foundation. He can't do that if he's fighting himself.

OUTER SECTOR

Creed, Milla, and Chayse follow Desyl from the cargo hold to one of the small crew quarters at the back of *Ares*. Chayse can't help but smile as he walks through the ship that was his home for so long. *Nemesis* is better than he could have ever wished for, but *Ares* will always feel like home to him.

As much as he's grateful to get a chance to board the flagship again, something is wrong. Gryffin should have met them not Desyl. The Commander had refused to answer any of their questions, stating Gryffin would do that himself, but that didn't explain his absence or why they were going in the opposite direction to the command deck and Gryffin's quarters. He glances over his shoulder at Creed and Milla, seeing the same worried look on their faces.

Desyl unlocks the door to the room and Chayse instantly realises what the problem is. Gryffin is inside, sitting on the bed with a nice new set of shiny implants attached to him.

The second Chayse sees Gryffin, he spins around and tackles Desyl to the ground. He pins him down with one hand and fixes his other around the Commander's neck. 'What the hell have you done!' Milla tries to pull Chayse off, but his anger is firmly in control.

He only calms down when a heavy metal hand grips his shoulder. Gryffin pulls him off Desyl and holds him against the wall. Desyl climbs to his feet and rubs his neck.

'What the hell did you do, Desyl?'

Chayse glowers at Desyl then looks up at Gryffin. The new eyepiece is far more hi-tech than his old one. The purple iris spins dizzily as Gryffin stares at him. When Chayse finally pulls his attention away from the eyepiece he realises something about Gryffin's other eye. It's blue not purple. It would only be blue if Gryffin was keeping control of himself.

'He's still in there.'

Desyl nods. 'Yeah. He's still in there.'

'Can he talk?'

'Of course I can talk.' Gryffin grabs his former aide by the neck, holding his feet off the ground as he looks at him. 'This was my choice. You want to beat someone, beat me.' He lets Chayse go, dropping him to the ground.

'Who's controlling him?' Milla asks.

'I am,' Desyl says. 'Well, technically he is right now. But if he can't for whatever reason, I can step in. I'm the only one able to give him orders. He can then relay orders to Boone, Trace, and Dante.'

'You know it could be a one-way deal for him,' Chayse says.

Desyl nods. 'He knows it too.'

'He is still here. Talk to me,' Gryffin growls from the corner.

'Sorry, sir.'

'Just Gryffin. Desyl is captain now.' He looks over at Creed and smiles, but it's barely visible. 'You accepted the role, High Commander?'

Creed grins widely. 'Of course. Wasn't going to step away from being High Commander. Helps that Rayde would have been well and truly fucked off about it. Big bonus. So, how much of you is still you?'

'I'm fighting the programming for now.'

'I guess that's a good thing then. The last time I saw you use that implant in your head, you put half the crew in the med bay,' Creed says. 'No offence, but how exactly is that going to help us?'

'It'll help because without it I'm dead. Four fully operational cyborgs isn't much against the numbers the Foundation have, but it's better than none.'

Milla sits beside him on the bed and leans closer to examine his ocular implant. 'Are you okay, Gryffin?'

'Yes.'

'I'll take that as a no then, cause no offence, you don't look okay. If you clench your fist any harder you'll break your fingers. So, where's Terra? I can't imagine she's over the moon about all this.'

Gryffin breaks eye contact, focusing on the floor instead of her.

'Gryffin? What is it?'

'She's on Earth. She's safe. The Dixon's will get her in a few days when it's clear for them to return. We need to get everyone together, but I want to talk to Aleena first.'

'She's on *Nemesis*,' Chayse says. 'Do you want to go to her, or should I ask her to come here?'

'I have to stay here in case I lose control. Can you bring her across?'

Chayse nods. 'I'll make the call.'

'Thanks.'

Desyl leans against the door frame still massaging his neck. 'After that we should all get together in the meeting room. We've got a lot to tell you.'

∞

OUTER SECTOR

Aleena pauses at the door to the training room but cannot bring herself to step inside. Milla had told her about Gryffin. His decision to upgrade his modifications is still difficult to accept.

If she knows nothing else about Gryffin, she knows he has a great hatred for each and every one of his implants. For him to make the decision to get more, their situation must be so much worse than she originally believed.

Before she can talk herself out of seeing him, she opens the door and walks to the railing. Gryffin is training with another cyborg, but she cannot remember the blond man's name. Desyl and a team of ten armed Nomad security are watching them train.

Desyl notices her and leaves the others to stand guard so he can join her on the upper level. He hesitates for a moment then hugs her, holding her close.

'You okay?'

She smiles and nods when he lets her go. 'As well as I can be considering. How is he?'

'As well as he can be considering.'

'He is fighting well.'

Desyl nods as he watches the men train. 'He's back on form, that's for sure. Boone is holding his own though. Needs a bit more work to get to Gryffin's level.'

'And the additional security?'

Desyl looks over at her and smiles, but it is forced. 'He's like a ticking time bomb, Aleena. The control implant and the programming are fighting him. He's holding them back, but it's taking its toll on him. He keeps zoning out. Almost like he's lost in his head somewhere. Each time he zones out, it takes longer to get him back.' Desyl stops talking but there is something on his mind.

'He is considering allowing it to take control.'

Desyl's head whips around. 'How the hell did you know that?'

'I know him. If he continues to zone out as you put it, he will be a liability when you eventually fight. He would not want that.'

Desyl snorts. 'Damn. You do know him. Yeah. He's considering letting it take over. Got to admit I see what he means. He only did all this so he'll be of use to us.' He kicks at the railing and scrubs a hand through his hair. 'I haven't got a fucking clue what to do, Aleena.'

She takes his hand and squeezes it. 'Your priority is *Ares* and her crew, not Gryffin. I love that man dearly, but this is bigger than him. Is it safe to speak to him alone? I would prefer not to have an audience.'

'He'll be fine. You know what he's like when he's training. It calms him.'

She follows him down the stairs and waits while Desyl stops the training session and instructs everyone to leave them alone.

Gryffin turns to face her and she cannot hold back the tears. She rushes over to him and throws her arms around his chest. Gryffin hesitates briefly before he hugs her back. Aleena cries against him, finally releasing the anguish she had been fighting to restrain since she heard of Roman's death. Holding his son brings it all to the surface and she does not try to hold it back.

Gryffin holds her until the tears stop falling. Aleena pushes back from him and takes a moment to compose herself before she looks up at his face. There is nothing in his expression. No sadness. No anger. Nothing at all. It is Gryffin, but without his soul.

She places her hand against the side of his face and examines his new ocular implant. That is the most noticeable difference. The eyepiece completely covers his own eye. Although judging by the size of the piece, she imagines it has replaced it entirely.

His other eye may be blue, but it lacks any of the warmth she is used to seeing. Gryffin may not have been a light-hearted man, but she could tell a lot about his mood by looking at his eyes. Now, they offer no insight at all.

'You okay?'

At least his voice is unchanged. She gestures to the bench beside the wall and watches as he sits and stretches his legs out in front of him. 'I am well. Is your new leg troubling you?'

'A little. It's getting better though.'

Aleena looks down at his prosthetic arm. The new limb has additional components attached to the side, making it appear larger than its predecessor. 'I am scared, Gryffin.'

'Of what?'

'Of everything that is transpiring. This latest revelation is not helping to soothe me at all. You should not have had to resort to such drastic measures. My heart is breaking for you, Gryffin.'

'I'm fine, Aleena. Really.'

'Stop lying to me, Gryffin. I have known you, the real you for many years. You are hurting and you are scared.'

'No I'm not.'

'Gryffin—'

'I'm terrified, Aleena.'

She covers her mouth with her hands and nods slowly. She was not expecting him to be so honest with her, but every now and again, he drops his wall with her when she least expects it. 'I wish I could help you.'

'You can.'

'How?'

'Look out for Terra for me. I don't think she'll stick with the Nomad after this is done. I need to know she'll be safe.'

'Of course. You do not have to ask. But I am sure you will be able to do that yourself.'

'Maybe. I don't want you anywhere near this fight either.'

'You cannot keep me from it, Gryffin.'

'We're going to Earth and there's a good chance not all of us are coming back. You need to live to keep the order when whatever's left of the groups return.'

Aleena understands what he is saying, and it does nothing but fill her with dread. 'So this battle with the Foundation is only the beginning. Is that what you are saying?'

'The Nomad and Hunters will go head-to-head. I'm guessing some of the Rogues will align with both sides. You need to be the voice of reason. It's going to get ugly and violent and there will be deaths. There's no way of avoiding it. Please get on the ship with the rest of the colonists and keep away from this. You're too important to me. I don't want you to die too. '

She cups the side of his face again and nods. 'Very well. I do have one condition though.'

'What?'

'I want you to promise you will join me for a cup of tea when this is done.'

He smiles and, for a moment, her friend is back again. 'Understood.'

She leans against his arm and stares at the wall opposite her. It was nice to hear him make the promise, but she knows there is a strong possibility she will never see her friend again once he leaves.

EPILOGUE

Gryffin is pulled out of his nightmare by someone calling his name. He looks up at Creed and instantly knows something is wrong. 'What is it?'

Creed crouches down beside his bed and glances at Gryffin's prosthetic leg and arm lying on the floor in front of him. 'We just got a transmission. Don't worry. It's not about Terra. It's... Well, it's from someone called Jada. She's a Foundation cyborg.'

Gryffin picks his arm off the floor and reattaches it. 'The Foundation are here?'

'Well, no. That's the weird thing. They claim they're working independently of the Foundation. Jada works with the cyborg, Nova, that Garvan encountered on Earth. Jada wants to talk to you. She says she can prove they're on our side.'

Without being asked, Creed lays Gryffin's leg on the bed and helps him slip the connectors in place. 'Is it a Foundation ship?'

'Yes and no. It's *Infinity*.'

Gryffin stares over at him. '*Infinity*? They've got my father's fucking ship?'

Creed nods. 'Yeah. They've surrendered to us and handed the ship back. But she's insisting on talking to you. It's your call, Gryffin.'

'Where are they?'

'In the cell on *Talos*. I didn't want them too close to you just in case they got in your head. You on for talking to her?'

'Might as well.'

Creed stands up and nods, but doesn't look thrilled about putting a group of cyborgs together on his ship. 'Fine. No offence, but I'll be putting a few security teams in with you. And they stay in their cell.'

Trace, Dante, and Boone are as uncomfortable about meeting Jada and her team as he is. He can feel their unease as they take a transport over to *Talos* with Creed and Desyl. Bray, Chayse, and Milla are going to meet them there, but he's been told they're just going to make sure nothing happens.

He's not sure whether they just mistrust the Foundation cyborgs or if himself and his team are included in that. When they're met by a six-person security team he realises it's not just Jada and her team they don't trust. He walks with the others to the detention area and steps up to the first cell.

The woman at the front steps closer to the bars, ignoring the security team who raise their weapons as she approaches him. 'I'm Jada.'

'No designation?'

'You would prefer I call you Thirty-Five?'

'No. What do you want, Jada?'

'We're not here to harm you. You must believe us.'

'You've got two minutes to convince me before we take down as many of you as we can.'

Jada steps forward and something hits Gryffin as he gets a better look at her. She's sad. Which doesn't make any sense. The new cyborgs have their emotions under the control of the implants. No human emotions should be showing. 'You've broken through the programming.'

She nods. 'We all have.'

'How the hell is that possible? They improved the design.'

'Yes. They learned a lot since your design was finalised. Fortunately for us, it is still flawed. Some of us have been able to fight the modification.'

'How were you able to bypass the programming?'

'Nova managed to break through. As we are all linked to each other, she taught the rest of us how to do the same.'

'You were part of the team that attacked Ultar?'

She nods, but her face drops a little. 'We tried to lessen the casualties, but there are only a few of us in control of our thoughts. The Foundation's hold on the others is too strong. I know you lost someone close to you—'

Gryffin slams his fist against the side of the cell, denting the metal. 'Don't say another fucking word.'

She nods and looks away for a moment. 'It will mean nothing, but the team member who killed Roman was going against Nova's orders. Nova made sure both Roman and the Nomad found a little way from him were buried in the town graveyard. She left the graves unmarked so they would be undisturbed.'

Gryffin reigns in his anger as her words sink in. 'She did?'

'Of course. He defied the Foundation. He deserved respect.'

He agrees with her on that point. 'What do you want?'

'We need your help, Gryffin.'

'You work for the Foundation. The only help I'll give you is to take you out of the fight - permanently.'

'More than anyone else in the Sector, you know first-hand how the modifications feel. How the implant pushes you out of your head, out of your thoughts. You know what it's like to be used by the Foundation. You know what the need for revenge feels like.

'We are done being used by the Foundation. The Council will not be happy until everyone in the Sectors bows in front of them. I don't want to be a part of that. None of us want to.' She moves forward, taking small cautious steps. 'I know you have little reason to believe us, let alone trust us, but we don't know what to do. We have a grip on ourselves, but if they find out their control is slipping, I dread to think what they'll do to us.

'The Foundation believes we died on Ultar. Our tracking devices were removed before we left the surface. Perform any test you wish. Do whatever you must to satisfy yourself that we are allies.'

'You want to join with us?'

'Yes. We want to fight with you. All of us do. But there is more. The other members of our team are still working for the council. They will maintain the ruse, stay within the Foundation until we need them.'

'How many more?'

'Seven, including Nova, our leader. She is the one who sent us to find you.'

Gryffin leans against the wall and crosses his arms. He's torn. Having seven additional cyborgs on their side would be a damn useful asset. If they could be trusted. Which is the problem. Too much of this relies on him trusting a group of cyborgs.

He glances up at Jada and a little of his doubt fades away. They've been through what he has, minus the mad scientist and filthy station. None of them asked for this. The Foundation decided their fate and they had no choice but to go along for the painful ride.

Gryffin examines each of the cyborgs in turn. They're all so young - early twenties to mid-thirties at the most. The Foundation clearly picked them for their youth. No doubt they were given combat training at some stage either before or after the mods. Garvan was right. They're a formidable group.

'Let me link with you,' Jada says.

Gryffin can feel everyone in the room tense at her suggestion. 'I don't think that's a good idea,' Bray mutters from behind him.

'Direct your weapons at me. If I try anything kill me. I just want to show you that I'm telling the truth. The only way you'll know for sure is if you link with me,' Jada says.

Gryffin turns to face a less than happy group of people. Only Creed seems to be on board with giving it a shot. 'You good with me doing this, Creed?'

'Me. Yes, but I don't know one end of an implant from the other. Probably not the best one to base your decision on.'

'She could control you,' Bray says. 'I'm not on board with this.'

'She's right though. It's the only way to tell if she's telling the truth. And we need this. We need more cyborgs on our side.'

Bray crosses his arms and stares over at the cell as he slowly shakes his head. 'I'm not liking this, Gryffin.'

Gryffin grabs two pairs of restraints from the wall and hands them to Bray. 'It'll take me a few minutes to get out of two sets. Enough time for you to take me down if anything goes wrong.'

Bray glares at him then grabs the restraints from his hand. 'I really hate you sometimes, you know that?'

'Yeah. You've said.'

Bray secures Gryffin's arms behind his back then steps back as Gryffin faces Jada. 'They will kill you if you do anything you shouldn't.'

She nods once and steps closer to him. 'I have no doubts about that.'

Bray removes the signal block from Gryffin's ocular implant and gestures to the cell. 'You're good to go.'

The link with Boone and the rest of his team is strange, but something he's slowly getting used to. This new link is like a thump to his gut. He stumbles back as Jada pushes into his head.

'There's something wrong!' Bray shouts from somewhere behind him. Gryffin shakes his head, stopping anyone from shooting her.

'It's okay.'

'Gryffin—'

'I said it's okay.' The pressure in his head reduces and he slowly straightens again.

'I apologise,' Jada says. 'I am used to linking with a much larger group. May I try again?'

Gryffin manages to nod without throwing up.

'Try to relax, Gryffin. If you hold me back it will just cause you more discomfort.'

Easier said than done. He doesn't want anyone else in his head. There are enough people poking around in there already. Gryffin concentrates on not blocking her and little by little the discomfort eases.

She's telling the truth. He sees everything play out as she said. Sees her with Nova when she gives the order to bury his father and Lucan. Sees Jada and her team escaping on *Infinity*. Then he feels her pain, her fear. She's a victim as much as he is. All the new cyborgs are.

Jada breaks the link and Bray quickly reattaches the block so she can't sneak back in. 'Well?'

Gryffin nods. 'It's all true. Looks like we just increased our cyborg army.'

∞

OUTER SECTOR

Gryffin leans back in the chair and looks around the table. He never thought he'd be sitting at the same table as Creed and Hardy. Hell, he never thought he'd see either of them again.

The Hunters, Rogues, and Nomad are flying together as one... for now. He's already spoken to Creed about what happens next and the new High Commander is set to fight whoever he has to in order to secure the future of the Nomad. The new ships were being prepped for battle and, if all went to plan, they'd be moving back through the Port in a few days.

'Gryffin?'

He looks up at Creed only noticing then that everyone is staring at him. He must have zoned out again. 'What?'

'What do you have in mind?'

'What?'

'Do you have a plan?'

'Yeah. I want to open the Port, both sides.'

'You mean like open wide for everyone to come through?' Sayber asks. 'Wide open so everyone with a ship can pop over. Are you out of your god-damned mind?'

Gryffin looks over at Sayber. He can see the same doubt on the faces of everyone else at the table. 'Thought you'd be up for it? Bring the fight to them for once.'

'I'm not saying I'm not a tad unstable, but going up against the Foundation in Foundation space, on Foundation soil, is nuts even for me.' Sayber looks at Bray, sitting to his left. 'You agree with big brother's plan?'

'I'm not a fan of agreeing with him, but to hell with it. I'm in. I'm done running and hiding. My family deserve to be able to go home. And if we manage to open the Port, we could have quite a bit of back up ready to come through.'

Hardy claps excitedly from her seat at one end of the table. 'I like this plan! It's about time we take the fight to them.'

'Should have guessed you'd support this,' Sayber says. 'You're even crazier than the Nomad.'

Hardy wiggles her eyebrows. 'I choose to take that as a compliment.'

'What a surprise,' Sayber mutters under his breath.

'So, you do know if we open the Port it's not just the good guys that will come through,' Milla says.

Gryffin nods at Milla. 'Everyone on this side is against the Foundation. That's all that matters. The Foundation have controlled that area of space for too long. Time to end that. See how brave they are against an army of pissed of Outer Sector ships.'

'So we're all agreed,' Creed says. 'We're heading back with our claws out. When are you thinking of launching this attack?'

'It's your call, High Commander.'

Creed smiles at Gryffin. 'I guess it is. We'll need another few days to finish with the ships. Could do with a hand, Sayber.'

The Hunter nods. 'I suppose we could help out. *Cronus* could do with a bit of a face-lift too. What do you reckon, Bray? She's your ship. You good to look after that?'

'Hold up. She's mine?'

'Of course. Even Gryffin would agree, right?'

Gryffin nods. 'You took her. She's yours.'

Bray opens and closes his mouth, completely lost for words.

Sayber brushes his fingers over his goatee as he leans across the table. 'If I was just handed a ship like that to captain, I'd probably make sure she looked... well, a little less Foundation and a lot more Hunter. Having her attack them flying the Hunter colours would be an extra kick in the balls.'

Creed smiles widely. 'That's sorted then. So, Gryffin. How are you and the other guys doing?'

'Our mods are all operating as they should,' Gryffin says. 'If we're to do what you need us to, we'll have to be on the ground up close and personal with the Foundation cyborgs.'

Creed leans back in the chair and examines Gryffin. 'All due respect, from what I hear they've got an unknown army of better cyborgs. Can't say I'm thrilled about sending eleven of you to your death.'

'We can handle it. Their cyborgs aren't thinking for themselves. They're following orders. That makes their reflexes a little slower as they process them. And we could use me to control them. I was able to link with Jada and her team. I could do the same to the others on Earth.'

Desyl nods. 'Yeah, but they could take you over too. And you've still got the control implant to think about. It that does what it's designed to do, you're gone.'

Gryffin stares down the table at Desyl. He's having a hard enough time convincing himself this is a good idea without Desyl pointing out that it could all be for nothing. He's barely keeping a grip of the implant. 'I'll deal with that if it happens. For now, we've got an edge they don't have. We all know how to fight. We've all faced the end of a gun or the tip of a knife. When was the last time you heard of the Foundation mounting an all-out battle?'

Gryffin pushes to his feet and goes over to the screen at the head of the table. The frozen image of the Council, each in their ornate robes and embellished masks, fills the screen. The Dixon's were still trying to find out the identity of each member, but so far this picture is all they have to go on.

He's not angry about Roman or Terra anymore. The anger had been replaced with a cold calm he hasn't felt in years. Gryffin tilts his head to the side then places his hand on the side of the screen as he examines the group in the image.

'They're calling us a threat to justify making more cyborgs. The Council is torturing innocent people because of me - the faceless monster who modified himself so he could threaten their peace. The people of Earth have no idea their beloved leaders made that very monster.'

He places his flesh fist against One's forehead on the screen and pushes until the screen shatters under the force. Blood oozes from the wound, running down One's face as he pulls his fist back. 'They're scared of me. Scared of what they created. That's good. They should be.'

Thank you for reading *Cronus*. I hope you enjoyed the book. There's plenty more to come!

The sequel, *Talos*, is coming soon.

Do you fancy staying updated with news about my books?

- Join my mailing list at: https://www.kafinn.com/

- Like me on Facebook: https://www.facebook.com/kafinnauthor

- Follow me on Instagram: https://www.instagram.com/kafinnauthor/

Also, if you have a moment, I'd appreciate if you could review *Cronus* at the store where you purchased it. The Nomad and I would love to know what you thought of the book.

Thanks for your support!

K.A. Finn

ARES

NOMAD SERIES BOOK 1

AVAILABLE IN EBOOK, PAPERBACK AND AUDIOBOOK

He wasn't expected to survive, and for 20 years, he has managed to stay off their radar. Until now. Until her.

Gryffin was the sole survivor of The Foundation's experimental project to transform human children into hybrid cyborgs - half human, half machine. The program failed and he was sent on a one way trip into The Outer Sector where he was left for dead. He has survived for 20 years by suppressing his human emotions and embracing his machine side.

Officer Terra Rush believes in her duty to the Foundation. The Sector needs to be prepared for colonization, and nothing can stop her from doing her job... except him. When Gryffin saves her from an attack, Terra uncovers a terrible secret. The Foundation has been lying to her... and maybe they still are.

They have labelled Gryffin a killing machine, yet he acts more human than many of The Foundation's leaders. He has awakened intense feelings in Terra that throw her loyalties into question, and even though he pushes her away, she is determined to find out the truth about the cyborg program.

Gryffin refuses to be a mindless soldier, yet escaping The Foundation's control and stopping the colonization of his home will require Terra's help. Can Gryffin overcome the machine inside and trust her? Or will getting in touch with his human emotions destroy him once and for all?

NEMESIS

A part of her died when she lost him.

Commander Terra Rush has spent the last eight months mourning Gryffin, believing he died when his ship crashed. When he returns to her, broken and scarred from months of torture at the hands of the Foundation, it feels like a miracle - at first.

His unpredictable mechanical side, reawakened by the brutality he endured as a prisoner, threatens to destroy him. He's lost the trust of the colonists. Has he lost part of himself as well?

Her need to protect her ravaged heart puts distance between them when they need to depend on each other the most. If the colonists are to survive, they need Gryffin to reunite the Nomad and stand with them...and he needs Terra's help to do so. But time and tragedy have changed them both so much. Can they find their way back to each other before everything they know is destroyed?

PERSES

CHAOS

Twenty-five years ago, two futures were changed.

Before becoming a Nomad and a Hunter, brothers Daegan and Brayden Sawyer were like everybody else on Foundation Earth. Then Daegan leaves for a school trip, a decision that would lead them to travel very different paths.

With his older sibling declared dead, Brayden's grief causes him to spiral out of control. After being banished by his family, he becomes even more self-destructive. When he's arrested and given a death sentence on the infamous Tyrat Prison, he realizes how far he's fallen.

However, Daegan is alive, though he may wish otherwise after discovering he's the latest recruit for the cyborg project. Years later, he finds salvation on the battleship, *Ares*. With their help, he becomes Gryffin and carves a formidable reputation for himself.

Chaos follows them as they fight their own demons and strive to find who they were always meant to be.

MANIA